SPRINGFIELD

Marian Eldridge is an award-winning writer and literary reviewer. She grew up on a small farm in Victoria and now lives in Canberra, where she is a member of the Seven Writers group. Her previous publications include the short story collections *The Woman at the Window* and *Walking the Dog*.

Other books by Marian Eldridge

Walking the Dog
The Woman at the Window

Amongst the Leaves: Prose and Poetry from Students' Workshops at Darwin High School (*editor*)

SPRINGFIELD

MARIAN ELDRIDGE

University of Queensland Press

First published 1992 by University of Queensland Press
Box 42, St Lucia, Queensland 4067 Australia

© Marian Eldridge 1992

© Elizabeth Eldridge for guitar music 1992

© Mike Jackson (Larrikin Music) for dulcimer music 1992

This book is copyright. Apart from any fair dealing
for the purposes of private study, research, criticism
or review, as permitted under the Copyright Act, no
part may be reproduced by any process without written
permission. Enquiries should be made to the publisher.

Typeset by University of Queensland Press
Printed in Australia by The Book Printer, Victoria

Distributed in the USA and Canada by
International Specialized Book Services, Inc.,
5602 N.E. Hassalo Street, Portland, Oregon 97213-3640

The words from "The Morning Side of the Mountain" (Manning) quoted in
chapter 62 are reproduced with the permission of Warner Chappell Music.
Poetry quoted on page 90 is from Coleridge, "The Ancient Mariner".

Cataloguing in Publication Data
National Library of Australia

Eldridge, Marian, 1936-
   Springfield.
   I. Title.

A823.3

ISBN 0 7022 2390 5

*For my children
and their children*

Acknowledgments

A good many people have contributed to the creation of this novel, and I am grateful to all of them. In particular I want to thank Paul Walsh, Sue Stockfeld, David Stockfeld, Seven Writers (the other six), Marion and Geoff Pollard, John Owen, Joanne Loughrey, Mike Jackson, Ken Eldridge, Elizabeth Eldridge, David Eldridge, Bernadette and Peter Carter, and Peter Campbell (PC Publishing), all of whom helped generously in various ways.

Contents

Part One   Marycote   *1*

Part Two   Glasshouse   *121*

Part Three   Fragments Dim of Lovely Forms   *237*

Part One

Marycote

> Deeds to be hid which were not hid,
> Which all confused I could not know,
> Whether I suffered, or I did:
> For all seemed guilt, remorse or woe,
> My own or others still the same
> Life-stifling fear, soul-stifling shame.
>
> – Coleridge, "The Pains of Sleep"

1 Some Time After Midnight

Some time after midnight a storm blew up. It rolled from hill to hill like heavy artillery, lashing treetops, flaying ribbons of bark and twigs and green leaves from their branches. It shattered a limb of the big manna gum right on the boundary between Springfields and Catchpoles. Where the line of the fence made a step around the old cottage called Marycote, the falling limb snapped strands of wire like tendons.

There was no one living at Marycote now. Its owner, Angus Springfield, a man in his early forties, lived across the creek in the shelter of the next valley. He was where he had grown up, in the fine old farmhouse an earlier Springfield had built as family and fortunes increased. Since his return to the farm some two years before, Angus Springfield kept most of the rooms shut up. He ate at the back of the house in the kitchen and slept across the passage in what was still known as the maid's room. Occasionally, to please old Mary Springfield who liked to drop by, he would light a fire in one of the other rooms and sit in there.

On the night of the storm there was a good fire blazing in the sitting room, its warmth reflected in the brass bars of the fender. Mary had lit it herself that afternoon on her way home from the town. "There!" she'd said, brushing ash from her fingers once she completed laying paper and then the kindling and the log. "You tuck into another pikelet, Angus, while I just put a match . . . It'll be nice and cosy when you come in again. It's going to be a nasty night. More like mid-winter if you ask me. This greenhouse business, I don't know, what do you make of it all?" She'd sat in one of the two leather armchairs – not the one Angus used, of course – and, before he'd had time to comment on the weather, had begun to tell him about her afternoon at the hospital. "She didn't know me," she said, then looked at him hesitantly. "But perhaps if you –" Angus, impatient to get back to the glasshouse, slapped dust off his trousers and sat down. "She hasn't known anyone for ten years, Mary." They were talking about his mother. The clock in the hall struck five. Mary jumped.

"Heavens! It can't be! They'll be wondering what's kept me." At this allusion to Catchpoles she'd smiled so apologetically that Angus had given her a hug. "You're a good scout, Mary."

When the storm broke, Angus was enjoying a nip or two of after-dinner Scotch by Mary's fire. He was sitting back in his armchair, just as his father and his father before him had relaxed after a hard wintry day in the paddocks. Opposite him was the empty chair with the less impressive arms where Mary had perched a few hours earlier. His mother's chair. Angus poured another Scotch. Must be weeks since I touched this stuff, he thought, savouring its bite on tongue and throat; he clean forgot sometimes. Lifting the bottle again, he felt the trembling in his hand. Jumpy, he was jumpy tonight. All that talk, greenhouse, glasshouse. He splashed whisky into his glass.

As usual when he used this room, it was unlit except for flames from the fire. They leapt up and burned a red spot of soot in the chimney; flickered over the saucepan at his feet. He leaned forward to glance at it. Hash, reheated. Pity it wasn't one of Mary's casseroles. He'd managed to get through only a few mouthfuls. The dogs could have the rest in the morning. For himself, he'd take the rifle tomorrow and get a couple of young rabbits. He was a dab hand at rabbit stew. And tomorrow, tomorrow he'd get over to the plantation and complete that bit of new fencing. Otherwise the sheep would finish off the seedlings next spring the first day he planted them out. Tomorrow he'd keep right out of the glasshouse. Pottering all day with the seedlings. Sowing, watering, pricking out. Watching the first two ant-sized cotyledons come bursting through the soil, and the sun shining through the forest of slender red stems that one day would be rough-barked giants that he couldn't stretch his arms around. He smiled, and the firelight made bright ridges and dark hollows out of the thin, lined face.

His gaze fixed itself on the handsome pair of brass firedogs his grandfather had picked up cheap at a forced sale. Behind them the log, an old fence post, had almost burned through. Soon it fell apart, flared a little and crusted into embers. The house shuddered; draughts gusted through the room, but Angus made no effort to push the coals together. He was listening: the sudden rain on the iron roof was deafening. He pictured the rain in action, beating into his glasshouse, gouging out chunks of the sodden creek banks where once blackfish had sheltered. Over-grazed all those wasted years when his agent had leased the farm to his neighbour Lou Catchpole, the land was making slow recovery. Whenever there was heavy rain, rivulets fled down the bare flanks of the hillsides, and clods of the thin topsoil tore loose and slid into deepening washaways. His shoulders sagged. When, finally, he'd made up his mind to come home, he'd been full of ideas: now the place good as had him licked. *Didi mau, Angus! Go away!* Was he an intruder here, too? Here, on his own place?

The clock in the hall struck once: the half hour, or one o'clock. He'd have one last drink.

The wind shrieked. Cattle and sheep, huddled under the few aged trees the early settlers had spared, twitched and shook their heads as though in disbelief. Around and above them, indifferent to their presence, indifferent to the man staring over his glass at the embers, the storm pursued its course.

Angus leaned over the arm of his chair to place his empty glass on the floor beside the bottle. He placed it carefully, very carefully, then heaved himself to his feet. Swaying, he took a tentative step and tripped over the saucepan. He steadied himself against the chair. Sitting over the fire too long, he told himself. Bloody knee playing up again, won't hold me up. Using the back of the sofa as a support, he moved across to the window and pulled aside one of the dusty velvet curtains. The rain had eased off temporarily, but the sky — moon, Cross, Magellanic Clouds — had gone long ago, wiped out in the storm's first assault. The heavy blackness replacing it was lit almost continuously by jagged blue light. They say there's a streak of lightning that rises from the ground at the same time, he told himself, straining to see it. Thunder exploded around him. As he began to soar on the old mix of exultation and fear, he clung to that idea — lightning streaking towards Earth and simultaneously rising to meet itself. But he could never capture the moment. Dropping the curtain, he made his way past the sofa and threw another log on the fire. Half filling his glass by its light, he settled back in his chair to stare into the startled flames.

About half a mile northeast of Springfield, on the farm known for many years as Valley View and now called Valley View Park, the wind tugged at the yellow brick two-storey house on the ridge like a tongue worrying a tooth. This was the Catchpoles' new house. Old Mary Springfield, distantly related to Angus across the hill, was wakened by lightning illuminating her room. She counted the seconds till the thunder. I do like a good storm, she thought. I've never been scared of storms. Great-grandmother and I used to go out on the verandah at Marycote and watch them together. Bother, she thought, her tongue probing, I forgot to floss my teeth . . . Well, I'm not getting out of bed just for that. And she laughed to herself, a little girl with a secret.

Forcing himself to bed at last, Angus Springfield lay listening to the screech of pine branches across the iron roof of the farmhouse. He hated the sound. It was like someone screaming, women, or a man . . . Metcalf. *Metcalf*. Should cut that big limb off, it's dangerous, he told himself. Fall on the roof one day. Should sleep in some other room. He shrugged at the bedclothes until the fold of the blankets was against his mouth. Could do with another blanket tonight, couple of blankets, three-dog night this one, better get up I suppose or I'll never drop off.

The blankets were in the linen press in the passage. He found his way easily without a light, then stood irresolutely. Do I want another drink? Might as well now I'm up, warm me up a bit, shouldn't have sat up keeping the fire company.

Waste of a good fire, though, turning in while it's blazing, risky too — sparks on the rug, or the chimney alight, the house, *houses, the village, walls and roofs made of straw and then the screaming — but turn away, turn away!* Decent of old Mary to drop by so often. She knows how to set a fire, Mary does. One match, turn your back and it's away *and then the screaming*

Oh Christ! Another whisky, and another whisky. Good woman, Mary. Wasted amongst that lot over at Valley View, Valley View Park I mean. Jesus!

In bed again, the extra blankets flung folded for double warmth, he sank into the constant roar of rain on the iron roof. Lambing weather, typical lambing weather, he thought, relieved that his ewes weren't due for another couple of months. Maybe this season we'll get a week or two of sunny weather at the right time. Could be lucky this year. Should shoot that fox I've seen playing round by the old cottage. Cheeky beggar. Come lambing she'll have cubs stashed away, up amongst the rocks or along the creek. Bloody foxes, bloody foreign pests. All they take is the tongue, and the tail. Big perfect lambs, they only go for the best.

He had thrown so many extra blankets on to the bed that he was starting to sweat. There was no relief. Forever sweating, and then the rashes. The everlasting heat. Useless thinking you could cool off when it rained; you could set your watch by the rain, every afternoon it came, warm as a downpour of blood.

Suddenly every object in the room stood out sharply in a phosphorescent glare. Thunder cannoned around him. The house shook. God, that one was close! Can't they knock the bastard out? Angus slid further down in his steaming bunker.

In Melbourne, a young woman who called herself Gita sat bolt upright. Where am I? she said aloud, or perhaps she dreamed that she spoke. Where am I? Where am I?

The storm's right over us, Mary Springfield thought, startled awake by a particularly loud bang. Turning her head, she caught her digital clock's red eye. The clock regarded her sternly: 2.52 . . . 2.53. Your teeth, Mary! The clock was her birthday present from the household. I do wish . . . I really did say a proper clock, just a cheap one, don't spend money on me, a proper clock with hands, and a tick. They could have listened. This ungrateful thought was followed as quickly as the thunder upon the lightning: for that I must make myself get up and floss my teeth.

Back in bed, she nudged at her doona. She never could get used to its lightness. She jumped as the wind brought half a dozen roof tiles shattering to the ground. Iron roofs, Mary thought, drifting back to sleep. I do like the sound of rain on an iron roof.

At Marycote, the cottage where Mary Springfield had spent her long-ago girlhood, a loose sheet of iron flapped in the wind, and a possum in the ceiling curled itself into a tighter ball.

Where am I? Where am I? the words forcing the solid darkness to retreat and revealing through the grey woven mesh of half-light the shapes of a window, a chair, another bed, and in it, breathing softly, the child. Gita's child.

Down, Metcalf! Down! Fuck you, get down! Angus shouted, scrabbling around on the blankets for his 222.

Voices. Women's voices. Women chatting in groups outside their houses. Children, and a few old men. The smells of things cooking indoors, tantalising smells, exotic, like the Chinese cafe at home but indefinably different, and the lazy smoke curling like mist, and out of the mist the child running, always running, running towards him, face lifted in welcome, You are num-bah one!, black hair cut in a fringe, trousers too big and shirt too small, You are num-bah one!, one hand outstretched and the other holding something, something for him and Metcalf entering the village ahead of the others – and this was a turnaround, this gift from a child: they were the ones who came armed with gifts, bits of soap, shaving cream, bubble gum for the kids — Metcalf in front of him, Metcalf moving ahead to take the kid's gift, Metcalf laughing, holding out his hand — in slow motion Angus saw it, again and again and again, saw the kid running, the women suddenly silent, watching, loud as a heartbeat the pattering steps, Metcalf holding out his hand, the watching women, the child's face lifted in ecstasy, then the arm bent, flick of wrist and himself and the child in that split-second throwing themselves to the ground, to safety — into a wheel rut, behind a smashed rubber tree oozing latex like blood . . .

Choking with dust. Choking with the heavy blankets. He hadn't even opened his mouth to shout Metcalf a warning.

2 At Last the Sky

At last the sky blew clear, and the treetops, and the paddocks. The child in the hearse was glad. His fingers picked with excitement at the frayed knees of his jeans. His lips danced a small song. Only in the distance, caught on a tall hill, tatters of mist still hung. Like washing, thought the child, or bits of dreams Gita forgot to dump in the ragbag. Now, as they drove past, the child, whose name was Jarrah, could see things — a hawk hanging from the sky, and big grey rounded rocks you could hide behind, or climb on, or maybe slide down, if only the hearse would stop. But it never would stop. Ahead of them, always ahead of them, the road ran uphill, drawing them forward, winding the old hearse on.

Jules was driving. It was Mark's hearse, reducoed white with the names of bands in fat bright letters the shape of your teeth when they fell out, and magic signs called the ASCII Code that Gita said was just old computer talk, not magic at all. That's all *you* know, Mark said. He'd fitted out the hearse inside with a tape deck and a heater and comfortable seats along each side for his friends, instead of flower racks with brass rails and rollers for the coffin. Ever since Mark had dumped himself at Gita's place he'd worked on the hearse in the back yard, when he wasn't practising on his drum pad or playing computer games. Sometimes he let Jarrah help on the hearse — maybe he might let Jarrah help, stand back, stand over there, just don't get in the way, okay? Today was the test run, Mark said. He'd put a tape in the new deck and played the beginning over and over full blast because of the drumming and then he'd turned it down and sung his own words again to make everyone laugh, " 'We're goin' to Grace Broz, Grace Broz,' we'll go into the country", and Jules had laughed, and Jarrah had thought good, that sounds good, I've never been to the country.

When they started off, it was Mark who was driving, with Jules in the front beside him. Mark was still singing. " 'From the desert . . . from the jungle . . . yeah oh yeah!' " he sang. When Gita hissed "He can never get the bloody words right!" he turned right round and grinned at her. " 'Don't cry-y-y, baby.' " Otherwise nobody talked much. Crystal and Gita and Jarrah were behind the two men, in the back where they used to put the dead people. Jarrah had one whole long seat to himself where he could stretch out flat. "Sit up! Get your feet!" Mark yelled at him through the rear vision mirror. I didn't hear that, Jarrah told himself. He swung his feet down very slowly and gazed at something behind Crystal and Gita.

Mark drove through the city until they came to the last of the big factories, and then he stopped and got out. Jarrah could see grass, lots of not-very-exciting dried-up white grass with a little bit of green underneath. This must be the country, he thought, waiting for something to happen. He hoped there would be a shop. He was starving. He'd woken up early at Crystal's place and finished off a packet of cornflakes and some cold chili beans in the fridge so that when Gita got up hours later he didn't want anything else but then somehow they missed out on lunch because Mark came to take them all to the country.

He looked around for the giant red box holding up the yellow M of a McDonald's. But all that was happening was that Mark was giving Jules a go with the hearse. Mark was always giving Jules a go with things. He never gave Jarrah a go on his Apple with Fantasy Zone or Wonder Boy or Rescue Mission. As Mark walked around the hearse and opened the other door, Jules slid across the seat into the driver's place. He glanced at the three in the back but his eyes didn't smile. As though we're some of the old chairs and things in his shop, Jarrah thought. Jules's skin was white as powder. His pale eyes were set so wide apart you felt that if they wanted they could see right round your face to the back of your head.

Jules's turn went on for hours — hours and hours and forever. When he came to the crest of the hill, Mark said "Let her rip, man!" but Jules changed into second gear and crept downhill towards a wooden bridge across a creek.

Mark punched Jules lightly on the shoulder. "Power, man!"

Jules took no notice. Jarrah was glad. When Mark moved in at Gita's place, he was always on at Jarrah about something, knock before you barge in thanks buster (and Gita let him say it), or stop that racket, can't you see I'm working, can't you see we're busy? I'm glad glad glad Gita and I live at Crystal's now, thought Jarrah. He stared at the back of Mark's head, where little bits of hair were pulled taut by the rubber band every time he moved his head. I wish I had a rubber band to snap, thought Jarrah, narrowing his eyes at Mark's plump neck.

Now Jules was driving even slower, leaning on the steering wheel to crane sideways past Mark. "See anything, anyone?"

"What are we looking for?" Jarrah shouted, peering from side to side then kneeling up on the seat to see better. "Mind that upholstery!" said the rear vision mirror. Jarrah pressed his nose flat against the window and breathed *hah* on to the glass. In the country there were lots of sheep, and two magpies blowing about in the wind, and the collapsed iron and one brick chimney of a burnt-out building. And, running through the grass, parallel lines of rock. "Like railway lines, Gita!" he exclaimed, turning to her. "Out there in the country, look! Next time me and you'll go by train, let's!"

But Gita's eyes slid over him like a train that won't

stop *veins across a green scalp, hollow veins rotting pumped full of green pus*

Jarrah stared at her, then turned away. To the north and west (he knew that by the sun, and wondered if the others knew it too, but couldn't be bothered asking them, I just couldn't be bothered, he told himself) to the north and west he could see right across a valley to a mist-covered hill in the distance. Now that the sun had stopped sulking, the clouds behind the hill shone like wet stones. "Valley View Park," he read aloud from a sign over a wide white gateway by the roadside. Water was running under the gate in little rivers and disappearing into a ditch. He sat around again. "What are we looking for? . . . Gita," he said, addressing the question to her maybe.

Gita didn't answer. Nobody answered. Crystal, who told him things sometimes, was too busy exclaiming "Just look at that yellow monster on the ridge!" Jules drawled "Why *do* people?" then laughed his special Jules-laugh that made Jarrah think of catching your just-cut toenails on the top sheet. He used to laugh it a lot when Gita and Jarrah were living with him. Jarrah decided he liked Mark better. Mark wasn't looking out for anything, he was rabbiting on about revs and things. As for Gita, she'd been in a shit ever since Mark came as arranged to pick them up at Crystal's place (and she'd put on her olive-green dress and her leather jacket with the studs and her black leather cap that she wore at the back of her head) and then she'd seen Jules in the passenger seat in the front and she'd said "All right then, Mark, in that case I'm bringing Crystal", and Crystal, who'd been working late at the refuge, had jumped out of bed even though it was her day off, grabbed Annie's overalls off the clothes-line because all Crystal's own things were in the machine, and was ready in a flash. It was supposed to be just Gita and Jarrah and Mark so that Mark could show off his hearse, and it ended up being five, with Gita in one of her moods.

What are we looking for? Jarrah repeated, in a mumbling burr to himself. Maybe when somebody sees it, Jules will stop and I can look for shiny stones in the creek − "Jarrah," said

Gita — or tadpoles under the bridge, or a lamb, I could catch a lamb for a pet —

"Stop it, Jarrah."

"I'm not doing anything."

"Yes you are, you know you are. He's always doing it, he drones, he does it all the time," she said, her face tight, so that Crystal patted her hand, pulled Gita's arm through hers and went on patting her hand and Gita let her. Gita just let her even though she hated people grabbing at her — Jarrah, or Jules when they were living with Jules.

"Will there be taddies in that creek, Gita? Gita?"

But it was Crystal who answered. "Too early yet, mate."

"Lambs? Lambs, Gita?"

"Too cold," Crystal said.

"I hate the country," Jarrah said.

"I had a foul dream last night," Gita began, and for a moment Jarrah thought she was talking to him. "I had a foul dream, I thought I was in a coffin," she muttered, staring at some spot on the seat beside Jarrah.

"Thinking about going out today," Crystal said drily.

"No." Gita shuddered. "It wasn't a coffin, more like a space capsule, you know? Only I *was* the space capsule, or the coffin, whatever it was, falling through space, through nowhere, just falling and falling, in it and not in it, dead but alive —"

"I dreamed that too!" Jarrah said, his voice growing shrill. "I dreamed I was in a little space, Gita, and then I woke up and I'd fallen out of bed between the bed and the wall, and I thought wow, I'm in a space capsule, I'm dead and alive, because I wasn't properly awake, you see, and when you're not properly awake you think funny things, even if you're awake enough to climb back into bed but you go on dreaming. I dreamed I was falling through space, Gita. I dreamed the same dream as you!"

"Liar!" said Mark over his shoulder, and Jules even though he was driving turned right around and laughed at him over the back of the seat.

Gita pulled her arm out of Crystal's. "He might have dreamed that, how do you know he didn't?"

Jarrah tried to catch her eye, smile friendly again at her, but she was staring past him out the window, she was saying to no one in particular, "Why shouldn't our dreams go out and mingle with other people's, get all mixed up, good dreams and bad dreams, bits and pieces, why shouldn't they?" She was staring past Jarrah out the window, talking to nobody, and nobody answered.

3 Now What Will We Do

"Now what will we do while Mummy and Daddy are away this weekend?" said Mary Springfield to the three children at Valley View Park.

"Mummy! Daddy!" scoffed Jane, who was, Mary Springfield kept reminding herself, at a difficult age.

Mary had been up since before dawn to help Lou and Belle get away. "At this rate we'll be hanging about at the airport for a good three hours, Mary," Lou Catchpole grumbled.

"Then you might be very glad I've filled a thermos, Lou."

The Range Rover shot away in a scrunch of gravel, a chorus of farewells echoing in their ears. Drive carefully! Have fun! Goodbye! Belle, your umbrella! Sydney's weather! What time do you think you . . . Take good care of Mary, kids! Mary, don't let . . . Watch out for . . . Come on Belle, we'll be gone two days not two years, girl! Goodbye! Goodbye!

Now it was mid-morning. Mary was at the stove stirring a batch of toffee, and the children, Jane and the little boys Elton and Keiran, were waiting to lick the saucepan.

"It's turned out so nice, chicks," Mary continued. "Hardly any wind, and the sun shining again."

"I know what you're going to say," said Elton. "Let's have a — "

"Picnic," said Keiran, looking at Elton then pushing out his own lip.

"You guessed!" said Mary brightly, trying to keep doubt at bay as she glanced down at their faces. "How would you like me to make you a special picnic lunch, apple and nut sandwiches . . . well then vegemite . . . strawberry jam – "

"Yuk!" said the children. "Yuk! Yuk!"

"And afterwards, just for special, toffee."

"I hate picnics," said Elton.

"We hate picnics."

"A walk, then? How about a good brisk walk?" She saw the boys grin at each other: her pace these days was much too slow for them. "Blow the cobwebs away," she continued valiantly. "It's been so drizzly, you've been cooped up inside all week. You could take Chomper." She smiled with wicked cunning. "On a nice long rope. He'd love that."

"You take Chomper. He's your dog."

But I don't love Chomper! Mary silently protested. That wretched animal. He was a white bull terrier with a black patch over one eye that gave him an unbalanced, piratical look. One Christmas Santa had brought him for Elton and Keiran, and three elegant spangled bantams for Jane. Somehow, by a process which Mary could never work out, the bantams had survived the puppy's chasing, and Chomper had turned into "Mary's dog". I don't need a dog, thought Mary, not a dog that digs, and chews rocks, running up to you with that silly grin, begging you to throw a rock for him to chase and pounce on and growl over, rolling it in his paws and grinding his poor teeth shorter and shorter right down to his gums.

Whenever I go out the door he's waiting for me, all short teeth and smile. Oh good heavens! Mary nearly burned herself, such a painful thought had clutched at her side. Do *I* smile at people like that?

The kitchen leapt around her with doggy grins.

"Anyway I want to watch the footie," Elton said.

"We want to watch the footie."

"I'm going to watch a video," said Jane. She added "In Mum and Dad's room."

Mary Springfield was about to ask "What video, dear? Did your mother . . ." but at the shape of Jane's mouth she said only "All right, no picnic. We'll have lunch here as usual and I'll go for a walk." And no toffee either, she thought, testing a drop of the creamy-gold mixture in cold water. I'll take the lot with me to Marycote.

"Did Mum say you could use all that butter?" said Jane.

4   The Massy Green

The massy green boobiallas overhanging the wooden gate were so thick that only Jarrah, looking past Gita's head as the road curved slightly, noticed the house set in the step of the fence-line. It was made of weatherboard, with peeling paint like Gita's place in the city, and it was much smaller than the yellow brick house that had shouted at them from the ridge. With its verandah roof pulled over its eyes like a sunhat, the house turned its face towards him like a kid at a new school who's going to let you play with him.

He leaned over and shook her arm. "Look, Gita, look behind you. Plenty of space for you there."

Gita's head turned the way a mother's does when she's not really listening.

"There!" Jarrah shouted. "Plenty of — "

It was Jules who took any notice. Stopping the hearse suddenly, he craned around to look back at Jarrah's cottage. "Victorian. Three chimneys. See that, Mark? Three chimneys means at least three mantelpieces. On yer, mate!" He grinned at Jarrah, then put the hearse into reverse. "We should have guessed there'd be a house behind all those trees. What are they, boobiallas?" Jules was asking Mark but Jarrah could tell he really knew the answer.

The tops of the old posts leading you towards the recessed wooden gate in the roadside fence were shaped like candle flames.

"Want me to see if it's locked?" Mark asked eagerly.

"No, mate. Just hop out and see if that's a hard patch behind the wattles there, this side of the fence. I'll put her in there, out of the way."

"Too many low branches, don't you reckon? I mean, the new duco and all that —"

"No worries, mate. No trubs." This was the way Jules talked when people started fussing.

Mark jumped out, tramped about gingerly in his new Doc Marten boots with the red laces (like Gita's), then came up to Jules's window. "No chance of getting bogged there, that's for sure, but I'm not too keen on all those low branches."

"Next time I'll bring the panel van," Jules said. "They're everywhere."

"You don't see too many about like this old girl," Mark said proudly.

"That's just what I mean, mate, that's just what I mean." Jules laughed, and after a moment Mark laughed too. Mark stepped back then, and Jules manoeuvred the hearse off the drive on to the firm tussocky grass beside the fence, between the wattles and the boobiallas and out of sight from both the road and the house. Jarrah, craning through the glass of the back doors, could see Mark looking anxious as branches scraped the bonnet and one side of the hearse. As soon as it was parked they all got out, stretching and looking over the gate. A drive, grassed over now except where rain over the years had washed out some deep ruts, ran up to the cottage and past it to an old garage leaning crazily like a man with a bad back.

Crystal nodded towards the bare hill rising behind the cottage. "Look at that, Gita. Typical, isn't it?"

"Give it a rest, Crystal, give it a rest," said Jules, untwisting the wire that fastened the gate to the post. He swung the gate open. "After you," he said, very polite.

"What is? Look at what?" said Jarrah to Crystal as they walked towards the cottage, since Gita hadn't answered.

"That hill, mate, behind the cottage there. Bare as a baby's bum. Not a tree left standing. Oh, they spared a few by the cottage, along the fence, see. That's something. Most old houses have exotics planted around them. Pine trees, or gross yellow cypresses."

"We're all exotics," Gita muttered. "You too, Crys."

Exotics, Jarrah droned, tasting the new word. He wondered why Gita sounded so grumpy. Crystal was her friend. "They're ji-normous, those gum trees," he commented, pleased that Crystal was telling him things again. That was maybe the best thing about being at her house, her telling him things. And having plenty to eat. His stomach rattled. He wondered if either of them had something to chew right now.

"Sure are big," Crystal agreed. "Gives you a good idea of what the bush was like before the farmers got to it, doesn't it? That's farmers for you, Jarrah."

Gita, trailing along with her head down, looked up then. "They came in and raped it. Is that what you're trying to say, Crys?"

Jarrah picked up a dried cow pat and spun it away like a frisbee. The women who dropped in at Crystal's house often talked this way, propped against the sink while Crystal made peppermint tea, or curled up in armchairs with someone else leaning against their knees. There were certain words at which their voices grew fierce. It was the same with everyone, Jarrah supposed. After Mark moved in, those words had been foresters and crops and profit. Mark and his friends in the band would talk furiously while Gita picked at her dulcimer or sat with it asleep in her lap like a baby. At Crystal's the worst word was rape. And Jules must have known this, because he had to have a go at her.

"You're dressed for the part at any rate," he said. "For farming I mean, Crystal, not rape. I thought that uniform was out of fashion now."

"What are you on about, Jules?"

"The old bib and brace, my dear. The old bib and brace." And he laughed, pleased with himself.

"What's going on today, Gita? What's Jules up to this time?" Crystal demanded as they followed him towards the cottage. "Mind the mud, you're getting those nice shoes soaked. You should have worn your boots." Gita glanced covertly at the slops of mud on her flimsy shoes: she had been wearing her Doc Martens with the red laces for the drive with Mark, but when he'd brought Jules too and she'd run back to get Crystal, she'd flung them across her room. "What's Jules up to?" Crystal repeated. "Gita, I don't like this."

Gita kept her head down. "Stay in the hearse then, Crys."

"A cottage this size is unusual in having three chimneys," Jules was telling Mark.

"Maybe they liked making chimneys," Jarrah put in, but nobody took any notice.

Around the cottage was another row of posts with candle-flame tops. The front gate was padlocked. On the other side of the gate, a zigzag brick path ran up to the verandah. But the front door was shut, and the windows on each side of it were boarded up.

"It can't see and it can't speak," said Jarrah, pointing. "Where are its ears, d'you reckon? Maybe it's listening to us. D'you think it's listening to us?"

This time Jules did respond. "See no evil, hear no evil, speak not of evil," he said, and laughed his nail-scraping laugh. So what's so funny, thought Jarrah. Jules always has to say something. Now Jules was leaning over the gate and nodding towards the uphill side fence. "Loose picket," he said. They walked around the fence, and Jules held the picket aside while each one climbed through. Crystal was last. "Go on," she said impatiently. "After you," he said, all over again. Bor-ing, thought Jarrah. Bang bang gotcha! This is an ace garden, he thought, picturing kids chasing one another in and out of the twisted trees shedding leaves the colour of blood. You could make ace hideouts. He ran up the front steps and tried to peer through the boarded-up windows, but wasn't tall enough to reach up to where one of the boards had fallen away.

The adults followed more slowly. Jules knocked, then gave the front door a light push.

"Do the old card trick, Jules," Mark said excitedly, as though he had only just learned about it. "You know, slide a credit card up against the tongue of the lock." He pulled out his wallet. Jules raised his eyebrows in the direction of the road. "There's no one —" Mark began.

"In the country," Jules interrupted, "isn't it customary to go to the back door?" He led the way off the low end of the verandah and continued along the zigzag path. "Handmade," he said, nodding at the bricks.

Show off, thought Jarrah.

Show off, thought Gita. "Someone lives here, they've been gardening, Mark," she said suddenly, leaning against his shoulder. "Just recently, see." She indicated the tiny, pointed leaves of spring bulbs and, beside them, a small heap of freshly pulled flatweeds. She squatted down and turned them over. "I could make soup from these," she murmured, using his hand to pull herself upright. "Mark."

"Soup? From grass?"

"They're dandelions, silly. You can use them for soup. Tea. Beer."

Mark turned to Jules. "You hear that? Gita reckons you can eat these weeds."

"You certainly can eat them," Crystal put in. "They're good for the liver."

"They stir up the blood." Gita laughed. "Mark? Stir up the blood."

"Pee-the-beds?" said Jules. "Great." He narrowed his eyes at Gita and Mark. Gita turned aside with a shrug.

At the back of the house was another boarded-up window where there wasn't even a knothole. Jarrah, trying to peer in, succeeded only in scratching his cheek on the secretive boards.

"That'll be the kitchen," old know-all Jules told him. "Because of the chimney we walked past round the corner."

Jarrah looked up, and read the word Marycote burned into a slab of wood above the back door. Unlike the front door, this one was closed with an old-fashioned bolt with a padlock attached. Jules knocked, listened, then lifted the whole bolt out of the grey splintery wood. They stepped into a passage that led to the front door. A small room to their left contained an iron bath with claw feet, a copper, and two concrete laundry troughs.

"You could have a bath in that, it's so big," Jarrah said, leaning over the copper.

"I daresay people did. Kids like you, once," Crystal told him. He liked Crystal.

Jules tried to rock the copper. "Nice one," he said speculatively.

Across the passage was a narrow room that Jules had said would be the kitchen. Jarrah went over to the large window he had tried to peer through from outside. Not even a knothole this side, either. Gradually their eyes adjusted to the semi-darkness. There were bird droppings over the floor and on the benches, and a strong smell as though some animal had made its home here. At one end of the room, on the outside wall, was an open fireplace with two tiny low windows, very cobwebby, set into the bricks of the chimney.

"Pine, without a doubt," Jules said, patting the high mantelpiece. "There's progress for you," he added, indicating an old-fashioned wood stove beside the fireplace and, actually standing in it, on the bricks, an electric stove.

"Maybe they liked the wood stove for winter and the electric for summer," Crystal said.

"Sure. Hot for winter and cool for summer," Gita added in the same argumentative tone.

Jules ignored them, of course. He bent over a pile of yellowing newspapers in a cardboard box by the stove. "Record number of strikes, pensioners hit hardest this winter, PM slates unions," he read. "Well, what do you know."

Mark flicked a switch by the door. "Sorry folks, temporary power failure due to industrial action." He grinned from face to face, urging them to laugh at his joke.

A bird suddenly darted from somewhere near the ceiling and out into the passage.

Jarrah pointed. "There's a nest on top of the light shade."

"That's a swallow's nest," Crystal told him.

"Nesting now? Is it nesting now? Lift me up, Gita. I want to see the swallow's eggs."

But Gita pushed him away. "Fair go, you're too big. Anyway, it's an old nest. It must be, they don't nest till spring. Do they?" she appealed to the others.

Mark was sliding out drawers and opening cupboards. "Take a look at this stuff, will you! Cutlery. Plates. Cups. Yuk — mouse droppings."

"You could walk right in and set up home," Gita said dreamily, running her finger around the rim of a rusted saucepan.

Jarrah pushed in beside the electric stove and peered up the chimney. Set in the bricks was a heavy bar the width of the fireplace. He pulled it; it swung out past the electric stove and over the hearth. "What's this bar for?" he asked. "Gita?"

"To hang kettles and pots on," Jules and Crystal said in unison. Then glowered at each other. "You used it in the old days," Jules told him. "Over an open fire," Crystal added. "In the olden days. For cooking on the open fire."

"Nothing worth anything here," Jules said. "Unless someone wants . . ." and he nodded at the plates and cutlery. "Let's have a look at those mantelpieces, Mark."

In the room behind the kitchen they could make out a couple of armchairs, one lying on its side, and a leather sofa with a castor missing.

"Worthless," Jules pronounced, running his hand over the sofa. "Woodworm," he said, turning over a chair. He beckoned Mark over to the mantelpiece. "See this? Cedar. Australian red cedar from the north coast. I thought it might be." He ran his hand gently over the mantelpiece. "Let's see what's on offer in the next room. There should be another fireplace sharing its chimney with this one." He was right: in the front room, smaller than the sitting room, was a third fireplace, and over the fireplace another cedar mantelpiece.

"Want the jemmy?" said Mark.

Crystal said sharply "Just what smart deal are these two getting you mixed up in this time, Gita?"

Jules, raising one sorrowful eyebrow, said "You just don't trust her, do you, Crystal?" and Mark added "Don't you think she might find that question just a little bit hurtful, Crystal?

Just a little bit nasty? You said the same sort of thing about the band."

"It wasn't the band. It was the way you both tried — "

"She knows a dulcimer's useless in a rock band, Crystal."

"And she has the voice, Crystal, the voice is perfect, if only she'd practise."

"Anyway, it's not the band I'm talking about right now, and you two know it." Crystal looked at Jules. "What I want to know is, just what are you involving her in this time?"

She! She! She! Gita said "Nothing I can't handle myself, Crys, okay?"

And Crystal: "Then I'm going for a walk."

"Oh for God's sake!" Gita slammed the door on the lot of them and went across the passage into the room opposite. In here there was a little more light. The room was half filled with bales of hay stacked in steps to the ceiling. Jarrah, sitting on a bale, was watching a bird darting to and fro. "Shh, Gita!" he hissed. "It's that swallow, isn't it? It's trying to find the smashed pane at the top of the window, see, where the board's fallen off."

Gita shut the door and pushed a bale of hay against it. "What a lovely smell," she murmured, climbing up on to a step in the hay and leaning back. "Like sunshine. I could go to sleep for a year." And she smiled at Jarrah, the old sleepy smile that he loved.

"Are we going to stay here, Gita?" he asked. "Just me and you, are we going to live here?"

"No silly, I've told you. We're staying at Crystal's for a bit and then we're going back to my place."

"With Mark?"

"Sure with Mark."

"D'you like Mark, Gita?"

"Sure I like Mark."

"Crystal? D'you like Crystal?"

"Sure I do. Hey, what is this?"

"An' Jules? Jules, Gita."

"Look, why don't you go out for a walk. Crystal said she

was going for a walk, why don't you go too. Find something to tell your new teacher."

"I don't like my new teacher."

"Hey now, come on. From Crystal's place you can walk to your new school."

"I like my old school."

"It won't be for long. I promise."

"You said that last time."

"Well excuse me, Jarrah, but aren't you being just a little bit selfish? We'll all be getting in the hearse and going home soon. Go on out and find something while there's still time, okay?"

"Find what?"

Gita laughed exasperatedly. "How should I know till you find it?"

Just then the bale of hay scraped across the floor as the door was pushed open. "So this is where you're hiding," Jules said. "Mark's gone off to look for you."

Jarrah stood up. "I bet I know what you two are going to do, you're going to smoke dope."

He went out.

5   Buttercups and Orange Peels

Jules shrugged, palms upwards, his long fingers, Gita thought, curling like wakening snakes. "Doesn't anyone trust me?"

Gita laughed. "So? Have you got some? Dope, I mean?"

"No, my dear. You know me, travel clean, make sure your jocks are darned in case you're run down by a bus. Songs my mother taught me. Didn't yours?" Gita laughed again, a hard little half-laugh that people seemed to use in Jules's company. Jules pushed the bale of hay back against the door and, coming across the room, leaned against the stack of hay and looked up at her. Smiled. Flicked back his dead-straight grey hair in a boyish gesture.

"Gita. Old friend."

It was true: she had known Jules for so long he was part of her own skin. Other people had dropped away like healed scabs. Many of them she had met at Jules's place: Jarrah's father, and Crystal — looking for a girl she thought might OD.

Everyone knew Jules.

But Mark — Mark she had found for herself. She smiled.

Jules said "Your slow-motion smile."

"I bet that's not original. I bet you read it somewhere."

"Gita!"

"Like the name of your house. You didn't think of that. Wyewurrk."

"Why think of something yourself if someone else will do it for you?" Gita made to slide down from the hay. He caught her wrist. "You're running away. Why are you always running away?"

"I feel bad about Crystal just now. I should go and apologise."

Jules laughed. "What's it like, all those fems together in the one house?"

"All those fems! Crystal and Annie and me. And three kids."

"Mark misses you, Gita. Don't you miss him?" Reaching up, he ran his hand over her face, as though it was a mantelpiece he had discovered. "Of course you do." He stared at her. He screws me with his eyes, she thought. She stared back. I won't look away first.

"Come over here," Jules said, turning his head towards the fireplace. He took her hands and jumped her down. We're the same height! she thought. It always surprised her. It was the way he stood, tight as a coiled spring. Lifting his feet up by his chin, Jarrah had once observed. "I want you to look at this mantelpiece, what you can see of it behind all this straw," he was saying. "Mice, damp, it'll be ruined if someone doesn't do something." She watched his hands run over the curves of the mantelpiece as tenderly as they had over her face. "Original," he was saying. "Just like the others." He looked at her questioningly. She waited. "You could make use of a mantelpiece."

"A mantelpiece! What are you on about this time? I've got no use for a mantelpiece."

"Of course you haven't, my dear. Not as such. Though others might."

"So? You've got someone with an old fireplace who wants an old mantelpiece." She ran her hand over the scroll as Jules had done. "They look fine to me here, in this place."

"And so does a fistful of dollars in that dainty hand of yours. You surely haven't forgotten?"

She sighed. "What are you on about, Jules?"

"I'd have a buyer tomorrow."

"And you would give me . . . You don't give up, do you?"

"For old times' sake."

"I'm not interested."

"No? Then I'm disappointed." She said nothing. "I thought you were smarter than that." Still she said nothing. "I thought you valued your independence."

"I do. Look, Jules, get this straight. I'll never be back."

"Cash in hand is independence. And a new leather jacket." He put his finger in the rip along the shoulder and tweaked the frayed seam.

"Stop it, Jules."

"Gita! Gita! Is that what they taught you when you ran away to that place? Is that what our friend in the overalls and all her fems in the femmery are telling you?" He took hold of her hand.

"I said stop it. You know what I mean. I want out. I am out. And Mark wants out. Him and me. Leave us alone, okay?"

"I suppose right at this very moment Mark up on the hillside somewhere might be saying the very same thing to Crystal. Leave her alone, Crystal. Or are they different somehow, Mark's friendship with me, and your being at Crystal's?"

"That's just for a week or two. While I sort a few things out. He understands."

"Does he? That's not the story I hear."

The swallow, which had been motionless for some time at the top of the hay somewhere, began to dart to and fro across the ceiling. The room, for all the sunshine trapped in the hay, was suddenly freezing. Jules's breath was warm on her neck. Her hard little laugh flew out. "Well isn't it good he's got you!" she sneered. "As thick as thieves, as they say." She laughed again, hot with the old wild feeling of power. I need nothing from you, she thought. I don't need anyone, Jules, least of all you. Not now. Not ever again. I am the strong one now.

He said softly "Sometimes Mark's not very smart about his contacts, Gita. Did you know he's using?"

"You are the user, Jules."

He laughed. "My dear Gita, there's using, and there's using."

"Meaning?"

"Meaning it doesn't use me."

She hated his patronising smile. "You're the worst sort of user, Jules. And if Mark doesn't wake up to you, you'll do to him what you do to all your friends."

"And what is that?"

"You squeeze them dry and spit them out."

If she hoped to offend him, she was disappointed. He laughed again. "Is that so? Like pips from an orange, you mean?"

"And the flesh, the flesh too! Because you want only the juice of the orange, not the good part, not the nourishing part, not the flesh!"

Jules raised one eyebrow. It was the first thing she had ever noticed about him, this trick with his eyebrows. Muscular control, he had said. Nothing but muscular control. Anyone can do it. If they want to. But try as she had, she had never succeeded. Jules was saying "What an interesting choice of images. I'm not sure that you're right, though." He put one arm around her shoulder and gave her a quick hug. "This is just like old times, isn't it? All the jousting."

"It's all a game to you, isn't it? Squeezing people dry."

"And you think I'm going to do that to your boyfriend?"

"I know you will."

"Well then . . . it's Mark, not the mantelpiece that you

want, is it? Yes?" The thin, greedy mouth was as mocking as ever. "You must love him very much."

"I never said anything about love."

"Neither you did."

"I need nothing from you, Jules. Not now, not ever again."

"We're two of a kind, you and I."

She shuddered. "Don't say that!"

Laughing, he pushed her back against the hay. His hands, busy with their clothes, her limbs, his own preparations, began a conversation quite separate from what his mouth was telling her. His words, she told herself. Concentrate on his words. It always worked, with Jules, with the others. "Though I'm a more orderly person than you," he was saying. "I like things in their place. But you . . . you . . ." The words faltered, as though he, at least, were listening to their flesh. "You, if you will recall, I found . . . unpredictable. Spontaneous but . . . unpredictable. That's what I find so attractive. Whereas Mark is totally — ah yes! — ah yes!"

See no evil, she adjured the blind window. Over Jules's shoulder she watched the trapped swallow. Suddenly it found the broken pane above the boards and swooped out. She felt exultant, as though she were the freed bird, then was seized by last night's dream and was afraid, emptied of everything but dread. She clung to Jules.

"That's better," he said.

Standing up, he brushed away bits of hay and straightened his clothes. "I'm reminded of something I came across the other day," he said as he helped her to her feet. "In an old school text in a box of books someone was trying to flog. Clear thinking exercises. Who'd want that these days? Anyway, I took the book home because it looked amusing, and something in it's just come back to me." He flicked a wisp of dried grass from her hair. "It might amuse you, my lovely Gita. Don't look so angry — my lovely Gita. Think about this little exercise instead. Just look at those nasty pieces of orange peel — or are they pretty buttercups?"

6   You Look Like a Parrot

"You come and meet me," said Mary Springfield to the three Catchpole children, "in, let's see, one hour from now. All right, an hour and a half. Not more than two. And then we'll have the rest of the toffee."

"Aren't you leaving it here?" "For us?" cried the two boys, watching Mary slip the hardened golden squares out of a cake tin into a paper bag.

"Jane will make sure you cross the road safely." The boys raised their eyes ceilingwards. "Won't you, dear? Jane? Jane dear?" Mary left three toffee squares in the tin and passed it to Elton. "I'll be over at the cottage."

"But that's in Springfield's place!" Elton protested, his mouth twitching sideways in an involuntary tic.

"What if ol' Angus's out after rabbits and takes a potshot at us? Give me my piece, Elton, you spaz!"

Elton roared around the kitchen, holding the tin just out of the smaller boy's reach. "Springfield's a spaz! Keiran's a spaz!"

Jane Catchpole watched Mary Springfield slip the bag of toffee into her coat pocket. It was an old Driza-bone of Lou Catchpole's that Mary wore for rough jobs like collecting kindling: would wear for collecting kindling, except that Valley View Park didn't burn wood. In the sunroom there was just the one huge fireplace the width of the end wall where the fire was rarely lighted: too much trouble, Lou said, too messy; stifling with a crowd. It was all electricity now, a heat cold as charity Mary thought whenever she recalled the big roaring fires in old homesteads she had worked in: many around the district, Marycote, of course, and Springfield when Angus was away and she'd been helping Belle out, and then the old Catchpole place called Valley View, before it was burnt down. She had never ached with the cold then.

Mary saw Jane staring at her as she rugged up – purple balaclava to protect her ears from the wind, green and yellow scarf, thick red gloves. The girl was at a difficult age. Mary put an extra kind smile on her face.

"You look like a rainbow," said Jane. "You look like a parrot."

Mary smiled. Smiled. The scarf around the balaclava protected her ears from more than the stinging wind.

She left the house by the front door. This way she might just manage to give that silly dog the slip. She tiptoed through the house, opened the door quietly, opened it wider — and there he was, tail swinging, eyes eager, tongue slavering and a round wet stone at his feet. As she watched, he picked it up, shook his head, and dropped it again.

"I'll fix you," said Mary Springfield.

Walking down the steps to the first rock-edged garden bed, she loosened a round rock much too big for his jaws and rolled it along the path. Away bounded Chomper. He caught up with the rock and lay with it between his front paws, grinding it, nudging it, grumbling fondly in his throat.

Mary slammed the gate. "You ridiculous thing," she said, more gently than she had intended.

She slipped a piece of toffee into her mouth.

7   Marycote

Mary climbed into the garden at Marycote by way of the loose picket. Unlike Crystal, she would have been charmed had Jules been there to hold it aside for her. At first she stood on the front verandah and looked around her, just as Gita was to do an hour or so later. Leaning on the wooden rail, she popped another toffee into her mouth and gazed over the creek and the road towards Jarrah's misty hill. It was a perfect autumn day, a perfect view. She stepped off the verandah at the uphill end and tugged at a few weeds that were choking the newly emerged points of snowdrops and snowflakes and sweet-smelling jonquils, old-fashioned bulbs that had been part of her great-grandmother's garden. The first Mary Springfield. Well I don't suppose they are the same bulbs, any more than I am that other woman, and yet we are, too. Bulbs divide, and they stay the same. Springfield, my great-grandmother said, that day I came home crying from school, my mouth full of the ashes of my mother's pitiful lies. Springfield, said my great-grandmother. Now there's a name. Have that name now, young Mary.

Mary straightened up. She wished she had a fork. The ground in spite of the rain was too hard. The flatweeds broke off at the ground, leaving the tough root to send up a new crop of flourishing leaves. Wonderful, thought Mary, picturing that powerful root, what goes on underground. She rubbed her back. Bending and pulling made her shoulders tired. And there was a niggling pain in her side again. Before the children arrived she would sit down to catch her breath. There was a spot beside the old mulberry tree growing against the high western wall of the cottage. It would be out of any wind. She walked around the house. If she had wanted to go inside she could easily have pulled the bolt out of the door frame. But why bother, when it was all there in her head. Her childhood.

She did pause to look up at the name burned by her great-grandfather into a slab of iron bark over the back door: MARYCOTE. For his bride. Here Mary's thoughts faltered, because that was unfamiliar country: she had never been a bride. And by the time Mary of Marycote's proud groom got around to having the name beaten into a bright sheet of copper, to be placed to the right of the front door, he had moved his fecund wife and his children to the shelter of the next valley where the lettering on the copper plate read SPRINGFIELD.

Marycote. And now Mary Springfield of Marycote lay in the churchyard overlooking the little town, dreaming of all the years of sweeping and scrubbing and boiling up the mud-stiffened work clothes, and the monthly rags, and bringing up the sons her husband had wanted, nursing them through accidents and sickness and burying some before their time; watching with awe as her husband with god-like power set the hills ablaze to clear the obstinate forest; jumping at the crack of a stick when bushrangers were about; giving (when her husband wasn't in sight) a loaf of bread and sweet tea or an old dress to a passing black woman; moving away to the grand new house in the next valley and later, widowed, moving back again to the cottage her husband had named for her. All these stories the child Mary had heard from the old, old lady who had given a home to the granddaughter, Mary's own mother, who had brought disgrace upon the family while hardly more than a child herself.

Such a pretty little thing that I was, thought Mary Springfield, who had seen the old photos. Of course all babies are pretty, she added hastily (though, having nursed many of the district's young mothers in their first days home from hospital, she was never quite convinced). And named after that kind generous woman, she continued, since this was a safer thought. Or was it the cottage I was named after? A child again, she ran inside the cottage. And what have you been doing, young Mary, said Great-grandmother Springfield, cutting thick slices of freshly baked crusty bread for the hungry child.

And how could she reply?

For what has my life been, wailed Mary at the locked door, but sweeping and scrubbing and baking and hanging out other people's washing and taking it in again and waiting to bleed every month till I dried up moons ago like a pool in a drought? And what has it all added up to? Answer, Mary, or you'll get the cane across your knuckles! She felt bad again: for what is life but the pleasure of doing things for other people? All the same I never dreamed the years would fly so fast like swallows at evening; at the beck and call of this one then that one, poor things all of them, ill, or old, or burdened with too many children, and I a single woman with no ties — how could I ever say no?

Poor Belle, for instance, when Angus came home and was . . . difficult. And him such a good man at heart! Poor bride, she did try. Coping like a good daughter-in-law with his parents, poor George crippled up in his body and Kate in her mind. Having to run Springfield because Angus wouldn't, and Belle not even farm-bred — who else was there to turn to except me? We did a good job between us, Belle and me.

There was the occasional hand from Lou Catchpole across the valley. Neighbourly, I thought at the time.

Perhaps when she'd left Springfield for good and George was dead and poor Kate in the hospital, I should have stayed on. Maybe he would have come home. He's never turned on me. A man needs a woman around the house . . . a *house* needs a woman, even if she is only some old distant relative. When he shut the place up I could have rented Marycote. If only I'd had the courage to ask. Instead, I ended up at Lou Catchpole's place. Who would have dreamed it?

Well, that is my life, thought Mary Springfield, looking up at her name on another woman's cottage. Turning away, she saw the huge limb of the manna gum that had fallen across the fence. Oh, she thought, now I will have to tell Lou and he'll start to fuss again about straightening that step in the fence, he'll go stirring up Angus. If only the boundary fence had been built in a straight line to begin with! If only one of the Springfields, Angus's grandfather, was it, hadn't sold the farm he called Valley View to Lou Catchpole's grandfather. Then there'd never have been years of argument between neighbours over a silly thing like a dog-leg fence.

If only our lives could be so neat!

I am very tired, thought Mary Springfield, continuing her walk around the cottage. Just a few minutes' rest by the mulberry. As it did every autumn, the tree caught her breath. It was a magic tree, covered with gold coins. I used to pretend they would take me anywhere, if I collected enough. How I loved gobbling the fat juicy mulberries in summer! How Mother would scold at the purple stains on my face and hands and pinafore! Poor Mother, so worried about stains.

Just a moment here out of the wind, and then I'll start out to meet the children. They really are funny about a chance meeting with Angus. She took out another piece of toffee. Soon her head dropped on to her chest. Her mouth fuzzy with sugar, she fell asleep. She did not hear the hearse pull in at the front gate, nor the four adults and the child come up to the house. They did not see her, because, like Mary, they entered the garden on the uphill side. She did not hear Jules knock on the door, but she did think, like Gita, I could sleep for a year, and she felt the house sigh with dismay when Gita clung to Jules.

8 Gita Fled

Gita fled to the front verandah. Leaning on the rail, she made herself hold on to the path's patterned brickwork, the lock on the garden gate, the willows growing along the creek, the road, the bridge. At a step on the verandah she turned abruptly. It was Crystal.

"There you are, Gita."

So that's where you're hiding! There you are!

"Yes, Crys. Here I am, Crys."

"There's a nice bit of bush left along the fence," Crystal said cheerfully, coming towards her. "I came across young Jarrah perched way up in the fork of a huge gum tree. There's a broken limb across the fence. He must have shinned up there and kept on climbing. He's a good kid, that. He's up a helluva long way but when I asked him if he wanted a hand down he reckoned he'd be just fine. He said to tell you he wants you to have a look at him first." As Gita said nothing, just kept on staring out across the valley, Crystal glanced at her keenly. "What's up, love? Listen, I'm sorry if I pissed you off before. Me and my big mouth."

Gita's hands lifted off the verandah rail and dropped back. "It isn't you."

Crystal sounded relieved. "Funny, isn't it, it's the women's guilt thing. I should know better by now but whenever one of my friends is grumpy I immediately think what have *I* done."

Gita hunched over the rail as though she had a cramp. "It's him. He won't leave me alone."

"About moving back?"

"Yes. Oh, he doesn't *say* so. But that's what he means — "

"Did you say you need more time, you're still thinking things through?"

" . . . so he thinks he'll get me by a quick fuck."

"You mean . . . just now?"

"At me and at me, just because *he* wants."

"Selfish prick!"

"It's all a power thing. A game."

"Of course it's a power thing. The whole patriarchal system is a power thing. And if he persuades you against your will, then that's rape, and no woman has to endure that, you know that, Gita, even if the guy *is* —"

At the word rape, Gita laughed bitterly, saying "He has never raped me, Crys. You don't understand. It isn't like that."

"Do you want to talk about it?"

"Oh Crystal . . . at that place we did nothing but talk. Yak yak yak."

"Sometimes it helps."

"Oh, we worked in the gardens too. I got quite expert at raising seedlings and planting them out. Cool day, water the punnet, seedling into the ground, press the soil down, water in well. Green fingers Gita, me."

"Seriously though, you don't open up much to your friends, do you? I've noticed. Bottling it all up inside you."

At the words I've noticed, Gita wanted to dive off the verandah, swoop like the trapped swallow into the sky, into nothing, freefall. She had to clutch at the verandah rail again. And Crystal was her *friend*. She said "I guess that's why I despise myself so much."

"Despise yourself?"

"I told you, it's a game. For me too, I mean."

Crystal said gently "You don't have to play."

"I know that."

"Each time you say no, it's easier next time."

"I know that, too. You want to hear what I said? I said I'm never coming back. I said I valued my independence."

"Just now in the cottage?"

"Yes Crystal."

"Good for you! So he didn't . . . you didn't —"

"Of course I didn't. I didn't let him touch me."

"Good. If that's how you wanted it."

"He just won't let me alone."

"He's bad news, that one. Bad news. What are we going to do, Gita? You could tell him to go, tell him to pack up his gear and piss off."

"Do you think I haven't tried?" How do you let something go that has made itself part of you? How do you let yourself go?

"You were there first. He took it on himself to move in, didn't he? You didn't invite him. You didn't even know him before he moved in."

Gita laughed again. Crystal thought she was talking about Mark, poor mirror-mouth Mark who like herself was nothing but a pale reflection of Jules. Shining with someone else's light, cold lifeless moons.

"He says a squat's a squat so he has as much right as I have to move in."

Crystal shook her head. "I like his logic. He's just a middle-class kid playing at slumming. As soon as the novelty's worn off he'll shoot right back with his dirty washing to his mum. You'll see."

"That doesn't solve my problems."

"Of where to plant your gear in the meantime?"

"Yeah, that too. I'm sick of the hassle."

"So what's wrong with my place for a bit longer? Sure, there's a woman coming down from Sydney next week with a couple of kids, but my place has elastic walls, you know that. Tons of room for you and Jarrah."

"Oh Crys." Gita threw her arm around the broad shoulder. "You know what you've just done, don't you? You've put out your hand and hauled me back." Inside that capsule.

Crystal hugged her. "Dear old friend."

9 Mexican Marigolds

Her eyes shot open. A boy carrying an old bird's nest was staring at her, a strange boy making a noise in his throat (not singing exactly, you could hardly call it a tune), but certainly not Chomper worrying a rock. A boy, not Chomper. You could hardly throw a rock for a boy to run after.

"Hello," said Mary Springfield to the boy. "Where did you spring from?"

"From a tree. Look." He twirled the nest on one finger. "This is an eagle's nest."

"Goodness, is it?"

"And that's a mulberry tree. Have you got silkworms?"

"No. Have you?" She rather liked this child: someone who knew one tree from another.

"I did, but they died. I only had lettuce leaves."

"What a shame. And what are you doing here? Looking for mulberry leaves?"

He shrugged. "Just looking." He turned away, picking at a feather in the nest.

"All by yourself?"

After a moment, when she'd begun to wonder if he was deaf, perhaps, he turned back to her. "Nuh. With the others. They're looking too."

"Did you all ride out from the town?" She thought she knew everybody in Currawong. Whose child could this be?

"Nuh."

"But you live in Currawong?"

"What currawong?"

Mary felt a sense of relief: not slipping after all. The boy was saying "We're living at Crystal's now for a bit, but mostly we live at Gita's. Before that we were at a place, and before that at Jules's, and before that – I forget."

"And who are *we* when we're at home?" Though it doesn't sound as though we have a home. Poor little mite.

"Me and Gita." He dug at a tussock with the toe of one sneaker.

The canvas was worn right through, Mary saw, and the poor child had no socks on. "Your shoes are soaked through, you must be freezing!" she exclaimed.

Ignoring this, he continued. "And Mark. Mark isn't at Crystal's though. It's only women there, and kids. He's at Gita's place. Because it's a squat. He says."

"A squat. What is a squat, dear?"

"Just a house you find. An empty house."

"And you move into it?" He nodded. Mary put a protective hand against Marycote's weatherboard wall. "And then it is yours?"

"S'pose." He frowned. He didn't want to think about all

the fights when Mark first moved in. "Till it's going to be pulled down. Then we all get chucked out."

Mary Springfield suddenly saw a minute front garden with a rusted hollyhock by the letter box; she was swinging on the gate and her mother was standing against the front door, arms folded, while neighbours gathered, and loud-voiced fat men pushed the gate open before Mary had time to jump off.

"And this is going to happen to you?"

"S'pose so. Pretty soon, I guess. Maybe next week." He saw the concern on the soft cheeks under the purple knitted thing, and took a step towards her. "Maybe tomorrow."

"And then what?" she breathed, remembering pillows and chairs and saucepans all jumbled together on the footpath, and herself sitting on a box, and her mother crying.

"Then we look for somewhere else of course, don't we?"

Great-grandmother will like a letter from you, her mother had said, bringing not Mary's slate but paper, and a real pen with a nib, and a bottle of pale blue ink. She doesn't know about you, her mother said. Won't it be a lovely surprise! Mary hadn't been too sure about that, because she had memories of another person she'd been told to call Grandmother who had shouted and wept and refused to kiss her. But Great-grandmother had enjoyed the surprise, evidently, because not long after Mary had struggled with blots and cramped fingers and her mother had let her put the letter into the grinning red mouth of the pillar box, she and her mother were at Spencer Street Station with their boxes again, were waiting for the country train, her mother said, to take them both to Great-grandmother at Marycote . . .

"And that's what you're doing today, is it, dear, looking for somewhere else?"

Bored now, Jarrah shrugged. After a moment he walked away, twirling the bird's nest. Mary Springfield struggled to her feet. She was so stiff she had to hold on to the mulberry tree. She'd let herself doze too long. Perhaps she'd imagined the boy. Perhaps he hadn't been there at all, like the make-believe boy she'd played with at Marycote because there was no street full of kids you could lark about with till dark and the mothers called everyone in for bread and dripping or, for a treat, bread and jam.

And then the boy was back again, and with him other people, two men and two young ladies.

"Good afternoon," said one of the men. "Is this your cottage? What a charming old place! Old cottages are a hobby of mine." He looked her square in the eye. He had a surprisingly young face under short thick grey hair, and a smiling voice. The younger man, on the other hand, slouched, and said nothing, and had his hair tied back like a girl's.

"It is lovely, isn't it?" Mary replied to the smiling man. "It's a bit run down at the moment, but nothing a little bit of elbow grease wouldn't put right. And the power's there, to the big pole, see? And the septic. You could nearly move in tomorrow. I used to live here, you know, when I was a girl, so I'm very fond of the place. I'd love to show you through." She hesitated. "Unfortunately Angus keeps the place locked." Seeing them exchange glances, she hastened to explain. "Angus is the owner. Angus Springfield. He lives just over the hill. You wouldn't have seen his house from the road. I'm Mary Springfield, by the way. I live on the next farm. Were you coming downhill? Then you'd have passed where I live – a new two-storey cream brick place?"

Again the four adults exchanged glances. She reddened. Was she talking too much? Lou called her an old gasbag when he wanted to rag her.

"Are you all thinking of moving here?" she asked. "The boy was saying –"

The fair plump woman in the sensible overalls was shaking her head. The slouching man grinned. "Just Gita and me," the child said loudly.

The pleasant man said "Oh, I think if one moved we'd all move, wouldn't we, Jarrah?"

"I see." Would Great-grandmother care for these people under her roof? Mary looked from the dark-haired thin woman whose flimsy shoes were soaked through like the boy's to the other young woman, and then at the two men (trying to work out who's the father, old stickybeak, thought Gita). "Well, as I said, it's a lovely old place, just right for two, or a family — or even for one," she added wistfully. "You'd have to talk to Angus, of course . . . but whether he'd want to let it — goodness, I'm sure it's never occurred to him — but then again . . . you'd have to talk to him. I can't show you much from the outside," she said, leading them around the house. "All the windows boarded up. This used to be my room. I lived here with my mother, and my great-grandmother."

"She must have been old," Jarrah said.

Mary Springfield laughed. "She was. But she did all the cooking. On the open fire. Have you ever sat round a big fire on a frosty winter's night and made toast on a long fork?" she asked Jarrah.

Jarrah shook his head. His stomach rattled. He could smell the scorched breadcrumbs, and the butter yellow as mulberry leaves melting through to the plate.

"Are you gardeners?" Mary Springfield was asking. "There used to be a wonderful cottage garden at the back here."

"Gita will be our gardener," said Mark as they looked at small bricks laid edgewise at an angle to make a saw-toothed border around beds overgrown with dock and sorrel and milkweed. "She's the expert. She'll grow organic vegetables and make wonderful hunza pies and pee-the-bed soup while Jules and I burn down to the city every day."

"And I'll catch taddies in the creek," added Jarrah. "Not to eat, of course. You don't eat taddies, you keep them —"

"Why not?" said Jules suddenly, and for a moment Jarrah warmed to him, thinking he meant tadpoles. "There's water in the creek. Just think of what we could grow. All the Mexican marigolds amongst the tomatoes, Mark."

"Aren't you a bit too close to the road?" Gita said drily.

"For tomatoes? Lines of tomatoes staked six feet high around the marigolds, Gita? Mexican marigolds, Gita."

Mark laughed a high-pitched whinnying laugh that meant he caught on.

"Oh stop it!" Gita shuddered.

"Don't be like that," Jules said softly.

"Are we really going to live here, Gita?" Jarrah asked.

"No," Gita said.

10 You Need a Good Belting

Just then three children appeared and, going up to Mary Springfield, demanded toffee. Jarrah didn't hear what she said their names were, his mouth was watering so much as she produced a bag of toffee from the pocket of her oily-looking coat and the strange kids hogged in. He was used to the children at all his different schools not sharing things, but the old woman made the girl offer the bag around. She's a sulk, she doesn't want to, Jarrah thought, looking at the girl's bent head. But when she came last to Gita, the girl stared. The two boys were staring, too. It was the gemstone in Gita's nostril, Jarrah realised; it glittered like a star. He touched the place on his own nose.

"Jane!" hissed the old woman. Then, after glancing in the bag – counting how many's left, thought Jarrah – she put it back in her pocket and said in the sort of voice kids use when they want other kids to play one more time: "Of course, to rent the cottage you'd have to talk to Angus Springfield."

"Perhaps some other time." Jules rolled the words around like a kid with a pocketful of allies who's going home now, but Mary Springfield rushed on: "He lives further down the road on the way into town. It's one of the finest old places in the district." Jules, who had turned away towards the road, turned back to her as she continued. "You can't actually see it from the road, you have to drive in a long way. There's no harm in asking, is there? I ought to come with you, it might make it easier," she added.

Jules said "Well, thank you, Miss Springfield, we'd appreciate that." Jarrah heard Crystal catch her breath as though she was going to hawk. "Wouldn't we?" Jules looked at the others. Mark grinned. Gita looked away.

And now Mary was full of doubts. She looked at Gita's shoes. "We could go across the creek and down through the bush, but it's pretty muddy just now, and there's a barbed wire fence. It's a fair walk round by the road, though. A bit late in the day for these little chaps," nodding at Elton and Keiran.

"If you and the children would care to come with us, we could drive round the road together," Jules suggested. "If you preferred to do that," he added with his most charming smile, to fill in the silence as Mary looked at him, summing him up, looking diffidently at the others. "We're parked down by the gate," he continued. "Beside the fence. Safer off the road, I thought. It's pretty narrow there where the road curves."

"Now that was thoughtful." Mary smiled back at this thoughtful young man. "I do think it would help if I introduced you, don't you . . . under the circumstances . . . you know?"

"Of course," smiled Jules. "There's room for all of you, and you could fill us in about the neighbourhood as we go, Miss Springfield. I've noticed quite a few old stone fences round here," he chatted to her as they walked towards the front gate. "Falling into disrepair now, aren't they. Pity."

"Isn't it! It's a real shame. No one builds them now, of course. Angus did have a go at repairing some of them at Springfield last year."

"I thought Mum and Dad didn't want us going over to Springfields," Jane said loudly. She was older than Jarrah, one of those big girls who would make a lattice with their fingers and then play tricks on you, look, put your finger there, then pinch it between their bony knuckles. "Mary!" the girl persisted, but all Mary Springfield said was "Quick sticks!" to Keiran and Elton who were dragging along behind the crabby Jane.

Quick sticks, said Jarrah to himself.

He looked longingly as the old woman passed the paper bag to the older boy who was nagging for more toffee. The boy had a habit of screwing up his face. He jerked his mouth and almost closed one eye. Jarrah stared. How did he do it? Jarrah blinked, and twisted one side of his jaw. The girl Jane, walking next to him, poked him with a sharp elbow. "Don't do that. You're not allowed to make fun." "I wasn't." "You were. I saw you. You need a good belting." The younger boy, staring at Jarrah, said "You need a good belting." He put one piece of toffee, then a second, into his mouth. "Can I have one?" said Jarrah. "No," said Jane, so when she wasn't looking Jarrah took the paper bag from the little boy and helped himself.

Mary tried not to sound impolite as she exclaimed "Is this your car? How big it is! Goodness, it looks like . . . looks like – "

"It is," said Jules. "Ever had a ride in one?"

"Well no . . . no, of course not." She tried not to giggle. As Jules opened the front door and handed her in, she said "This'll be a bit of practice for the future, won't it?"

"Practice. Oh yes, I see what you mean!" Jules laughed, laughed gently, holding the old woman's eye until she laughed back at her own wit.

God how I hate him! thought Gita. Everything's a game to him, even conning some old duck into thinking we want to live in the country. We're all nothing to Jules, shells, husks, rooms he forces his way into and ransacks.

"Gita?" he was saying softly, holding out his hand to assist her into the hearse.

11   Stone Axehead

From the road they drove in along a winding track with pinoaks planted on either side, grown so large now that they formed an arch over the track. The leaves on the trees and in piles on the track itself were a mass of scarlets and golds and rich browns. Toffee brown, thought Jarrah. He was sitting next to the crabby girl. The old woman twisted herself around over her seat to try to make the girl tell him something. "Your silver-spangled Sebrights," she urged. "They're bantams. Tell him about them, Jane."

"Silver-spangled Sebrights," repeated the girl.

Jarrah tried the words against his teeth, hissing softly.

"Ah, now there's a house!" Jules exclaimed suddenly. Standing on a small rise was a large, hip-roofed house with wide verandahs and elegant wrought-iron lace. As the track curved, it disappeared behind a mass of shrubbery and leafless trees. All they could see was a grey shed with a steeply rising red roof and red shutters instead of an attic window, and the dark shape of a huge tree hanging over the spot where the house must be.

"That's a pine tree, Crystal!" Jarrah shouted. "That's *exotic*, Crystal!" When she grinned and nodded, he tried again. "Lots of chimneys there for you, Jules!"

"*Isn't* it?" Mary Springfield said in response to the enthusiasm in Jules's voice when he'd said now there's a house, any doubts she might have had about driving around with strangers quite disappearing. "It's a shame to see it so neglected, no woman there now of course." She said suddenly "You mustn't mind Angus. He's a bit . . . abrupt at times."

"He's a deadshit," said Jane. As Mary turned sharply, she added "Dad says."

This time they went straight to the back door, following Mary along a path through heaps of crunchy leaves that made Jarrah think of walking through a bowl of cornflakes.

"He's home," Mary said, pointing to a pair of mud-encrusted gumboots by the back door. She knocked. When there was no answer she knocked again and opened the door slightly. "Angus! Only me, dear. I've got some people with me who'd like to have a word. Angus? May we, dear? . . . Come in," she hissed, beckoning. They followed her into a large kitchen. At the table a tall thin man was cleaning a rifle. As they entered he stood up, leaning back against the table as though, Gita thought, they were crowding him. Crumbs and cereal packets and dirty dishes were mixed up on the table with spread-out oily newspaper and a tin of gun oil and a rag for pulling through the barrel. For a moment no one spoke. The little boys pressed close to Mary Springfield. A blowfly buzzed, caught in an ancient sticky flypaper hanging from the ceiling. Who was it told me those sticky papers poison the atmosphere? Gita asked herself, staring up at the struggling fly. Crystal, it's sure to have been Crystal. *Was* it Crystal?

Mary exclaimed "Goodness, Angus, you must let me get to those socks!" Nine pairs of eyes swivelled down to the man's feet and stared at the holes in the heels and toes of mismatched socks.

"Thanks, Mary," the man said, looking up again from his feet, and Gita thought That's a gentle voice, not like Jules's, mocking, or Mark's, babbling. "But it's okay. I usually wear a second pair as well, upside down."

Jarrah laughed. He went up to the table. "What have you been shooting?"

The man indicated a pair of skinned rabbits lying on the table. They were still wearing grey furry socks. Their pearled flesh shone.

Elton crowded up close beside Jarrah. "Clean through the head!" he said admiringly.

"This is Angus Springfield," Mary began, and waited. When again none of the others offered their names, she hurried on. "They're interested in the old cottage, Angus. Living in it, I mean. So I brought them over because I thought, I mean, it seems an idea, a tenant would look after it for you, keep out thieves and vandals . . ." Her voice trailed away.

"It's a fine old cottage, fine example of its period," Jules began all over again. Crystal gave another impatient tuh! with her tongue. Gita saw her turn away to the bench by the sink where the children, bored with all this talk, were turning over the heap of things on the bench.

"I've been storing hay in it. It's full of birds and mice now. Possums too, probably." That gentle voice again.

And memories, Gita thought. She must have spoken aloud, because the man glanced at her and, behind her, Jules laughed.

"There's no electricity connected, of course," Mary said, eager now it seemed to support Angus Springfield's objections.

"In the kitchen fireplace there's one of those bars that swings out to hang pots and kettles on," Gita said dreamily.

This time it was Angus Springfield who laughed. "You could see that through the boards across the window, could you?" he said, so that Gita, caught out, hated him.

Jarrah tugged at her arm. "Look at this. It's an old axehead, Crystal says." Gita looked down at the small greenish-black oblong stone he was holding. It was sharpened and polished at one end. She took it into the palm of her hand and turned it over, smooth rock skin against her own. "It feels good," she said, giving it back to him.

"Crystal says it shouldn't be here, it should be put back on the ground where it was found," Jarrah said, turning the stone in his palm the way Gita had done. "Do you think that, Gita?"

"Why? What for?"

"Because it doesn't belong to him. Us, she means. It belongs to them."

Gita shrugged. "Us and them. Us and them."

"Just think," Crystal murmured beside her. "Now it's a whitefeller paperweight."

"All those trees!" mocked Gita. She sighed. Crystal! Crystal! Always something. She turned back to the three men.

Angus Springfield was saying "Well, I don't know. I'd need to give it a bit of thought, people living in the cottage." And Jules: "I'm a sucker for old houses, always have been. It was just a sudden idea, an impulse, you know?"

So the game was over, at last.

Mark had to put in his oar. Turning with a grin to Mary, he said "Your enthusiasm's catching. It had us all swept off our feet there for a bit."

So that Mary, looking alarmed, began to stumble through a dozen apologies, saying "I hope I haven't, perhaps I, Lou says I always . . . oh dear!"

Gita felt almost sorry for the dithery old thing.

Jarrah dodged around Jane who was hovering at his elbow, hissing "Give me that rock, put it back!" He said to Crystal "D'you think they used this axe to chop up rabbits?"

"There probably weren't too many of them still around when the rabbits came, mate. The settlers had hunted them all away. Or shot them."

Jarrah narrowed his eyes at the man's rifle on the table. Suddenly his arm was pinched. "You better put that rock back now," Jane hissed. The little boys, jostling, shouted "No, give me a hold of it! Me! It's my turn!" The axehead fell with a crash.

Gita saw Angus Springfield jump violently at the sudden noise. Looking behind her, she saw the four children scrambling around on the floor.

Mary Springfield was calling "That's enough of that, chicks, it's time we left Uncle Angus in peace. Jane! Elton! Keiran! Enough of that, now. Jane, dear!"

"Hey, Jarrah," Gita murmured.

Jarrah, standing up, saw Jane's hand closing around the smooth axehead.

"You don't want to be scared of Uncle Angus, chicks," Gita overheard Mary saying to the little boys as she helped them into the hearse. Gita recalled the way the man had stood up as they all trooped into the kitchen — pressed back hard against the table as though he wanted to get away. She recalled his violent start when one of the kids dropped something heavy.

It's the other way round, Mary Springfield, she thought. It's Uncle Angus who is scared of the chicks.

12 Why Shouldn't Our Dreams Mix with Other People's, Gita Said

dreams in your veins

                                                            where am I?

      I look like a parrot

                                      where am I? where am I?

veins full of green pus   *didi mau!*

the old man weeping the crop flattened Go away, old man! *didi mau!* go away!

                                    I will never I will never

and then the screaming

                      didi mau!   fucking-well serves you

didi mau! didi mau!

13   Some Weeks Later

Some weeks later, Lou Catchpole of Valley View Park, taking a look at his cattle in the paddock next to Marycote, discovered the big limb that had fallen across the boundary fence between his property and his neighbour Angus Springfield's. Mary Springfield had not told Lou about the smashed fence, indeed had said nothing at all about coming across strangers at Marycote and going with them to Springfield; and the children had not mentioned it either: Jane was preoccupied with a boy with whom she was doing a project on rocks, and Elton and Keiran had discovered a new pastime, smoking rolled-up bits of bark in the shelter of the hayshed.

It *would* be the one bloody tree in the bloody middle of the fence, thought Lou, running his hand over the weld on the end of one of the long coach screws inserted into the tree trunk. Who but some bloody Springfield years ago would have saved a tree and used it as part of the fence? Sheer bloody-minded, he thought, examining the broken wires. If it had to fall, why couldn't it have been a tree on Angus's side? Then Angus'd have to repair the fence all on his own. Now we'll have to do it between us. Pity the whole tree didn't come down over the cottage. Maybe then he'd be a bit more inclined to put a bulldozer through it and straighten the bloody fence the way anyone in their right mind would want it. Who else but Springfields would have a fence with a kink in it when the rest of it's straight as a die? Those extra few acres are bugger-all use to Angus, and it sticks out into my place like a sore thumb. It's . . . it's untidy. That's what it is, thought Lou. Untidy.

He'd go straight home and give Springfield a ring, pin him

down to making a time for repairing the fence. Half a day's work between the two of them. Better still, rather than trying to deal with him by phone, he'd go over there right now and have a chat. Stubborn coot might be more reasonable these days. He'd had enough time, hadn't he? How long was it since he first came home? Fifteen years? Twenty?

The ill-feeling between the two men ran deeper than a family feud over a boundary fence. Angus Springfield had once tried to beat up Lou Catchpole in a pub brawl. Well, the publican put a stop to that quick smart: threatened to have Angus run in if he didn't take a running jump at himself. Sober up, get stuck into working the farm. It was hardly fair on Belle and old Mary to leave everything to them. I lent a hand when I could, said Lou to himself. He'd got the lease of Springfield soon after old man Springfield croaked. Angus had disappeared by then. Put his farm in the hands of an agent and cleared off. Didn't even come back for the funeral when his old man carked it. People reckoned he was up north shooting crocs — he was a crack shot, wasn't he? Others reckoned he'd been sent to the funny farm. And years later when he decided to return, just like that, out of the blue, he put it about that Lou had eaten his pastures dirt-bare to get the last blade of grass into his sheep before he had to move them off Springfield.

Lou glanced around his own paddock. Sure, he always grazed more heavily than Angus did. Angus under-stocked. By walking across the creek and down over the next hill through the bush instead of driving around the road, he could get a closer look at Angus's sheep. Angus had his ewes in lamb at the back there, behind the big house. Not too far off lambing, by the looks of some of them. You had to hand it to him, he kept his stock in good nick. Last year he'd had the best drop of lambs in the district, close on a hundred per cent, though Lou thought it was a sheer waste of energy putting in as much time as Angus did, going around the ewes twice a day, mothering a twin lamb on a ewe whose own lamb had died. Survival of the fittest is my motto, thought Lou, coming towards the house through that patch of useless bush the Springfields had never got around to clearing. Just gum trees and wattles and kangaroo grass. I like it like that, old man Springfield had said, when old man Catchpole had chivvied him about it.

Sheep dogs, chained at their kennels outside the garden, barked as Lou walked through the back gate. What a jungle! he thought, pushing shrubbery aside in order to follow the path. Needs a slasher through it. He knocked a couple of times at the back door, then called out. Can't be home, he thought. He was about to have a gander through the window when he caught sight of Springfield, watching him from the doorway of the glasshouse. Christ! As Lou walked towards him, Angus turned away and was bent over a box of seedlings on a bench when Lou entered the glasshouse.

" 'day there, Angus," Lou said finally, as Angus went on watering things in little pots.

" 'day."

"Busy there, eh?" Morose bastard. Can't he even look up? "Something for the garden?"

"Yellow box. Blackwood. Grevilleas."

"Pretty big garden, eh?"

"You could say that."

"I'll tell you what I came over about, Angus," Lou said impatiently, since courtesies were getting nowhere.

"You do that, Lou."

Christ! "You know that big tree in the fence near the old cottage?"

"The big manna gum?"

"Yeah, well, whatever. I'm not up in the trees like you, Angus. What I'm trying to tell you is, it's dropped a bloody great limb on the fence. Smashed the wires and a couple of droppers. Must have been in the last day or so, eh, if you didn't see it either?" Lou was fishing; he didn't want to admit to Angus that he hadn't been around his property since before the big storm. Angus said nothing, for the same reason. He'd looked over the ewes in lamb, but that was all. Time had run away with him in the glasshouse. "The stock haven't started pushing through yet," Lou continued. "I thought we might make a time to do it up. What do you say?"

"Yeah. Okay."

"So what day suits you? This afternoon?"

That would be a miracle, thought Lou, himself planning on going into Currawong after dinner. As he'd expected, Angus said "I'm busy this afternoon." Too busy to give himself a shave, thought Lou, running his hand over his own chin. I bet the house is a pigsty.

As though he had read his thoughts, Angus, wiping his hands on his trousers, said "Cup of tea, Lou? Reckon it's about time."

To Lou's surprise, the kitchen was tidy, swept, the kitchen table scrubbed, the bench neat and cleared of mess. He glanced through the servery into the dining room: the fire was set ready for the evening. Did the sly bastard have some fancy woman stashed away? "Now Angus," he said, helping himself to another of Mary Springfield's rock cakes made with ingredients from Lou's own pantry. "Now Angus, about this fence. What about tomorrow? Or the next day? I've put a few branches in the gap for the time being."

"In that case, Lou, I'd rather leave it till I get a job done here, if that's okay with you."

It was the most agreeable way he had spoken since Lou arrived, so Lou was moved to say, neighbourly, "Oh? Got something on, eh?"

"Ahh . . . just a job in the glasshouse. I should be right by Sunday."

"I like to keep Sunday for the family, Angus." What would you know about that, you solitary bastard.

"Saturday then."

"Jesus, Angus, you like to make things hard, don't you? Saturday mornings I like to cheer the kids on at Little Aths. Okay, Sunday it is. I'll bring the chainsaw if you'll bring the wire. If we make an early start, we should be all done by midday."

Angus pushed his chair back from the table. "Sunday it is, Lou."

Lou Catchpole returned to Valley View Park fuming. "He's off his chump. He's downright uncivil. Ask him a simple thing like fixing a time and he has to make a great song over it. What sort of farmer does he think he is, filling up that glasshouse with little pots of trees, hundreds of them? What does he think he's doing?"

"Starting up a nursery?" suggested Mary Springfield. She would ask Angus next time she called in on her way home from the hospital.

Lou ignored Mary. "He's crazy, I tell you, Belle."

"Do you think I don't know?" said Belle.

14 On Sunday

On Sunday, Angus was already waiting at the cottage when Lou Catchpole drove up the track from the road. Jane and the two little boys were with him in the truck he used for rough work. The children stared at Angus. Angus ignored them.

"Sorry to keep you, mate. I'll just spread this hay, then I'll be right with you," Lou said, heaving two bales of hay across the boundary fence for his cattle which had come crowding and bellowing as soon as they heard the truck. Maybe if he's in a good mood he'll listen if I bring up that business about the dog-leg, he thought, as he climbed through the fence to spread the hay. Maybe I'll tell him he can keep my share of the wood. He made a point of shouting another apology for keeping Angus waiting. He almost added that he could get started with the chainsaw if he liked – Lou's chainsaw that he never lent anyone! – but decided there was no need to lay it on.

The hay spread, he went over to the truck. "Get away from under that limb," he heard Angus shout. "Your father's starting the chainsaw. Hey! Move!"

Lou began to fuss, unwilling to have Angus's good mood challenged, and cross with himself for not having noticed the children first. "Take those kids back to the house, Jane. You hear me? Tell Mary to find something for them to do. And what do you think you're doing, Keiran? Put those matches back in my coat pocket."

"Mary's going into town."

"Then tell her to take you all with her."

"To church? She'll love you, Dad!"

"Look, will you just hold your jaw, Jane, and get going, and take Elton and Keiran with you or I'll give you all a good clip on the ear."

The two men worked on in silence, Lou cutting through the smashed limb, Angus hauling logs and branches out of the way at a furious pace. Lou's words of last week were sawing at his temple. Saturday mornings I like to cheer the kids . . . I like to keep Sunday for the family . . . Why Catchpole? Why *Catchpole*?

Surly bugger, thought Lou, catching sight of his neighbour's face. And couldn't help having a go at him. He paused, pushing off his ear muffs. "Half each, I reckon, don't you, Angus?" he shouted.

"It's what I'm doing, isn't it?"

"Never said you weren't, mate, never said you weren't."

"I've brought a thermos," Angus said mid-morning. He rubbed his knee; it was playing up again, and he wished he'd brought ear muffs like Lou against the noise of the chainsaw. He let his eyes rest on the distance: the boobiallas and eucalypts and wattles, and above them — a cloud of dust settling.

"*Metcalf!*" he said.

"What? What's that you said? What?" Lou followed Angus's gaze. "Good Christ! That's smoke. It's coming from my place. Stir yourself, will you!"

The two men jumped in Catchpole's truck. Lou crunched gears. I can't stand this, Angus was thinking. Cooped up with Lou Catchpole, I'm going to jump out. "It's not your house, too far to the left," he made himself say, to keep his hand from turning the door handle. "Hell, it's your hayshed!"

Shadowy figures running. Then the whoosh of flames The two men drove as close as possible then ran to the shed. *No men in sight, they've all disappeared into the jungle. Springfield and Metcalf running* but the heat is too much, they have to stand back, move back *run but his legs are heavy, he can't move, no use, no use, no use, the words scream in his ears, the flames engulf him*

"No use, Angus," Catchpole was saying from a great distance. "Nothing we can do here. Useless calling up the brigade at this stage, what I had in there's well and truly fried now." Angus followed as Catchpole walked closer to the shed. Heat from the steel posts hit their faces. "Shed's okay, thank Christ. No damage to the roof, I reckon. Not enough hay in here for a really big blaze." Catchpole's voice swinging closer shouted at Angus, then settled to everyday level. "It must have burned for a good twenty minutes before I noticed it."

I noticed it, Angus thought, picturing the first tiny flame skittering across loose bits of hay, then dividing, spreading, probing like a hundred hungry tongues into holes in the bales, burning hotter and hotter and at last sending up a cloud of dense black smoke. *I* saw that smoke, Lou.

"How d'you reckon it started?" His voice faltered.

Catchpole was evidently as shaken up as Angus because he said outright "Ahh . . . my own bloody fault, I reckon. I remember opening a new packet of smokes when I was loading that hay on the way over to Marycote. I must have dropped the butt." He kicked at a scorched bale. "Just as well I only had a few bales left because what little there was is either burned or useless."

"Yeah. Cattle won't touch smoky hay."

"Looks like I'll have to buy some in sooner than I'd planned. Who'd credit it, eh?"

Angus was shaking with relief to find himself safe, whole, no one injured, only a heap of grass destroyed — and what's a shedful of hay? A day's work, a new crop next spring. "I've got a roomful of old hay in the cottage that needs being eaten, Lou. You're welcome to what's there till you're right again if it's any use to you."

Catchpole, amazed by this generosity, decided that, all things considered, he would postpone the matter of the dogleg. He said "That's decent of you, Angus, real decent. Thanks, mate."

"Nothing we can do here," Angus said. "How about we get on with that fence?"

Lou kept saying "That'll teach me to be more careful when I'm smoking. It's all my fault. Who'd credit it? It's all my fault." *my fault my fault my fault*

Angus felt such a surge of anger he almost hit him. "You going to keep that up for the rest of your life, Lou?" he shouted.

15 She Tiptoed Lightly

"Didn't you see that fire in the hayshed, any of you?" Catchpole asked his family over midday dinner. "She was a beauty!"

None of them had noticed the smoke, they said. "We were back at the house with Mary," Jane said promptly. "We weren't looking out any windows," said Elton. "Were we, Keiran?" "I was in town all morning," Belle Catchpole said. "Having my hair done. Gaylene's doing a few of us from home now she's had the baby." She patted a stiff gold curl. "You might have commented, Lou." "It's very nice, dear, very pretty," Mary said to Belle, and to Lou: "I didn't get back till just on lunchtime. I'd popped the cass in the oven before I left," she added, looking at Lou anxiously. The truth was, she had taken longer than she need have because on her way to church she had slipped in to Springfield to tidy the kitchen.

"Hang on, hang on," said Catchpole, dropping his fists on to the table's edge. "Just a minute. What time did you say you got back, Mary?"

"A quarter to one, I think. Not much later. The casserole —"

"Yeah, okay, okay. And what time did you leave here?"

"Oh Lou . . . about ten, I think. Yes, ten, I know it was ten because I can remember switching on the car radio so I could listen to —"

"Never mind that now. That fire started a bit before ten-thirty, I reckon, because we'd stopped for a cuppa when I saw the smoke. And you say you were back at the house with Mary by then, Jane, you and the boys?"

Jane stared at him, a bright pink spot on each cheek.

"But Mary says she was on her way into town then, Jane," Belle said.

"So? She wasn't in the house, but we didn't know that, did we? We were in the house. Weren't we, Elton? Weren't we, Keiran?"

The younger boy began to bawl. He hauled something out of his pocket and flung down Lou's box of matches.

"Oh Janie," cried Mary Springfield. "What stories have you been getting your little brothers to tell?"

"Leave this to me, Mary," Catchpole interrupted. "Jane –!"

The girl turned furiously on the older woman. "Stories?" she raged. "So what about you? What about you, taking us over to Springfields with those funny people you found at the cottage when Mum and Dad were in Sydney? We aren't supposed to go over to Angus Springfield's place but I bet you've never told Mum and Dad about that!"

"What's this? What people?" Catchpole asked.

"Hippies!" shrieked Jane.

"Hippies," echoed Keiran.

"We all went in a hearse," added Elton.

"A hearse! What is all this? Would you just explain, Mary, please? Would you mind throwing a little bit of light on the situation? You went over to Springfields, you and Jane and the boys, and you went with strangers, with a bunch of hippies, in a *hearse*?"

"One of them had a ring in her nose!" shouted Keiran, with a conspiratorial simper at Jane.

"Stupid, it was a stud," said Jane. "Like in my ears."

"Oh Lou!" cried Mary. "They were quite nice people really –" She turned to Belle.

Belle Catchpole was studying her fingernails.

Any minute now, thought Jane Catchpole, any minute now, Dad'll be shouting at Mary and Mary'll start crying and then Mum'll start in on both of them.

And she tiptoed lightly from the room.

16 Spencer Street Station

In Melbourne, Gita at her place was sorting through a heap of clothes she had dumped on Jarrah's bed. Her thick jumper, her tracksuit, her jeans and her Doc Marten boots with the red laces, all went into a rucksack. Jarrah's green jumper with the prickly neck and his patched jeans went into a cardboard box. His too-small brown jumper, her Indian dress that she was sick of, any socks with holes in them went into a heap on the floor.

"What are we doing, Gita?" asked Jarrah, who was sitting on the bed, perched on the pillow out of the way of his and Gita's clothes. "Are we moving again? Are you and Mark splitting again?"

Splitting, thought Gita. Like the halves of one whole. A cell dividing. Your other half. Your better half. Little half-chick. God save me.

"Where are we going?" persisted Jarrah, watching his sneakers going into the cardboard box. "Are we going back to Crystal's again? Are we taking everything back to Crystal's? That's why there isn't any food at this place," he droned. "Because we're going back to Crystal's."

"There isn't any food here because no one's been out to get any."

"I'm hungry."

"Are you? Go out and get something, then."

"I haven't got any money."

"Well don't look at me." She went on sorting.

"Jules's? Is it Jules's? I hate Jules. It's Jules's place, isn't it?"

"No."

"Where then?" He reached down and fished his old brown jumper from the heap on the floor and put it on top of the cardboard box. "Don't you know where?"

"*You're* going to your father's place."

"I am not. My father's in Adelaide."

"Well, now he's in Melbourne, isn't he? And he wants to see you."

"He does not! He never wants to see me! You said so yourself."

"So he's changed his mind, okay?" The child was silent. She looked up, then came and knelt on the floor beside him and pulled his head into her shoulder. "Listen Jarrah, your father's come to live in Melbourne for a while. Because of his job. So now he wants to see you. That follows, doesn't it?"

He pulled away. "How long's he been in Melbourne?"

"Oh . . . a while. I don't know. A few months, I guess. And he'll be here soon so why don't you help sort out what you want to take?" She frowned over his brown jumper, then tossed it aside again. "You remember him," she continued. "He came to see us when he was in Melbourne on business trips, don't you remember?" And you two always ended up fighting, he thought. "And now that his firm's posted him to Melbourne he can see a lot more of you, can't he? He says he'll get you a dog. A big woofy dog, Jarrah." He watched her thin, quick hands folding the flaps of his box, pushing each corner under the other over the bulging contents. "Shit, they're just bending. You'll have to hold it. But you'll be in the car."

"Aren't you coming?"

"To your father's? No thanks."

He was silent again. Then he said "I hate dogs. I'd rather have a bantam."

"Oh shit, Jarrah! Give me a break, will you! The reason I'm going somewhere by myself for a bit is 'cause I'm full up to here with hassles like that, and I'm not telling anyone where I'm going, not Mark, not Crystal, not even you, so that if someone asks no one'll be telling lies when they say they don't know." Won't let it slip, she meant. Won't have it wormed out of you by Jules or Mark or your rotten sod of a father if he suddenly decides he's pissed off with doing his share for a change.

"Just for a bit, mate," she said. Pleaded.

He shrugged.

"Good kid. Put anything in your box that you specially want, okay? Quick now."

Quick sticks, thought Jarrah. What had that old woman said that crabby girl had? Silver-spangled Sebrights. He ran the words around in his head until they sang on the roof of his mouth.

"I wouldn't mind a bantam," he said again, going across the passage to his room in which open drawers were spitting out clothes. Under his bed he found an octopus strap for his box. He glanced around once more, picked up a toy soldier he'd pinched from a shop.

"Yes well we'll just have to see, won't we," Gita muttered absently, riffling through the pockets of the St Vinnie's coats she was leaving behind. She found a few coins and a five dollar note. There were more coins under the bed. She picked them up, then went across the passage and up a half-flight of stairs into Mark's room. He kept his drum kit in here, and his computer. Amongst the heap of papers on the glossy desk he'd brought with him were fifty and twenty dollar notes. She opened a drawer. Heaps more notes. You dumb sod, Mark. She remembered going into Jules's room when she was moving out of the place he called Wyewurrk. In the end she couldn't bring herself to pick up even a cent there, such an eerie feeling she had that Jules himself was watching her with his clever, cunning eyes.

From the street a klaxon horn clamoured. Jarrah's father. Snatching handfuls of notes from the drawer, she fled downstairs. "It's only for a bit, mate," she said to the child as she caught sight of his face. "He is your father. Grab your things," she said, hoisting the rucksack on to one shoulder. "You'll have an ace time, you just wait."

"Fuck me dead, that's not that same old leather jacket, Gita?" said Jarrah's father.

He put the rucksack and the box behind the front seat of his sleek white sports car. The car sure looked as though it would go but there wasn't much room in the back for a passenger, even a small one, Jarrah thought.

"Alfa Romeo, Jarrah. GTV two litre. Classy, eh?" his father said, but he was looking at Gita.

He gave Jarrah a six-pack of Mars Bars. "I've got a surprise for you later," he said, pulling the front passenger seat forward. "Hop in the back, kid. All set, Gita?"

"Hang on, I forgot something." She hurried back to the house. In the kitchen that smelt of gas and stale fat, she found a leaky biro. "Gone with Jarrah's father," she wrote on the back of the unpaid electricity bill, and put the note on the table under the tahini jar. A weight lifted from her shoulders. She drew in her breath, felt it fill her lungs. Breathe deep, deep. Float away, free as an escaped balloon that grows smaller and smaller as the balloon-fliers run with upstretched hands . . . *Breathe with your diaphragm* says Crystal at her shoulder. Snap! The balloon's string is seized, the balloon bobs and tugs. Yes Crystal. Yes. All right. I do remember. Snatching up a packet of lemongrass teabags and a half-eaten packet of dried pawpaw, she slammed out of the kitchen.

In her hurry she almost fell over Mark's ten-speed Peugeot leaning against the laundry troughs in the porch. He never rode the bike anywhere now he'd got the hearse going. It wasn't locked. She wheeled it out to the car.

"Hell, not a bike!" Jarrah's father exclaimed. "Jesus, Gita!"

"Give me the rucksack. I'll ride."

He ignored this, and began to remove the Peugeot's front wheel. "Got a rag of some sort?"

She leaned into the car and took hold of Jarrah's old brown jumper that he had stuffed under the octopus strap around his box. "He'll buy you a heap of new things, mate, don't you worry," she said as he made a grab at it.

"Get that stretchy strap the kid's got, too," Jarrah's father said as he arranged the jumper so that the bike, hanging over the number plate, wouldn't scratch the duco.

"The boot's to hold a champagne breakfast, not a bloody bike." Jarrah's father rubbed her shoulder with his as he took the strap. "I wouldn't do this for anyone else."

Gita turned away. "Shove over," she said, and slipped into the small seat beside Jarrah.

Now that Gita was behind the passenger's seat instead of

in it, Jarrah's father had to push his seat forward to make room for Jarrah.

"Where can I drop you?" he asked, not too friendly, looking at Gita in the rear vision mirror through blank silver sunglasses. She should have sat in the front, Jarrah thought, tearing at the wrapper of his second Mars Bar. Gita leaned against him.

"Give us a bite, mate."

Jarrah held up his wrist. "Look what he give – gave me while we were waiting for you. It isn't a Mickey Mouse watch like Jimmy Smith's got but there's an alarm and everything." He leaned up to whisper. "Don't you like it, Gita?" Then "I'm timing something. Want to know what I'm timing?"

"Where are you headed, Gita? Where can I drop you?" Jarrah's father repeated, so that Jarrah didn't have a chance to say what he was timing.

"Spencer Street Station. It isn't out of your way, is it?"

The man laughed. "You never were much chop at direction, were you?"

"Forget it, then," Gita muttered. "I've told you, I'll ride." Jarrah looked at the second hand of his watch.

"Hey there, sunshine, don't get thingy. Sure it's out of the way, but I can drop you off at Spencer Street, if that's what the lady wants."

"Here we go again," muttered Gita. Droning, Jarrah thought. "So what's new?"

"What's that?" The man's glasses were empty in the mirror.

"Oh forget it!" Gita threw herself back against the seat. Again Jarrah looked at his watch. He was timing how long it took these two to start fighting.

"Spencer Street it is," said the man, doing a rapid U-turn. Jarrah laughed as tyres squealed.

"Spencer Street," he murmured, careful himself not to drone. He tore the paper neatly down the side of another Mars Bar. "Spencer Street Station."

17   Lemongrass Tea

Catchpole was right: he had much less grass in his paddocks than Springfield. He understocks, Catchpole reassured himself once again. I'd be all right, too, if we'd had steady rain early on this autumn instead of those useless storms washing away my good topsoil. I was banking on decent rains. Shouldn't have to be handfeeding like this. He had found a few unscorched bales in his shed, and when these were finished he had made a start on the hay stored at Marycote. It was very convenient. All he had to do was lump a couple of bales out of the cottage and spread them in clumps on the other side of the fence.

One cold Sunday morning as he went to lift the bolt out of the rotting lintel, as Angus had shown him (locks to keep out honest people, Angus had joked, still in a good mood), Catchpole found that the bolt was hanging loose, pulled right out of the wood. That's funny, he thought. Maybe I didn't shut it properly last time. In the dim passage he stumbled over a rucksack. In the front room, wrapped in a sleeping bag on the hay, there was someone — a tramp — asleep.

"Hey!" he yelled. "You cheeky bugger! What the hell do you think you're doing here?"

It was a woman who sat up. She blinked like a startled bloody owl, dark hair straggling round her face, bits of hay clinging to it.

"What are you doing here?" Catchpole repeated, less loudly this time.

She frowned at him over the edge of the sleeping bag as though he were a tiny figure at the wrong end of a telescope. "What's it look like to you? I'm trying to sleep."

"Sleep? It's twenty-five past eleven. Even if it is the Sabbath." He leaned against the doorway. When she would not drop her eyes, he grinned. "On the run, are you?" She said nothing to that, just looked annoyed. He took a step into the room. "Well, you've found yourself an out-of-the-way hole here, that's for sure. No one's likely to come here looking for a girl on the run. Though I'm not so sure I want someone hanging about. I'd have to think it over. Before I said yes. Terms and that." He was enjoying himself.

"But it isn't your place to say yes to, is it?" she said softly, pert, cheeky as young Jane.

Riled, he tramped closer. "I've come for a couple of bales of hay," he said. "I'm handfeeding cattle in the next paddock."

She shrugged, huddled inside her sleeping bag as he backed against the pile of hay and eased a bale on to his shoulders. "It's okay," he said, grinning down at her. "It's only hay I'm after."

Riff-raff, he thought, dumping the bale over the fence and climbing through. The cattle milled around, bellowing and tossing their horns. Not a bad looker, though, what he could see of her, not much more than her forehead and nose. Probably not in Belle's class, got a bit of decent flesh to her, Belle has. Christ, look at that bullock, its ribs are staring out of its coat. Damned autumn drought!

As he went to flick the twine off the bale, his hand touched something rubbery. He glanced down. Fucking hell, it was a used frenchie! He recoiled in disgust. One of the cattle could have swallowed it, choked to death, caught AIDS, passed it on through the abattoirs to some poor unsuspecting family tucking in to their Sunday roast! He picked up a stick to carry it to a heap of wood covering a dead beast that he intended to burn sometime. He glanced at it, pathetic worm on the end of the stick . . . thought of the bloke who had used it, left it beside the girl when he'd finished with her, what sort of bloke was that, what sort of woman, he pictured the two of them, rooting and gasping in the hay, and what was left of that other bloke now but this pathetic piece of spent rubber?

As he walked back to the cottage for the second bale of hay he felt a growing anger against the woman.

She was out of the sleeping bag now, busy in the kitchen boiling up something on a little spirit stove. Catchpole watched her from the doorway. Good-looking filly, in spite of the tracksuit, and those steel-capped bovver boots that young Jane was so keen on, and a man's jumper that came almost to her knees. To fill up the silence he told her again that he was handfeeding cattle. "Every weekend I come over. Have to, this weather."

She made no reply. Pulling the sleeve of her jumper over her hand, she lifted the saucepan off the stove and called loudly to someone — more than one? — evidently still asleep behind the closed door of one of the other rooms.

"Water's boiling! Wake up!" she shouted, pouring hot water into three cups.

Taking a teabag from a fancy packet, she dunked it in one of the cups and began to sip. Catchpole came over to the table and picked up the packet. " 'Lemongrass'," he read. " 'For a clear skin and bright eyes'." He laughed, then wrinkled his nose at the tea's fragrance. No thanks, not in my line, if it's all the same, thanks. Give me a real cup of tea any day, he prepared himself to say when she offered him a cup. But she did not offer him a cup. She leaned against the kitchen table and drank her tea.

As she lifted her head he caught the glitter of the stone in her nostril. "I know who you are!" he exclaimed. "You're that lot that were over at Springfield's some time back wanting to rent this place."

He took her silence for agreement.

"And he's let it to you?" Silence again. "Well I wish you joy of it," he said, looking around at the bird droppings and the cobwebbed windows. "Well, I haven't got all day, I'll pick up that other bale and be off. Like I said, I'll be over for hay good and regular."

18   The Age-old Dance

"I can't get over a good-looking girl like that getting round with a pair of bums," Catchpole said yet again as Belle dished up Mary's Irish stew.

Belle's serving spoon hovered. "What did they look like? The others?"

"I told you, I didn't see them. They were in one of the other rooms, dead to the world. At midday!"

"But they were there?"

"Well of course they were. You don't think a woman's going to live in a tumbledown cottage on her own without electricity or a fridge or the phone or a bloke, do you?"

"Great-grandmother did, after Great-grandfather died, before Mother and I went to live there," Mary said.

"Well there you are, she had to have *someone*."

"I should call in," Mary said, ignoring the jibe in Lou's none. "Newcomers. I could take a cake."

"I wouldn't bother," Lou said dismissively. "My God, Mary, you'd feed every hayseed that lobs into town if you could." Seeing the old woman bridle, he added "And out of my pantry, too."

Belle said impatiently "He doesn't mean it the way it sounds, Mary."

"Oh don't I!" said Lou.

"Then why . . ." Mary began, then gave up because the only one listening was Jane, her eyes as eager as Chomper's.

"You'll be going over to the cottage every other day, did you say, Lou?" Belle was saying, narrowing her eyes at the serving spoon.

"Till I buy in some hay of my own, yes. It's pricey right now."

Belle crumbled a piece of bread. "I don't know what Angus thinks he's doing, letting hippies into the district," she said. "The morals of people like that."

"Yeah, well, he always was a funny sort of coot. Decent over the hay, though. Thoughtful."

"Is that what you call it, Lou?"

Sometimes, thought Mary, exchanges in this house are like Chomper bounding after a rock. Chaw, chaw, tempers and good teeth wearing away.

"Hay's one thing," Belle was saying, a strident note creeping into her voice. Chaw chaw. "Hay's one thing, Lou, but did he give any thought to what he was doing inviting a heap of troublemakers to move into Marycote? Did he give any thought to these young ones . . . to Jane?"

"What do you mean, to me?" Jane objected. "D'you think I'll be over there sharing needles?"

"Oh hush!" breathed Mary.

"It's the example," Belle said, flicking a glance at her daughter. But it was Lou she was aiming at. "It's all right about hay. A few bales of hay. What about loose-moraled people right on our boundary fence not five minutes from this house?"

Catchpole scratched his head. "The woman seemed okay. But I'll have a word with Angus sometime, if that's what you want."

"I should think you should. I think you should tell him how we view it from here, Lou."

They finished their meal in silence. The children hurried out of the room. Catchpole reached for his hat.

"I daresay you'll find him in right now, Lou," Belle said, with a nod towards the phone. Catchpole sighed.

Springfield's phone rang for a long time. Lou felt a sense of reprieve. Just as he was about to hang up, the dialling tone stopped and Angus said "Yes?" Catchpole jumped. He put his hand over the speaker and hissed "All he says is yes! Not good-day like anyone else would. Just yes!"

"Oh dear," murmured Mary. She began to scrape and pack the dinner dishes.

"Good-day there, Angus, how are things?" Lou began. "Catchpole here, Angus." He winked, and gave Belle the thumbs up. "I've been meaning to tell you, decent of you over that hay, Angus. I've been making good use of it. As a matter of fact I was over at the cottage again this morning. I met your tenants."

There was a small silence, then Angus said "Moved in, have they?"

"That's about the strong of it."

As Angus made no further comment, Catchpole, with a desperate glance at Belle, said "It's your business, of course, mate, but I reckon you want to be careful what you do over there. Mary got the feeling you weren't going to let anyone in, else I'd have said something to you on the subject that day we were fencing, since it concerns me too, the cottage being right on my boundary, I mean." He paused. Again Angus said nothing. Typical. Catchpole heard himself growing shriller as he bounded on, grinding away at the silence. "I mean, tenants, well that's okay, I suppose, if they're local, locals have been here for years, but people from out of town, I mean, you know, that's a different horse, come summer they'll probably set fire to the place, yours as well as mine, have you thought of that? And this lot, driving round in an old hearse — I would have thought they were the last sort we'd want in the district, I mean, you know — and you can guess what I found in the hay this morning." Too bad if he thinks I mean a heap of needles. "I mean, people taking over your patch, taking over, I would have thought where that dog-leg was concerned you of all people —"

The phone clicked, and went dead.

Catchpole swore under his breath. He turned on the table. "For God's sake, Mary, d'you have to rattle those bloody dishes every time I get on the phone!" He crushed his Akubra on to his head. "He's so bloody-minded, I feel like thumping him!"

"I wouldn't try that on again, Lou," Belle said drily.

19 The Forests Protect

Angus took his rifle from its place on the wall behind the kitchen door and, going over to the bench, rummaged for ammunition amongst used nails, stubs of pencil, the spirit level Mary had dropped in when he'd mentioned one day that he couldn't find his, buttons, biro tops — all of which he knew Mary itched to tidy. As he scrabbled, papers scattered to the floor — bills, receipts, torn newspaper articles that he meant to read sometime. Jamming them back on the bench, he looked around for the stone axehead that he used as a paperweight. Mary, he thought. She must have moved it. I wish she wouldn't. I just wish she bloody wouldn't.

Slipping several rounds into his pocket, he set out for Marycote. Once he would have walked straight up the scrub-covered hill behind the house: now, he chose to go the long way, moving cautiously through the yellowed winter grass at the edge of the timber. *The forests protect our soldiers but encircle our enemies.* It was a Vietnamese proverb. He first heard it from the woman they caught creeping out of the village with a basket of fish and fruit and vegetables. For someone hiding up in the hills, no doubt about that. She was the girl from the mama san's. The one with the glittery stuff in her hair. After weeks of nothing but the stink of death in his lungs, her fragrance at the mama san's had unnerved him. Let's get out of here, he'd said, pushing a heap of notes into her hand "for your family". He'd taken her out to dinner and they'd talked. He'd talked. He'd told her about the old man with tears jumping out of his face as they'd chased charlie through the paddy fields. He wept for his harvest, she told him. I know, he said, I'm a farmer too. Then why are you here? she asked gently. I love my country, she said. Our paddy fields have run with blood too long. Her singing voice haunted him still. *Que cha dat to, noi chon nhau cat run*: the place where your ancestors are buried and your umbilical cord was first cut. You will go home, she told him. I bloody better! he said. How could the woman they picked up for questioning be the girl from the mama san's? Logistically, it was hardly possible. Was he one of those foreigners for whom all locals looked alike? Her face came back to him in nightmares, gentle and reassuring then fierce and defiant. *You of all people,* he thought, Catchpole's words tangling with the singing tones of the spy from the mama san's. People taking over your patch, he thought angrily. Marching in, pushing you around, bloody foreigners *you got what you deserved then, didn't you!*

20 Upon a Dulcimer

Angus could hear music as he came around the side of the cottage. A woman was sitting on a rucksack on the front verandah, playing some stringed instrument and singing in a high, clear voice. A guitar, they all played guitars. He paused, silent as a forward scout, and looked across the fence. It wasn't a guitar; the highly polished, narrow-waisted instrument was too slim. The notes shone, like a rain cloud in front of the sun, or the creek in the gully in full flow, rushing and ringing.

She must have sensed his presence *you developed a kind of sixth sense that betrayed another's presence* because she stopped singing and lifted her head. *Eyes* he was conscious of unseen eyes as he continued along the fence towards the loose picket.

you had to be quick you survived through surprise What's going on here? he intended to say — shout — as he stepped on to the verandah. Alert, wary, she was no longer singing, though she continued to pluck echoes of her song from the flat instrument.

He said "What do you call that?"

She had been planning to say, aggro for aggro, So what's all the hassle, one night camped in a dump? Or, if he were as she remembered him, on guard, backed against his kitchen table, It's okay, Mr Springfield (she couldn't remember his first name), it's okay, I'm all packed up. His question disconcerted her, and she dropped her gaze.

"It doesn't have a name. It's just something I made up."

"I meant the instrument."

"It's a dulcimer."

"A dulcimer," he echoed, so strangely that she stared at him. "So that's what a dulcimer looks like." What was that thing old Waxford had made the class read aloud in turns two lines at a time? Angus had learned the lot off by heart because he'd liked its strangeness but he'd never found out just what a bloody dulcimer looked like.

" 'In a vision . . .' " he mumbled. " 'Could I revive . . .' "

"What?"

He must have been thinking aloud. You forgot when other people were present. He looked around. "Where are the rest of you?"

Too late she remembered the trick she had used with the other guy. "There's only one of me."

"Two blokes and another woman and a kid. You all came to the house some time back, with Mary. And Catchpole said there were more here when he came for the hay this morning." He frowned. What had Lou said exactly? Again he went over Catchpole's words, trying to extricate sense from the babbling roar over the phone.

" 'And he a pleasure dome'!" he exclaimed.

Lectures, nagging, Gita had grown up with. Aggro. Try-ons. She had to deal with that sort of shit every day. But this, this was weird stuff. It was the chill fingers of fear. The fall through space. The rasping fingernails on the roof last night, the thundering steps, the harsh kkh-ck-ck-ck-ck, kkh-ck-ck-ck of the beast that would not let her sleep.

She fixed on the rifle with the telescopic sights. This she could deal with. Men with their phallic toys. "Is that thing loaded? Mr Springfield?"

"Loaded? Of course not. I don't climb through fences with a loaded gun."

"What did you bring it for, then?"

"What?" He looked at the rifle, and for a moment seemed puzzled. "Thought I might see a rabbit." Or a fox. Foxes were going to be bad this lambing. Why else would he have his 222 with him on his rounds of the paddocks if not on the off-chance of sighting a fox? Or a rabbit. "Ever had rabbit stew?" *If you didn't blow the bastard's brains out in a frenzy of rage or grief within the first few minutes then he was safe, he would live, you couldn't shoot him at all* He rested the rifle against the verandah railing. "No, you'd be a vegetarian, wouldn't you?"

At this talk about food, Gita remembered that since leaving her place in the city she'd had nothing to eat but some dried pawpaw and the lemongrass tea. When she got off the train she had intended to cycle in to the town to stock up using Mark's money, but in her haste to get to Marycote, to sanctuary, she had pedalled straight out to the farm.

"You can tell vegetarians just by looking, can you?" she said, sharp with hunger.

Easily offended! he told himself. "What are you cooking on in there?"

"This." She got off the rucksack and pulled out the spirit stove.

He examined it. "Not much good for more than a cup of tea, is it?"

"Look, what time's the next train to Melbourne?" she asked. He didn't reply. "Hey, I'm sorry about all this," she said. "It was a stupid idea. I guess I didn't think. And the cottage was empty." Still he said nothing. "Can you tell me what time's the next train?" she repeated.

"Ever cooked on a wood stove?"

"No."

"People soon get used to them."

She looked at him warily. "I tried to get the open fire in the big room going, but it nearly smoked me out."

"Chimney needs cleaning. Full of soot. Birds' nests. Possums maybe. Plenty of possums round here. That chimney isn't safe the way it is. You might have burned the whole lot down."

"I wouldn't want to do that. It's a nice old place."

"Good vibes?"

She scowled, certain this time that he was laughing at her. And then she wasn't sure, because he said "Must be pretty cold in there without a fire. I could make a start on the chimneys this afternoon."

"You mean I can stay? Mr Springfield?" Mr Springfield, Mr Springfield. He was making her beg, he was no better than Jules, he used silence to force people to beg.

Angus hesitated. Had he meant that? Is that what he'd meant, that this oval-faced hippy with the long neck and the stone in her nose could stay? Catchpole's shrill words rang in his ears: I'd have thought they were the last sort we'd want in the district. Angus smiled grimly. *Then you got what you deserved, didn't you . . . Lou?*

"I don't see why not," he said. And laughed.

21 Women's Voices

Gita, wiping down the bathroom walls in long, slow sweeps, gave a plus to this guy Springfield for not asking her a string of questions, what brings you here, how long are you staying, where's the kid. She stopped cleaning and leaned her arm against the door frame *the unremembered dream in your veins for hours*. Angus, on his way outside with a possum wrapped in a hessian bag, hesitated. You okay? he was on the point of saying, then shrugged instead and continued on his way to the foot of the nearest manna gum. It was the tree from which the limb had fallen. "Off you go, little feller," he said, unfolding the bag. He'd been surprised to find a grey ringtail actually sleeping in the ceiling. Usually they spent the day in holes in dead trees, and scampered about at night on roofs or in ceilings where there was a sheet of loose roofing iron. Maybe the storm breaking the limb had disturbed this one. He watched it dart up the trunk, its white-tipped tail swaying. Reaching the safety of a huge fork, it crouched, peering blindly down at him.

"You'll be surprised when you come back tonight," Angus told it. "No more cosy ceilings for you. You've been displaced, old son." Maybe he should have shown it to the woman. She might have been interested. Nah. He turned back to the cottage. Why was he bothering? He'd met her sort often enough, up on the North Coast before he came back to the farm. He knew all about women like her. *How did you get that damaged knee, Angus? True? Then it fucking-well serves you right!*

She'd be off the minute she was through with the earth mother bit. And this old place a wreck, roofing iron loose, spouting fallen off, broken panes of glass, birds and mice everywhere. Though nothing basic, nothing wrong with the foundations – nothing that couldn't be put right easy enough with a few days' work. Pity to see old places like this just rotting way. Weather. Vandals. Thieves after fittings. Lou Catchpole at him to bulldoze it. Catchpole! He laughed. So why not have a tenant right on the bloody boundary. *You got what was coming to you, didn't you, Lou?*

He paused, staring up at the high cleared hill directly behind the cottage. He should move the ewes over; there'd been no stock on the hill for a couple of months so there was a fresh pick now. He turned and looked across the creek. They could go over to lamb on the little hill; plenty of shelter there for lambing ewes, behind the big rocks and under the yellow box and the stringybarks.

He looked back at the cleared hill, and for a moment saw it timbered again with red-veined seedlings, with saplings, with forest giants. He sighed then, and thought about the job in hand. Just what had he let himself in for? Earlier, after he'd hurried back to his house and returned in the Suzuki with tools and buckets and brooms, the woman had said vaguely "Do you want me to do anything?" "How about making a start on the bathroom?" he'd said sharply, handing her a couple of buckets. "I'll come down to the creek with you and help you carry up some water. It'll be creek water for everything for a few days. Boil it well, won't you?" He spoke brusquely. The woman said nothing. "I'll get stuck into the spouting tomorrow," he told her. "For rainwater. That's just for drinking and washing up. Bore water for everything else, soon as I get a chance to look at the windmill. Till then the pit toilet out the back's okay." A fine mist was drifting downhill, and he'd said "Haven't you got something better than that tracksuit to keep yourself dry?"

Just below the cottage was a clear deep pool in the creek. He'd begun dipping the buckets. "There are springs further up the gully. You can swim in this pool come summer." What on earth was he telling her that for? His voice became curt again. "No running hot till the electricity's connected. Think you can manage without in the meantime?" To soften his tone he'd added "There's an old chip heater in the bathroom I could try to get going for you. So long as you don't go and blow yourself up." And then he'd glanced at her.

She was watching the running water as it gleamed and tugged at weeds held fast in the creek. Mist like glitter was caught in her hair.

"Come on," he'd said, turning away with his buckets. "This rain's getting thicker."

He had walked swiftly back to the cottage, letting her struggle uphill at her own pace with her buckets. When she had reached the cottage he was busy in the ceiling, crawling silently across the rafters towards the unsuspecting sleeping possum.

Evidently she felt she had done her share by poking a damp cloth at the bathroom, because when that was done she went into the kitchen and started playing the bloody dulcimer. Angus, cleaning the chimney in the sitting room, recognised the song she'd been singing on the verandah earlier that afternoon.

> A spider sits in the corner of the window
> she sits and spins
> she spins and waits
> every night spinning
> she grows thinner and thinner
> until she is nothing but a little new moon

Angus flung down his broom and came into the kitchen. "Cup of tea going, by any chance?"

"You want a cup of tea?"

"If it's not too much trouble." Christ, and he was doing the place up for her!

"I can use the stove now?"

"Fair go. I've been up in the ceiling and on the roof and I've just cleaned out the chimney in the sitting room." Didn't she have eyes in her head? "You'll have to make do with that little stove of yours." He went back into the sitting room, where she could hear him crashing tools around.

She brought the steaming cups into the sitting room. "It's lemongrass. This is dried pawpaw."

He looked in the paper bag she was offering, and saw two pieces of brownish sugar-encrusted fruit. "I'll give it a go. Bit on the sweet side, isn't it?" As he put the bitten piece of sugary fruit on to his saucer, he saw her eyeing it. "You like that stuff, do you?" She nodded. "What was that thing you were singing out there in the kitchen?"

She shrugged. "Just something I made up."

Gita was rather pleased with her song. It was the first she had tried again for a long time. And her very first piece for the dulcimer. When Angus didn't pursue her reply, at least show something on his face — surprise maybe — she added "Last night. I made it up last night. When I couldn't get to sleep."

She looks past, not at you when she's talking, Angus thought. And her replies don't come at once, they seem to come from a long way away, lived on her own a lot maybe. He wondered if that was how he sounded to other people. Remote. Distant. You could almost say uninhabited, like a farm where the family's been forced to walk off. "You say you made that up last night?" he asked, more to remind himself that he existed.

"Yeah. I could see the moon in the corner of the window, in a web."

"Sounds like I better get stuck into a bit of window-cleaning, eh? Unless you want to?"

"I like them. The spiders."

"Talk to them, do you?"

He saw her shoulders tighten. Well so much for trying to be funny. He put down his empty cup and stood up. "Thanks. That was good-oh. Back to work now, eh? No rest for the wicked."

She took the cups and the saucer with his bitten piece of pawpaw out to the kitchen. To his surprise she brought the dulcimer back to the sitting room. He glanced at her.

And thought she was chewing.

Ionian Mode

A spi - der sits in the cor - ner of the win - dow. She sits and spins. She spins and waits. Ev - 'ry night spin - ning, she grows thin - ner and grows thin - ner un - til she is noth - ing but a lit - tle new moon.

* *

Before he went home, Angus dragged out some old dry fence posts stacked under the high side of the cottage and, taking his axe from the utility, chopped small lengths for the stove and larger pieces for the open fire. The woman had drifted outside and, coatless despite the thickening rain, was walking towards the trees on Catchpole's boundary. He didn't see her return, but later, when he was in the kitchen again, coaxing the stove to light with a twist of old newspaper and a handful of chips, she appeared from the sitting room.

"The trick with the stove", he said, adding two short lengths of split post, "is not to let it go out. Now for the open fire." In the sitting room doorway he stopped. "You've already set it!" He took it in: back log, small amount of crumpled paper, dry bark (she'd evidently searched carefully up on the hill), small sticks, larger sticks, light log across the top — just the way he would have done it himself, or Mary. The woman was standing beside the fireplace, watching him. "That should burn all right," he said, crossing the room. "You've done it before, haven't you? Country girl, are you?"

She shook her head slightly, and again looked past him with that curiously drained expression. Being nosy, was he? He said hastily "What have you got for a light for tonight?"

She smiled then. "Fire flames."

Women's voices. And then the running, and the whoosh of flames, and the screaming

"Listen!" he said, grasping her arm. "I don't want this place burned down . . . no fire-guard, all that hay . . . people live in this house!"

She pulled her arm away and rubbed it. "*I* live in this house! I don't want to be fried, do I?"

the screaming

And now she was looking at him with the dull uncomprehending stare of the women in the village. Horrified, he began to plead. "I'm sorry. I'm sorry — I never realised. I wasn't thinking. I should have brought over a hurricane lamp. And a fire-guard. I'll go back and get them. What else do you need?" He hurried away from her into the kitchen on the pretext of looking around. On the table he saw, sharp as a nudge, the screwed-up empty bag she'd had the pawpaw in, and his used cup with its saucer now empty. "Hang on," he said, going back into the sitting room where she was standing staring out the window. "Just what have you got to eat here?"

She shrugged, without turning around. "I was planning on riding into the town and stocking up."

He glanced out the window. There was a squall building up. "Getting a bit late in the day for that, isn't it?"

She muttered something. He had to ask her to repeat it.

"Tomorrow. I'll go tomorrow."

"How about if I bring you back enough to see you through till then? Bread, milk, butter. I'll drop them back with the fire-guard. Okay?" She nodded. He glanced around the room again, at the broken furniture, the linoleum curling up at the walls, and said carefully "If you'd like to come back to the house and have a bite to eat? Stew, I've got a heap of stew."

Gita thought of another night without food. She thought of the nightmare on the roof crying kkh-ck-ck-ck, kkh-ck-ck. To Angus's surprise she turned around. "Okay." He has kind eyes, she thought. Like Mark's. But a strong mouth. She felt a vague stirring of desire, unfocused, easily set aside. "Thanks. But no hassles, okay?" *I'm too tired, too tired, too tired.*

"Sure no hassles," he said gently. "A decent meal, then I'll drive you straight back with the fire-guard and something for your breakfast." He ventured another joke. "I'm a farmer, don't forget. I know a starving beast when I see one." And this time she did smile.

They drove back to his place in silence.

22 Catchpole Woke Up

Lou Catchpole woke up in the middle of the night with the solution crystal clear. Of course! What a mug not to have twigged sooner. There's no one else living in that cottage.

Just that woman by herself. All that yelling out to some bloke. I should have opened every bloody door in the place and checked it out for myself. I'll do just that the next time I go over there for hay.

Beside him, Belle breathed evenly. He gave her haunch a light slap. Bloody hippies. He'd slip across to the old cottage first thing in the morning.

23   The Forests Protect

She was wakened by the thumping on the roof. Someone was up there on the roof. As she lay, tense as a spring, the noise stopped. All she could hear were little creaks in the walls of the house, as though Marycote was resettling its limbs, and a hiss from the smouldering fire. Was it still up there? Or had it slid down? When her ears ached with straining, she shuddered down inside her sleeping bag and tried to go back to sleep. And then the other noise started. Kkh-ck-ck-ck-ck, kkh, kkh. It was still up on the roof. Who? Springfield? That weirdo Catchpole? Some other maniac she hadn't seen yet? There was a tremendous banging across the roof, as though there were two of them up there, and in the distance that ghastly kkh-ck-ck, and then silence.

She lay for a long time, listening, but the creature didn't return. She couldn't get back to sleep, even though she had something she told herself she'd always wanted, a fire to doze off by. Springfield had brought a big log back with him and thrown it on to the fire. "That should keep you going," he'd said. Funny guy. You think he's a deadshit like that kid said that day and then he smiles. She lay watching the glowing coals. Palaces. Mansions. I could walk right in there.

She felt the darkness growing softer. Finally, when she was sure she was no longer shaking, she climbed out of the sleeping bag and scrabbled around for her sweater and tracksuit. She would make a cup of lemongrass in the dark. She wouldn't light Springfield's hurricane lamp, and she'd shield the dancing blue flame of the spirit stove so that if the creature was still outside it couldn't see her.

Hot tea warming her, she sidled around the walls and peered out.

And in the half-light saw the trees, saw their silhouetted shapes surrounding the cottage, solid trunks with rounded feathery crowns, presences surrounding her, bending towards her. How lovely they were against the lightening sky. She had an overwhelming sense of a living, joyful presence. The sky was grey now — no, gray, she told herself, because there was a pinkish tinge to the fading darkness, and that, Jarrah would say, was g-r-a-y not g-r-e-y which, Jarrah would tell her, made you think of blue, the blueness of steel. See, Gita? Sure, she would say, and this is a pinkening sky, a tender, female sky, but strong, and as enduring as steel.

Until now she hadn't given Jarrah a thought since she'd sent him off with his father.

24 Using

Angus looked under the shed at Springfield for spouting for Marycote. He found what he needed, stacked away beside lengths of timber, sheets of roofing iron, coils of used fencing wire, steel posts, collapsed frames of old chicken coops. Belle used to get cranky with him for hanging on to all this old stuff. The accumulation of years. It's junk, Angus, get rid of it. Oh . . . I dunno. Might come in handy one of these days. You're hopeless, Angus.

He loaded the spouting on to the utility, then on an impulse went back into the house. He'd take over a few things to make a tenant more comfortable, a wardrobe, a couple of decent chairs, a small table for the sitting room. He hadn't mentioned these things last night. To be truthful, he hadn't thought about them. The woman had disturbed him. Oh, there'd been no hassles. He'd fed her and dropped her back at Marycote, just as agreed. No, it was her manner. The thousand yard stare, the blokes used to call it.

He went into the closed-up, unused part of the house for the things he wanted for Marycote. Furniture had gathered dust in the maid's room until his return from up north, when he'd dumped it in another spare room. He opened the door of this room. It was the room with the double bed. Its chillness struck him like a blow. He bit his breath. Tried to silence his heart beats. Behind him, the house listened. Concentrate on the job in hand, he told himself. Bed frames stacked against the wall. Might as well take over a bed frame. Pile of mattresses here. This mattress feels damp. Everything's damp. Everlasting damp. Could ask Mary to air things. Not fair to, really. This mattress: I'll tell the woman at Marycote to give it a good airing by the fire.

I don't even know her name . . . and all at once was surrounded by unseen terror which pursued you so silently you never saw it until you stepped out face to face. Angus swung around. The vines receded. It was only the empty bedroom with its bitter memories.

"It's you, is it?" she said. Well who else, he thought. "Come on in." He followed her through the kitchen into the sitting room. "Like some toast?" she was saying. "I'm making it on the open fire. On a forked stick." He sat in one of the old chairs; the others from Springfield were still on the utility, parked out of the drizzling rain in the falling-down garage. "You can do the buttering," she said. "Want honey?"

He nodded. The chill fog of that closed room at Springfield began to evaporate. ". . . your own hive?" she was asking.

"No. It's bought. Local, though. Yellow box." It crossed his mind to tell her that the tree's botanical name meant "honey-scented", but she was speaking again.

"It's good. So is Paterson's Curse. Do you know it? Paterson's Curse, Salvation Jane — don't you think that's funny? The same plant, I mean." Perked up today, have you? thought Angus. All you needed was a good feed. Gita was on the point of telling him Jules's story about buttercups and orange peels, but decided not to. She didn't want to be reminded of Jules. She said instead "I've always wanted to keep bees. They don't sting you if they know you."

"Is that so?"

"It's true," she insisted. "Like a cup of tea with your toast? The kettle should be hot by now."

He surprised himself by saying "I'll make it if you like."

"Sure. Everything's out there. I'll do more toast."

"That log you brought over last night was still going this morning," she told him when he came back with the tea.

He raised his slice of toast to catch a dribble of honey with his tongue. "Yellow box. I thought that old stump might burn all night. It came off the little hill across the creek. I pulled it out last summer."

"Maybe I can learn some of the trees while I'm here. I'd like to do that."

Yeah? he thought. "Why not?" he said.

She glanced at him. "That's right. Why not?"

Scratchy! he thought. "Across the creek, up amongst the rocks, there's yellow box and stringybark. Along the fence here, in my place and Catchpole's, that's manna gum."

"The big ones near the cottage?"

"Yes. They'd be a good two hundred years old."

"Here before the white people," she said, remembering the stone axehead Jarrah had shown her in the kitchen at Springfield.

"That's right. And then there's all the wattles." To his surprise, he heard himself offering to identify them for her if she really wanted to know. He knew most of the trees on his place. But what he was saying was drowned by a shout from the kitchen.

"Got a fire going today, I see. Not in bed this time, are you?"

Catchpole! What the hell! Angus glanced at the woman. She hadn't moved. She had that secret look again. Sullen. He tried to recall on whose face he had seen it before. Suddenly she bounded up and went out to the kitchen. Angus heard her say, loud enough even for his ears to catch, "We're having breakfast. Would you like a cup of tea?"

"We?" Catchpole sounded puzzled. "Then there really are —"

"Sure. What did you think?"

Catchpole pushed past her into the sitting room.

"'day, Lou," said Angus drily.

"Oh! Oh, g'day. You look comfortable enough there, at any rate. Didn't see your ute."

"It's there, Lou. In the garage." He laughed as Lou raised his eyebrows.

Catchpole turned to the woman. "Came over for hay. For the cattle, remember? Like I told you."

"I thought you said once a week," the woman said, sitting down again.

"Yeah, well some of them are feeling this cold spell, aren't they?" Catchpole went to sit on the sofa, felt it wobble, lowered himself gingerly. "Breakfast time, is it? So what's offering?"

"I said. Tea."

"Yeah, sure. Always one for a cup of tea. So long as it's not that scented stuff you were drinking last time."

Gita sulked out to the kitchen. Angus, watching her retreating shoulders, smiled wryly. Men! Expecting you to wait on them: he'd heard it all before. Good thing he'd volunteered to make the tea there a while back! When she returned to the sitting room he was saying " . . . so I'd be pleased, Lou, if you'd take what you need back to your hayshed and that way I can clean up the room and get rid of the mice."

"It's a lot easier for me just to chuck it over the fence from here," Catchpole objected.

"But not for my tenant, Lou."

"Hell, she's not reckoning on staying, is she?"

Angus shrugged.

"And the rest of them, are they planning on moving in, too?"

Again Angus shrugged. Gita glowered: this was another of those conversations as though she were not present.

Catchpole turned on her. "Are they?"

She thought of saying yes. She glanced at Angus. "No."

"Must be a bit lonely all by yourself, isn't it? Girl like you, used to the bright lights. I give her two weeks, Angus, three at the most, and she'll be hot-footing it back to the city just as quick as she can go. You see if I'm not right. If the possums don't scare the shit out of her, the silence will."

Angus breathed out h-h-h-h. "Just lay off, Lou, will you? Just let her be."

Catchpole laughed. "If that's how the land lies, Angus."

Gita jumped to her feet. "I'm off into the town now."

"Can I give you a lift?" Catchpole said. "I'm on my way home actually, but I'd be more than happy to turn round again."

"Thanks, but I'm going on my bike."

"A bike, hell! Hop in the Range Rover and I'll have you there in a flash."

She shook her head. "I like bike riding."

"You do? Suit yourself then. I'll go and put out that hay." He turned back to Angus. "You're serious about this letting business, then?"

"I am, Lou."

As Angus heard the Range Rover start up when Lou had finished feeding the cattle, he recalled the way that prick had swaggered into the sitting room, saying things like tea time *again,* not that scented stuff *again.* He hurried out to the front verandah. Lou went, not back to the farm, but in the opposite direction, downhill towards Currawong. Lying bastard. By now the woman was out of sight though she wouldn't have got far down the road. He strained to hear whether the Range Rover's engine stopped long enough to load up a bicycle. He couldn't tell. And that was another legacy of his tour abroad: damaged hearing. *Fucking serves you*

He went slowly back into the cottage and paused in the sitting room, going over in his mind all there was to do to make Marycote habitable again. It had been unoccupied for years, since the deaths of two aged distant cousins, and its needs muttered at him. Secure door locks for starters. Spouting and glass and paint and rewiring and new floor coverings. But not for this woman. She wouldn't stay. He looked at the empty chairs; he could almost see the two of them still sitting there, eating honey and toast and talking about things close to his heart. By the fireplace, socks and skivvies trailed out of the rucksack. The dulcimer on her sleeping bag looked as though it was asleep. He went across and twanged the strings. Christ, what had he let himself in for?

25 And He a Pleasure Dome

The next morning Angus had a copy of Coleridge's poems with him when he arrived at Marycote. "That dulcimer," he said. "It's in a poem called 'Kubla Khan'. I thought — but maybe you know it. I mean, you know, seeing you're always playing the thing. I've put a marker at the page."

He didn't tell her that, before leaving Springfield just now, on another impulse he had gone into the library to look for the book. From behind the locked glass doors of the bookcases in that tall quiet room, his parents' and his grandparents' books had looked down at him. Had looked down kindly, he'd thought, even eagerly. He'd flung back the curtains of the unused room and had left them that way.

"That's weird stuff," the woman said, when she had read the poem.

"It was an opium dream. He was hooked."

"On opium? Heroin?"

"He tried to write his dream down when he woke up but something interrupted him and later on he could only remember bits here and there."

"Yeah. Heroin fucks up your head."

"A lot else fucks up your head too."

Does it? What would you know? Did this woman say that, or was it the other one: the woman up on the North Coast, the spy with the glitter in her hair, his wife, conniving with the invader ... all women, no woman? *Then it fucking-well serves you*

"What would you know about it!" Angus sprang back at her. Then looked up in alarm. She was reading the poem again. "I better go and put in that new ball tap," he muttered, to test her hearing. She smiled at him vaguely. "The fixture's okay," he went on more loudly, "but I should dig out the septic sometime. Well, that's a farmer's life, isn't it, shovelling shit?"

She said "Heroin's called shit, did you know that?" And laughed, at some private scene.

Angus laughed too, with relief. She didn't hear me, after all: didn't hear me attacking her. I didn't attack her; I didn't even open my mouth.

26 Candle

Once the main restorations at Marycote were completed, Angus came to the cottage less frequently. For several days he had worked till dusk like someone possessed, but now he came only for an hour or two at a time to finish things off: tightening the springs under the armchairs with new webbing, replacing the castor on the sofa, restoring a chipped door knob.

He got used to her being there in the same room, plucking chords from the dulcimer or just staring into the fire. Funny, he would think, catching sight of the pale, oval face as he straightened his back, I learned a whole poem about a dulcimer and I never knew till now what it sounded like. And, bending again to his work, would become absorbed in what he was doing.

"You're a perfectionist," she commented one day. Her voice startled him.

"Ahh . . ." He shrugged. "I like to get things right, that's all." But was pleased, nevertheless.

One afternoon, when he was working on the sash in the sitting room window and she was sitting lotus-fashion in front of the fire, he noticed a candle on the mantelpiece. He came across and rubbed the blackened wick between his fingers. She'd found an old cracked flowerpot somewhere, filled it with soil and stood the candle in it.

"Sorry to interrupt." He waited until she looked up. "Candles. Flaring. Too dangerous in this old place." Too dangerous for someone like you to fool around with.

She looked at him abstractedly. "This place is safe. It doesn't flare here."

"No?"

"If it ever did I'd be careful, extra careful I mean."

"You would, would you?"

His tone evidently stung her, because she replied sharply "Yes I would! Because it would be a . . . be a . . ." She broke off.

"Be a what?"

"A sign," she muttered.

"A sign? Sure, sign of a draught." She shook her head slightly. "No?" He stared down at her.

She looked uncomfortable. "I told you. To take care."

"That's for sure. Take care of draughts."

"No, not just draughts. Something . . . wrong. Or going to happen. I don't know, it's hard to explain . . . that you have to take care."

"Just as well, messing round with candles. Listen, I want a cottage standing here, not a burnt-out shell. Signs!" Laughing, he picked up the new sash cord.

"There's more than one way of knowing things," she said obstinately.

He turned around. "Tell me more!"

But she just looked sulky, and went on staring into the fire.

Angus slid the window up and down. She won't see it out over summer, he told himself, but my next tenant will want a cool breeze through here without the risk of breaking his arm. And he'll want a cottage that's intact.

He straightened his back for a moment, envisaging Catchpole's fury at having strangers in that step he was after, right on his bloody boundary.

Every time he pictured Lou's face as he repaired something else, he would smile to himself.

Gloating, he's gloating over something, Gita would think,

lifting her head from a tune she was working out on the melody string. And would feel too chilled to continue.

27 Rush

Gita looked out to a threatening sky and the discovery that she'd run out of kindling. Reluctantly she put down the dulcimer; the strummed drones had taken her over. She loved their exhilaration — you could lose yourself in that — and, above the drones, the melody, clear as a glass of spring rain. But, if she wanted a fire in the bedroom to go to sleep by, she'd have to get busy right now. Jules had liked that about her, her busyness, her ability to get what she wanted. Pulling on her tracksuit and her boots, she hurried over to the manna gums along the fence in the step. There was still plenty of small stuff on the ground here, bark and sticks that she'd better dry out for the fires tomorrow while she was about it.

It was raining already, soft big drops that clung to her sleeves and hands. She looked up, and felt them cold and gentle on her forehead and mouth. And it wasn't rain at all, it was snow. She put down her sticks and walked into the open. How beautiful the flakes were, dropping quietly around her and on to her hair and shoulders and outstretched hands. Some of them settled on the grass like visitors, others melted away as soon as they touched solid earth.

Perhaps it will snow all afternoon, she thought, perhaps I will walk in my red-laced boots in a white landscape where all the stumps and lichen-covered rocks and little hollows I am coming to know will be smoothed away like a pillow of sleep.

A small wind got up. She caught one of the whirling snowflakes and licked her fingertip. As she did so a shock of familiar warmth rushed through her, flooding her breasts and belly, tingling the backs of her heels and the soles of her feet.

Then, fulfilled craving had been as sweet as falling snow: here, snow at Marycote brought back all the yearning.

When she looked out her bedroom window next morning, the

snowfall had melted away while she slept. Remnants clinging to the shadows fled as the sun climbed. Across the creek, sheltering against a big rock, was a lamb, birthed and abandoned overnight, but it, too, grew gradually smaller until by midday it had quite disappeared.

28 Runaround

Angus came into the kitchen at Springfield and threw a pair of freshly skinned rabbits on to the table.

"Well Mary, at it again? There's no stopping you, is there? A bloke turns his back for five seconds and you're darning his socks or turning his old shirt collars."

He was cheerful this morning, talkative even, so Mary pulled the kettle to the centre of the Aga for a quick cup of tea together. When Angus was in this mood there was nothing she liked better than a bit of a chinwag. He was one of the nicest people she knew, when he wasn't in a mood.

She placed the rabbits on a plate and wiped the freshly scrubbed table again. "How are your new tenants getting along?" she asked, spreading a small cloth, and bringing the tea things and a jar of apricot jam she had made last summer and hot scones straight from the oven.

"Fine, as far as I know." He helped himself to another scone. Watching him heap on butter and jam, she recalled the bread and dripping of her youth. "Good batch today, Mary," he was saying. Mary was known all over the district for her scones. "They get better every time. If that's possible." She looked surprised and pleased; as usual murmured something self-deprecating. "Yes. In the end only one turned up," he continued, his cup half way to his mouth for several seconds.

"And he's settling in?" She caught her breath at a twinge of lumbago: didn't she love the old house as much as that smiling man?

"I think so. It's a woman, actually."

"A woman? On her own? I must call on her." As a consequence of Lou's harsh words over her slackness in exposing the children as soon as his back was turned to a bunch of hippies, yobbos, weirdos, she had shied away from her usual hospitality to newcomers. But a woman! And alone! She pictured what she would take, scones, or a nice boiled fruit cake. Better still, a six-egg sponge you were supposed to beat by hand till your shoulders ached. "I'll go this afternoon. Right after lunch. She'll be thinking we're an unwelcoming lot." Since the child and the younger woman had seemed to be together, he must mean the other one, the older woman, the one who came sensibly dressed, in a thick coat and overalls. "A country woman, is she?"

Angus laughed. "Spent her entire life in the city, I should think."

Oh but the land had called! Marycote called! And Springfield had called poor Angus back from his aimless wandering up north. "Even so, it must seem very quiet. Lonely." Perhaps she and the newcomer would strike up a friendship. In Mary's memory Crystal appeared older, closer to Mary's age . . . a retired teacher, perhaps, or a widow, though Mary couldn't remember a wedding ring, or a spinster like herself but one with no ties, no commitments, wealthy no doubt (and here the friendship faltered), a self-confident woman, a woman with time and money to indulge a whim . . . a garden! Mary saw her doing all the things she herself daydreamed about — or even yanking out all Great-grandmother's bulbs! Angus was usually so busy (preoccupied, she meant, self-absorbed) he wouldn't even see the mess a wild gardener was making. "What exactly does she have in mind at Marycote, I wonder?"

"Nothing, I reckon. Keeping the stove alight. Playing the dulcimer."

"Dulcimer?"

"Variation on playing the guitar, Mary. They all do it. Now you mention it, she did say she was interested in finding a bit of work if she could, cleaning, barmaiding, anything if I recall. Don't hold your breath, I told her."

As he repeated those words don't hold your breath, an unremembered dream of the previous night came back with the clarity of nightmare, the stink of death in his veins for hours but the details just out of reach, *over the horizon over the next rise the enemy around the next corner* and in a flash recalled something else by that opium poet, another verse he'd learned by heart — no, hadn't needed to *learn* —

> Like one that on a lonesome road
> Doth walk in fear and dread
> And having once turned round, walks on
> And turns no more his head
> Because he knows a frightful fiend
> Doth close behind him tread.

He shifted abruptly, staring at Mary. Her lips were pursed together. She hadn't noticed his unease.

Barmaiding, she was thinking. The blonde young lady grew powerful biceps, her hair turned brassy, her ears rang with the foul language of swilling men.

"Dear," she said gently, leaning towards Angus. She did worry about him. He was the son she would have liked, if marriage and children had been part of God's plan. "That little problem . . ."

He knew what she meant. "What problem, Mary?"

Now I've gone and spoiled things! And we were having such a nice chat. She began to flutter. "On your own, dear. I can't help noticing when I'm tidying up. The temptation."

He made it hard for her. "You mean women? Or the lack of them?"

"I can't help noticing the level in the bottle, Angus, when I'm tidying up."

So you add a bit of water, Mary, don't you? You don't fool me. "It's nothing I can't handle."

"That's good, that's good, Angus. But on your own," she repeated. "Fine with other people, but on your own, dear . . . the temptation."

He could see tears in her eyes. "So what are you suggesting this time? I hit the wagon?"

"If our own prime minister, Angus . . ."

He laughed. "That weeping hypocrite!" Here was Mary holding up as an example a man whose party she wouldn't vote for in a million years, while he who had voted Labor since he was twenty-two was coming more and more to despise everything its present leadership stood for.

Wounded by his laughter, she said primly "It's none of my business, Angus, of course. Though I must say, in my book tears don't always mean weakness." She started shaking again. Lou's quite right, I poke my nose in far too much. Marycote is none of my business. I won't call after all. No, I definitely won't call on the new person at Marycote.

She felt a surge of relief at not having to face a rough sort of woman. And just as quickly was shocked at herself. Who was she, Mary Springfield, to be critical of someone forced to earn her living as best she could? Anxious to atone for such a lapse into uncharitableness, she looked around Angus's kitchen. She often hurried through her hospital visiting in order to give herself enough time at Springfield. A woman with muscles would have this place spotless in a flash. She said timidly, hoping this idea might serve as penance, "If you were ever thinking of looking for a cleaning lady . . . I mean . . . this house is so big, isn't it? Of course I know you've said don't bother about the rooms you don't use but if you had someone in on a regular basis, and I don't have time to get over as often as I should, do I?"

"I should do it myself, Mary." He spoke gently, alarmed that he might have offended her. He thought she was trying to say that she was tired of coming over to Springfield. They worked her pretty hard over at Valley View Park, and she wasn't a young woman. Once a week, oftener, was it, she stopped by on her way home from town in her old blue runaround, and swept and washed up and ironed whatever she could lay hands on. You shouldn't do all this, Mary, he would say. Nonsense, it gives me something to do. The devil finds mischief, Angus. And he would laugh. You are the least idle person I know, Mary. Oh Angus (again that timorous smile)! What a nice thing to say!

It occurred to him that it would kill two birds, having his tenant do a bit of the cooking and cleaning instead of poor old Mary. Solve the rent business as well. I'll give it some thought, he'd said when the woman had mentioned it. He had no idea how much to ask. His first thought on letting the cottage was to irritate Catchpole. He hadn't gone much beyond that. How much do you reckon? he'd asked her. She'd shrugged and mumbled It's up to you, or something equally unhelpful. Sulky sort of girl. And not likely to be thorough like Mary. Still . . . "I don't use that much of the house, do I? Just the kitchen mostly."

"And your bedroom and the bathroom and the fires when they're set! And the laundry to chuck your muddy boots in!" Plenty to keep even a young woman busy. And Mary felt better about the bad thoughts she'd been having. Her life was a series of small atonements.

"Don't think I don't appreciate all you do, Mary," Angus hastened to reassure her. "It's wonderful to come home to a clean house with the stove stoked up and something hot in the oven, believe you me."

"There you are, then. Get this lady in regularly . . . only a thought, of course, Angus. She mightn't . . . she might . . ." Her voice trailed away. A barmaid might bring with her the odour of liquor and tempt him to start drinking again! Oh Angus, what have I done? She must get across to Marycote immediately and see for herself. "But I've quite forgotten what you said her name was, dear."

"I didn't. To tell you the truth, Mary, I don't know."

"Don't know!" She added hastily "Of course not dear I thought you'd told me but now I put my mind oh my poor forgetful mind! It was Lou who mentioned Lou did mention some name." Since Angus was staring at her, she said "Oh dear, I've stayed too long again, I mustn't hold you up, I'll let you know her name, shall I . . ."

Driving the short distance from Springfield to Valley View Park, Mary could hardly see the road; her eyes had gone all blurry, as though a chill draught had crept in and was tearing at her eyes. Lou Catchpole, seeing the blue runaround weaving along his drive, thought it was about time the old girl gave up driving.

* *

Mid-afternoon was the time to call. As Mary went out the kitchen door she heard Lou, hunting through a drawer for a spirit level, remark to Belle Catchpole "A sponge cake. She's spent the afternoon making a bloody great sponge cake for some bunch of dole-bludgers over there at the cottage."

Mary poked her head around the door. "It was only twenty minutes, Lou. And of course I'll pay for the ingredients. And the use of the Mixmaster."

"For heaven's sake, Mary," Belle Catchpole intervened. "No one's asking you to pay for a few eggs and a bit of flour out of your pension." She lowered her voice. "Why can't you leave your stupid comments till she's out of hearing, Lou? You know Lou didn't mean anything, Mary. He's in a foul temper because he can't find something, that's all. If you were more tidy with your things, Lou – "

"Christ, I know the spirit level was here. It's been in this drawer for years. It's always kept here."

Mary came back into the kitchen. "I'm sorry Lou, I really am, but if it's the spirit level . . . I borrowed it."

"You borrowed it? What the hell would you want with a spirit level?"

Mary's colour rose. Her memory again! She'd quite forgotten to ask Angus if he'd finished with it.

"Well!" barked Lou. Standing there staring at him like a bloody loon.

Mary said timidly "Isn't there another one out in the shed? I'm sure I've seen . . ."

Lou swore at her.

"Lou!" cried Belle. "Mary, he –"

Mary was so offended that Lou would swear at a woman, an older woman at that, that she forgot entirely about turning the other cheek. "Since Angus's tenant is looking for work in the district, Lou, I hardly think she can be labelled a dole-bludger. I suggest you mind your mouth."

Before her trembling knees could give way, Mary went out and shut the door.

Lou and Belle heaved exasperated sighs at each other.

"She gets worse and worse," Belle sighed.

"She won't last forever," Lou soothed. "You should see the way she's been driving lately. Sooner rather than later, I'd say."

But Belle had just recalled Mary's comment about the tenant: one tenant, a woman. She stopped loading the dishwasher. "What do you mean, sooner rather than later?"

"It stands to reason, doesn't it?"

Belle's voice grew shrill. "Are you wishing she was dead? Mary! Is that what you're saying, Lou?" Him knowing all the time who was over there at the cottage! "You utterly calculating, callous . . . Words fail me!"

"All I'm saying — "

"And to think how welcome she always made you whenever you just happened to drop by round meal times! Or have you forgotten, Lou? Lou, I'm talking to you! All those months she and I were in charge at Springfield because his parents were a pair of crocks and God knows where *he* was. One old woman and a girl trying to run that bloody farm and not a useful man in sight!"

Lou swore again, under his breath this time. Coming over to the dishwasher, he rubbed himself against her. "I didn't hear you complain too much then that I didn't have my uses."

Belle laughed. Her voice dropped to normal. "Get away with you. Can't you see I'm busy?"

"Come here! Nothing wrong with my memory."

Mary Springfield, standing on the verandah to adjust the waxed paper covering the cake, heard the first part of this exchange: Belle's raised voice, though not her words, and she thought they get worse and worse, I couldn't go through it all again. I don't know what I'm going to do, I really don't.

To Mary's surprise, the tenant at Marycote was the thin girl with the dark hair that Mary remembered fell curling about her face. Today, however, she'd caught it into one thick plait, not down the middle of her back as Mary had once worn hers but, Mary thought, in a much more adventurous way, to the side over her left shoulder. Now Mary could see her right ear clearly. Not only did she have a gemstone in her nose, she had little gold rings all the way up her ear, five of them, right into the gristly part! It made Mary's own ears hurt just to see them.

"You have such pretty hair," she said hastily, in case the girl thought she was staring. Before she could stop herself she added "Aren't you worried plaiting it will take out all the curl?" And then she blushed, because the girl just looked at her.

She began to wonder whether perhaps she had made a mistake in coming, after all, because although she said "I'm Mary Springfield, you might remember . . ." and then waited politely, she had to ask the girl for her name. No wonder Angus . . . ! And the girl didn't smile the way Mary and all the people she knew smiled when they had a visitor. In fact, she looked at Mary in much the same way as young Jane sometimes looked at her: as though she was an old piece of furniture that Jane would much rather wasn't in the same room.

However, Gita did say "Come on in," and she took her into the sitting room where Mary decided she'd better sit down without waiting to be invited or she might stay standing until it was polite to leave. And Gita, taking Mary's sponge and putting it not on the table but on the floor between the two chairs, did ask if she would like something to drink. Herbal, ocker or decaf coffee? So that was all right. While Gita was out in the kitchen Mary settled back in her chair and looked around the room. Window cleaned in here too, ceiling repaired, pile of firewood in a box, that fire-guard, that's one from Springfield. And the table. Angus has certainly been busy. But goodness, what a mess, clothes everywhere! I do hope she remembers to put her smalls out of sight if Angus has to come in. I could do a lot in this room, Mary thought. The windows for instance . . . velvet drapes. The old velvet of my day used to last forever. And lace curtains, of course. I could run up a pretty curtain in a jiff . . .

"Your little boy's at school, I suppose?" she asked, sipping at rosehip tea from a chipped cup, one of her great-grandmother's, she fancied, only she didn't like to say so in case her memory was up to its tricks again. I must bring her another cup, she thought, running her finger around the rim and catching her nail on the chip while she waited for Gita's reply. One of that rose-patterned set. Belle won't notice. Belle likes all-white these days, with next to nothing served up on the plate, just a drizzle of sauce to fool you.

"That's right, he's at school," Gita said.

"Well isn't that nice! I wonder if he's in the same grade as little Elton Catchpole. I must ask Elton tonight."

Gita said nothing.

Mary lowered her voice. "And your husband – is he . . . ?"

"The boy's father? Adelaide."

"Adelaide!" At least not dead.

"Yeah, but he's in Melbourne for a bit right now."

"He knows a lot about old houses," Mary said, thinking of Jules. Separated, then. What a shame.

Gita laughed. "Jules, you mean? He knows a lot about a lot of things, Jules does."

"Some of Lou's wood?" Mary asked, to fill in the silence that followed. Just yesterday, running into town for something, she had passed Lou turning into the Marycote drive with a load of firewood, and had meant to say something to him later about his kindness to the people at Marycote.

The girl gave her such a look!

"No. Angus's."

This was not true. Actually the fire was burning brightly with two of the logs that Catchpole had dropped off. But Gita had no intention of giving this old busybody the satisfaction of hearing that they'd come from that creep. She'd been miles away in front of the fire yesterday when there was such a banging on the kitchen door that for an instant she knew it was a bust.

"Asleep again, are we?" And Catchpole had grinned, and taken his time in telling her the reason for his visit. She knew the sort. "What do you want?" she'd said. Flat. Looking past him. "I've come to take the rest of the hay, like the landlord said. Sorry I didn't get back sooner" he'd flung at her back as she retreated to the sitting room "but it looks like you're not sleeping in the hay now, anyway. Curl up by the fire, do you?" Grinning and grinning. "Seems like you've set yourself up here nice and cosy," he'd continued, leaning against the doorway. "Planning on a long stay after all, eh?"

Gita had shrugged. "I'll see what happens." And made the mistake of meeting his eye.

"You'll see what happens. I see. You'll see what happens." Grinning. Holding her gaze until she was forced to drop her eyes. Drop her eyes to this creep!

"How would you like a bit of firewood?" he'd continued. "Course you would. And then I'll load the hay. Come and show me where you want the wood. Come on. You want to get outside a bit more by the look of you, put a bit of colour into those pearly white cheeks. Now come on, where do you want this wood put?" She had stalked outside. "This'll burn well," he'd told her. "Dead stuff that's been lying round in the paddock for years. Should have cleaned it up long ago. I'll finish tidying up the rest of that limb that fell on the fence one of these days, seeing as Angus hasn't got round to it, all the rubbish, sticks and leaves and that. Should take the whole tree down actually, and replace it with a proper fence post."

"The whole tree? Why?"

"Well, dangerous, for one thing. Might drop another limb. Should get rid of the whole lot along the fence by rights." In sudden terror she'd thought my trees, my lovely morning trees, my friends! She must have looked upset because he'd laughed then, whuh whuh whuh. "Now don't tell me you're one of those greenies, never fell a single tree but thanks very much for the firewood and the use of the weatherboard cottage." His voice licking at her ears had both excited and repelled. "Must be a bit of a change for you, all by yourself here. Nice quiet place like this."

"It's a change."

Still laughing, he'd jumped up on to the truck. "And you'll see what happens, eh?" he'd shouted at her retreating back.

Standing to the side of the kitchen window, she had

watched the wind blow his hair and wrestle with his shoulders as he tossed the logs off as though they were sticks. When he came in with an armful of wood, saying "Now for the next business", she had offered him a cup of tea. "Work before pleasure," he'd said, stepping over her things on the sitting room floor in order to throw one of his logs on to the fire. So she'd sat down by the crackling flames and from under her cloud of hair had watched him as he lumped the heavy bales past the dooway.

"Last load," he'd shouted, and she had stalked out to the kitchen to make the tea. "Not that scented stuff," he'd said, brushing hay from his hands and seating himself opposite her at the small kitchen table. "You know what it reminds me of, that smell?" Ignoring this, she'd passed him the cup. "Hey! This is the real thing!" he'd exclaimed, slurping his tea. "Always been a sucker for the real thing." Grinning. Slurping. Under the table his knees had touched hers. She had moved her legs. Again, his knees. "Like the real thing, do you?" she had mocked. Flat. Brazen. And he'd jumped. Swallowed his tea. Stood up hurriedly. "Off now," he'd said loudly. She'd laughed inwardly, laughed until she felt sick. Come the heavy then back off shitless. She knew the sort.

The girl kept smiling at something. Mary couldn't recall what she had said that was funny. Something about Angus. She had to strain to hear the girl's replies. She did wish young people wouldn't sit with their heads half turned away. She'd come all ready to like her new neighbour, but the visit was harder work than she had expected. Perhaps Gita was shy. Perhaps she was missing her friends. Mary decided to say something nice about the people who had been with her that day at Marycote and Springfield. Were they good friends?

"Yeah." Gita sighed. But the old woman had brought her a cake. Staring into the fire, she said in a flat voice "Mark plays percussion in a band. I sing, at least I used to. Crystal . . . sure, Crystal's a good friend. She works in a women's refuge some of the time. Lots of people stay at her place, women I mean, because they haven't got anywhere else to go. You know?"

"She sounds like a very good friend to have," Mary said wistfully, wondering whether to tell this young woman about her great-grandmother who was another good woman, and then deciding against it: the young didn't want to hear about the old, they wanted to talk about themselves. So she said instead "What interesting friends you have. You must miss them."

Gita threw herself back in her chair. "Right now I just want a break from all that. I just want my own space. You know?"

Mary nodded eagerly. "Oh yes indeed! That's exactly how I feel sometimes. My own space. That's why I come over here now and then and potter round in the garden. Or rather, I used to. Of course I won't while there's someone living here."

"Feel free," Gita said, cutting another piece of cake for herself, then pushing the plate towards Mary.

"You're not a gardener?" Mary asked hopefully.

"Me? The only thing I grow is grass." Gita's lips curled into a laugh. She glanced at Mary.

Mary said innocently "I don't think this garden is really suited to lawns, though, do you?"

It was too easy to take the mickey out of this old duck. So Gita said "How's that?" as though she really wanted to know.

"Well, it's more beds of annuals, and shrubs, and native things, isn't it? I think it's a nice combination, myself. A nice balance. You'll find something similar over at Springfield, though when Angus's father was alive he was one for begonias and ferns. They were a great hobby of his. Of course he couldn't do much else towards the end. He spent all his time in that glasshouse. Angus likes the glasshouse too, but he doesn't seem keen on begonias. But the garden! It's a shame to see old gardens neglected. I wish I was younger. You should see this place in the spring. All the wattles up on the hill, and the plums round the house. And then in summer the fruit, plums for jam, and even nectarines off that old, old tree out the window here."

Fruit straight from the tree, the dew still on it, sliced on to your muesli, did Gita eat muesli, Mary had a new recipe, barley instead of oats, much nuttier-tasting, Mary found a couple of tablespoons each morning kept her right . . . Gita let the voice flow over her. If she didn't have to answer a string of questions, questions with loops and hooks and barbs, the old woman's presence was quite pleasant. Soothing.

"This is a great cake," she said, when Mary paused for breath. "My grandmother used to make cakes like this." Did she? Gita had a hazy memory of a grandmother, or was it an old aunt, but Gita guessed she'd made cakes.

"I can give you the recipe if you like," Mary said, warming to the girl. "It's so easy, really. Just eggs and flour and hot water, and don't breathe when you open the oven. Angus says you play a musical instrument?"

So he's been talking about me. I wonder what he said. "That's right."

"That will be an asset at the school. They're sure to be after you to help with the Christmas concert."

Gita sighed. "Well I don't know how long I'm staying here, do I?"

"Oh." And to Mary's shame she felt a wicked shaft of relief.

"I'll see what happens," the girl was saying.

"Angus mentioned you were looking for some work in the district."

"That's right. Give me something to do, I suppose. Nursery work, that'd be good." All that talk about gardening. Green fingers Gita.

Mary smiled, thinking she meant working with children. "You might pick up something in the town, I suppose, the solicitor's wife's just had a new baby . . . though I don't know, I think her own mother . . . Or the doctor's wife, someone like that. You could slip in and out of town easily enough, I suppose, especially on fine days. Angus says you have a bicycle."

Gita watched a flame curling around a glowing coal. Angus says, Angus says.

Mary took a deep breath. "Of course, *Angus* wants someone to clean his house and do a bit of cooking, a good hot nourishing dinner, you know." How was it she was abandoning poor Angus? This room was as messy as any man would keep it.

The girl definitely looked interested.

"Why don't you mention it to him?" said Mary Springfield desolately. "Or I will if you prefer, next time I see him."

Walking back to Valley View Park with the empty cake plate, along the washed-out road edge where she wrenched her ankle, through the fancy gate and up the drive, Mary Springfield wept. She wept for Marycote; she wept for Angus; she even wept for herself. Gusts of wind rocking between the farm buildings mocked her. Lou Catchpole, seeing her stagger, drew back into the shelter of the garage. I'm right, he thought. Too bloody right I'm right. She's slipping fast. She's on the way out.

29 Why Shouldn't Our Dreams

He hadn't been near the place for a week and the first thing he said was "Where did you get that wood?"

Pardon *me!* "Your neighbour dropped it off when he came for the hay."

"Catchpole brought you that wood?"

"That's right. No law against it, is there?"

He said nothing to that, not even "All right if I go in?" as he usually did: he just barged through the cottage and began ripping up the linoleum in the sitting room. She sat down by the fire again and tried to go on working on her melody. She wouldn't move from this chair till he fucking-well asked. It was her place, wasn't it? But she couldn't think, couldn't hear the song with her fingers. He had brought too much anger with him. She could feel it right across the room: anger sharp as barbs, enclosing him, catching at her, tearing her fingers. That place had been full of people like him: silent ones coiled inside their misery, noisy ones shooting off their mouths. Session after session of them. She just couldn't handle it in the end.

With a desperate look at his back, she threw one of Catchpole's logs on to the fire.

One afternoon Mary called in with a nice little cass for Angus's poor tenant. Gita, brooding over the fire, was so ungracious that Mary tried again a few days later with a boiled fruit cake and a sample of Nottingham lace she'd found at the draper's (thirty-five per cent synthetic these days, but it couldn't be helped). She fancied it might make really nice curtains to go across the windows, with a velvet drape at the side if she could find some, if Gita liked it . . . would let Mary . . . "And if you're a churchgoer, I can easily pick you up of a Sunday, Gita, whatever time," she added.

Through a mouthful of fruit cake the girl muttered "Thanks, but no thanks. I don't go for all that Jesus stuff."

Angus, busy measuring up the sitting room that afternoon, thought why the hell does Mary bother. But that was Mary's way: if someone was grumpy, she just tried all the harder. Out of their longstanding camaraderie he said quickly, to tease her, "Whenever people mention Jesus, Mary, you know who I think of? Yassa Arafat."

Mary squawked. "You don't mean that little man in the tea towel, surely!"

"That's the one. Devoted to his cause, loyal band of followers, price on his head, the eternal survivor —"

"But Angus! He doesn't even bother to shave!"

The two of them laughed. I might as well not be here at all, Gita thought. She flung down the dulcimer and went out to the garden.

Mary had brought a small gardening fork with her. "Just in case I have a moment," she had explained with that deprecating smile Gita hated. "I'd like to have a go at that wretched couch grass," she had continued, moving some of the edging stones to get at the roots. "Before it gets away in the spring."

My place, Gita thought. Pausing by the garden's edge, she could see dozens of minute transparent creatures, no bigger than her little fingernail, disturbed earlier by Mary and now moving slowly over the stones in search of new shelter.

Stamp on those, said Mary at her shoulder. They're baby snails.

Gita looked around. There was no one else in the garden.

Through the soft transparent shells of the snails she could see the living tissue of their bodies. She lifted her eyes, and for a moment saw the garden as Mary had described it, first the deep pink prunus, almost out now, see, then the pale one whose tart fruit made delicious jam, and the white . . . like a bride with her bridesmaids, Mary had offered timorously. And the bulbs! All those golden faces lifted to the sun. Gita felt a tremor of delight. And up on the hill, Gita, all the wattles, gold everywhere, and later on that bit of bush that he's got fenced off, such a mass of wildflowers, that lovely scented white heath, Angus, you really should show her in spring. Jesus! You silly old woman, shut up and take a look at his face. He's just dying to, isn't he!

Under a clump of leaves she noticed something white. She picked it up and turned it over in her hand. It was a shell, pitted and bleached bluish-white, all the nacreous gloss grown dull: an ugly, empty thing.

That's a snail shell, Gita.

Thanks but no thanks. Any fool can see that.

Before the real Mary could come out of the cottage on her way home, Gita put the shell in her cardigan pocket and hurried down to the creek. She felt a cold trickle through the thin soles of her shoes, or perhaps it was only the chill of the mud. Leaning down, she trailed her fingers against the tug of the current. Water has no beginning and no end, she thought, not like a leaf, a leaf has shape, it has edges. Lifting a handful of water, she let it fall back as droplets. Where was each droplet now? She leaned against a willow trunk and stared into the swirling brown water.

* *

What a shit you are, Springfield! Crystal would eat you . . .
"Do you think I could get some sort of work around here, Angus?"

"What sort of work?"

"Anything. Waitressing. Barmaiding. Avon lady. I've done the lot. Surely some of these rich farmers need a cleaning woman." You, maybe?

He had laughed. "Don't hold your breath. I'm about the only bloke without a wife round here, and I do my own cleaning."

Without a wife. Crystal would eat you.

. . . Jules isn't so bad, Gita. You just have to look after yourself around Jules. And he can get us a couple of gigs, he knows people, Gita, but you'll have to go back to the guitar, you know a dulcimer's useless in that sort of group. Come on, Gita, get your act together, we haven't got a good singer, we're relying on you, Jules has booked us the gigs.

. . . Jules. Jules putting his mocking arms around her. Jules laughing. Attaching his price-tag. Moving inside her, moving slowly then more insistently then suddenly stopping – pausing to look down *gloating* because however much she vowed *I will never I will never* her faithless body despaired until he chose to continue.

"My lovely Gita. Our joustings always end with a good fuck, don't they?"

. . . Just for a few days, Crystal. Of course, Gita. Any time you need. And then the talks, the talks, get away from that scene, you've been there before, you can't take the risk. Yes Crystal, no Crystal, I should do that Crystal, yes Crystal yes Crystal yes Crystal, like droplets into the rushing stream.

Or a caught leaf rotting in a pool.

An empty shell. A husk. A hollow vein.

And the road that had led to this cottage? Just one more worn-out vein.

Dreams in your veins the dreams came back *holding your breath until you reached the surface struggling pushing yourself up towards the light then waking gasping screaming the unremembered horror in your veins the details always out of reach over the horizon over the next rise beneath you in the tunnel hardly daring to breathe learning the details in the darkness feeling your way pushing yourself along everything just out of reach the enemy around the next corner* Who was the enemy? She was afraid to know he secured himself in his roll of barbed anger *don't hold your breath!*

I thought at Marycote I could begin again but the terror on the roof stalks me every night . . .

The evening was closing in. She shivered, and pulled her cardigan closer.

There was a shout. Angus was hurrying towards the creek. She hadn't noticed his limp before. "Want to come and look at something?" he called. "Up the hill a bit." He came level with her. His blue eyes shone with excitement. "I was taking a look through the binoculars just now on my way home — Mary said to say goodbye, by the way — and I happened to look up at an old dead tree and I could see something moving on it so I went and took a closer look. I haven't seen them in years."

She hurried to keep up with him. "But what are they?"

"You'll see. We'll get over the fence at this strainer post. Let me go first, then I'll give you a hand."

The fencing wires hurt her feet through the worn soles of her shoes. At the top of the strainer post she teetered, then jumped unaided. He shrugged, but couldn't help asking "Where are your boots?"

"I didn't know I was going bushwalking, did I?"

They continued up the hill. "Look," he said. "On that dead tree, about half way up. We won't go any closer. Here, use these. I always carry them in the ute. In case I see something, an early lamb, or a ewe down. Usually not something like this, though."

She adjusted the heavy binoculars and, in the half-light of early dusk, saw them. Saw eight or ten grey feathery creatures with long dainty tails blowing up and down the tree like puffs of smoke. For as long as she could hold the binoculars steady she watched them, one after the other running up the trunk and out along a branch then with a leap gliding down and running up again. One after the other, up the trunk, along the branch and skimming down.

Her arms began to shake. She handed the binoculars to Angus. "What are they? Flying mice? They're lovely."

"Gliders. Feathertails. Probably got a nest inside that tree. They come out at night for insects and nectar. I think that lot are just playing."

"They don't seem to mind us." She took the binoculars again. When she gave them back she smiled at him. "Thanks, Angus. They've made my day."

He muttered "That's how we get by, isn't it? Seeing things like that? One day at a time. Settling for the little things" then returned to his previous tone as she looked at him quickly, the tone he used with Mary. "It's pretty rare to see feathertails, unless the cat brings one in. They're around, but they're nocturnal. We were lucky to see them just on dusk." She liked him in this mood. "Hollow limbs in dead trees like that one are used by a lot of birds and animals," he told her as they walked back to the fence. "Parrots, kookaburras, possums — there are two or three sorts of possums round here. I'll take you out spotlighting one night if you're interested."

"Spotlighting? Shooting?"

He laughed. "With a torch."

"Whose paddock are we in?" she asked suddenly.

"Catchpole's."

"That tree with the gliders is his, then?"

"That's right. Why?"

"He might want to cut it down for firewood."

"He might. But I doubt if he'd be bothered going to all the trouble." She remembered the trees along the fence at Marycote, and felt a surge of relief. "Plenty of wood on the ground that he can pick up," Angus was saying. He sighed. "You'd be surprised, though, at the number of things that make use of the stuff on the ground. Get disturbed when it's cleaned up, I mean. Skinks, beetles, spiders, centipedes, you'd be surprised."

She thought about the little snails, dislodged by Mary's gardening. "So what do *you* burn, then?"

"Yeah, sure. I burn wood, of course I do. I just get fed up with Catchpole."

Whuh whuh whuh She shuddered.

"You cold?"

"No. Just a ghost on my grave." *Always been a sucker for the real thing* She wrapped her cardigan tighter.

They came to the fence. As before, he climbed over first and waited to help her. This time, because she was jumping downhill so that the drop was further, she braced herself against his arm as she jumped. And, in her thin shoes, stumbled, little light steps that brushed her against him. His hand on her arm tightened. She smiled, lifting her face.

He dropped her arm, saying abruptly as he turned away, "Come on. You're not dressed for this cold wind."

Well, screw you! she thought.

They walked downhill in silence.

What the hell's the use, he was thinking.

She was thinking much the same thing.

30 Shell

So what about my new linoleum? Gita thought, slopping across the bare boards in the sitting room. Screw him, she thought. If he'd bothered to ask *me*, I'd rather have polished wood. Maybe I've scared them off, she thought, as the days went by and neither Mary nor Angus dropped in at the cottage. And the place, settling and creaking around her, became more her place. She still heard them on the roof at night, those hammering cries of dread, but alone within the walls of Marycote she felt safe. No one laying claim to her, measuring and hammering, taking her over, taking over her house, strangers checking the wiring, well maybe *you* don't want the power on, they told her, but the boss does, you won't *have* to use it, staring, checking her out . . . No one recounting bits of Marycote's past, look I dug up this chip of old plate under the nectarine, see the blue flowers . . .

nothing but a little new moon

She would stand at the porch door and breathe deeply, filling her lungs with the needle-thin frosty air. And with each breath there would return that lightness of spirit that she'd felt as she fled from that greasy kitchen at the squat. She had done it, she had floated away, floated until she was an infinitesimal speck, safe from all those upstretched, kind, concerned hands. Her place. *Her* place.

Sometimes she thought about the little gliders blowing up and down their tree: joyous, self-contained creatures, like the trees outside her window that morning when she had woken to the presence of horror. Sometimes she recalled what Angus had said: That's how we get by, isn't it? One day at a time. Settling for the little things. One evening she would walk up the hill again and recapture the experience – one evening, soon. Not yet.

She did not venture out far from the cottage, except to gather kindling under the trees along the fence, or to cycle into Currawong when there was nothing left to eat. There she would stock up with as much as she could carry and walk the bike back to Marycote. If she had to be out on the road, she preferred days that were overcast. She would keep her eyes down, concentrating on the road at her feet or a few yards ahead, feeling herself dissolve into the mist that hung over everything like sheets over the contents of a room. To her relief she did not run across Catchpole or Angus or Mary in town. The stares of the shopkeepers she no longer minded, indeed welcomed: they proved that nothing could touch her.

She discovered the whitened snail shell in her cardigan pocket, and put it on the sitting room mantelpiece where she looked at it sometimes.

31 Mulberry Cycle: May, June

Sometimes, late in the day, Gita would stand at one of Marycote's western windows and lose herself in the sky. The winter sunsets were violent, great red and purple welts that rose and spread then faded to a pallid streak. *Leaking blood* If she were at the window across the passage from the sitting room, she had to look through the twisted leafless branches of the mulberry tree. *Like blackened veins* And on a scrap of paper she began to make a new song. She remembered the tree on the day she had first come to the cottage. It was autumn then, and the mulberry was a mass of gold leaves. Like dollar coins. *Hey! Funny money!* By the time the last light had faded, the paper was covered with scribbling and crossings-out. She took up the dulcimer and, cross-legged in front of the fire, tried out chords.

> *May*
> Hey! funny money!
> she's wild with fat gold coins
> she needs her fix

She scrawled through the last line, then put it back again.

> *June*
> A scribbled page
> a web
> torn net of blackened veins
> the sky leaks blood

She laughed to herself at the morality of it. "Mulberry Cycle", she decided to call it.

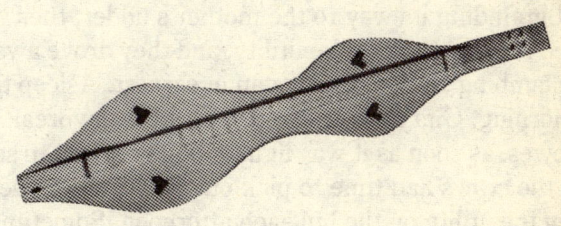

32 Lambing

One afternoon Gita saw Angus's utility up on the hill. She saw it stop a short distance from a small mob of sheep. Angus got out, a dog jumped off the tray at the back, and together the man and the dog walked the sheep towards the fence. Each time he whistled – a short, piercing sound that carried downhill to the watching woman – the dog would move to the left or the right. If a sheep made to bolt from the rest, the dog was there instantly to head it off. When he had the sheep in a tight bunch against the fence, Angus ran in and caught one of them. Gita wished she had a pair of binoculars. When he stood up again a lamb had been born. She saw the sheep nuzzling it, then turning abruptly towards the dog as the lamb struggled to its feet. Gita at the cottage and Angus a few yards from the ewe stood watching until the lamb had succeeded in finding its way to the mother's udder, then Angus whistled the dog back to the utility, and they drove away.

The lambing season now began in earnest. Asleep till late each morning, Gita missed Angus doing the daybreak round of his ewes, as soon as it was light enough for him to see and before the crows had time to pick out eyes and tongues. But she saw the utility on the hill each afternoon. Sometimes she saw Angus tie the feet of a ewe and lift her on to the tray.

Sometimes he would take a limp lamb and fling it up, letting the ewe run off searching and bleating.

Gita started to walk further for her kindling. At the top of the rocky little hill on the Springfield side of the creek she found plenty of light firewood. If she was wearing her boots, she would splash from tussock to tussock across a shallow part of the creek; if not, she would walk uphill and go around the springs. The late afternoon sun slanted with a golden light across the grass. She would look up at the trees, their yellow buds swelling amongst long grey-green leaves, and recall that Angus had offered to identify them for her. Or had he laughed at her? She couldn't remember.

One afternoon she came upon a ewe giving birth to a lamb, then to a second lamb. It was a bitterly cold day, with patches of rain and sleet, and a south wind blowing down the bare flanks of the cleared hill. Amongst the trees and the massive boulders, however, where the ewe had chosen to give birth, there was little wind. Next day Gita was out earlier than usual. She wondered if the twin lambs had survived overnight. She found the ewe in the same spot, grazing under the shelter of the trees. She stamped her foot at Gita, the lambs close by her side.

As Gita made her way back to the cottage, across the creek and down the bare slope, she came across another ewe giving birth. She could see the lamb's head. When the ewe saw Gita she jumped up and walked away, then lay down again. Silly thing, thought Gita. I'd have chosen the rocks and trees across the creek. She returned to the cottage with her armful of sticks and bark and laid them on the kitchen hearth to dry out. Then she walked back up the hill. The ewe was lying where she had left her. Every few minutes she strained, her head flung up, her haunches heaving. Gita's hands flew to her own belly. I'd like to have had a sheltered rocky place to hide in, she thought. All those people telling me what to do.

Returning to the cottage, she threw another piece of yellow box on to the fire and, sitting on the floor in front of the flames, took up the dulcimer. The bright brittle notes flew out. But soon they grew silent; she leaned towards the fire, seeing only the lamb's head that would not be born. Jumping to her feet, she went to the window. Wind was lashing the treetops. She hurried back up the hill.

The ewe had not moved. She crept towards the straining animal. Hadn't she watched Angus catching sheep? If this one would let her . . . and if she took hold of the lamb's head and tugged at each contraction . . . She moved closer. At once the ewe scrambled to her feet, moved a few steps, then lay down. Each time Gita approached, she dragged herself to her feet. You poor thing! cried Gita, watching helplessly. You poor, poor thing. Maybe you never even wanted that lamb!

If he persuades you against your will it's all a power thing a game but you never were much chop at direction can't you see I'm only trying to help you goddamn you you bastard!

She turned and ran, up the hill a little way then across the creek, stumbling, slipping, chill water soaking over the tops of her boots as she scrambled from one reed clump to the next. Out of the water, up through the bush she ran, wind and twigs whipping her face, then down the other side of the hill. The grassy slope, oozing water, was so slippery that she skidded and fell. She lay for a moment, breathless, as cold water soaked through to her skin. What the hell was she doing this for? She hadn't been to Springfield in the daytime except that first afternoon with Jules and Mark and Crystal; she turned mistakenly in the direction of the road. When she came to the avenue of pinoaks she realised that she had missed the house. Goddamn you, Gita!

At last the shed with the red shutters came into sight. Hens squawked and scattered as she ran through them. Rounding the shed, she nearly collided with a dead thing hanging from a gnarled tree, its red legs sticking out helplessly, its headless neck dark with congealed blood. At their kennels Angus's dogs began to clamour, a series of strong healthy barks and a thin wiff wiff. Shrubs in the garden caught at her, sending showers down her neck. She clattered on to the moss-slippery path that led around the house.

Angus came out of the glasshouse. "Hello, what's the panic? Haven't set fire to the place, have you?"

She said, unsmiling, "It's one of your sheep. I think she can't give birth."

He looked surprised. "That was good of you to come over. Thanks. I'll go and have a look at her."

Gita thought of the ewe distraught in a birth she had never wanted. "Can I come with you?"

"Sure. I'll drop you back at the cottage on the way."

"I mean, come with you to the birth."

"If you want to." He looked at her closely. "Hell, that's not just rain, you're soaked through."

She nodded, shivering. "I fell in the creek." Good as.

"Didn't you cross above the springs? Come into the house and get out of this wind."

She took off her boots and Mark's socks at the door. Inside, her wet foot made a print on the floor, a sign from the rushing creek whose water was never still. She took another step, and looked down at the solid print.

Angus watched her, curious, then concerned. "You'd better have a shower here and something hot to drink, warm yourself up a bit. You look chilled through."

She nodded. "But what about that poor ewe? She's been trying to give birth for ages."

"I'll go and have a look while you have that shower."

"I'd like to come. I'll survive like this a bit longer."

"You really want to come back to the paddock? I'll wait for you. She'll be right for the time it'll take you to have a shower. Though it's probably too late for the lamb by now, from what you say. Sure you still want to come?" She nodded. "Well, you better get into that shower or it'll be too late for you too. This way," he said, getting the least worn towel he could find in the linen press. "In here. There's a trick with the taps," he began, turning to her, then swinging back to the taps because she was already peeling off her wet things, tracksuit, jumper, skivvy, as though he didn't exist. "I'll look for something dry for you to put on and leave it outside the door."

He hesitated, then made himself go into that chill room with the double bed where he forced open drawers swollen with damp. He took a long time selecting things for this woman: socks, woollen slacks, long-sleeved woollen skivvy, warm viyella shirt, jumpers, a pair of fur-lined gloves he'd given Belle for that last birthday together. He hesitated over underclothes. Belle had always been fussy, satin and little ribbons and lots of lace. Not this woman's cup of tea. What the hell! he thought, the dainty material catching on his work-roughened hands.

The shower had been turned off. He hesitated, then knocked on the door. "These might do for now . . . Gita."

That's the first time he's ever used my name, she thought, hugging the thick towel around her.

"These are fine," she said, coming into the kitchen.

He didn't look up. "Good." He swept crumbs to the floor, pushing aside the morning's dishes and the cereal packets. "Here's a drop of soup. Get that into you before we go. Bit of bread to go with it? Like the crust?" Belle had always liked the crust.

"Thanks. Aren't you having some?"

"In a minute. I've just remembered something else for you." He went out to the laundry and returned with a pair of red gumboots. "Try these," he said. If she said "Red boots! Whose are these?" he would say "My wife's" and if she continued "What! She didn't take them with her?" he would strike back: "A pair of bloody boots! She left me here, didn't she?" But Gita didn't say this. She had lived for years amongst people who travelled light, shedding possessions as easily as a coat on a summer's day . . . beds, fridges, friends, unpaid bills. She said "I had a look in the town but there's no St Vinnie's, is there?"

"You're welcome to them, Gita, if they're any use to you."

Using her name, he discovered, took away some of the past's bitter potency. He looked at her then. "I'll get you another towel for your hair, you don't want to go out with wet hair in this wind." Relief flooded through his voice. Because it wasn't Belle he saw, she hadn't turned into Belle by wearing Belle's clothes. It was Gita drifting across to the stove for another helping of soup, her face with the clinging damp hair more oval-shaped than ever, her thin neck even longer. He wanted to take her head between his hands and towel her hair dry himself.

They found the ewe and unborn lamb where Gita had left her. "Bess!" Angus said quietly to one of the two black and white border collies watching eagerly from the back of the utility. The younger-looking dog leapt down. Angus nodded at the other one, the grey-whiskered, rheumy dog he'd had to lift on to the tray back at the house. "Old Shep's past it these days, he likes to come along for the ride."

With Bess's assistance he caught the ewe easily. "She's tired now, so the contractions have stopped," he said, taking the lamb's head and shoulders and pulling. When it was free, he pummelled it gently, then swung it around his head. When he laid it on the ground again, the ewe licked it but it didn't stir. Gita touched it. It was damp, covered with yolk, and still warm. Only its head was cold and swollen, its lips blue. "Come on," she said, rubbing it with Belle's good gloves, feeling for its heart, trying to will life into the still form. "Come on, come *on*."

"No use," Angus said, adding sharply as she persisted: "Give up, Gita! It's only a lamb." Not a dead marriage.

"But so . . ." She looked up at him.

"Yeah. Shame. It was a fine big lamb. That was the trouble. Too big for her, especially the head. These merinos are often like that. Some farmers don't bother going round their ewes at all. The weak ones die and the strong survive."

"But wouldn't the mother have died as well if she couldn't give birth?"

"Sure. And then next year she wouldn't be round to have trouble again, or drop a lamb that'll grow up to do the same thing. Survival of the fittest."

"That's cruel."

"It's practical."

"But you don't do that."

"No, well . . . if you talk to some of the farmers round

about, they'll tell you I'm —" He shrugged. "Come on, this wind's freezing. It's dead, Gita." He caught the ewe again and, tying her feet together with twine, lifted her on to the tray. He's gentle with his animals, Gita thought. The dead lamb he placed beside the ewe's head, where she could smell it.

"Where are you taking the mother? I thought you just let them go."

"Did you?" He glanced at her, and she felt caught out again. She'd hated him that first time, when she'd let slip seeing the swinging bar behind the boarded-up kitchen window and he'd laughed. Now, when she said nothing, he continued "I'll take this old girl back to the house. There's a ewe with a pair of twins in the house paddock. I'll catch one of them and park it on this ewe. See if she'll take it in place of this dead one."

"Won't she know the difference?"

"Want to come and watch?"

"Sure."

It was warm in the cabin of the utility. For a moment he breathed in its various smells: wool, and old Shep (relegated to the tray this afternoon), and the yards, and today sharp as grief the faint muskiness of the woman. "I had a heater put in," he told her, busying himself with the ignition key, breathing her in. "Luxury. By the way, that lamb would have died not from the cold but from suffocation. As soon as the head was born it would have started to breathe, and the ewe's contractions would have crushed it."

Killed by its own mother! "So I should have come over when I first noticed her?"

"Probably too late even then," he said gently, in response to the rising note in her voice. He smiled at her. "Not worth falling in the creek and freezing to death for. Anyway, you'll be right now with the gumboots, won't you? They look like a pretty good fit."

Again using the sheep dog, he caught the ewe with the twins, and then one of the lambs which he gave to Gita to hold. Its heart under its flexible skin was beating warmly. She rubbed its nose with her finger, then held its warm head against her cheek.

When she glanced at Angus, he was watching her. "Don't pat it too much, you put your own smell on it," he told her, turning away. "Bring it over to the shed."

In a small pen inside the shed the ewe was on her feet, her head bent protectively over her newborn dead lamb. Angus leaned over, picked up the limp form and rubbed it over the head of Gita's lamb. "The mother recognises that," he explained. Then, taking a sharp knife from a shelf, he carefully skinned the carcass and cut five slits in the skin. "One for the head and one for each of the legs."

"That thing hanging near the shed is a sheep, isn't it?" she said, looking at the skinned lamb. "Part of a sheep? I nearly ran into it."

"Did you? It's an old ewe that died. Dogs' meat now."

"Doesn't it get fly-blown?"

"Not in winter." *Maggots in a corpse sing, did you know that?* Dear God! But he hadn't said it — he hadn't said it. He steadied his breathing. Then, taking the lamb from her, he dressed it in a neat little coat that hung down over its tail. "That's where the mother sniffs when it's drinking. So she can tell some intruder isn't having a go. They do, you know, some of them, either by mistake or if they think they can get away with it." He laughed to himself without humour. "Taking over someone else's patch."

He placed the lamb in the pen beside the ewe. At once it went to drink from her. She moved away. Again it tried, and again she moved. Each time it butted its head around her legs, she stepped aside. "Here Bess!" he called. Bess jumped into the adjoining pen. "Sit! Stay!" Angus commanded. The dog lay on her belly, facing the ewe, which stamped her foot and turned her head watchfully, shielding the lamb with her flank. This time she let the lamb drink. Its tail wagged vigorously as it sucked.

Angus moved back, motioning Gita to do the same. "Stay!" he repeated to the dog.

33   Brittle as Glass

"It might work," he said as they walked towards the house. "Having the dog there makes her protective. Brings out her maternal instincts. I'll run you back to the cottage, then I'll get round the sheep again." He glanced at the sky. Should be on his way right now. "How about some more soup first?"

She nodded. He smiled, then turned and stood for a moment looking back at the shed, the hill, the house paddock bright green in the late slanting light. Half a dozen lambs were playing, running follow-the-leader in proppy bounds on to the top of a stump, then leaping off.

"It's a good life, Gita."

Maternal instincts! "Slaughter and breeding."

He looked at her sharply. She was staring at the playing lambs.

"No. Breeding and slaughter," he said drily, and walked on.

She turned to see his retreating back. Hey! What did I do? She almost had to run to catch up. As they passed the glasshouse she glanced through its walls. Could do with a good wash, she thought. She recalled something good from that dark country, her past.

"What are you growing in there?"

"Trees," he said abruptly. "Stuff from round here mostly."

Back in his kitchen, he poured the soup in silence.

"Mary's?"

"Yes."

"She certainly likes feeding people, doesn't she?"

"Yes."

"She's gone and made me some curtains, two sorts for each window, striped cotton for the sides and lacy stuff to pull across."

"Yeah?"

Moody! she thought. Sunshine one minute, sleet the next. Well, screw you, Angus! "We should settle that rent business," she said irritably.

118

He sighed. "I've been meaning to give it a bit of thought. You worked out how much?"

She shrugged. "Dunno. I told you, didn't I, it's a long time since I paid rent." And she owed Crystal money. No hurry, Crystal had said. Just whenever you can manage it, Gita. Good old Crys. She'd write her a letter one of these days. Maybe she'd better start looking for a job. Soon. Not yet. There was still some of Mark's money left, and when that ran out she could see about her pension again, maybe not supporting mother's any more but the dole maybe. She was in no rush but all the same she said "I heard you were looking for someone to do some work over here."

"Well . . . no. Yes." Angus hesitated, recalling the discussion with Mary. In lieu of rent, he'd thought. But did he really need a woman to clean his house? There was next to nothing to do, as far as he could see. Mary liked pottering around, but as for actually paying someone . . . to do what? "Why? Are you interested?"

Clean the house and do a bit of cooking, the old woman had said. Gita sighed. Housework pissed her off. "What do you mean, no you're not looking for someone?"

He stared at her. Bright and hard, brittle as glass the idea came to him. Why not have her work with him on the seedlings? Get them out of the punnets into pots before they got any bigger. The job was urgent. It was almost too late. If he was really serious about it, if he wasn't just kidding himself, he could use someone fulltime. Pay them a really good rate. If they were any good at it, that is, and it was someone he could work with, someone he could trust, someone who wouldn't shatter him with criticism and mockery.

"I meant yes. I said yes, didn't I?" He intended his usual dry joking tone; in his excitement the words came out harshly.

She looked at him in alarm. Don't spoil it, Springfield. I've had enough hassles for a lifetime. "Just what did you have in mind?"

He saw the expression on her face, and thought she was put out at the suggestion of doing some work, or come to that, paying rent. Though she was the one who'd brought the subject up. It had slipped his mind completely. Better forget the glasshouse idea if that was her attitude, just forget all about it.

"Mary seemed to think you could do the sort of thing she's been doing. In lieu of rent. A bit of cleaning, mostly."

"*Mary's* been doing . . . I thought you said you looked after yourself?"

"So I do, mostly. I'm a dab hand at rabbit stew. You should know, you had some, remember? Mary used to drop by and do a bit extra sometimes, but evidently that's got a bit too much for her. She's been in bed with the flu these last couple of weeks. She does a hell of a lot over there at Valley View Park."

"Well, to balance out the rent . . . what rate did you pay her?"

"Mary? Nothing, of course. I didn't pay her anything."

Gita laughed. "You had someone housekeeping for you and you never paid her?"

"I told you, it wasn't exactly housekeeping. She liked to drop by occasionally. Once a week or so. I can just imagine what Mary would have said if I'd tried to pay her."

And I can just imagine what Crystal would say if she could hear you now! "So you never tried."

"I see. We're going to have that sort of discussion, are we?"

Look, I don't want to have that sort of discussion, either. "Seems like, doesn't it?"

He sighed. "Let's get this straight. If you want to do it this way, you do a bit of housework over here in return for living in the cottage. Otherwise, pay cash, I suppose. But whichever way you decide on, *you* find out the going rate and let me know. I've got more on my plate than I can get through at the moment." He sighed again. She won't stay long. I know the type. *Fucking-well serves you*

Part Two

Glasshouse

And here were forests ancient as the
   hills
            – Coleridge, "Kubla Khan"

34 Green Fingers

Gita took the soft broom and swept the kitchen floor. She didn't bother to move the chairs, just pushed the broom around their legs. She kept forgetting to ask Angus for a dustpan, so she swept the crumbs of mud and food on to the heap in front of the stove and put one of the empty whisky bottles on top of them. When she found all the bottles gone one morning, she used a length of stove wood.

He'd said just the back of the house, kitchen and passage. Swirling the broom in the doorway, she listened: no sound of him. She'd have another explore. Opposite the kitchen was the tiny room with the narrow unmade bed and clothes strewn about. His room. It smelled of him: sweat, and Velvet soap, and an odour that was recognisably his, like a fingerprint Jules said. She breathed him in again *breathe with your diaphragm.* Funny sort of guy. Where did he get to all day? She glanced at the dressing table. Still the same letter on top of the pile, some of them never opened: "Dear Mr Springfield. Your subscription to . . . due 1 January . . ."

There was a photo in a cheap frame pushed behind all the letters: Angus, tired and stooped, until she looked more closely at the woman and boy with him and decided that the dark-haired thin child looking eagerly at the camera had to be Angus — something about the eyes. She had no old photos of herself. Would she look out of the past with the same fixed gaze?

In the passage again, she glanced in the big cupboard crammed with towels and sheets, the dunny with the wooden seat, the enormous green-tiled bathroom where the claw-footed bath looked ready to scuttle towards her. She closed the door and slipped around a corner into the hall. The hall was just about wide enough to drive a car down. There was a little dead organ under wraps in here, and a heap of carved walking sticks in a holder, and a clock that frightened the life out of her when it struck. Just seeing if you wanted me to set the dining room fire again, Angus! . . . The ceilings over here seemed about twice as high as Marycote's. There was a chandelier in the dining room, d'you mind, its crystals weeping dust on to the table. The room wasn't used much, evidently. Her fire was still set.

Next, the big lounge room, its curtains drawn, its heavy chairs and sofa shrouded with sheets except for two leather chairs by the fireplace. Behind the shining firedogs (was *she* supposed to polish them?) spidery heaps of soot had fallen on to the paper and kindling as though it was a long time since he'd sat in here. Boring. Back up the hall was the library with its curtains still open (well, that was something); she'd have a good poke through the books one of these days. By the door was a drawing of three naked cherubs floating in a circle; today, when she looked more closely, she saw six — no, seven — little boys, their arms and legs as plump as a baby's. And then three again.

Beside the library was a room that said Office. Holding her breath again, she sneaked another look through the open desk. Boring boring boring. He was still doing his tax. She'd never filled in a tax form in her life, not even that time she'd had money coming out her ears. Last time, digging deeper through the heap of papers, she'd come across a harmonica. Well, what d'you know! Did he play, then? She'd thought she heard the kitchen door and had shoved it back under the papers. Her fingers riffled carefully. It was still there. She blew a few tentative notes, then buried it again.

She hadn't got as far as this bedroom before. Even with all the stuff stored in here, the room was huge. It had to be what the ads called the master bedroom (why not a mistress?): double bed, fancy dressing table with three mirrors, big flat-piled patterned rug in front of the fireplace. Where had she seen such patterns before? At Jules's. She pressed her forehead against the mantelpiece. *Original just like the others you could make use of a mantelpiece what are you on about this time Jules I've got no use for a mantelpiece of course you haven't my dear not as such*

She swung around, ready to make up some story. The room stayed silent.

She wasn't alone, even so. From every wall stern couples

in heavy dresses and suits watched from sepia eyes. On a stand were a matching jug and basin. I wouldn't mind these, she thought, her fingertip caressing the raised green and white roses and the gold-leaf. Her finger came away covered with the fine dust of moths' wings. She rubbed it clean on one of the shrouds covering the furniture.

She opened a wardrobe. Wow! So much stuff! A clinging perfume stole around her as she pushed the hangers along the metal rod. She tried to imagine Angus in this room, masterful in his master bedroom, Sit, Bess! Stay! but it remained empty of his presence. She wouldn't mind wearing that fancy thing to sing in a gig. She held it up in front of the mirror. All black and silver see-through. Would he mind, if she asked? Next, the chest of drawers. Piles and piles of stuff, shirts, jumpers, skivvies, earrings. He's got his own St Vinnie's, all right. No one'll miss these. She took a handful of Belle's lacy briefs and went back to the kitchen.

As she washed up she daydreamed out the window, losing herself in the small gum trees on the rise behind the house. Their leaves danced and flickered. Angus had said he'd identify the local trees if she was interested. He'd said he'd take her spotlighting, too. She'd never seen a possum, apart from the feathertails on that dead tree at dusk. He said there were two or three sorts of possums around here. Maybe she'd remind him.

She was just about done in here. She could go back to Marycote now. She sighed. Gather more kindling; stoke the kitchen stove, if it wasn't out already — she'd couldn't remember whether she'd closed the damper before she set out for Springfield; wash a heap of clothes (but she could put that off for a bit now that she had all those briefs); make a list of things to get in town, she was running short on just about everything; try the new song again but it wasn't working, she felt depressed each time she picked up the dulcimer *doggerel howls for the moon/ always beyond its reach.* Maybe Mark was right, maybe she should concentrate on the guitar; get back into the band; maybe she'd write him a letter; that meant cycling into town to post it, it meant writing it: Mark honey/Hi Mark/Mark.

She wondered again where Angus was. No matter how quietly she went into the kitchen when she arrived (and she'd tried wearing her thin-soled shoes, and holding the back door so it wouldn't bang), he would always turn up from somewhere, but after he'd given her a brusque good-day he would disappear and she wouldn't see him again that day. Mary came once a week, he'd said; Gita had been coming over more often than that, every two or three days maybe, morning or afternoon as the mood took her. Sweep a bit, make a pot of soup from the vegetables she found at the back of the fridge. There was hardly anything to do but it got her away from her obstinate song *dreams in your veins the details always out of reach over the horizon over the next rise* and if it paid her rent — if Angus was silly enough — she wasn't going to argue while it lasted. She sighed. While it lasted.

Maybe she'd find something else to do here before she went home. Wash down the walls of the glasshouse, maybe. In the laundry she found a bucket and a rag and some metho to make the glass shine. As she made her way past a thorny pomegranate holding fast to its hard scarlet fruit, half a dozen parrots rose with shrill cries of alarm. The garden was full of birds. Maybe there was a bird book in the library.

At the entrance to the glasshouse she hesitated. She had never been in here. The benches were covered with seedlings. Some were growing singly in pots; others, crowded together in punnets, twisted in a mass of stunted red stems towards the light. Their poor roots, all cramped up, Gita thought. Angus was standing leaning on his arms, head bent over the punnet on the bench in front of him. When he didn't move she said "So what's all this, then?"

He swung around. "How long have you been standing there?"

"Oh . . . half an hour. Hey! About ten seconds, Angus. I came to tell you I'm off now." She plonked the bucket on the ground.

"Are you?" He took a couple of steps, then rubbed his

knee. "All this . . ." He indicated the benches. "Just an idea I had."

"They're quite a size, some of those seedlings."

He rubbed his knee again. "They should have been pricked out into pots weeks ago. One seedling each, see? Hundreds of them. They're almost too big now to transplant, some of them."

"Want me to give you a hand before I go home?"

"I'm pricking out these acacia and eucalypt seedlings — wattles and gum trees to you —"

"I know what they are, Angus."

Do you? he thought, glancing at her. Prickly! he thought. But I knew that. He picked up a small square plastic tube. ". . . into these pots. Tubes. They're all filled with sterilised soil from the bin by the shadehouse, that's it out there, but I work in here in the cold weather."

"You don't fill the tubes in here, do you?"

"No." Again he glanced at her. What would she know about the risk of spreading fungus through spilled soil? "But pricking out in here's okay, it's not a messy job. Now, look. You hold the seedling by the leaf . . . like this, see? Poke a hole in the soil with a pencil . . . like this . . . put the seedling in, tamp down the soil, water it in. That settles the soil round the rootlets and gets rid of air pockets. You've got to take care that the tap root goes in straight. As well as you can, it isn't easy. If it's crooked the root'll go on growing with a kink in it and the adult tree'll fall over in the first good gale." She looked interested, more interested than he'd expected, and her question about where he filled the tubes was sensible, so he went on talking. "What I do is, I take a small bundle of seedlings from the punnet and trim the tap roots . . . like this. That helps. What you're really after is a good strong root system all the way down the tube."

"Let's have a go." She smiled to herself. Green fingers Gita. Why let on?

"Got it in one!" he said admiringly. "Women are best at these fiddly jobs . . . It's true! They've got better muscle coordination. Forestry departments round the world employ women for finicky work like this."

"And pay them less, I suppose."

He grimaced. If she was another one going to pick him up over every harmless bloody thing he said till he hardly dared open his mouth . . . well, he could put up even with that if it meant getting this job done.

"I'll pay you whatever the going rate is per hour, Gita. Overtime, too, if you want to come at weekends."

"Fine by me."

They worked on in silence.

She liked this work, a thousand times better than sweeping and washing up. Anyway, why couldn't he do those things for himself? Any woman living on her own cooked and cleaned her house as well as doing whatever paid job she had to do.

"Are you going to sell these?" she asked, when his silence began to nag at her. She'd had enough of silence. If there was too much silence she got scared those others would join in . . . Crystal, the people at that place, Jules. She had to switch off to escape them. And if she switched off too far, that scared her, too. What if she switched right off one time and couldn't get back? That could happen.

"Sorry, what did you say, Angus?" Help me get back, Angus.

"I said no. Plant them out myself."

"Where?"

He shrugged.

"Up on those bare hillsides?" she persisted.

"Yeah. That's what I had in mind. And smaller things for the understorey — correa, grevillea, wirilda, hakea." He waved his hand at another bench.

"Good names, aren't they?"

"Yeah." Sort of thing she'd go putting in one of her songs. He added a couple more. "Prostanthera, dillwynia, bursaria. They all do well round here. But it's quite a job. You see it all getting ahead of you and after a while you lose heart." Sometimes in nightmares his own forests hunted him down. "Like I said, it was an idea I had when I first got back. Before I got here, actually. That's what got me going in the end, made me come back, I mean." He glanced at her apprehensively. She'd be asking him a heap of things next, where were you, what were you, why.

She was peering through the mud-splattered glass wall, a look of delight on her face. He followed her gaze: eastern rosellas in the old rose bushes.

Maybe she hadn't been listening, after all.

"Young birds," he told her. "Would have hatched last season in some hollow limb round here."

The breasts of the young birds were a ragged red, their backs a threadwork of blacks and greens and yellows. *That's* what the rug in that bedroom reminded me of, she thought. The patterns in the feathers of the rosellas at Springfield! Not something out of the past. Not Jules! Not Jules!

"Over there at Valley View Park," Angus was telling her, and he seemed to find something very funny, "Mary puts out birdseed for the rosellas because she likes birds in the garden — so what happens then? They get stuck into the new rose shoots." He laughed again as he pictured them: edging sideways along the thorny stems, snapping off the sappy red shoots, letting them drop to the ground. Lou's prize roses.

Gita couldn't see anything funny, but said all the same "You know what you call that, Angus? Buttercups and orange peels."

"What? Sounds like one of your songs, is it?"

"Yes . . . no. Something a friend told me." Some friend. "You see a patch of buttercups and you think how pretty and then you find they're just bits of rotting orange peel so the question is, before you knew that, were they horrible or pretty?" He listens with his eyes. "To make you think. This friend said."

He laughed again, this time with relief: she wasn't trying to dig him up.

"Wise fellow, your friend."

"Fellow! Fellow, was it?" Laughing herself now.

"Sor-ry! Wise woman."

"It was a man."

"We seem to be going in circles here."

He was startled by her sudden change in mood. "He's a bastard. He wrecks up people's lives."

"Yours?" he said gently, forgetting that she, too, might be sensitive about the past.

"He scares the shit out of me." She stared at him. "He uses people. It's a power thing. A game. You know what he says? There's using, and there's using. And *he* uses *people*. That's worse than using a substance, isn't it, using people? Using a substance is just one person's business. Isn't it?"

He wanted to put his arms around her, he wanted to say it's all right, girl, you're safe here with me. Safe with him! Jesus, Gita, help me. *His fingers sank into decaying flesh. He flicked a sly maggot from his hand. The corpses sang stickily. The whole place stank of death*

As he recoiled, so did she.

What's he so scared of? I've had all the tests!

"Tomorrow then? See ya!" she said brightly, picking up Belle's jumper and swinging it over her shoulder so that, watching her walk out of the glasshouse, he thought it's all right, she didn't notice anything, it's all right, I'm all right, I'm not going off my head.

35 Sunshine and Sleet

He was a funny one, all right. Abrupt as anything next morning when she turned up all in a rush to get on with the seedlings. He was still in the kitchen, finishing his breakfast after the morning round of his ewes.

He hardly looked up at her, just said curtly "What's all this? You're early."

She'd woken with the leaves flickering and the wind blowing the sun across the sky and she'd felt such a rush of joy she couldn't wait to get busy before the day clouded over. Well thank *you*, Angus!

As she turned away she stumbled over a bottle.

"Thought you wanted a hand with that job in the glasshouse before it was too late." Watching it spinning.

"You really want to, then?"

"I said so, didn't I? Thought I might give the glasshouse a wash down while I was about it . . . Look, if you'd rather I didn't —"

"No. No, go ahead. I should've got round to it after that big storm a while back."

But when she had found the bucket and the rag and the metho again and was off out the back door, he said "Hold on, would you, I'll be right with you."

"I'll have something to eat first, then — *if* you don't mind."

He looked up at that, and she was shocked to see how grey his face was in the morning light, the skin drawn taut across his temples, blue-black rings like bruises around his eyes. She glanced down at the floor. That was a whisky bottle she'd sent spinning.

As she reached for the teapot she added, to soften her sarcasm, "I forgot about eating at home."

"Sorry. Sorry, Gita." He pushed back his chair. "Here, what would you like? Eggs? Cereal?" He touched her arm briefly. "Sorry if I sounded . . . I was —"

"That's okay, Angus," she said gently.

Now he was in his good mood again, the one when they'd eaten toast and honey together at Marycote before Lou Catchpole came barging in. It lasted all the time they were washing down the glasshouse and filling tubes in the shadehouse.

"If you've got a good understorey," he told her, rubbing at splatters of bird shit, "not just a plantation of, say, eucalypts, then you'll have birds coming to the smaller things for nectar and insects and that way you'll have much less insect damage to the crowns of the trees and a healthier forest all round."

"And that's what you're aiming at?"

"Well, you know the old saying, the road to hell."

"The road to hell?"

"Is paved with good intentions."

"No Angus, I don't know that saying." She laughed. "When I'm busy, I'm busy."

"I've noticed."

Talking to her, it all seemed possible. "I'd like to plant up a lot of that hill behind your cottage," he said. Your cottage: she liked that. "Eventually. This year I'm concentrating on an area I've fenced off the other side of the hill behind the house here. It's starting to erode pretty badly. And making a start on getting the understorey stuff back into some of the bush . . . Well, that's the cleaning done. Hell, what a difference! Thanks, Gita. Come and I'll show you the shadehouse. I'll fill some more tubes while we're out there."

The shadehouse, behind the glasshouse, consisted of posts and beams covered on three sides and the top with shadecloth. The south side was open, and Gita shivered in the chill wind.

"I'll be right back," Angus told her. Funny thing, he didn't mind leaving someone in the shadehouse. When he returned, he was carrying a worn oilskin coat. "Try this for size. That south wind's like a knife . . . Okay?"

She poked her hands into the deep pockets and smiled at him. "Okay."

From a wooden bin outside, he shovelled soil into a barrow and wheeled it into the shadehouse. Watching her sideways as they filled tubes at the bench, he was struck again with her enthusiasm. Funny sort of girl. Mary ran rings round her with a broom.

"My father spent a lot of time in here and in the glasshouse," he told her. "He loved the farm, but the sheep got too much for him in the end . . . old second world war injuries . . . so he pottered round in here growing begonias. Not my cup of tea . . . I did have a go recently at something he always wanted to do. Patching up the stone fences on the property . . . till I realised things in here were getting out of hand. They're years old, those stone fences. Seems a pity to see them just collapsing . . . Once the coping stones go, the rest goes."

Same with people, he thought.

This time he must have spoken aloud, because she said

"Yes. Coping." And then, before he had time to get nervous, she asked him if he wasn't worried rabbits would eat the seedlings.

He showed her a roll of strong plastic sleeving to be staked around each seedling. And the stakes. And the special tree spade for planting the seedlings.

"I've still got to do the spraying, though, otherwise they'll just be choked out by weeds. I guess I've been putting that off." His face brightened. "One thing I have done in good time, and that's the ripping. Along the contour," he added, as she looked puzzled. "Where the trees are to go."

"What for?"

He glanced at her. She really did want to know. "Rain'll collect in the ripline and soak deep down and then the roots'll go down deep, too. For the moisture. That way they'll withstand the summer."

"Yeah, right." She went on filling tubes. She was thinking all this roots into tubes, roots after moisture, good strong root system, and neither of us makes one smart-arse crack. After a while she said "A lot goes on, doesn't it? In here, and up there on the hill."

He nodded. And smiled at her. "Time for a cuppa, Gita. Ocker? Or ocker?"

And then, sometime during the afternoon, his good humour evaporated. It was when she saw parrots dipping through the garden again, different ones today, all crimson breasts and blue tail feathers. They came to rest in a leafless tree, globes of brilliance against the overcast sky.

"Crimson rosellas this time," he said when she asked.

"They look like a painting. Red on grey."

"Yeah. Blood on mud."

"Well! Great."

Her voice seemed to startle him. "Don't take any notice of me, Gita. I'm pretty poor company, you'll find."

He half expected her to reply "Don't worry about it!" with the petulant emphasis on worry that was fashionable these days, suggesting the opposite of the words themselves.

She said nothing at all.

"You'll be back again?" he asked, at the end of the afternoon. "You will come back?"

She smiled to herself. "I'll see what happens."

He said the same thing each day. "You'll be back?" He couldn't help himself. Just come when you feel like it, he'd told her. It was a kind of insurance against the time when, like a green paddock come summer, her enthusiasm dried up. He knew her sort. So he kept telling himself. But all the same was disappointed when some days she arrived late, or left early, or didn't show up at all. Given up on him, had she? Where the hell was she?

He couldn't bring himself to leave her in the glasshouse to work by herself, even though she was clearly a natural with plants. He had his tax to finish in his office, lambs to mark, the spraying in the plantation to do, but he kept putting them off. It made him too jumpy, the thought of someone else in his glasshouse. So he stayed and worked with her, and found having her there easier than he'd expected. She didn't ask a string of questions, and she was quick, surprisingly quick for someone who was usually so vague. Sometimes he forgot altogether that she was there. And then she would disappear into the house for something, the loo or a drink of water, and when she didn't come back promptly he'd get jittery again and have to go and look for her. And she'd be in the kitchen, dreaming into the garden, or, today, looking at an old art book in the library.

"I thought you must have fallen down the dunny."

She wasn't at all bothered by her long absence. "Look at this, Angus — these old paintings done when white people first got here. Take a look at these kangaroos!"

The book smelt musty, like the room. He laughed. "They couldn't see what they were looking at, could they? And the trees — English trees. Pictures of what they'd been taught to see. Borrow the book if you'd like to."

"Thanks. Maybe I'll just drop in here sometimes. If that's okay?"

"Of course it is. Do the old room good."

They went back to the glasshouse. On her time sheet, tacked to the bench, he wrote "− 20 min". He was the one who'd ended up keeping tally. When he first came to pay her for sweeping the kitchen, saying "How many hours do I owe you for?", he'd discovered each had left that part to the other; he'd made some sort of guess, upon which she'd scowled and said he was being ridiculous, she didn't want charity.

"Minus twenty minutes . . ." You had to be careful with Gita. Her voice startled him.

"But what if we don't see them as they really are any more than they did? What if we see only what we've been taught to see?"

"What?"

"The kangaroos. What if what we're seeing now, even in a photograph, is no more true or less true than what those artists saw?"

"There are kangaroos in the bush over the road," he told her. "We'll take a look one of these days, if you want to."

"Sure. I'd like that."

She wondered if he'd remember. Hadn't he suggested going spotlighting one evening? And learning the local trees? But smiled at him. He was in his good mood again.

That day she worked long into the afternoon.

"Hell, time's slipped away, I'd better get going," he exclaimed, looking at the low grey glow of the sun. "I'll run you back in the ute. Want to come round the ewes with me first?"

"The lambing's well under way now," he told her as they drove around the hillside where large lambs were playing.

"It takes a long time, doesn't it? How many weeks now?"

"You could actually have all the ewes lamb in the one week. Save weeks of time doing this. But then you could get a really bad patch of weather, blizzards for instance, and you'd lose most of the drop in one hit." He stopped the utility. "Here's one little lamb that wouldn't stand up to a blizzard. Its mother was having a bit of trouble this morning. Still looks a bit knocked about, doesn't it, that lamb? I'll take them back to the house paddock and keep an eye on them. Here, Bess!"

The ewe stamped her foot. As the dog approached she charged. Angus ran in, headed her off, plunged as she turned again, and caught her. Swinging her on to her rump, he happened to glance up — and was jolted by Gita's expression. And for a moment was twenty again, full-forward for the local team, proud of his strength, his speed, his appeal to girls . . . this girl . . . stolen, the bloody lot stolen.

He spoke harshly. "How about catching the lamb?"

"You talking to Bess, Angus?"

"Sorry!" He busied himself tying the ewe's feet together, the echo of his words and her dry response ringing in his head. He stood up. "I'm not much good at talking to women, Gita. As you must have noticed."

Hey, you aren't feeling sorry for yourself? "Don't worry about it." She laughed lightly. "Anyway, Bess thinks you're okay."

"Bess?" The dog, waiting head on paws by the ewe, lifted her head. "Bess's used to me."

"Well . . ." Gita grinned. Maybe I'll get used to you, said her look. If you'll let me.

Leaving the ewe on the ground, he came across to her. She saw the fine lines around his eyes, and his eyes, vulnerable as a child's. "Gita —"

Before this conversation got out of hand, out of her control, she said "You know what's good about being with you? You don't hassle people, Angus, you don't put the hard word on them. We're working together on something really good, really worthwhile, and I like that, it's good, it's special, it's what I've needed."

"Sure. I understand." The lamb was nuzzling around its mother. He reached down and spent a moment scooping it up. Hands off, Angus: that was clear enough. "It's what I've needed, too, I guess."

* *

"Are all your ewes good mothers?" she asked as he put the spindly lamb into a little box in the cabin.

"No. Sometimes they mightn't have enough milk." He lifted the ewe on to the tray. "Hop back in, I'll run you down to the cottage."

"I meant, look after their lamb like that old girl there."

He glanced at her. "Not all of them. Not by any means. Some of them desert them as soon as they drop them."

"What do you do then?"

"Cull them. Sell them."

"Who to? Another farmer who'll have the same problem?"

"Some of them go overseas on the sheep ships."

She said no more until they reached Marycote. He turned to her. "Gita, you won't . . . you will —"

"Be back?" She hopped out and ran around to his side. "I seem to, don't I?"

"We're going well," he called, leaning out of the window. "We're catching up."

She turned and walked backwards. "I like the work."

"You've certainly got the right touch."

"Green fingers Gita, me." She waved and walked on, then shouted over her shoulder "Maybe it's the teacher!"

She had never told him about the nursery work at that place. But, through working in the glasshouse at Springfield, the feeling began to grow that that earlier experience, miserable as she was then, had been worthwhile after all . . . some of it. She might even tell him about it one of these days. Sometime. Not yet. She would choose the time.

36   Barbs of Anger

You don't open up much, do you?
Crystal, that's just not true!

Two or three times in the glasshouse she was on the point of telling him. And each time Angus went and blew it. Like the time they paused to watch a magpie pulling worms out of the garden and she commented without thinking "White-backed magpies. I've seen them with black backs somewhere."

"Have you? Further north, was it? They're black-backed further north."

Done a bit of travelling, have you? said his look — and nailed her tongue to the roof of her mouth.

And again just now: she'd been standing staring out across the garden, tapping the pencil lightly on the bench, and suddenly she could feel him watching her and that gave her goosebumps usually, made her hunch her shoulders and pinch her face and think herself somewhere else. But this time when she turned around she smiled because his eyes and his mouth were as doubting as a kid's.

She would tell him. She said "You're lucky, you know."

"Lucky?" Yeah, lucky's right, half my life wasted. Carried home in a bodybag. Dead lucky. "You think so, do you? How d'you make that out?"

She ignored the derision. She would tell him. She lifted her hand. "All this. It's somewhere . . . to be."

"Be! Be what?"

The kind look had vanished, timid sunlight streaking behind a cloud. She mumbled eventually "Whatever you want, I suppose." That wasn't what she'd meant.

"Whatever I want! God, Gita, whatever I want . . . Remember what you said that day you came across to tell me about the ewe that couldn't lamb? Slaughter and breeding, you said."

"I said? No, that was Crystal, the very first time we met you. Crystal said that. Angus, it wasn't me."

He wasn't listening. He was good at that, not listening. Well, screw you, Angus! *I* didn't say that about slaughter and breeding!

"I've seen enough slaughter to last me a lifetime, Gita." She stared at him. "What's it all for?" he went on, his voice agitated. "Where does it all get you? I'll tell you where: round and round through the same patch of bloody jungle, that's where it gets you. Look at all this." He waved his hand. "Look at it, Gita, hundreds of plants to get into the ground this spring, hundreds more in punnets still to be potted, I must have been mad, sowing all this seed, there's enough work in here for ten men, let alone two and one of them a woman."

"Well thank you very much!"

She couldn't stand working beside him in this mood. She couldn't take these barbs of anger. Why didn't he piss off out of the glasshouse for a while and leave her to get on with it?

37 You Want Womans?

The child in the too-big shirt is about ten and his sister maybe two years older though it's hard to tell, they are such a small, fragile-looking people, how do such tiny women ever manage carrying a child and then the birth itself? He feels like a giant in their country, an ungainly, sunburned, sweating giant. You want womans? the boy says to him, and he is repulsed: is this what years of struggling against invaders has brought these people to? He is about to give the boy a shove, *didi mau!* when he looks again at his sister and she's the woman at Marycote, she looks at him enigmatically and he wakes up, he makes himself wake up and she is coming towards the narrow bed you want womans? and then he wakes properly and it's only a moonbeam gliding across the floor of the maid's room.

38 Ringtail

Gloomy, then all of a sudden cheerful . . . sunshine and sleet all right.

The ringtail, for instance. She'd worked late again and then there'd been problems with a couple of ewes lambing so that by the time he dropped her off at Marycote it was well and truly dusk. She saw the animal first, small furry body, pointed face, white-tipped curling tail, in one of the big gum trees along the boundary fence.

"Possum," he said, getting out of the utility. "Ringtail." He handed her the binoculars.

"It's much bigger than those little gliders."

"They were good-oh, weren't they? Wonder if they're still there. We should take a look sometime. Right now I should get these old girls and their lambs back to the shed." She gave back the binoculars then, and he trained them on the possum again. "Ringtails, they're all round your place – over at my place too. Not bushytails, the big brown fellows – you don't see them too often these days." He sighed. There were dozens about when he was a kid. Or so he remembered it. Shot out. Wasted. Search and destroy. What was it all for? Maybe if his tree-planting ever got going, some of these animals would start to come back. Maybe.

"We should try spotlighting," she ventured. He *had* said.

"Spotlighting? Sure." As he smiled she glimpsed someone as elusive as these shy possums. "I'll have to get a new battery for the flash," he was saying. "Bet you pick up spiders' eyes!"

She laughed.

Your place. She was glad he'd said that. She'd look up ringtail tomorrow in the marsupial book in his library.

39   J Curve

And then furious with her – yes, furious, his face pale, even the warm blue of his eyes fading hard with anger, and all because, poking around in that lovely big bedroom which was just a dumping ground anyway, she came across something she wanted: a china candle holder with a hollow rounded handle on each side of the saucer, and this time she asked if she could borrow it.

He knew she'd peeked in all the rooms. He'd caught her in the library, hadn't he, and he'd said she was welcome there. So why all the fuss this time?

"You'll burn the bloody place down," he said, grabbing the candle holder. "There are standard lamps and bedside lamps laid on in this house. If you want more reading light you only have to say."

"I just like candles," she pleaded. She'd arrived at the glasshouse earlier than usual because he'd said the job was getting desperate, and then she'd gone into the house to have a pee and as usual got sidetracked. She glanced at the candle holder. She should have just taken it. "Angus, listen, I've burned candles for years. In old kindling-dry places, too. Marycote's not the first old house I've lived in. I know how to be careful."

"We've been over all this before. There'll be a sudden draught, Mary's lace curtains will blow and the whole place'll go up. Haven't you ever watched a candle flaring?"

"Yes," she sulked.

"There you are, then."

"I've told you, I'm careful. I don't put it anywhere near Mary's curtains."

"You *don't* . . . you mean you've been burning candles over there since we talked about it anyway?"

She flushed. He'd caught her again. "Yes I have! Beeswax. Stuck into one of your whisky bottles. I'd much rather use this candle holder," she gabbled, alarmed by his expression when she'd said whisky bottle. She reached out and ran her fingertip over the candle holder, over the rounded handles. "It's quaint. Look. It goes with the house." She bit her lip. "And if a candle starts flaring, I'm extra careful, I told you that ages ago."

"Oh yes, I remember: because it's a sign."

"What you're scoffing at might be real enough for someone else."

"Like Jesus?" He couldn't help this dig, remembering her derision that afternoon Mary had offered her a lift in to church.

"Jesus?" She frowned. How did Jesus get into this? She glanced at him again. He wasn't so cross-looking now. Her eyes flickered over the candle holder. Keep on talking, he might let her have it. "Like, for instance, you're thinking about someone, they keep jumping into your head, and suddenly there they are. That can happen. It's happened to me."

"Because while you were busy conjuring them up, your feet took you to where they were most likely to be."

"It could be someone I don't want to see."

"Sounds like a heap of mumbo-jumbo to me, Gita." Laughing at her. But gently.

She smiled. "I know it does . . . to you. There are more ways of knowing things than you might want to believe, Angus."

"This isn't getting us anywhere, is it?" He was suddenly angry again. *Where the hell does anything get you? Round and round through the same patch of jungle, eyes, eyes everywhere, eyes watching, boring into your forehead, into the back of your neck, eyes out there waiting then PIOW! K-TNK! K-TNK! but you're safe — safe — your body unbidden dives to the ground* "We've wasted enough time over this, will we get back to the glasshouse? And as for using candles over at Marycote, I'd be pleased, Gita, if you stopped putting my property at risk."

He saw her mouth tighten. He shouldn't have said that about property. He was starting to read her thoughts.

"You are," he told her, less than ten minutes later, watching her slender fingers take a single seedling by its leaves and ease it into the dibble hole. "Of course you are."

She finished tamping, then looked up, about to say something.

"Careful, I mean," he said quickly, conscious that he'd been standing there gawking. "Those tap roots should stay good and straight."

"I've just had a brainwave, Angus. Have you got any tweezers?"

"Tweezers? Yes. Should be some somewhere. Might take a bit of hunting. What do you want them for?"

"Go and get them and I'll show you. Something I've just —" remembered, she was about to say. She bit the word back.

He hesitated. He'd have to leave her in the glasshouse. But

he could hardly say you have to come with me while I tear the place apart trying to find a pair of tweezers.

"Long ones, not too springy," she said hastily, to cover up her unfinished sentence that he seemed to be waiting for.

"Will these do? So, what's the brainwave?" he said abruptly, his heart thumping with relief that . . . what? The glasshouse still stood?

"You know how careful you have to be that the tap root doesn't make a J curve when you're pushing it into the hole?"

"A J curve? Where did you come across that term?"

"I guess I heard someone —" She stared at him. Caught. You could see that through the boards across the window, could you? And couldn't bring herself to tell him: at that place, Angus. From our teacher the nurseryman, Angus. You've got green fingers, Gita, he told me. "It's the shape, isn't it? A J?"

"It doesn't matter," he said gently, surprised at the sudden colour in her sallow cheeks. "Go on, Gita. It doesn't matter."

"Well, I was thinking, if you used tweezers to pick up the seedling . . . like this . . . that would squeeze the tap root a bit, wouldn't it, damage it a bit, I mean, just enough to get the side roots growing, wouldn't it, which you said is what you wanted, and then you could use the tweezers to push the seedling into the tube . . . like this . . . instead of having to trim the tap roots and dibble a hole and fill it in again and tamp it down. You'd be saving time and you'd have less risk of . . . J curves. What d'you reckon?"

"We could try it," he said doubtfully. "Show me again . . . You know, Gita," he said after a while, "I think you might have something there. Let's have a go."

She handed him the tweezers and watched him put her idea into practice. Well, not her idea, exactly. It was standard practice in that other nursery . . . at that place.

"This'll work," he said after a while. "This'll be all right. This'll be good, Gita." He smiled at her. "Why didn't I come up with this myself?"

"It takes genius, Angus."
"You might be right at that."

40   Two Separate Streams

He was easier to take when he forgot she was there. He's like Mary Springfield, she thought, filling a tray of tubes with carefully mixed soil. Or Mark when he's talking computers. He just yaks and yaks. The first few days he said nothing and now there's no stopping him.

. . . forgot . . . fell back into his old habit of talking out ideas with himself, arguing. But with this difference: now, because there was someone present who was restful, who wasn't lying in wait like a snake in the leaf litter, he relaxed enough to offer these ideas aloud.

"That unctuous manner," Gita heard one morning, dragged back from a bare hillside upon which, in a patch of wintry sunshine, she and he (sure, just the two of them and one of them a *woman*) dug holes and heeled in each seedling (she supposed that was how it was done), and she watched the sturdy little seedlings send their roots down to explore the cool earth the way she went exploring through the house sometimes; and their leaves thrust up to glitter in the healing sunlight, their trunks growing sturdier and thicker until her arms could hardly meet around them.

"That unctuous manner. It says it all. Don't you reckon? But the tide's turning. Look at that last by-election. Don't you reckon?"

Gita nodded. "Maybe." What was he on about now? There were days when what she said and what he said were two separate streams running side by side. "How do you keep up with all this stuff, Angus?"

"Oh, telly mostly. It's in the kitchen, haven't you seen it? I sit up pretty late some nights." He laughed. "Keeps the monsters at bay." He glanced at her anxiously: he hadn't meant to say that.

She grimaced. "You want to know something? I don't even

vote. I've never enrolled. It's just another way the government catches you, putting your name on a list."

Mark's friends who came around to give him a hand on the hearse ran like streams, too, bubbling, rushing, shouting at one other — while she washed a pile of dishes so there'd be something to eat off. That's a form of politics too, Gita. The men setting the world to rights, the woman at the sink. Sure is, Crystal!

On the other hand, if something important was happening, friends being evicted from a squat, say, then she'd join in with everyone in the street to yell at the heavies sent in to toss all the bedding and the sad broken-down couches on to the footpath. But *politics* — the word left her with a feeling of emptiness, a huge yawning boredom that frightened her — what did it matter? The hoardings outside the newsagent in Currawong said the same thing as the hoardings in Melbourne yesterday tomorrow sometime forever. Where did it all get you?

"On to the dunghill of history," she said, recalling a phrase he'd used yesterday.

"That's right!" he exclaimed. And was off again. "But Gorbachev is riding a tiger and you know what they say about people who do that, don't you? He who —"

"*She* dare not dismount," said Gita drily, since that saying had come up yesterday, too.

Angus, absorbed, didn't notice her tone. "And President Bush is riding it too, dangling a carrot in front of the tiger because that's about all the political sense he's got."

She couldn't help laughing at that.

"But you wait," Angus said. "You just wait. He'll want to be first cab off the rank on the silver screen, won't he? Especially if there's votes in it. He'll have to do something dramatic soon. Another little war somewhere. Bring all your friends."

"Don't you like Americans?"

She saw his face grow sombre. "Ah, they get people into a hell of a mess."

"*They* do, do they?"

She jabbed the tweezers into the soil. Crystal's right, men just want a woman to pour things into.

"Hey careful!" Angus said. "What's happened to you today?"

He'd loved a good talk about politics once. He and Metcalf used to talk for hours. It was up there they first started thinking about things. Things that mattered. Really thinking. Told each other they'd been conned. He could hear Metcalf to this day: Hey Springers! Get a load of this. Chaplain says to me And how was your leave in Vung Tau, my son? (Metcalf could take him off to a T.) Fine, Father, fine, I says. Very peaceful. Very restful. Good, very good, my son! And what were you doing? Well, Father . . . I spent two days with a woman. My son, you shouldn't have done that! Fornication is a sin against God! Christ, Father, I shouldn't fuck someone but it's all right if I go and kill them?

Metcalf God, he missed that bloke. There'd never been anyone since he could really talk to. Trust enough to talk to. He'd never talked to Belle. Before he went away, when they were just kids, not even married then, they were too crazy for each other to bother with words. Golden girl Belle. She couldn't begin to understand why after only three weeks R and R he signed up for a second tour of duty. And when he came home for good . . . He'd tried, hadn't he? Of course he'd bloody tried. And how did his golden girl react to that? She said he was just using her. Especially, she complained, in bed. Where *was* he, what had *happened* to him? But if ever he tried to tell her, she'd get scared, she'd say she couldn't cope with it. So he'd shut up, and then she would say he was sick.

And that woman on the North Coast, he couldn't talk to her. He was a *male*, wasn't he? All she wanted to do was draw out his ideas like a snail out of a shell so that she could jump on them.

He caught Gita watching him. So intense were his thoughts that it seemed she must be able to hear them. He muttered "I thought I could trust her. What a mug I was!"

"Someone made you really mad, huh?"

He hesitated. "I guess I never was the easiest person to put up with." They worked on for some minutes, then he said "I've eased up on the drinking, that's something."

"Sure. That is something." She thought about the drawers and the wardrobe full of clothes in that big bedroom. "Maybe she'll come back."

"Not likely. She's got someone else. He'd been hanging round her for years. It took me a while to wake up."

Tampering with his property. "So you reckoned that was it?"

"She was having his kid."

"Tough."

He glanced at her quickly, not sure whether she was mocking him.

"Yeah. Well. That's how it goes, eh? That's how the cookie crumbles. But I gave that rotten bastard what was coming to him, you bet I did." He laughed harshly.

Gita looked up from the seedling tray. This didn't sound like the guy she watched caring for his animals.

He glanced at her sideways. She was looking surprised. He hadn't meant to give away so much about himself. And he had no intention of going on about the pub brawl with Lou Catchpole. "Anyway, what about you? What about your family?"

"My *parents*!" Gita said, with a click of contempt. "You really want to know?"

Sometimes, when people asked things like this, she would say she'd been an only child and that her parents were dead. Or were in Perth. Overseas. That her father was one of those high-powered executives who was never home and her mother a secret drinker. A deserted wife. A widow. That she told Gita I've taken in each of your sisters and their babies and I've had enough. You're pregnant, you look after yourself.

After a moment's perplexity Gita said "I've forgotten, Angus. What does it matter?"

"It doesn't matter." Gentle again.

She turned on him as though he'd insisted on knowing. "The kid – Jarrah – he's with his father. About time that lazy sod took a turn . . . Some women are cut out for being mothers, and some aren't. I'm guess I'm one of the ones you'd cull for the sheep ship, huh?"

He reached for the watering can. "You said it. I didn't."

41 Stretching Thin and High Like a Scream

She couldn't get off to sleep that night. Fling herself to this side or that as she tried, bits of their conversation kept prodding her like sticks. *That's how it goes, eh? . . . The kid's with his father . . . I gave that rotten bastard . . .* She sat up, shivering, and reached down to the floor to light the candle. Behind her, as she sat up again, her shadow moved hugely. She stared into the candle flame. Beside the bottle was her week's pay. He'd given it to her that afternoon as she was leaving. She'd forgotten it was pay day. He hadn't. He never did.

She hugged herself; she was freezing. Swinging her legs over the side of the bed, she reached for her sloppy jumper and pulled it on. She ran her fingers across her breasts. Under the thick wool her nipples were taut with cold, hard little unharvested fruits.

. . . He paid regularly, and he paid well, deducting the rent that she'd suggested. *You* find out the going rate, he'd told her. She never had, just said something off the top of her head when he'd asked her again.

She scooped up the notes and let them slide over her hands to the floor. She had quite a stack now, poked into a tin out of sight with the accumulated dirt of years on top of the kitchen dresser. There was bugger-all to spend money on round here, except food, and the laundromat when there was nothing clean left at Marycote, and occasionally something that caught her eye in that shop in the fancy arcade, earrings mostly, and her moon chart, and one time the beautiful red and green paper moth in the passage that fluttered its long wings in every draught.

Kneeling, she gathered the notes together, then took the candle and went out to the kitchen. As she moved across the passage the candle flared. She placed it on the kitchen table and stood protectively between it and the door. Draughts, Angus said. Nothing but draughts.

All the same, she listened intently. Nothing. The flame calmed down, grew fat and unmindful. But as soon as she stepped on to the chair for the tin at the top of the dresser, it flared again, stretching thin and high like a scream.

Her hands began to shake. The money, it was the money. What else could it be? She refused to look further, to go scrabbling around in her mind amongst dust and dead cockroaches and mouse dirt. The money. Put it somewhere else, said the candle. What if some shit busts you? But where? At the bottom of my sleeping bag? In the springs of the sofa?

Not here, said the candle.

Where, then?

In a quiet place, said the candle. Why not?

Why not? she repeated.

She could open a bank account.

The flame grew calm, and so did she.

Who said there was no such thing as signs?

42 Politics

In the morning she woke refreshed, gathered all the dirty clothes and sheets she could find, pushed them into her rucksack and cycled into Currawong. The money business came first. She spent some time cycling up and down the main street, eyeing off the banks. The best looking was a two-storeyed building, yellowed as old lace, with square corners and tall, spare windows. Here she stood in queues, filled in forms, wrote her surname for the first time in how long. She stared at the two words. Her name. Herself.

"Everything all right?" said the teller.

Gita looked up. The teller, anxious to assist, was very young, with that fair skin that is almost transparent. Gita gave him the old slow-motion smile. And smiled again to see him blush. "Just reading the fine print."

The teller nodded approvingly. She handed over the signed form with a flourish.

At the laundromat she filled several machines, then decided to have a drink in the pub across the road before going to the supermarket. The Iron Bar, the pub was called. It was the only pub in Currawong that she'd been in so far. She and Jules and Mark and Crystal had dropped in for a drink on their way home that day they'd met Angus, and Jarrah had come marching in to the bar because he'd finished his chips and was sick of waiting in the hearse. She didn't blame him.

Outside a pub could be a good place to start busking as soon as the weather warmed up. Try out some of her new songs. She'd suss out the Iron Bar now. Might be interesting. Might be someone who wouldn't brainwash her with politics.

It was midday, and the pub was busy. Men stared, then looked away if she met their eyes. Gita found an empty seat at the bar. The barmaid, the only other woman there, went on joking with the men in front of her although she half turned towards Gita as if to signal I've seen you, I'm on my way.

"Good-day," Gita said to the guy on her right, who looked more promising than what was offering on the other side. She had to speak to the guy's left ear. All she could see of the rest of him was soft yellow hair cut short over his ears and long on top, and a soft black coat shrugged high on to his neck.

He didn't bother turning his head. "Is it?"

He was so lugubrious that she laughed. "Isn't it? Looks okay to me so far. Busy in here today. Must be a popular hole."

"Sale day."

"I guess everyone comes in here on sale day." Everyone except Angus. "Oh come on misery, give yourself a holiday!"

His shoulders shook with silent laughter. Clear as cold water they said why should I bother?

Well, screw you, Gita thought, as he hunched into the bar and said nothing further. The barmaid came up to her. Gita asked for a bottle of stout.

"Like that stuff, do you?" muttered a voice on her other side.

She turned around. "Sure. Ever tried it?"

"Nah. Beer, beer's my poison. Name's Blue. Blue."

"Gita. Hi, Blue."

"That's nice. That's a nice name. New round here, aren't you?"

At least this wizened old redneck was trying.

"Sure. I'm working here for a while."

"Working. What's that thing you got in your nose?"

"A stud. Lots of people have them."

"Do they?" He leaned over and touched it. "Nice. Nice."

Gita moved her head. She heard the guy in the black coat laugh.

"Nice skin, too. Nice hair." Blue touched her face again. "Eh? Gita?"

"Come on, Blue, that's enough," said the barmaid.

"Sorry, sorry," Blue muttered, and ordered another beer.

Gita smiled gratefully at the barmaid, but the woman wouldn't meet her eyes.

She looked along the bar. There wasn't another stool available. But why should you move, Gita? Stay where you are. You're bloody right, Crystal!

"What did you say your name was?" Blue was asking her. And he started again. "Nice. Nice ears. Jesus, how many earrings?"

"Hands off, Blue. I want to drink my drink." She tossed her head to avoid his muttering fingers. "Piss off, I said. Look, just fuck off, will you!"

She glared at him.

"Don't you talk like that!" Blue raised his voice. "Hey! Lady's bein' rude. Lady's swearin'."

"What's up, Blue?" someone shouted.

"Lady keeps lookin' at me," Blue complained, as Gita continued to glare.

There was laughter around the bar. "Hard up, is she, Blue? Send her over here. I'll show her something to look at."

Gita stared into the long mirror above the bar. Shits! Shits, the lot of them. And found herself looking straight at Lou Catchpole. He was sitting with a group of men at a small table against the wall, a glass in his hand, a grin on his face.

He stood up and pushed his way over to the bar. "That'll do, Blue. Come on, shove off. Leave the lady alone."

"You know her, do you, Lou?" someone shouted.

Catchpole waved his glass in acknowledgment. The bar fell silent, then resumed its normal hum of conversation. He pulled himself across the empty stool. "So . . . what are you drinking — lady?"

"The name's Gita."

"Sure. And how's life out there on the farm — Gita?"

"Fine. Busy."

"Busy, eh? I wouldn't have thought there was a lot to keep you busy at the cottage. Beer for me, Jan, Coopers for the lady."

"I'm working for Angus in the glasshouse."

Catchpole whistled. "Are you really? Just what is going on in that glasshouse? Or shouldn't I ask?" Whuh whuh whuh.

"You can ask, sure. I'm putting seedlings into tubes for transplanting round the farm as soon as the ground warms up."

"What? Windbreaks? He's planting windbreaks?"

"And understorey in the bush."

"Understorey? What's wrong with what's there?"

"It's been grazed out. Or burned out. He wants to get the bush back to what it used to be."

Catchpole whistled again. "Is that so! I was wondering what crazy scheme he had in mind this time."

"How come you haven't asked him yourself, since you're so interested?"

"Ah . . . Springfield and me, we don't always see eye to eye."

"You amaze me."

He didn't like that. "Want me to show you something? Look at this." He pulled up his shirt-sleeve to the elbow and turned his arm over.

She glanced with distaste at the purple scar like a grin on the pudgy underarm. "Angus did that?"

"In this very room."

With his fingernail he tapped her bottle of stout, tap tap tap.

I've eased up on the drinking, Gita, that's something. "You're not going to tell me . . . with a broken bottle?"

Catchpole grinned triumphantly. "How come you don't ask him yourself . . . since you're so interested?"

Gita stared. I gave that bloke what was coming to him, you bet I did. Was this the guy his girl had chucked him over for? Chucked *Angus* for? *Catchpole?*

"Why would he want to do that?"

" 'cause the bastard's crazy. Haven't you noticed? Or does everything just float across that pretty little head of yours? He came back crazy and he's acted crazy ever since. You want to watch out when he's in one of his moods . . . Yeah, he went away a hero and he'd have been welcomed back a hero only he decided to go off his bloody head, didn't he?"

swift and strong running in, catching the ewe, putting the lamb to the udder and watching till it struggled to its feet

She smiled. "He's okay."

"Have it your own way. Anyway, what brings you into town?"

"Dirty laundry."

"What, not washing it in public, are you?"

"Think that might be interesting?"

"Could be." He grinned, and she laughed. Lou Catchpole. She could manage Lou Catchpole. She put the bottle to her mouth and held it high like a fanfare. "I'm thinking of doing a bit of busking — singing," she explained. "On the pavement. How does that grab you?"

"Singing for your supper, eh? Do a bit of that, do you?"

"Sure. When I'm hungry."

"Get hungry often?"

"Now and then."

"Good at it, are you?"

"Want a demonstration?"

"Could be interesting."

"You'll have to make a donation. Coins in the fountain — Lou. No such thing as a free lunch."

"Course I'll make a donation." He leered. "If the performance deserves it."

It's all a power game, my dear. He's eating out of your hand

"So how are you getting home with your laundry?" Lou Catchpole was saying. "On the bike again, are you?"

Gita sighed. She wasn't looking forward to pushing a heap of wet washing all that way. She never used the dryers at the laundromat. Someone — Crystal — had told her that their heat was a source of germs. The return journey from the laundromat was always harder than the trip into town.

She nodded. "The bike, sure."

"Like a lift back? You haven't had a ride in the Range Rover yet, have you? That's it outside the pub." He looked at his watch. "I want to see a bloke in here shortly, go to the bank, then head off. Suit you?"

"Sure . . . Another beer, please, Jan. And a Coopers for me . . . Hey!" She tossed her head at Lou. "Good family man giving lifts to strange women — aren't you worried people will talk?"

"About me?" He laughed, and glanced around the bar, where everyone was immersed in his own conversation. "Ahh, they all know me in here."

"They went off their brain when I came in. Haven't they seen a woman in a public bar before?"

Catchpole laughed again. He was enjoying himself, elbow on the counter, drink in his hand, good-looking girl all ears. He slapped down the empty glass and nodded at Jan. "Course they did," he said to Gita. "Course they went off their brain. No offence, mind you, but . . . for starters . . . Jesus, girl, that thing in your nose!"

"Great."

"And you're out at Springfield. Well, Marycote. Everyone knows Angus."

"What does that mean —" she put the bottle down carefully — "everyone knows Angus?"

"I told you. Crazy. Off the air. Oh, he might be okay right now. Maybe you've got . . . umm . . . the magic touch? Eh?" He stared at her. She stared back, expressionless. "Yeah . . . well . . . maybe you want to watch your step. He's a crack shot. Didn't know that, did you? He was in a crack regiment knocking hell out of those slanteyes up in 'Nam . . . 'Nam. *Viet*nam." He stared at her again. "Bit before your time, eh?"

"I was a kid then." To show she wasn't a political moron, she added "Poor guy, I suppose he had to go. They did, didn't they?"

"Conscript, you mean? He wasn't a conscript. He volunteered, girl. Well, he was conscripted the first year, yeah, sure, but when that was through he volunteered. Signed on for a second tour of duty. Jeez, I'd have given my eye teeth to've had his chance."

"So why didn't you volunteer?"

"'cause . . . well, like I was needed on the farm, wasn't I? I had to give a bit of a hand on his farm as well as my own, didn't I? I tell you what, this great country of ours wouldn't be crawling with the buggers now if I'd been over there. If you'll pardon my French."

"Crawling with what buggers?"

"Asiatics. What d'you think?"

She said, very caustically so that even Lou Catchpole couldn't miss her meaning, "Don't you mean slanteyes? Slopes? Nignogs?" Words scrawled more and more frequently on walls and bridges around Melbourne. You couldn't miss them. She looked around the bar very deliberately. "I don't see too many *Asiatics* in here. What did you guys do, run them all out of town, like the Aborigines a hundred years ago?"

"Hey, keep the volume down!" He leaned towards her. "You better listen to me. You just good and listen, Gita my girl. Don't you go saying things like that round here. Me, okay. I'm a pretty tolerant sort of bloke. Others mightn't be. If you want my advice, don't even mention Aborigines round here. There's a few old folks still alive that can remember things they'd maybe rather not remember and their families don't want a lot of do-gooders and greenies and pinkoes from out of town asking a lot of nosy questions."

"You, maybe? Your family?"

"Jesus! You don't take a hint, do you? As a matter of fact, no. Not my folks." He slumped back, grinning. "Maybe the Springfields?"

43 Using

Gita's head was spinning as she left the pub. She'd drunk too much stout. Keeping even with Lou's shouts. What in fuck had induced her to accept a lift with him? A fast walk home was what she needed, not more of Lou Catchpole and his grinning innuendoes. And she still had to go to the supermarket, and that little shop in the arcade. As she crossed the road to get her bike, she saw Mary Springfield walking up and down outside the laundromat. Mary waved, and waited for her.

"Hello, Gita. It was you I saw coming out of the hotel."

Jesus! "That's right. I've been having a few drinks."

"Have you? That's nice, dear. Was it a nice girl at the bar?" Before Gita could answer, Mary rushed on "Are you in at the sale, too? I thought perhaps Angus . . . Lou came into the sale today."

I know. He's just been nudging my knee. Gita shook her head. "I came in to do a heap of washing. Behind you, in the laundromat," she added, as Mary looked blank.

"Oh. Yes. Can I give you a lift home? I'm just popping in to the doctor's." She nodded at the old house adjoining the laundromat. "I'm early. Lou laughs at me. I'm always early. I don't know why I get so het up whenever I come in to the doctor's. All he has to do is take my blood pressure and write out another scrip so I can sleep."

"I'd love a lift home with you." Gita glanced across the road. No sign of that deadshit. "Why don't I come into the waiting room with you? It's easier waiting with a friend."

"That is nice of you, dear. Are you sure —"

"Can we put the washing in your car rightaway? And the bike?" Too bad about the groceries. She unlocked the bike from the surgery fence.

"Of course, dear. I'm just round the corner, out of the traffic. Can I help you with something? Let me wheel the bike . . . Goodness, what a load!" she exclaimed as Gita came out of the laundromat with her washing wrapped in the plastic tablecloth she'd found in a kitchen drawer at Springfield.

Again Gita glanced across the road, then staggered as quickly as she could to Mary's car. "The front wheel comes off. Like this, see? There'll be room, Mary."

She didn't relax again until they were safe in the doctor's surgery.

The receptionist waved to them to sit down. "Doctor won't be long, Miss Springfield."

Mary shifted, easing her back against one of the cheap office chairs lining the walls. "I remember when this was a lovely old room," she whispered. "The Collinses lived here then. And when Dr Bryce set it up as his surgery, he always had a fire going in the fireplace, and a fresh flower on the mantelpiece."

Gita looked at the worn, ugly carpet, and the thick string-coloured lace and dark drapes turning daylight to dusk.

"It's seen better days, that's for sure."

Why on earth were they both whispering? There was no one else in the room. Eventually a man of Mary's age came in and sat down. How are you, Stan. How are you, Mary. Ah . . . shouldn't complain. Rotten weather. Yes, rotten weather. This is my friend Gita. How are you, Gita.

Two elderly women came in after Stan. How are you. Rotten weather. This is my friend Gita. After this exchange, they all sat wrapped in silence as thick as a winter coat. Gita sighed. I could be back at Marycote now. I could be at my place, not mixed up in this hassle.

The inner door opened, and a man of Angus's age looked out. Skin like damp pastry, Gita thought. She was surprised when Mary got stiffly to her feet, saying "Good morning, good morning Doctor."

The doctor nodded. Mary followed him into his room.

A fly buzzing faintly at the window reminded Gita of Blue's persistent muttering in the pub. Hurry up, Mary! Let's get out of this place.

At last Mary came out. Gita, too busy checking Lou wasn't in sight, was unaware of Mary's silence on the way to the car. Thank God, she thought, as they left the town behind and drove along the leafy road towards Marycote.

Suddenly Mary said "Oh heavens, I'll have to go back. I forgot to post Lou's letters. I'm so sorry, Gita. I could run you home and come back again . . . All right, if you're sure . . . Oh, I am an old fool!"

Gita laughed. "I'm always forgetting things."

She glanced at Mary as the old woman reversed, crashed a gear, bounced the car forward again. She sure looked upset. Maybe Lou would give her a hard time, if she didn't catch the post. Lou! She couldn't help saying "Anyway, if they mattered so much, why didn't Lou take the bloody letters – the letters?"

"He's very busy, Gita."

"Well, aren't you? From what Angus says . . . "

"Angus? Did he?"

Gita was amused at Mary's tone. It was like colour running back into a white face. He's your blue-eyed boy, all right, isn't he, Mary? And the blue eyes turned on Gita *the ewe left lying on the ground . . . Gita! . . . no hassles I'm too tired too tired too tired*

Mary was heaving a great sigh. "Oh well, I just have to get used to it, don't I?"

"Used to what? Hey, mind the road! Maybe you'd better pull up for a bit."

As the car juddered to a halt, Gita looked at the old woman in alarm. Lifting her hands on and off the steering wheel, her face set and pale.

"The letters. Lou's letters. That just goes to show."

"Okay, so you forgot them. It's no big deal, Mary. Hey! Don't cry! It's not worth crying about!"

"I told him, I said Doctor I'm getting forgetful, I'm getting very forgetful and he said Mary, you know what it is, don't you, it's ageing senility. I said *senility*, Doctor! and he said that's right Mary: ageing senility. Now go home and forget the word."

Gita almost laughed. You say something like that and then you say now go home and forget the word!

"Maybe the sleeping pills are making you forgetful. Have you thought of that? What are they — valium?"

"Oh, I couldn't sleep without them, Gita. It's awful, you know — but you wouldn't know, a young girl like you — waking up at two or three in the morning and lying there for hours . . . The thoughts that go running through your head!"

How do you know I haven't been there too? Gita thought, irritated by Mary's unintentionally patronising manner, but she said only "Have you tried something else? Ginseng maybe? Hot milk?"

"I don't think Doctor would want me to do that unless he'd —"

Gita sighed. "Then how about changing your doctor? I've heard there's a good woman doctor just moved into town."

"But would a woman —"

"Yes Mary, a woman would!"

"I don't know — I wouldn't like to do that, Gita. I've always gone to that clinic. I'm sure old Dr Bryce wouldn't have sold his practice to someone who was . . . was . . ."

"A prize shit?"

But Mary looked so upset, either at the thought of being disloyal or at Gita's language, that Gita said no more, just threw herself back against the seat and stared out the window. If some old woman was silly enough to keep on with a doctor who was a prize shit, what business was it of hers?

44 Property

"I've got to do that spraying in the plantation," Angus said to Gita when she arrived at the glasshouse early the next morning. "I'll have to run into town for the herbicide. Want to come for the ride, or — " he took a deep breath — "are you happy to go on by yourself in here?"

She muttered something he didn't catch, and he thought well, of course she is, she doesn't know what this means to me. All the same, he'd have liked some little sign, some acknowledgment. He glanced at her hopefully. Her face was like a frost at midnight.

"Get out of bed the wrong side today, did you?"

God, the corny things he came out with sometimes! She looked up. Sighed at him. "My period's due. Okay?"

"Sorry. Sorry, Gita." Then he frowned. Hadn't she said the same thing only a week or so ago when she'd been snappish over nothing much?

"Anyway, I was in town yesterday," she added. "I'm not in a hurry to go back."

"No?"

"Haven't they caught up with the calendar in that place yet?"

"Could be. What happened?"

"I went into the Iron Bar and the jerks went off their rods."

"The Iron Bar? Did you? Can get a bit wild in there at times."

"Don't they know women have been drinking in public bars since I started drinking?"

He laughed. "That wasn't it. Women drink in there."

"What was it, then? You tell me."

"They don't know you. You're a stranger. You're different."

"Oh. I'm different. Great."

"Like me," he added.

"What do you mean, different like you?" she snapped. Before he could reply she rushed on: "And another thing. Some stinking old barfly was bothering me —"

"Blue Foster, was it?"

"Maybe. I don't know — how would I know? — and everyone thought that was the funniest thing since Rough Riders till another guy came up and sort of *rescued* me and that was all right then, wasn't it, no one hassled me any more, did they, because I belonged to someone then, I was taken over, I was property!"

"Oh, come on!"

"You think I'm making this up?"

"I think you could be making a bit too much of it."

"You weren't there, were you?"

"I'm sorry I wasn't."

"Oh? I'd have been your property then so that would have been all right too."

"No. They could have had a go at me instead."

Whichever way, I'd still have been rescued. By some man.

He took her silence for a question, and went on to answer it: "All this, for one thing." He nodded at the seedlings. "All very trendy, plant a billion trees by the year 2000, but who really gives a stuff? Eh? Really? Greenies, and nuts like me. And if you do it properly, replant your farm, get right out of something you reckon's harmful — there was this bloke I met up near Mareeba who'd switched from tobacco to sweet potatoes —"

"And something else!" Gita interrupted. "The barmaid — the only other woman in there — she looked at me as though the whole thing was all my fucking fault anyway!"

"Listen," he said. "This town's no different from a lot of other places in this country we're expected to give our lives to defend. Racists the lot of them. Aren't they?"

"They were all Anglos in the Iron Bar, that's for sure."

"I'll tell you something that happened to me when I was up north a few years back — up on the North Coast, I mean. I got to know a migrant family a bit. They were running a restaurant. Came out with their parents just after the Second World War. Italians, Yugoslavs, I never worked out exactly. Doesn't matter, anyway. One night they got talking about the sort of things people used to say about migrants back in the fifties. They stick together too much. The women wear black. They won't learn English. The men fight with knives —"

"A broken bottle was more respectable, was it?"

Angus ignored this, or hadn't heard it. "And then another night their daughter started talking to me about the Vietnamese boat people coming in to town. They work too hard, she said. They gabble this sing-song to one another and you can't understand a word. They're all buying houses in the same street and turning it into a ghetto. Exactly the same things that Anglo-Australians were saying about her family thirty-odd years before!"

"Did you tell her?"

"Of course I didn't." I was too damn' busy trying to strip her of her damn' Catholic upbringing. "You're the only person I've told that to."

"Thanks."

He wasn't sure whether she meant that or was being caustic. "Well, I'll get on into town. You'll be right here while I'm gone?"

"Sure."

He went out of the glasshouse, then came back. "Can I get you anything while I'm in there?"

She pulled a scrap of paper out of her pocket. "I forgot to do my shopping yesterday. Maybe you could get these?"

He glanced at the list, surprised that she even had one. "Okay."

Again he set out, and again he came back, leaning against the doorway. "Sure you'll be okay here on your own?"

"Quit worrying, Angus. I know exactly what to do."

Driving into town, he went over her list in his mind: F&V (fruit and veg; he'd have to make a guess at what she'd like), rye, butter, soy milk (so far so good), kahlua, patchouli (what the hell was that?), incense — *incense* — where would he find that in Currawong? — tofu, *tampons* . . .

They'd have him with a harem out at Springfield.

* *

Of course he managed her shopping without any trouble. Try the health food shop in the arcade, the girl at the supermarket told him. Incense — what fragrance did he want? Ambrosia? Aphrodisia? Good God. He chose Sandalwood. School pencils used to be made of sandalwood. An old fragrance but one of the best, the woman behind the counter assured him. It's especially good for sensitive people, the intuitive, psychic types, you know? Because it protects the aura. A drop of sandalwood oil on the third eye —

"Patchouli?" he interrupted.

Patchouli came in a small bottle like a flavouring or a food dye. Unscrewing the cap, he took a sniff. As the subtle musky smell filled his head he recalled a bin full of oats; good healthy oats into which he had plunged his hand and, lifting it, let the plump grains slide whispering back to the heap. He read the wording on the label. "Imbued with the stillness at the heart of nature, the primeval earthy quality of this fragrance calms the mind's busyness and draws the wearer into creative renewal." He smiled, and was feeling cheerful, talkative even, when, Gita's shopping done, he went to buy the herbicide.

Normally he would have gone to the other end of the town to the old hay and grain store where he had an account. It was one of the oldest continually operating hay and grain stores in the state, a high weatherboard building smelling of oats and bailed lucerne and chicken pellets. You could buy tough workshirts in here, and gumboots, and these days leather saddles and Akubras. Springfields had always done business here. From the footpath you walked up five wooden steps, and there on your right was the manager's office. This was a tiny room, with a high old-fashioned desk taking up one wall, and a sliding interior window opening on to a worn counter on which, for as long as Angus could remember, one manager or another had leaned out for a yarn.

Behind the hay and grain store there had once been a malthouse, demolished during Angus's schooldays. Every time he came this way he could recall the rich smell of the malt as surely as if the old malthouse still stood. He liked this end of the town. Made a loop around those dead years between his youth and the present.

Today, however, happy with Gita's shopping, eager to get back to her, he went to the nearest place to buy herbicide, just a step or two from the arcade.

The manager was out on the pavement, watching a signwriter at work on the window. Angus greeted him cheerfully.

"'day, Les. Nice day."

The manager nodded. "'day, Angus. So so, so so."

"I'm after some Roundup, Les."

Les grunted. Couldn't get it where he had his account, had to come here, did he?

They walked into the store together.

"Doing a bit of spraying?"

"That's right. Preparation for some tree-planting. Putting back a few of the natives."

Les turned away to the shelf where the sprays were kept. "Got your work cut out doing that, haven't you?"

"That's for sure. I've got someone giving me a bit of a hand."

"Is that so?" As he bent over the till he said "How's that tenant of yours making out? Living in the old cottage, isn't she?"

"That's right. She's the one giving me a hand with the windbreaks, actually."

"Is she now? Good worker, is she?"

"Women are naturals when it comes to finicky work with plants, Les."

Les chuckled. "Naturals at a lot of things, I reckon."

"That's true."

"She came into the Iron Bar yesterday."

Angus's head gave a thump. He said carefully "She did mention that. Someone pestering her. Blue Foster, was it?"

"I believe it was."

Angus said even more carefully "Blue's like dog shit. How did she get rid of him?"

Les, his hands resting on the Roundup, gave him a sly glance.

"Latched on to one of your neighbours. Like you say, women are naturals at some things."

Angus's head gave another thump. "Phil Reynolds?" Phil Reynolds lived on the other farm adjoining Springfield. He was a sixty-year-old bachelor who lived with his mother and went into town on sale days and Sundays.

Les laughed. "Phil'd run a mile I reckon, Angus, before you'd find him getting chatted up in a bar."

He watched Angus hurry away, then went outside himself to scrutinise the signwriter's work.

She was in the shadehouse.

"Here's your shopping." He placed the plastic bags on the bench.

"Thanks." She glanced in the bags. "These aren't mine." She took out the bottles of Scotch in their black cartons.

"No, they're mine." He took them from her so abruptly, shoving them under the bench, that she looked at him in surprise.

"I didn't say anything, Angus."

"Did I say you did?"

His face looked pinched. "Got a headache?"

"Yes."

"Came on in town, did it? No wonder."

"I get migraines now and then."

"Know what you should do? Rest for a bit with the tip of your second finger pressed against the middle of your forehead. Like this." She demonstrated on her own forehead. "It's very relaxing. Really. It's where your third eye used to be."

"Gita!"

"Don't you believe me?"

latched on to women are naturals Catchpole latched on to Catchpole

"I don't believe rubbish when I hear it, Gita."

Her shoulders tightened. "Perhaps I better go home."

"Please yourself."

She wheeled the barrow outside, piled in soil from the bin, struggled with it back to the bench.

"Aren't you going home?"

"Some people *try* things before they condemn them."

"Poking your fingers in your eye to make you feel better — lovely!"

She banged a filled tube on the bench.

"Go home if you want to, Gita, I can finish this."

She turned slowly, her chin lifted in disdain. On her neck was a tiny mole like a flyspot.

"Just say the word and I'll go."

Turning away abruptly, he knocked something over in one of her bags. The bottle of kahlua. He set it upright. "Sorry." He was forever apologising for something these days. To his shame he thought he was going to weep. He fought his voice steady. "Look, this is no good. Bickering about nothing." Nothing! "Tell you what, why don't we give ourselves a holiday? Want to come for a drive? If you like I can take you over the rest of the property. And then we could come home along some of the back roads. Want to?"

She smiled.

His glasshouse girl.

45 Green Moonlight

While he collected milk, teabags and sugar, then cut bread and thick slices of cold meat for mutton and sauce sandwiches, she filled the thermos and set about selecting fruit. He watched her picking over the oranges, turning this one in her thin fingers, putting down that one. It astonished him that someone so efficient and quick with the seedlings could be so dreamy over a bit of fruit. He saw her smile.

"We'll take a picnic," she said. "Into the country."

Memories of her first venture into the country touched her like whispers of cloud.

They drove out along the Springfield drive where the pinoaks still held on to their autumn leaves, waiting for budburst before they shed them. Across the road was another gate which led on to creek flats where red and white cattle lifted curious heads from grass and clover ankle-deep.

"Yours?" she asked in surprise. "You've got a lot of land."

"I'm what is known as comfortably off." His tone was ironic. She pictured the closed-up house, its rooms as comfortable as a graveyard, Angus in the kitchen eating last week's rabbit stew.

"What do you do, stash it away and gloat over your bankbook?"

"No." He made a sweeping gesture. "We're driving on it." He laughed. "Stash it away and gloat! Is that your idea of me?"

She thinks I'm fishing, he told himself when she said nothing. I am fishing. What the hell does it matter what this woman thinks? They're all the same. Men too — they're all the same. I should have rotted in the jungle.

An image came to mind: a bloated corpse twitching like something alive. Charlie, they mouthed one to the other as they picked their way through the vines. Of course it's dead, Angus told himself, putrefaction's making it jerk. But in nightmares it cried out to him, its eyes agonised.

He glanced down at his hands: steady on the steering wheel. His feet were easy on the pedals, he could hear himself telling her "Too wet on the flats for sheep. That's why I run Herefords down here. Dry cattle, mostly. That one's in good nick, look at that!"

Two separate streams: death, and you waded on thigh-deep through the sham of living.

He turned to her. "I'm starving. How about you?"

He pulled up on a stony patch. While he reached for the picnic basket, the cane around its handle untwining with age, Gita looked around her.

"And the bush on the hill across the flats? Is that yours too?"

"Yes. It runs back into state forest."

"Is that where we'll be planting the little stuff, the grevilleas and things?"

"That's what I had in mind." He was pleased she'd said we. "If we can persuade the kangaroos not to eat them."

She had never seen kangaroos in the wild, only in a caravan park once when she was living with some guy in his panel van. She recalled the big grey roo lying on his side by the taps, flicking soft bored ears, a prisoner of flies and gawking kids pushing hunks of white bread at his proud thin mouth.

"Let's walk up there, hey? Let's have our picnic in the bush . . . Angus? Don't we have time?"

"Yes, sure, we've got time. All the rest of the day, if we want." He was surprised at her question. He hadn't realised his reluctance to go in the bush was so obvious — that it still existed. How in hell was he going to plant up the understorey if he couldn't bring himself to walk there?

"Sorry, I forgot . . . maybe your knee's bothering you today?"

"No, it's okay. Let's go."

"There's a bit of a cave up on the hill — just a rock overhang really but it'll be out of the wind," he told her as they squelched across the flats towards the bush. Talk, keep talking, then you won't remember. "I remember camping up there with a mate when I was a kid. A little kid, I mean. You know, having the big adventure. Sleeping bag, flashlight, supper as well as breakfast in case we got hungry. Packed by my mother in this very same picnic basket. I don't know who was more nervous about the whole thing, Mum or us." He stopped so suddenly that she nearly walked into him. "I guess I was always one for a bit of adventure. Till I learned more sense." Before she could say anything, ask him, pin him down, he said hurriedly, looking at the ground, "I went through a bad patch a few years back. Couldn't seem to settle to anything. So I took off. Spent a fair bit of time knocking about up north. In the tropics." He turned and walked on, stepping silently over rocks and around saplings. "Did you know walking through jungle's like walking through green moonlight?"

"Green moonlight," she mused. "I'd have liked that."

"It was the wrong light," he said abruptly. "I mean, for a person from this part of the world."

"Green moonlight?"

"Yes. Australia, I'm talking about Australia." He glanced at her anxiously. "Queensland. The Top End. All across the north. Doing whatever turned up. Barman — that didn't work out too well. Stationhand. Working on the roads. Out west of Kununurra. But I couldn't get used to the light."

"What was wrong with it?"

"Up there it's not blue-grey like down here, it's a pinkish-green." *Blood. Like a film of blood* "Because of the red soil and the bright green foliage. It just didn't . . . feel right. To me, I mean. To the Aboriginal blokes I was working with it was fine, they were born there, it was home . . . They were good to me, those blokes . . . They think these whitefellers wandering round on their own are a funny bunch. They couldn't make me out. Not wanting to go back to 'my country' as they put it."

Again he stopped abruptly. She could smell his sweat, and overlaying it something else, something she'd smelled in that room in Melbourne when they'd held their breaths knowing it was a bust.

He was talking again. "Back to the place where my ancestors were buried and my umbilical cord was cut. A woman said that to me." Listening, he seemed to be listening. "I mean, I could come back here any time I wanted, no whitefeller park ordinances, no triple-padlocked gates stopping me." He laughed. "Well, that was a matter of opinion, wasn't it?" He moved on again, swiftly, quietly. "When you've been . . . away . . . for any length of time, there's a hell of a lot of catching up to do." *If you can ever catch up with a purloined life.* "You know what finally made up my mind? I was working in Queensland by then, round Cairns, and I was looking at this range of mountains. By moonlight. Like I said, by day the colours are different from down here, but by moonlight the mountains are sort of floating blue-black, same as here. Is this making any sort of sense?"

She nodded.

"And I realised I was looking at the Great Dividing Range, the same range we're this very minute walking on. All the way from Cape York to the Grampians. The same range with the same moonlight." He glanced at her again. "Leading me home. If I chose to go."

She nodded again. Maybe she'd been looking at the same dividing mountains when she was wandering around in that panel van.

She felt a prickle of irritation when he laughed apologetically, self-deprecatingly. Like Mary Springfield, she thought, tightening her lips.

He saw the grimace and said quickly "People like me, on their own a lot, they grab someone's ear and they don't know when to stop. Anyway, we're here now. This is the overhang." He breathed with relief. He hadn't realised how jumpy he'd be with someone following behind him. "Not very big, is it? When I was a kid it seemed like a real cave."

The ground in front of the overhang fell away sharply into a gully. Across the gully was another scrub-covered hillside like the one they had walked up.

He took off his oilskin coat and spread it on the ground, then opened the packet of sandwiches and passed it to her.

"This tastes good," she said, stretching her mouth wide for the thick bread and meat. She poured hot water into the thermos caps and dunked teabags. "Here's your tea."

"Thanks. Especially when you're hungry," he added, watching her eat. He looked around the overhang, reached up and laid his arm against the solid rock. "People reckon the Aborigines used to camp up here in the old days. Dry, out of the wind. Bit far from the creek, though."

"Any rock paintings in here?"

He shook his head. "Not round here. My grandfather did find an axehead near the house. Lovely thing. Nice to hold in your hand. Really hard greeny-black rock, ground at one edge. I'd show it to you when we get back to the house but it disappeared some time back . . . Like the people who used it," he added.

Don't you go asking a lot of nosy questions. Don't even mention − "How do you feel about that?" she asked, taking another sandwich.

"How do you think I feel?" He looked at her. She

shrugged, waiting. And then she didn't want to know, because he said, staring across the gully, his sandwich untouched, "The world's drowning in blood. That's how I feel sometimes. All the blood of all the dead for generations. Slaughtered like cattle."

She looked at her bread, soaked and stained with his generous dollop of sauce. She stared at her red gumboots, stretched out in front of her like gobbets of flesh; heard herself squelching across the slippery flats; lifted her eyes and saw the severed edge of the overhang where droplets slowly gathered and fell.

And heard Jules's voice *Save yourself, my dear. You know what to do*

Startled by her expression, Angus said "Sorry — sorry, Gita. I'm not much of a companion for a holiday." And gave a rueful smile. "I get carried away."

She made herself laugh. "I've known worse."

He picked up a twig and snapped it into little pieces. The walk up through the bush, that set him going. *Tell her*.

He said instead "Did you know it's possible to film a streak of lightning rising to meet itself, did you know that?"

She held fast to that. Wrinkled her forehead at him. "What's that got to do with anything?"

"Dunno. It's interesting." Laughing himself now. "Isn't it?"

She grinned. "Real holiday talk. Where do you pick up all this stuff?"

"Telly."

"Telly. No wonder you get gloomy."

"Hey, there're some good things sometimes." An idea struck him: if he let her know when there was a nature programme on, maybe she'd have a bite to eat with him again like that first night —

She was watching him. "Ten cents for them." Holiday talk. Jules receded.

"Oh . . . just thinking." And, as her face relaxed, *tell her, why don't you tell her?* "Remembering, really."

"Huh?"

"The first time I got home. None of this —" he gestured:

the overhang, the trees, the sunlit hillside across the gully — "seemed . . . you know, real." TV in the sitting room with his parents, the blonde girl mad about him. He glanced at Gita. "Everyone down here talking about, oh, football, who was getting married, who topped the market. None of it had anything to do with *me*. My girlfriend — football — the lot. And that scared the hell out of me. So first chance I got I went back to my mates. Can you believe that? I felt safer up there than I did here!"

Safe. Oh yes, I know about that, Angus.

Angus breathed a sigh of relief. The words belonged to that earlier experience but she hadn't taken him up, she hadn't jumped on him, hadn't abused him. Hadn't she noticed?

"But you feel safe now?" she was saying. "Back here? You feel safe here?" I feel safe, Angus, at my place. At Marycote.

"You know," he said after a long silence, "I reckon if I didn't force myself to go on some days, I'd have shot myself long ago."

She thought of the glasshouse, full of bright green seedlings in their tubes, waiting to be planted out as soon as he said it was time. She said, her voice rising, "That isn't all it is, is it, just forcing yourself to do things?"

He didn't reply.

"Well!" She made herself laugh, nudge his shoulder with hers. "We're a pair, aren't we? Little half-chicks, both of us."

"Little half-chicks?"

"Don't you remember the story, she had one wing and one eye and one leg and in the end something got her, the fox, wasn't it?"

He picked up her hand and, putting it upside down on his knee, smoothed her fingers open. "That sums me up all right, but it's hardly you." Smooth strong fingers. He put her hand down.

"No?" She picked at her sandwich, thinking over all the different ways you could make yourself safe. Escape deadshits at you and at you. *Tell him.* "You want to know what I do when I feel hassled? I disappear. Go right away outside myself till I've disappeared, till there's nothing there."

"Gita!" The thousand yard stare. The abandoned farm. "Not all the time?"

She shook her head. "I've found something good to do here." She took a deep breath. "What I've got here, it seems . . . like you said, real. You know? Meaningful." Meaningful. A meaningful relationship. Was that what she and Angus had going together? Working together in the glasshouse? She watched a band of sunshine moving steadily uphill. His hand on hers had felt warm — dry and warm and solid. A good solid working relationship. "And no hassles," she added softly. "No hassles."

Okay. Hands off. You don't have to remind me. He laughed harshly. The story of my life.

"What's the joke?" she demanded, silky fingers of fear stroking her again.

You know what to do, my dear

"Don't you reckon it's funny," Angus was saying, "whenever you see Mars written, or Venus written, it's capital M, capital V, but Earth's always written with a small e, a *small* e, Gita. That says it all, doesn't it? Drowning in blood."

"Maybe you can't bring the dead back," she said agitatedly. "But you are doing something good about the land. *We* are. Aren't we?" Don't spoil it for me, Springfield. *We* are.

"So what happens when I die? Some developer will axe every tree, put up wall to wall horse boxes."

"Hey! Remember what you said about the moment *now*?"

"Trees aren't for the moment."

Subtle as a haemorrhage she began to seep away, OD'd, free fall, a drained thing spinning. Her footsteps echoed on the hollow wrung globe.

Help me, Angus!

The hand holding his uneaten sandwich was shaking. She laughed her hard little Jules-laugh. "What's wrong? Got that headache again?" Cunning with fear, skilful with cunning, she took hold of his shoulders. "Relax, I'll massage your neck. If you won't try the forehead thing yourself, let me have a go at your shoulders. Hey, relax! I'm good at it."

Her fingers were clever with men's taut muscles. She held fast to her fingers.

"Relax, relax," she kept telling him. And to herself: it's okay, you're here, you're here, Gita, it's okay. "Relax, Angus. Don't be so jumpy."

He twisted around to look at her. "God, Gita! Relax! D'you think I'm made of stone!"

"No," she said. "I don't." And then under her breath: "Hey! It's all right. I'm clean, I'm clean. I've had all the tests."

"Christ! . . . So have I — it isn't that." He dropped his head forward, rested it against her breast. He could hear her heart: a-live, a-live, a-live. Don't laugh at me, he begged her. Because he had this horror . . . whenever he got close to someone . . . brought death . . .

Not to me, Angus. Not to me.

You can't kill something that's already dead.

I'm a shell, Angus. A shell. A husk. Oh, I'm clever, when I'm with you, you think I'm alive. When I'm with Crystal . . . or Jules . . . When I'm with Jules . . .

I'm dead, Jules. Dead. Dead. Dead.

You seem bent on convincing me, my dear. So what does it matter? Spread your legs, my dear. One can't harm someone who's already dead

Oh Jesus, Angus!

She flung out her arms and he grasped her, hesitantly at first, not quite believing, then frantically as he began kissing her, her throat, her ears, her eyes . . . opened his mouth over hers so hungrily that she thought he's starving, he's like a man who doesn't care what's on his plate.

They sank on to his coat, knocking the thermos over and spilling the rest of the hot water.

"Hey," she said gently.

She drew a small packet out of the worn pocket of her leather jacket. "Better use one."

"Here?" he said. "Now?" Still not believing. But holding her closer.

"It's a nice day for it."

"You're unbelievable." He laughed shakily. "Kiss me."

"A hussy, you mean?" She was laughing herself, pulling off her jumper and bunching it under her head, unzipping her jeans.

He opened the packet. "No. Wonderful — unpredictable — I don't know . . . Kiss me!"

"Next time," she said, wincing as she sat up and rubbed her shoulder, "Next time we won't go pioneering. And we'll take our time — if you want to, that is."

"If I want to! You're unbelievable," he said again, holding her quietly now, breathing in the good smell of her, feeling the texture of her skin. Unbelievable, he kept thinking. His glasshouse girl.

46 Bandicootin'

Back in the utility, as the engine warmed, he said wonderingly "You know, I can't quite believe this."

"Jesus, Angus, you sound like you've never screwed before!"

She was joking. But when he didn't answer, she turned and looked at him. He was staring through the windscreen. Leaning forward, she put her hand on his knee to massage it. His hand closed over hers and held it so that her fingers couldn't move.

"Could be." He turned and smiled at her. "Oh — there are such blokes." Phil Reynolds his neighbour, maybe.

"What do they do instead? Use a milk bottle?"

"Work! Work till they drop!" Phil Reynolds.

"Is that what you've been doing?"

"No. You saw me. Mooching around in the glasshouse getting nothing done."

"Well, now you are. We are."

He turned her captive hand over and again smoothed the fingers open. "I'm no good on my own. You saw that. I need to be with someone. Work with them. People need friends."

"That's for sure."

"Someone they can trust."

"Someone they can trust," she repeated.

He drove out a gate at the other end of the flats and along some of the back roads. They left the bitumen, winding higher along narrow gravel roads with glimpses between the trees of farmhouses nestling into the hillsides.

"Good potato country," he commented. They didn't talk much. At last he pulled off the road where it curved steeply and began to drop away again, flattening out to the south where pewter clouds shone dully.

"Melbourne," he said. "We'll come up here one night and look at the glow."

She laughed, thinking about the spotlighting and other things he'd promised. "I'll have to remind you."

He thought she meant she was eager to come. "Miss it, do you?"

"City life?" She considered: her songs for the gigs. Mark and her, working over and over them. How about this way? Maybe. No. Hey! I've got it! Mark was good, when he wasn't spun out. "Miss it? Sometimes. No, not really. Things didn't work out for me there, Angus."

She glanced at him: *maybe now, tell him now* . . . but he was smiling, thinking about something else.

He said "Tell me something."

"No promises. What?"

"When we set out —"

"Mmm? When we set out?" She looked at him, smiling lazily. "You ask a lot of questions, don't you?"

He leaned across and kissed her.

No, now wasn't the time to tell him about something that hadn't worked out a lifetime ago.

They stopped to buy new potatoes advertised at a small weatherboard house hidden behind a clipped cypress hedge. An old woman whose face was as wrinkled and brown as a seed potato took them over to the big shed where the potato crop was bagged.

"My son grows the best spuds in the district," she boasted as Gita handed her several dollars from Angus's wallet.

Gita glanced carefully over the change the old woman fumbled from the pocket of her faded apron.

"Grows them up in the hills, does he?"

The old woman began to laugh. She laughed silently around shrunken gums and blackened teeth. "Huh! I'm not tellin'. If I let on where they're growin', you might come back one night the pair of you and go bandicootin'. Eh? Mightn't you?" She went on laughing. She was enjoying herself. "You don't know what I mean by that, do you? Bandicootin'?"

Gita watched Angus lump the heavy bag out to the utility. She watched him turn, ease it on to the tray. He smiled, catching her eye.

"Digging them up, I guess," she murmured.

"Not diggin', girl. Not diggin' with a spade. With your bare hands. See?" She scrabbled in the air with her wizened hands. "Bandicootin'!" And she laughed, out loud this time. As they drove slowly from the shed to the road, they could hear her laughing and talking to herself all the way back to her house.

"Bandicootin'," Gita said, laughing herself as she picked out several of the red potatoes to scrub for dinner. Some of them were an odd shape, and she laughed again as she took them into the glasshouse where Angus was looking at the seedlings.

"This one is you," she told him, setting the potatoes out along the bench. "Obviously." She ran her fingertip over the protuberance.

Angus grinned. "Then this has to be you . . . Hey, what's up?"

"Here's me again. See this lump? Me and Jarrah, that has to be Jarrah."

He put his arm around her. "You're missing him?"

She shook her head. "He's better off with his father. I hope the poor little bugger's okay, that's all."

Later, when he went inside to give her a hand with dinner, he suggested that she ring Jarrah's father to find out.

"Yeah. I should do that. Except I don't have his number."

"Ask Information. The phonebook's there on the bench." As she hesitated: "You know his name, don't you? His surname, I mean?"

"Sure. I know his name." But she did no more about it, just left it at that, and Angus, intoxicated by their sudden leap over unbridgeable chasms, forgot about a kid that wasn't anything to do with him.

47 The Age-old Dance

"Let's use the rug in that big bedroom," she said, and he was jolted: next time was now. "Eh? Screw on that patterned rug in front of the fire. After dinner. Let's. You get a good blaze going while I cook these potatoes. Otherwise —" she turned and grinned mischievously — "one of us'll get a cold bum again." As he hesitated, she added "Baked cheese potatoes — how does that grab you?"

"All right."

"Don't you like cheese potatoes?"

"Yes I do. I mean I've never had them. I mean — that's fine. That room'll be fine. Just fine." He kissed the back of her neck, and felt a tremor run through her. "I'll go and see to the fire . . . Hope the chimney's not blocked." Her sly response startled him. "*What* did you say?" he said.

She laughed. "You heard me."

At the doorway of the double bedroom he hesitated. Why this room? He became frantically busy, dumping the spare furniture in the hall, lighting a roaring fire, airing the bed. As he selected the smoothest sheets from the linen press he recalled her crude joke just now, and smiled.

"You don't shave your legs."

"That's right. Do you?"

"Just an observation! They're always covered by jeans or black stockings or something."

"So you wondered, did you?"

"Yes."

"What else did you wonder?"

"All sorts of things."

"And now you don't have to wonder any more."

"Looks like, doesn't it?"

"You approve, then?"

"What do you think?"

"I think you do. But I can't tell whether *you* shave *your* legs, can I, if you don't drop your trousers . . . My God, Angus, your knee!"

"That? An accident. Years ago."

"Some accident. Car? Tractor? Did the tractor roll on you?" She recalled how, in the utility, his hand had refused to let hers touch that knee.

"Something like that."

She knelt down and kissed the scar, the hollows, the lumpy tissue. Head against his thigh, absorbed as when music-making, she drew sure fingers upwards, over his hip's sharpness, into the soft skin of his groin.

"Like a candle," she murmured. "Hey? Like a flaring candle."

"Flaring's right."

He dropped to his good knee and let his own hands resume their inspection. Gita's body: a farm that before today he'd only been able to look over from the roadside. Slender, firm, as he'd imagined . . . hardy. His hands moved slowly. We'll take our time, she'd said. Firelight turned her skin shining and golden. Like the sweet potatoes on that farm at Mareeba, he told her. Ever seen them when they're fresh out of the ground? Not like the stuff you get down south.

She laughed. Her hands began again: his scarred knee, the long sweeps upwards. Cupping him with her delicious fingers, she said "And now I've got that candle holder. You wouldn't let me have it, would you, remember?" She sat back from him. "Holding a flaming candle." She laughed again, a lazy laugh as knowing as her fingers. "I could look at you all night."

"Don't make me wait all night."

She rolled away. "Come here, then."

She ran her hands over his back, exploring with her fingertips muscles grown lean and strong with outdoor work. She slipped her hand between their two joined bodies and felt where he disappeared inside herself, smooth, neat, two little half-chicks — *careful*, Gita! You're going over the top.

"What are you doing?" he murmured.

"Thinking."

"With your fingers?"

"How else do people think when they're screwing?"

He pulled her closer. "Why do you call it screwing? It's the wrong movement."

"What do you call it, then?"

"Oh, I can think of several good old farming terms."

"You would."

"Kiss me."

She grasped his buttocks; he heard her breath snag. She began muttering to herself, as she had up on the hill.

And at the same instant shrieked, pushed him away, sat up.

"What is it?" If he hadn't held on to her, she would have leapt right away. "Gita! Tell me! What's the matter?"

"That noise! That noise!"

Kkh-ck-ck-ck-ck, kkh, kkh-ck-ck-ck.

"What noise?"

"Can't you hear it? Listen, Angus, listen!" Kkh-ck-ck, kkkkh, kkh-ck-ck-ck. *Sometimes you're not very smart about your contacts, my dear* Jules's mocking laughter. "It's over here too!"

"That? That's just a possum. Up on the roof."

"A *possum*?"

"Yes. Hey! It's all right, come on now, calm down. Just a ringtail," he soothed. "Like the one we saw the other evening near the cottage, remember? Telling another ringtail to get the hell out of his territory."

"Are you sure?" She couldn't stop shaking. He was shaking himself. She clutched his arm. "That noise — over at Marycote — it scared the shit out of me."

"Why on earth didn't you tell me?"

"I thought maybe . . . " She stared, caught in the glare of the unspoken words . . . all in my head.

"*Gita.* Possums, just possums. That first afternoon I came over to the cottage, didn't I show you the ringtail I found in the ceiling? I should have."

"Yes, you should have." She tried to push him away. "I want to go home."

"Gita! You're all right, you're safe. You're with me."

She shook her head.

"You can't just leave me like that! For Christ's sake! Is it this room?" This bloody room!

But she wouldn't say, just went on insisting she go home, home.

"And if you hear the same noise there?"

She said nothing, gazing around the walls and the high ceiling of the bedroom as though they were insubstantial.

He sighed. "All right, I'll take you home." She hadn't said she would stay all night: it was he who had assumed . . . hoped. He leaned forward, pouring frenzied kisses over her belly, her breasts, her face. "At least let's finish this, let's finish, then we'll go. *Please*, Gita. Put your arms round me." She sank down; they began again the age-old dance of lovers.

When he drew away she lay there wide-eyed, listening, scarcely aware of him. Oh God. He shouldn't have insisted. He should have taken her home straightaway. But it was only a bloody ringtail!

At Marycote he said "Will I stay here with you?"

She shook her head, as he knew she would.

He nodded. "Well . . ." What could he say now? Thanks? It's been a good day? Sleep well?

She was standing under the carved name, Marycote, the door open, her hand on the latch. "Angus —"

"Yes?" he said eagerly.

She leaned against him for a moment. A-live, a-live, a-live. Only a possum, she kept telling herself. Only a possum, going about its possum business, chattering at some intruder. "Good night." She shut the door.

48   Crack Shot

The fire in the double bedroom was still blazing when he returned to Springfield. Better wait till it dies down, he thought, anyway I can't sleep now. He opened a new bottle of Scotch. When he woke some hours later, startled by a loud noise, he was lying across the kitchen table. There was a slithering and scampering across the roof. Christ! That bloody possum! He stood up, steadied himself against the table for a moment, then took his rifle from behind the kitchen door, a round from the bench amongst the heap of papers, and went quietly outside. *Green moonlight* Noiselessly, keeping to the shadows, he edged around the house. The possum was on the ridge, black against the white sky. He raised the rifle, took careful aim, fired. And heard, as it fell almost at his feet, the rattle of the dogs' chains as Bess and Shep fled into their kennels.

He knelt over the possum. The long tail with the silver tip was still. There was a thick oozing patch on its head. He stood up again, ashamed, sickened. He'd been living with possums for years. He went over to the shed, speaking gently to Bess and Shep on the way, and found a hessian bag in which to wrap the dead animal. After placing it in the laundry, he went inside and huddled in his bed in the maid's room where wild dreams tormented him.

Next day he was up early, found a spot under a gum tree to bury the poor stiff corpse, hurried around his ewes then walked down to Marycote and knocked on the back door.

After some moments he heard her voice on the other side of the door, and his heart thumped like a kid's.

"Who is it?"

"Me. Angus."

He heard the door being unlocked, and then she stood there in the doorway, her hair hanging in uncombed loops around her face, her oversize jumper reaching half way down her thighs, her legs and feet bare.

He waited for her to ask him in. When she said nothing, he said "I came to see if you were all right."

She nodded, pushing the heavy hair off her face. "Fine. Just not awake, that's all."

"Sorry. Got you out of bed, did I?"

"It's early, isn't it?"

"Gita . . . I'm sorry about last night."

She shrugged. "Don't worry about it."

"I wanted you to stay."

Again she nodded, but whether she meant yes you did, or yes so did I, he couldn't tell.

He dropped his gaze. Below the sloppy jumper her feet and knees were blotched with cold. He thought of the lovely body by the fire last night; wanted to draw her against him, run his hands under the clumsy jumper, feel the smooth skin warm to his touch as it had last night before that bloody possum got in his way.

"Maybe . . ." he began, then hesitated. She was looking at him from such a great distance. Maybe we can try again, he wanted to say. "Maybe you could give me a hand in the plantation over the next day or two," was what he said. And turned away, wincing as his knee protested at the sudden wrench.

49 The Girls Don't Care

When she didn't turn up at the plantation he wasn't surprised, but all the same he returned early to the glasshouse. Maybe she'd be there. Might have been there. She knew what to do. For three days he worked like a madman in the plantation, for three days flung down his tools mid-afternoon and hurried back to Springfield. Well, that's how it goes, he thought, as the empty glasshouse mocked him. I've thought really hard about someone and suddenly there they were. Load of old codswallop. Better to be like Phil Reynolds — what had she said? — use a milk bottle. He laughed. She had a nice way of putting things. It's a fine day for it. Was that all she'd wanted: the moment? Why hope for anything else? Then he told himself he'd rushed her, up there amongst the rocks. Frightened her off. No: offended her. He knew what such women said — he'd had it thrown at him up north, hadn't he? That coastal woman's voice was as clear as though she were there at his elbow — or underneath him. You men just want to be serviced. You've got it the wrong way, he'd joked, stung nevertheless. It's the bull that services the cow. She hadn't laughed.

> They ache with lust
>   the girls
> lift glass-green, grass-green skirts
> the girls don't care

So what happens? He gets all stirred up again wanting to root some obliging woman, drinks too much, shoots a harmless bloody possum —

50   And Then She Turns Up

— and then she turns up, Gita, she just bloody turns up as though nothing has happened, shakes the mist out of her hair and says "Thought we might have a cup of tea . . . Ocker or camomile?"

"Ocker," he said, his head thumping again. God, he was a fool sometimes!

51 Mulberry Cycle

> As green as love
>   as leaves
>   as glass
> the girls appear
> *Gita! Gita!*
> lift glass-green, grass-green skirts
>   they ache with lust
> *Gita!*

"Gita! Gita!"
The dulcimer clattered to the floor.
"Jarrah! How did you get here?"
"Train. And hitched. Hey! That's a mulberry tree out there, did you know? Can we have silkworms?"
"Jarrah!" She shook his arm. "You didn't tell them, did you? You didn't leave any notes around saying this was where you were headed?"

52 Loud as a Heartbeat

He stood up to ease his back, and saw a child coming towards him.
face lifted in welcome
loud as a heartbeat the pattering steps
Angus stared.
The child kept coming.
He didn't do a thing about it.
fucking-well serves you
"I'm Jarrah," said the child.
Angus breathed. Gita's boy. "Jarrah, eh? . . . Where's your mother today?"
The child shrugged. "She's coming."
Angus glanced down the paddock, but could see no sign of her. "Talking to your father, is she?"
"Nuh."

With the tree spade he made a neat hole the size of a seedling tube. "I'm Angus."

"I know. She told me."

"Oh? Did she?" What else did she tell you, I wonder. "Been here a few days, have you?" That would account for her absence these last three days, but why on earth hadn't she said . . . let him know . . .

The child looked at him oddly. "I just got here, didn't I?"

"Oh? . . . How *did* you get here?"

"Walked." The child looked bemused. "You saw me. I walked up the hill where you've been digging."

Talking at cross-purposes. Angus splashed water into the hole he'd just dug. "I mean from Melbourne. With your father?" That would explain things, too.

"He doesn't know I'm here. I just left."

Jarrah! She grabbed his arm and really pinched him. As though he was dumb enough to go leaving notes around!

"I didn't tell no one," Jarrah explained all over again. "I came by train and then I hitched."

Angus said nothing, just shook a seedling in its wad of soil free of its plastic tube and dropped it neatly into the hole.

"Don't you want to know how I knew where to find her?" the boy prompted.

"I can see you're bursting to tell me."

"I guessed!"

"You what?"

"I caught a bus and a tram over to Gita's place and Mark was there and so was Jules and they said they didn't know where she was and I'd better go back to my father's or they'd call the cops. So I went up the street and I rang Crystal and she didn't know either – they all thought she was at my father's with me. So then I just worked it out."

Angus put down the tree spade. "You worked out she was here?"

Jarrah nodded two or three times, basking in the man's disbelief. "Want to know how? That last time me and her left her place, she asked my father to let her off at Spencer Street Station. She had Mark's bike with her and everything. And I remembered the name. Spencer Street. That's the station for country trains. And the only town in the country me and her'd ever been to was Currawong. I remembered Currawong too." He waited.

"*Did* you?" Angus whistled.

Satisfied with this response, the child continued. "So I got a train timetable and I found Currawong on it and then I bought a ticket, my father's always giving me money — his girlfriend goes mad, she goes don't do that don't do that, you're spoiling him rotten, what about me — and I got off at Currawong and then I asked where this place was. This place," the child repeated, pausing to let Angus appreciate this. "I could remember all the names, Springfield, Valley View Park, Mary something or other — and a man called Phil said he was coming out this way and he give me a lift."

"My God!" Angus shook his head. "She must have been surprised to see you." A horrible thought struck him. "So what are you two going to do now? Pack up again?"

Jarrah shrugged. "Dunno. Play with those kids I met the first time, I guess."

"The Catchpole boys?"

"I don't know what they're called. Anyway, here's Gita."

Angus looked up, startled. She was standing beside him. While he was intent on the child's saga she had come up on his deaf side. Willed into being.

She smiled, but mostly at the boy.

"*Gita.*"

She turned to him.

"Thought we might all have a cup of tea up here, Angus. Seeing you weren't at the house."

And you just went into the kitchen and prepared it! He watched her take teabags and a small jar of milk and a plastic cup from the pockets of Belle's old oilskin, unscrew the two cups from the thermos, set them out against a tussock. "Ocker or camomile, Angus?" she was saying. "Jarrah? I didn't know you'd bought herbal tea, Angus." He couldn't take his eyes off those thin capable fingers; he could feel them still . . . massaging his shoulders, stroking his balls.

He gripped the tree spade. "Is this all true?"

"Sure. Resourceful kid, huh?"

"Like his mother."

Gita ignored that. Maybe she hadn't heard. She was too busy smiling at the kid again.

"I missed you," Angus ventured, "those days you didn't come over."

She nodded, and said in her vague way "I've had things to do. Catch up with."

"She's got a new song," the boy said proudly.

"Maybe she'll sing it later?"

She, she. "Maybe." Gita looked cross.

Jarrah thought the song wasn't ready, Angus, ready with a quip, didn't notice. "... *see* what *happens.*" He said it at the same time as she did. He caught her eye. They both laughed.

Jarrah, watching, narrowed his eyes.

Later, back in the man's big kitchen where that girl had pinched the stone axehead, Jarrah overheard the man say "Aren't you going to let his father know he's here?"

Jarrah's toes felt funny. They went soft like that cheese he had to eat at his father's. Why did Angus want Gita to do that? Didn't he want him here? Gita said he would. Gita said he was okay.

"Let him sweat," Gita said. "I mean that. The kid's had a rotten time there. His live-in girlfriend gave the poor little guy a really hard time."

His live-in girlfriend ... Angus was amused at the contempt she put into that phrase. "Even so ... they won't just say oh Jarrah didn't come home tonight, too bad, what's on telly, will they?"

"Won't they? That sod'll be so glad to be free of the responsibility he'd do anything."

"Well, it's your business ... but my bet is he'll call the police."

"He wouldn't do that! ... Would he?"

"Look, if it was me I'd give the boy's father a ring. They can't trace the call, Gita. Just say Jarrah's with you, everything's fine, and then there'll be no police, no publicity —"

"Publicity! Other people finding out!"

"Are you two fighting?" Jarrah muttered.

Gita threw her arms around him and held him tight. "No, mate. We're fine here. Just fine. Nothing's going to happen. Is it, Angus?"

Angus shook his head.

"I'm going to have a go on my skateboard." Jarrah pulled free. "And if you tell my father I'm here I'll just run away again."

He went outside. Angus turned to Gita. He wanted to put his arms around her as she had put hers around the boy, say it's okay, you really are safe, you're safe with me, Gita . . . and so is the boy, of course. But she wouldn't meet his eye, or if she did, just looked vague. Eventually she came up to him and said "Would you? . . . Or Jarrah could."

"Would I what?"

"Ring him. Ring Jarrah's father."

"Gita! He'd think I was a kidnapper or a child murderer or something. Or if Jarrah talked to him, that I was standing there twisting his arm . . . Well, as I said . . . it's your affair. But if you want to, you know where the phonebook is."

He went out to the glasshouse and fiddled about with the watering can. I'll be damned if I'm going to get involved in other people's messes. Kids' messes. God knows my own life is mess enough.

After a while the child came into the glasshouse.

"Angus!"

"What?"

"There's nowhere to ride a skateboard round here."

"Isn't there?"

"The ground's too rough . . . Angus!"

Angus looked up. The boy looked troubled. Poor little bugger. Under each eye was a blue half-moon. "Have you tried the verandah, son?"

He moved a couple of the punnets, pulled out a dead seedling. When he went back to the house, Gita was on the verandah watching the boy ride the skateboard.

As he opened his mouth to say — what? did you get through? does he want the boy? does he want you? — the boy swooped up on the skateboard.

"Want to have a go, Angus?"

"He never lets anyone ride his skateboard," Gita told him. "What have you done?"

"God knows. I'm pretty useless when it comes to kids. Or women."

"Is that right?" she said.

Her face was expressionless. Perhaps she thought he was fishing.

The skateboard plunged at them, stopped dead. "I'm going in to the kitchen to watch the Cosby Kids," the boy said, displaying the heavy watch on his wrist.

"We're going home now," Gita said firmly.

"Everything okay?" Angus asked her casually, indicating the kitchen . . . the telephone.

She nodded.

And that was all she ever told him about the matter of Jarrah's guardianship. But the boy remained with her at Marycote. He came over to Springfield when she did, turned on the telly without asking; fiddled with the things in the glasshouse — or might fiddle; threw a frisbee around in the garden until Angus yelled because it landed on the roof.

53   Jarrah at Springfield

"He doesn't say much, does he?"

Gita gave him a quick hug. "He's all right."

"He's got a lamb in the shed."

"Did he let you feed it?"

"Nuh. The sheep was feeding it. Why's he got it in the shed, d'you think?"

"Didn't you ask him?"

"Yeah, but he just walked away."

"You should have asked him again."

"I did."

"He's a bit deaf, Jarrah. It's a weak lamb, probably, or the mother is. He puts them out in the paddock after a day or two."

"Guess what else he's got in the shed?"

"Couldn't. What?"

"In the garage part. Behind the big doors."

"Mercedes? Mirror? Hang glider?"

"Nuh."

"Give up."

"He's got a tractor."

"Reckon you could drive it?"

"Sure."

"Better not try. It mightn't be the same as the other one."

"At that place? At the nursery?"

"Mmm."

"It isn't. It's bigger. Much bigger. That was just a toy tractor for mowing the gardens. But I'm bigger now, aren't I? Anyway all tractors are the same. You don't know nothing about tractors, Gita. I was good, wasn't I? I was good at driving that tractor? I was the best, out of all the kids at that place that had a go, I was the best, wasn't I? Gita?"

Gita sighed. "Yeah. You were the best."

54 Ocker or Herbal?

He said "I've told you, there's no need to pull out that stuff by hand. It's all going to be sprayed like the rest. Gita! Why are you bothering?"

That wasn't what he wanted to say.

He wanted to say Gita, I'm not Phil Reynolds. He wanted to say . . . when you came back here with mist like gemstones in your hair, saying "Thought we might have a cup of tea, Angus", it was as if time stopped that day you said "We'll take a picnic into the country" and everything that followed never happened. You haven't made one reference.

And I haven't dared . . . He touched her shoulder briefly. But I know that body, under that jumper and the jeans and the red gumboots, I know you, Gita.

He said "Gita . . . maybe we could try again?"

She stood up, a heap of horehound in her hand. "Try fucking again, you mean?"

Christ! There was more expression in her voice when she said "Ocker or herbal?"

He glanced around. The boy was stalking a magpie down the other end of the plantation.

"It would be better next time," he pleaded.

"Would it?" She slid away, water over a creek stone.

"You'll see what happens, will you?" He couldn't keep the sarcasm out of his voice. She knelt again, and he watched her hands scrabbling amongst weeds and stones. "If you don't want to tear your nails to pieces, put on a pair of gloves!"

55   He Says, He Does

"He swore at me!"

"You swore at him."

"And he yelled."

"Course he did. He's told you, hasn't he, don't touch his things in the shed? And what did you do? You took that horrible sharp butcher's knife he uses for cutting up the dogs' meat, and you started chucking it about outside. Against rocks."

"He didn't need've yelled."

"No. He shouldn't have done that, Jarrah."

"Hey! I didn't mind! . . . Guess what, he said I can help him burn a big heap of cypress logs. He says cypress is no good for firewood, it just spits, he says. Even with the fireguard. So he's going to burn it in the paddock as soon as he gets round to pushing the heap together. That's what he does with cypress, he says — Why d'you reckon he wouldn't take me round the lambs this afternoon like he usually does, Gita? He's an old grump."

"He, he, he!"

"Don't you like him?"

"Look, do you think you could do something to help with dinner instead of just giving me a headache with all that yakking?"

"Don't you like him? Gita, don't you like him?"

She gave one of her long sighs. "He's okay."

56 Zap!

"Zap! You're dead!" Jarrah flung himself into the sitting room. "Zap!" He grinned, laying the stick carefully across a chair, then picking it up again. "Don't you go burning this ray gun. Will you?"

Gita, lying on the sofa, looked at him tiredly. "Where in hell have you been! I've been wondering all bloody day. I can't take the hassle, Jarrah, I just can't, you know that, you selfish little sod."

"Don't start screamin' or I'll run away. I told you I was sick of going with you. There's nothing to do over there. Just sticking silly plants in the ground. There's nowhere to ride the skateboard except the verandah and he gets mad if I go back to the house by myself. He's scared I'll bust something."

"Well where *have* you been?"

"Playing with those boys."

"Who? The Catchpole boys? They'd have been at school in Currawong. Weren't they at school? Listen Jarrah, if you're having me on . . ."

"Ow! Let go! Jeez you've got sharp fingers! I was with that old lady till they came home on the bus if you want to know."

"With old Mary Springfield? She'd have sent you packing!"

"No she wouldn't! She made me brandy things with cream in them. Here – she sent this over to you. For tea. I told her you felt too sick to look after me so could she. And she said she wanted to come straight over to see you but I said you didn't want anyone, you had to be by yourself."

"Jesus, Jarrah, you're a number one story-teller!" Gita laughed: they'd think she meant alone with Angus.

"Well you *were* sick yesterday. You said don't pester me Jarrah you're making my head scream Jarrah. Didn't you? You did, didn't you? You're dead!"

"Will you stop pointing that thing!"

"Elton's got a gun. Zap! Zap!"

"Stop it, Jarrah."

"You should see Elton's new ray gun. Can I have a ray gun?"

"No . . . Tell me more about Valley View Park. Who else was there? Did you see Mrs Catchpole? What's she like?"

"Cranky."

"What did you do?"

"Nothing. She was cranky with the old lady, wasn't she? She goes is this another one of your good works, Mary, and Mary goes by my deeds shall ye know me. And then she had a fight with Mr Catchpole."

"Who? Mrs Catchpole?"

"No, the old lady. She got me to throw some old biscuits on to the compost heap, and Mr Catchpole said what are you throwing away there – no, first of all he said who are you, and I told him, and *then* he said –"

"Yeah: what are you throwing away there, and *you* said – and then what did he do? Hey! He didn't thump you or anything, did he?"

"Course he didn't. He goes rushing into the house in his gumboots and the old lady goes (here Jarrah wailed) oh Lou my lovely clean floor! and *he* goes bugger your floor Mary, what do you mean by putting biscuits in the compost, we've got more mice in the house than we can deal with this cold weather. And *she* goes then in that case, Lou, biscuits in the compost might encourage them to stay outside."

Gita laughed. "So what else happened?"

"Mary's got a dog. It chews rocks. She doesn't like it much. She said I could have it –"

"Oh did she! Thanks very much, Mary!"

Jarrah said hastily "It was digging up her best bulbs and she said she wished someone would just take it. We could, couldn't we? I'd rather have a bantam, though. Jane's got bantams, Gita."

"Has she?" Gita said absently.

"They've got silver patterns on their feathers and they're very special, Jane says. Elton says she never looks after them unless someone yells at her, but. How can I get a silver bantam, Gita?"

"Don't ask me. You're the smart guy." She picked up the dulcimer. " 'Oh my little aubergine!' "

"Mary says I could go to school."

"She did, did she!"

"She says Currawong school's nice, Elton and Keiran go there, she said are you still playing the dulcimer, the school's always looking out for mums and dads for Friday activities."

"I'll murder you, Jarrah."

"Angus has got a gun."

"I know he's got a gun. It's for rabbits and foxes."

"Mary says it's all right if you don't point a gun *at* someone."

Gita sighed. "It's the same thing. You know what people use guns for? To kill other people. It's horrible."

"She said I could visit her again."

"Well just don't wear out your welcome, hotshot. Okay?"

57 When Jarrah Didn't Return

Next day, when Jarrah didn't return to Valley View Park, Mary hesitated about calling in at the cottage to see if Gita was feeling better. The boy had been so insistent she wanted to be left alone. Mary decided to pop in at Springfield instead. Angus might know. And he could tell her what he'd like for his birthday. Mary had a long list of people in the district whose special days she liked to remember. She'd already added her new friend at Marycote; poor little mite; yesterday when Mary made brandy snaps, he told her he'd never had a grandma before. She'd hugged him them. The memory brought tears to her eyes. As she went to put her arm around him, he'd flinched — as though he expected people to hit him. Who? Surely not his mother? The girl was much too . . . tolerant, was the word Mary selected from half a dozen less charitable adjectives. His father, then? The boy never talked about a father. Just like me, Mary thought. How could I? Mother wouldn't say a word, not a single word. Mary blew her nose, and spoke to old Shep as she went into the garden.

She was pleased to find Gita busy in the glasshouse. Recovered, then. Angus greeted Mary warmly, just as he always did, but Gita . . . Mary couldn't make it out . . . the girl was so pleasant that day at the doctor's, a real friend-in-need . . . but now! Was it something Mary had done? But what? Burst in on the middle of some special chat with Angus, perhaps? She went over what had been said. Good morning, Angus . . . and he'd looked really pleased. Relieved, even. Mary! Long time no see! . . . Good morning, Gita. Hi, Mary. Are you feeling quite well again, Gita? Fine thanks, just fine, thanks for entertaining Jarrah. (That flat tone!) You don't want to overdo things, Gita, don't let Angus drive you the way he drives himself . . . And then something about what she was wearing . . . that *is* a nice dress, Gita; going somewhere special, are you? That was all right, wasn't it? A question after that to Angus about the plants, and he'd spent a few minutes showing her the different sorts they'd been putting in plastic tubes, egg-and-bacons and mintbushes, lovely things to attract the birds. He was always so patient with a forgetful old woman. Next, to Gita: And how's my little friend today? Gita must have thought she said where's my little friend. This was Mary's first inkling that she'd done something wrong because first of all Gita stared and then she said in that awful what-business-is-it-of-yours voice: Not here, is he. And then the hunched shoulder like a fist in the face.

I wasn't meaning to pry, you silly girl.

Mary didn't say that bit, of course. Dreadful things she'd *like* to say just jumped into her mind. She turned away to

Angus who was looking . . . concerned? puzzled? and said, a little more stiffly than she meant, "I can see you're busy, Angus, I won't hold you up any more, I just popped in about your birthday. Can you think of something you'd like, dear?"

Angus was one who received a little present as well as a card. Even when he'd been away she'd always sent a small something care of his leasing agent in the hope that it would find him somehow. He'd never said anything when he got back, and she hadn't liked to ask. He might think she was looking for thanks.

"Some little thing you wouldn't bother getting for yourself?" she added.

"Mary! There's no need . . ."

"But I like to, dear."

Angus thought for a while. "How about a pair of socks?"

Men always said socks. Mary laughed. The prickle over Gita disappeared. "Socks! That's not very exciting."

"It's just what I want — what I'd like, I mean. Wool. Not too lairy."

"Well of course wool, dear."

Angus gave her a warm hug. "You're a good pal, Mary. You'll have to remind me when it's your birthday."

"*My* birthday!" Mary laughed, then protested, brushing Angus's hands from her coat collar. "Angus! Don't you dare put dirt —!"

"Soil, Mary, soil. Lovely healthy soil."

"Soil or dirt, it's all the same on my collar." She threw a quick forgiving smile at the girl, half hidden behind the squall of hair. "And when's your birthday, Gita?"

The girl didn't look up, just mumbled "My *birthday*!"

There was a small silence.

"Well, that's settled then, Angus," Mary said brightly. She was on her way back to Valley View Park, where Lou would be expecting his hot dinner dished up, but all the same she hesitated. She was dying to look inside the house. "You certainly look busy," she repeated. Angus smiled; the girl said nothing. "How about if I make you a cup of tea?"

"Sure, go right ahead. You know where everything is."

"You don't mind if I make myself at home, dear?"

Angus glanced at her, puzzled. "Of course not, Mary."

The kitchen was a real mess. Mary set to with brooms, ash bucket, dusters.

58 Dreams in Your Veins

Men! Expecting you to wait on them

As soon as Mary was out of the glasshouse Gita said "Doing her womanly work as all good women should."

"Who – Mary?"

"Yes – Mary!"

each time you say no, it's easier next time

Angus laughed. "What's your grouch with Mary?"

"Fussing over birthdays. Rushing off to the kitchen." Looking after Jarrah. Bloody asking where he is *cull for the sheep ship* You selfish little sod, Jarrah, I can't take the hassle, I just can't take any more hassle.

"Mary enjoys it," Angus protested. "And when Mary does something, she doesn't do it by halves. No holding back with Mary."

open up you don't open up much spread your legs my dear I didn't let him touch me, Crystal

"It's true, Gita! You had a taste of her generosity yourself, didn't you, when you first came?"

She sighed. Yes, and yesterday too, when she sent a pie back with Jarrah.

"So what's the problem, Gita?" *Answer me, Belle!* "Just what's the problem?"

cull for the sheep ship I need nothing from you cull for the sheep ship I don't need anyone "All this . . . this . . . caring and nurturing," she muttered at last.

"So that's it, is it?" He gave a short laugh. "And what's wrong with a bit of caring and nurturing?" Her silence riled him *golden-girl Belle* he was getting nowhere *you had to be quick you survived through surprise* "Anyway, who says women have the monopoly on caring and nurturing? Eh? Who says? Women, I suppose. Women like you have a monopoly on truth, too, don't they? . . . Cat got your tongue?"

Later, going over and over what followed, he scratched at the thought till it bled: Why the hell couldn't I have left it at that? *So you got what you deserved, didn't you?*

"Gita! I *said* what's wrong with caring and nurturing?"

She muttered something at the bench.

"What? I didn't catch that."

I don't need anyone She raised her voice. "The female role. I *said* the female role. As − defined − by *men*!"

The bitterness jarred him *fucking-well serves you latched on to Catchpole* He laughed harshly. "That's not the female role."

He was sure she would look up eventually. And she did. "So?" she said coolly. "You tell me what it is then. What is it, Angus?"

"You really need to ask?" *You of all people* "You?"

Crystal! Crystal! I didn't let him touch me! He saw her lips curl in triumph as though she'd just proved something.

"What a shit you are, Angus."

"So what have I said now that's got your hackles up?"

"You really need to ask?" she mocked. "You?"

He flung away, his elbow catching the box of seedlings they had just finished potting. She laughed as it fell to the floor. He slammed out of the glasshouse. Mary − he'd go and see how Mary was getting on. Mary didn't set people up; Mary didn't deliberately set out to drive you into a corner. He found her running up one of her batches of scones. She nodded at the brooms.

"I hope you don't mind − I could see she hasn't got around to doing in here yet, Angus."

He sat down heavily at the table. "Hasn't she? I haven't noticed."

Mary slipped the tray of scone dough into the oven. "I suppose she's not as fussy as me. Fussbutton Mary, they call me over there."

"You're very loyal, Mary."

"What do you mean?"

"Blind Freddy could see the kitchen hasn't had a broom near it in days."

She felt that for all his apparent defence of her, underneath he was rousing on her. Her eyes filled with tears. Angus, glancing up, saw her expression and jumped to his feet. "Here, come and sit down." He pulled out a chair for her. "Give you a hard time over there sometimes, do they?"

"I didn't say that, Angus. I didn't mean — "

"I know you didn't. You wouldn't. You looked a bit upset just now. That's not like you."

She smiled, wiping her eyes again. He was really the kindest person. "I don't suppose three generations ever get on well together under the one roof." She frowned. "Not these days, any shakes."

"You've always been loyal, haven't you? Look how you've stuck by . . . by Belle all this time."

"I've tried not to take sides, Angus."

He concentrated on running his thumbnail along a crack in the wooden table. "I know that."

"I don't think I was ever blind to her faults. But she needed me more than you did. She had Jane. And *he* was never easy, right from the start he wasn't easy."

Angus let that pass. "But does she need you now? You want to be careful they're not just using you over there."

"I think that's quite wrong, Angus. Quite wrong. I stay there by choice."

"Of course you do, of course you do," he soothed.

"Besides," she said, looking around helplessly, "where would I go if I wasn't there?"

"Have you ever thought of renting a little place in Currawong again? You've got lots of friends in there, lots of activities. You're always running in and out in that little blue bus of yours."

Mary sighed. "I'm not too sure how long that'll go on, either. It's getting so hard to start." She laughed. "Like me."

"The runaround?"

"Yes. Just rr-rr-rr sometimes."

"Probably nothing much. Maybe the points. I'll have a

look at it for you — don't let me forget, will you? We won't keep you off the road, Mary."

"That is good of you, dear. I was beginning to think we were done for, me and it both."

He laughed. "Not a bit of it. What you need is a holiday. Get away from things for a bit." Space, your own space, that was how Gita put it.

"A holiday? Wherever would I go?"

"Well, if it was a change you were after, you could always move over here for a bit. They say a change is as good as a holiday."

He winced when Mary said "This is a sad house for me, Angus." She had never spoken so freely about her time with him and Belle and his poor sick parents.

"We didn't make it easy for you, did we?"

"You tried, the pair of you, I'm sure you did. I know you did. Don't think I'm criticising you, or that I haven't been happy coming across to tidy up or darn a few socks. I was. Very happy. I liked to see how you were getting along. In some ways you're the son I never had." Angus looked at the floor, embarrassed. "But as for moving over here . . . I wouldn't want to do that. I couldn't live here again."

"I wasn't thinking for good, Mary," he said awkwardly. "I was thinking more for a breather. Space, you know."

"I don't think I could live in a town now, not after all this time. I'd feel . . . hemmed in. You're right about the space. How many years is it I've been living on farms? Space all round me. I've got used to it. Housekeeping for that old cousin of mine, till he passed on. Milking a cow, he was. Just went to sleep, leaning against her flank. And then to Springfield to help out while you were . . . away. It wasn't easy for a girl to look after George and Kate *and* run a farm."

Again he winced. "There was always Catchpole hanging about," he couldn't help saying.

"That's not quite fair, dear. That didn't start until you'd moved right out of the district."

"Is that what you think, Mary?"

"I'm not saying she wasn't at fault in some ways, nor Lou

either, but she was young, Angus, and lonely too, I expect. She'd been very loyal to you —"

He cut her short, saying "Because you're naturally a loyal person, you shouldn't assume the same of everyone else."

Mary changed the subject hastily. She was on her way home from a round of hospital visiting, so she said "I saw your mother this morning. She looks very well. The nurses keep her hair combed very nicely. And someone had just painted her fingernails. Very nice, though I must say bright red nails didn't seem quite like Kate."

"No. I don't ever recall Mum with painted nails. I must get in there again myself."

"Yes. Why don't you? But don't be disappointed when she doesn't know you."

Angus looked up, startled by the sharpness in her question. Someone's been giving her a hard time, all right. He sighed. What was the use of sitting with someone who didn't know you? He stood up and, putting his arm around her shoulders, said "Kettle's boiling. How about I make the tea? Camomile, rosehip, or lemongrass — like to give it a go?"

"Goodness, my scones!" Mary exclaimed, hurrying to the oven. "They'll be burned to a frazzle. Oh dear, I'll have to do another batch. If you've got time to wait?"

"If you've got time to make them, Mary."

"Of course I have. They hardly take me a minute. Dear me, Angus, I do believe you've put dirt on my dress this time, giving me a hug. Go and wash your hands!"

"Gita?" he said softly.

She looked up, her dark eyes lustreless. She had swept up the spilled soil, every crumb of it, and was busy repotting the seedlings.

"I'm sorry," he said. "I'm sorry if I said something that upset you just now."

She picked up the tweezers, placed a seedling carefully.

"I've come to apologise, Gita."

He might be talking to a stranger. "Gita! Don't be like this! Don't *do* this to me!"

She turned slowly. "Don't do this to *you*!"

"I've said I'm sorry. And I mean it. What more do you want?"

"Don't worry about it, Angus."

He couldn't bear that expressionless tone with its tinge of contempt, like fading daylight. "Mary's made some scones."

"I'm not hungry. And I've got things to do at home."

"You've worked hard here, every day, that's for sure . . . Gita —"

"Mmm?"

He couldn't stop himself. "You will come back?"

She smiled in a tired way. "I'll see what happens."

"She's gone home, Mary. She had something she had to do."

Mary wasn't disappointed at having him to herself. The girl made her nervous with her silences and her sharp looks. She wouldn't remind him about the runaround, not rightaway. No hurry about that: they'd chat over their tea a bit longer.

"I hate the idea of moving into that home," she said suddenly. "All the people seem to do there is sit around waiting to be wheeled out to the cemetery."

"But you aren't thinking of moving there yet, Mary, are you?"

"We have to think ahead, Angus."

He said suddenly "Marycote would suit you."

"There's already someone living there, Angus," she reminded him drily.

"That mightn't be for long," he said morosely, chasing a crumb with a dab of butter on the end of his knife. He looked up, then at his plate again. He couldn't bear to see the sudden hope in the old woman's eyes. "We'll see what happens, Mary. We'll just have to see what happens."

59 Spread Your Legs, My Dear

Spread your legs Of course he said it. As good as said it. If he didn't say it, he meant it. Isn't it what we've talked about so often, Gita? He's running true to type.

True to type. Yes. But what am I to do?

Do, you have to do. It isn't enough to *be*, women must *do* as much as men do.

I know that. But how can a woman *do* until she *is*? I thought here in the glasshouse I was safe . . . until with those three words he shattered me.

The bastard. Tell him to fuck off.

Yes. But then what? Crystal, Crystal, then what?

Leave that glasshouse. Forget you ever saw it. Shut the door and leave it behind you.

Yes. But where do I go? What do I do?

You come back here, of course. Come back to me. You know there's always room.

Oh . . . Crystal!

So, my dear! Who's playing a power game now? Has it never occurred to you, Gita my dear, that women play a power game as much as men do? It's the way the world wags, my dear.

Yes Jules.

At least she will be safe with me, Jules. Safe out of your clutches.

My clutches, Crystal! You do amuse me. Tell me something, tell me just one thing. Is that what she really wants? Have you ever stopped to ask her?

She *is* asking me, Jules. Can't you hear her?

She, she, she!

Come back! I want you to come back.

Is that what I want to do?

Yes.

It should be clear by now . . . clear . . . (As though she'd plucked a wrong note, Gita started again) . . . *crystal* clear, I might say – laugh, my dear! – clear by now my dear that your good friend lusts, not for men, probably not for women (not even when the woman is yourself, my dear) but as we all do — yes, as we all do, even you, my dear — for power.

I don't lust for power.

Of course you do. Never more so than when you invaded Springfield's fragile glasshouse.

Come back! I want you. Come back!

What a shit you are.

At least I am honest.

You, Jules? Honest?

Yes, with whom it matters. With myself.

And I am not?

No, because you don't admit it.

Admit what? I don't understand.

Admit you play games. Green fingers Gita, for instance. Your little flutter with the fems, for instance. What comes out of your mouth is an echo to amuse yourself.

Gita eased her shoulders; they were beginning to ache. The rock she was sitting against was hard, and the south wind, even here, even in the shelter of the rocks, was as chilling as Jules's thin laugh. Be honest with yourself, Gita, said the wind. You know, Jules — she fought back — I don't think you are the logician you like to think you are. If a person isn't honest with herself, just *isn't*, then how can she admit it *without* being honest with herself — tell me that!

She looked up triumphantly. And it wasn't Jules standing over her. It wasn't Jules saying but I've won, my dear, now spread your legs.

It was Angus who was standing there, staring down at her in silent concern.

60 Squatter

"Hey," he said gently, squatting down in front of her. "All by yourself in the cold here — what on earth are you doing?" He'd nearly tripped over her when he'd walked around the rock. He touched her cheek with the back of his hand. "Can't you make it back to the cottage?" After her first surprised glance, she wouldn't look at him. Was this what Mary found each time she sat with his mother? And Mary went to the hospital each week!

He took her hands between his and began to chafe them. Are you feeling quite well again, Mary had said. It flashed across his mind that she was pregnant, that she was sick with an unwanted pregnancy, had fled to Marycote like a sick animal. He hadn't noticed anything, but that didn't mean much; she usually wore that thick sloppy jumper. He felt pleased with this sudden perspicacity, and then ashamed, because when she was feeling sickly and snappish all he could do was snap back at her. He wanted now to comfort her, hug her as he had hugged Mary, but was afraid of another tongue-lashing. So he said instead "Come on, I'll help you get back to the cottage."

When he stood up she let him lift her to her feet as though she were weightless.

He slipped off his coat, wrapped it around her and turned her in the direction of Marycote. "Mary's sent you some of her scones," he said, to ease over the silence. Mary said she always chatted to his mother in case Kate understood, although no one could tell. "I thought I'd better drop them over to you while they were fresh." It was he, not Mary, who had thought of the scones. Unable to settle to anything after Mary had gone, he had decided to go across to Marycote and try again.

As they walked around the springs and then turned downhill he stopped. Gita stopped listlessly beside him.

"Hello," he said. "Visitors."

A panel van had pulled in at the gate by the road, and a man was opening the gate. Angus frowned as the van drove through and the man shut the gate.

"I'm glad he thought to shut the gate," Angus commented, walking on. Gita walked on beside him. "Lose a few sheep on the road otherwise." His words echoed oddly, as though he'd caught himself talking to himself.

"Making himself at home there!" he continued, as the van drove along the rutted track and into the garage.

The man who had opened the gate was jogging up the track towards the cottage. Angus saw him stop, pick up something, a stone, and fling it with a boyish gesture back towards the road.

A man with grey hair came out of the garage and walked towards the cottage.

Gita clutched Angus's arm, pulling him to a standstill.

He looked at her in surprise. She was staring at the driver of the van with what he thought was dread.

"What's the matter? Do you know them? Gita? Is it someone you know?"

She laughed dully. "You've met them. That day we came across to your place with Mary."

"Them, is it? I remember. Interested in old houses, weren't they?"

"One's a dealer and the other's a hacker."

"What?"

"One runs an antique shop and the other does computing."

"Have you been expecting them? Is that what's upset you today?"

"They don't know I'm here. Nobody does. Unless Jarrah — no, he wouldn't, he just wouldn't have! Oh I'll murder him if he was the one. Nobody knows I'm here!"

"Then what —"

But before he could finish his question, or she answer it, there was a shout from the man on the track, and Mark came bounding towards her.

"Gita! It can't be you! It is you! Hey, Jules! Here she is! Jules!"

"So . . . what are you two up to?" Gita said, warming her chin in her soup mug. "Or can I guess?"

Her eyes moved the length of the mantelpiece which was a clutter of odd-shaped stones, bits of paper, jars of wattle bloom and gum leaves standing on the toes of socks and fancy lace briefs drying over the sitting room fire.

The grey-haired bloke smiled indulgently, the younger one grinned.

Angus frowned. Leaning forward, he pushed a couple of logs together until they sent up a crackle of sparks. He had just lit the fire. You'll stay, Angus? she had said. If you want me to, Gita. Recalling how up on the hill her fingers had dug into his arm in fear, of course he had stayed. She seemed happy enough now, sitting there cross-legged to drink her soup, her olive-green dress bunching between her knees and over her calves to the floor. Every now and then she arched her back like a cat's against the arm of the younger bloke's chair. The other one, flicking a husk from his mug into the fire, asked her something. Firelight jangled off her earrings as she lifted her head. Angus shot a quick look at the other two: three males, gathered around a female. There's something unnatural about her, he thought, watching her as intently as they did . . . something false, forced, taut as that material pulled across her knees. Going somewhere special, are you, Gita?

Or expecting someone?

She'd assured him no one knew she was at Marycote, and yet hadn't the older bloke — the more personable one, the other was just a big puppy — hadn't the older one said we came to see you, Gita? And she'd made them welcome all right, hugs and kisses all round, the younger bloke and her with their arms round each other's waists as they walked towards Marycote. Angus's coat had fallen to the ground; he'd picked it up and, since he still had the scones, had followed them into the cottage.

Hey! My bike! I thought it was stolen! the younger bloke had exclaimed, looking at Gita's Peugeot leaning against the copper. Maybe it was, said the other man drily. Gita's laugh had trilled out like a cuckoo's call. What have you brought to eat? she'd asked, once she had them all in her kitchen. *Real* pumpernickel? *Goats'* milk cheese? Quick, Mark, go and get it! I'll heat up some soup. Angus — you're staying, aren't you? Don't go, her eyes had pleaded. Would you light the fire for me? she'd asked him.

He recalled how she'd frightened him up at the rocks, and now here she was *inhabited* again. By a squatter, he thought suddenly.

He knew nothing about her, nothing. Images rushed at him. What after all had he discovered that night of the possum? He looked down at his hands: now he thought about it a bit more, that he was probably wrong earlier thinking she was pregnant — he would have realised, wouldn't he? We'll take our time, she'd said.

"What *are* you up to?" she was asking the others again. What are *you* up to, Gita? *And now I've got that candle holder. You wouldn't let me have it, would you, remember?* "What I want to know is, what the fuck you two are doing here."

Don't make me wait all night. And she'd rolled away. Come here, then

"Gita, my dear. Do you really think we could drive past your gate without saying hello?" said the older bloke, the one she called Jules. He turned to Angus. "I'm in the antique business, so I go to a lot of clearing sales. Deceased estates. Forced sales. Marvellous what you can pick up."

Angus nodded, dragged back from memories threatening to close over his head.

"Mark's giving me a hand for a while," Jules was saying. "As a matter of fact we're planning on spending a few days in this district."

"You can't do that!" Gita exclaimed. Jules raised one eyebrow. She muttered "I thought you had a shop to look after."

"I have a good manager, as always when I'm on the road. You know that." He turned to Angus. "We've just been to a big sale up north. Lovely stuff. Cedar, silky oak." He nodded at the dining chair from Springfield. "That's a nice example of reverse tulip legs you've got there, Gita."

"The rest of them are over at my place," Angus said drily. He should go — get out of here — leave her to whatever plans she had. Are you going somewhere, Gita? No, Mary, I just felt like a change. He went on sitting.

"Are they, indeed?" Jules shot a quick look from Gita to

Angus, then leaned across and shook Mark's knee. "The squat was never like this, was it, old son?"

"Are you still there, Mark?"

"He's moved in with me for a bit. It seemed like a good idea. Under the circumstances."

"What circumstances?"

Jules merely smiled, spreading his hands in a gesture that said isn't that obvious?

The cords stood out in her thin neck as she craned her head upwards to look at Mark's face. "Have you really?" She leaned against Mark's knees and nudged him. "Mark? Have you really?"

The young man nodded. He looks pretty miserable about a good idea, Angus thought.

"To Wyewurrk," Gita said, with dry emphasis. "And you're on vacation now, are you?" Mark shrugged. "Hey . . . you've chucked it in! I thought you really liked it."

Again the young man shrugged.

Jules laughed. "Now don't jump to conclusions, Gita. My dear. She always was one to jump to conclusions," he joked, turning to Angus.

"She, she, she!" cried Gita, upsetting the remains of her soup over her dress. Angus went out to the kitchen to find a dishcloth. While he rinsed it he could hear one of them asking her something. And her voice in reply, low, vehement. He strained to hear.

At that moment Jarrah appeared at his side. Quiet as an owl he had opened the back door. Angus jumped. "Don't do that!"

"Sorry. Thought you saw me . . . Is she very mad this time? Angus? Is she mad at me?"

"Mad at *you*? Why would she be?"

"'cause I've been to school. In the bus with Elton. And the teacher said where's your transfer papers, where's your mother, no one comes without transfer papers, no one just brings themselves to school!"

"You mean – Gita didn't know?"

The boy shook his head, owl eyes staring.

Angus laughed. "You take the cake," he said.

"Is there cake? I'm starving. I didn't take any lunch." He hesitated. "Who's in there? Who's Gita talking to?"

"People you know. Jules and Mark."

"Not *them*!"

At the look on his face, Angus gave the boy's shoulder a squeeze. "Yes, them."

Back in the sitting room, after the first one sharp glance from Gita, no one appeared surprised, or angry, or relieved, or even particularly gladdened to see the boy. He retold his day's venture.

"You're a canny kid all right," Angus said, to fill the silence when the saga was finished. He thought Gita glanced at him gratefully, the first real expression on her face all afternoon apart from when she was asking him to stay or quizzing Mark about something. So he added "Like his mother. Resourceful."

Mark looked more miserable than ever, and Jules began to talk to Angus about clearing sales again, and antiques, and old houses. "I remember your place as a particularly nice example of late nineteenth century."

And so the afternoon passed.

61 Kiss of Life

Angus looked out the window. "Hell, time to get round the ewes already!"

"Why don't we all come with you?" Gita suggested. "He's a whizz with animals," she told the others.

"Really?" said Mark, grinning. If he makes some adolescent crack about animal husbandry . . . thought Angus, but Mark said nothing further, so Angus said "We can walk from here, if you really want to come. There are only a few to lamb now. Nothing dramatic these days."

And then, having said that, he had to lamb a ewe after all, up on the hill amongst the rocks. "Oh dear," said Mark, as the afterbirth came away. "It's all rather messy."

Gita, holding the ewe for Angus while he tried to revive the lamb, laughed to herself at the look he gave Mark. Poor Mark. It was good to see him again. She saw Angus frown as he felt for a heartbeat. The lamb's head was blue and swollen. As they all watched he wiped away the yellow yolk, put his mouth to its nose and blew into its nostrils.

"Oh *dear*!" repeated Mark.

Angus spat, wiped his mouth with the back of his hand, then laid the lamb by the ewe. Its legs thrashed, its head beat the ground in a spasm. "Last gasp, I would say." But he picked the lamb up and blew into its nostrils again. And this time, when he put it down, it lifted its head calmly and tried to struggle to its feet. He glanced at Gita. She was looking at him, maybe even a touch of pride there, he thought, and felt a taut band snap in his chest. He squeezed a few drops of thick yellow milk from the ewe's teats and put the lamb's mouth to one of them.

"Well done," Jules said as they moved away, leaving the ewe and lamb in the shelter of the rocks.

Jarrah raced in ever-widening circles, shouting "What did I tell you, he's a whizz with animals, what did I tell you!"

"You were showing off," Gita murmured at Angus's side. "You did that to impress them."

Angus laughed. "I impressed myself."

"Well, that's it," he said, at the top of the hill. If he shut off his mind, if he stuck to his precept of one day at a time, then the afternoon had been a success — the talk with Jules as well as helping Gita out, if that's what it was that she'd wanted — and then taking them with him around his ewes and putting on quite a turn for them. He spat discreetly at the memory. The kiss of life. He was reluctant to leave them, to go back to the solitude of what even Mary called a sad house. He hesitated. "Would you all like to come over and have something to eat later? Pretty simple basic stuff." He held Jules's eye. "Gita can tell you."

Maybe he shouldn't have said that. Maybe Gita had other plans. Maybe she didn't want them hanging around any longer at all. But before they could reply she said promptly "Fine. We'll do that."

"Bring the dulcimer," he said to her.

"All right. If you'll play something too."

"Me?"

"Yes, you, Angus."

"What could I play?"

"You'll find something. A harmonica, maybe?"

He looked at her. She was laughing. She's been through my desk, he thought.

"I'll see what I can do," he said, suddenly happy.

62 One of Life's Minor Tragedies

Afterwards, some time after midnight when they'd gone back to Marycote and he was alone again, alone as usual by a dying fire, alone with a bottle of Scotch and an aching patched-up knee, he tried to recapture the feeling of joy, of elation even, that had warmed him as surely as whisky while they were with him at Springfield . . . the hastily prepared curry he'd scratched together from the left-over leg of lamb, and Gita helping him, Gita familiar with everything in the kitchen, here's a knife to chop the onion, Mark, you can do the tomato, Jarrah. She had diced the apple, turning the waxy fruit in her fingers as slowly as she'd turned those picnic oranges . . . or himself. He'd nicked his hand, watching her as he cut the cold meat.

The young bloke Mark wouldn't eat meat, of course; he had to make do with pumpkin and fried roast potato . . . Angus hadn't thought to ask . . . Mark should have spoken up sooner . . . or Gita, Gita could've . . .

He'd changed out of his work clothes into sports trousers and a clean shirt, and for the first time in God knows how long — years? — he'd lit both fires, dining and sitting room.

"This should warm up the old place," he'd told them (Gita), indicating the back log on the sitting room fire. "Off the big hill, this one. Part of a yellow box stump I pulled out with the Ferguson a couple of summers ago."

Gita had stared. "You remember where each log comes from."

Her laughter was fingertips walking up and down his spine. Flames leapt and glinted on the heavy crystals, one round, one oval-shaped, that swung from her ears. The chandelier in the high ceiling glittered with unshed tears, the surface of the rosewood dining table rippled and flowed.

Jules touched the tabletop delicately; turned over one of the chairs. "So here are the rest of them, you've got the whole dozen," he said, caressing the chair. "Reverse tulip legs. William the Fourth. Surely?"

Angus laughed. "You'd know. It's been in the family for years, I do know that."

Over the table he threw one of his mother's tablecloths from the linen press in the passage, darned with her almost invisible stitches and smelling faintly of mildew.

"Can I set it?" Jarrah asked eagerly.

Again Angus clapped him on the shoulder, as he had earlier at Marycote over Gita's visitors. Jarrah beamed up at him.

"We'll use the good stuff for once, will we, mate? Do it in style? Over here in the sideboard. Hell, it needs a bit of elbow grease!"

Angus smiled to himself as Jarrah, conscious that this was an occasion, laid the least-blackened knives and forks in carefully crossed Xs.

From the sideboard Jules took the heavy wine glasses with the lozenge-shaped pattern, examined them, and sent Mark to rinse them in the kitchen. "If you don't mind a red this evening, Angus?" Then he uncorked two bottles of wine and set them to breathe.

"Granite Hills," he told them. "Know it, Angus? Cabernet Sauvignon '82. Great year, '82. I picked up a dozen yesterday. Some good stuff locally."

"You don't say," Gita said softly.

Jules raised one eyebrow.

* *

"Anywhere, sit anywhere," Angus said when it was time to eat, himself going automatically to the head of the table where his father had always sat. He became conscious of Jules steering Gita to his right and waiting to lift in her chair. Jarrah made a dive to Angus's left. Jules sat next to Jarrah — from where he can watch each of our faces, Angus realised.

Holding up his glass against the light of the weeping chandelier, Angus felt that the room had come alive again. "I remember when we had to use all three table leaves," he said suddenly. "Christmases when I was a kid, with all the cousins coming from miles away. My God, these wintry days you can hardly credit the heat! Or were summers hotter then? My mother'd be in the kitchen basting chickens and stirring bread sauce and checking on the water level in the biggest saucepan with the pudding lolloping away in it. I used to love that sound." He caught Jarrah's eager gaze. "She'd've been up since daybreak, been to church, decked the house out with Christmas lilies — madonna lilies — and those big red poppies, huge ones, with the pepperpot seed boxes —"

"Opium poppies?" Jules suggested, his voice like the white sap that oozed from the poppy stems.

"Probably were. I remember they always had that old-fashioned hospital smell." He glanced at Gita. She was staring at Jules.

"Go on!" Jarrah prompted. "What did the kids do?"

"The kids? Oh — we'd all be racing round outside in the heat, chasing cicadas — that's another sound that always brings Christmases back, that shrill screaming, cicadas, I mean." He stopped again.

and the screaming

He frowned. "Dad used to keep the beer and soft drinks cool in a bucket down the old well."

Mark snickered. "My old man would've been so pissed he'd have gone right in after them head over toss."

"Every Christmas I'd beg Santa to bring me a horse." This was from Jules. "And all I ever found at the bottom of my stocking was a lump of horse turd. And my old man'd say bad luck son, he must have got away."

Angus laughed politely. He'd heard that old chestnut before. He caught Gita's eye. "Talking too much again, am I?" he said apologetically.

"No, Angus." Her voice indicated surprise that he should ask her. He saw Jules raise an eyebrow.

"Go on, Angus!" Jarrah said impatiently. "Go on about the kids."

"Working up an appetite — we were working up an appetite." He got going again. "Greedy little beggars! We'd have at least three helping of Christmas pudding because there was money in it, real money. Out in the kitchen there's a hook in the ceiling," he told Jarrah, who nodded importantly, full of love for Angus who was telling him things. "That's where the pudding hung for weeks after it was cooked to improve the flavour."

"Can we do that? Can we have pudding with money, Angus? Can we ask the Catchpole kids?"

"The Catchpole kids? We'll see." Angus's buoyant mood flagged. And he'd caught sight again of Jules's mocking eyes.

Christmas! Christmas with Gita!

"Ever thought of growing grapes, Angus?" Jules asked, refilling glasses from the second bottle.

"I have thought of it, yes. I've got a northerly spot I reckon'd be ideal, sheltered, good bit of basalt."

"One thing at a time!" Gita said, so that everyone stared at her. "He's got enough on his plate in the glasshouse right now."

Jules raised his eyebrow — the other one, this time.

His plate mopped clean with a thick slice of bread, the boy vanished out to the kitchen to watch telly. The others went into the sitting room where Angus stirred up the fire and Gita in that strong clear voice sang "Go Tell Aunt Rhodie" and "Barb'ry Allan", then something Angus didn't recognise. " 'They never met, they never kissed,' " she sang, " 'for he lived on the morningside of the mountain —' " drawling mou . . . ntain like some Appalachian hillbilly — " 'and she lived on the sunset side of the hill.' "

Now there's one of life's minor tragedies, Jules said, as the song concluded. Did you make that one up too? Angus asked. That seemed to startle Jules. That one too, he'd said. Evidently the bucolic life is agreeing with you, Gita — glancing in Angus's direction. He'll make her wild if he's implying it's got anything to do with me, Angus thought, rather hoping he'd hear one of these blokes cop a bit of her sharp tongue: make him feel better over that glasshouse business this afternoon. Gita, tuning the dulcimer, seemed unaware of Jules's comment. She smiled at Angus, her comfortable old-friend smile. It's an old pop song, she told him. Don't you know it? I like it, I like what it's saying. You could write a whole story about it, couldn't you, a whole book: him on one side of the mountain and her on the other, going about their lives, getting crabby and old, lonely as hell, all because neither of them ever thought to take a look over the mou . . . ntain.

They laughed. One of life's minor tragedies, Mark repeated. By the way, it's twilight — twilight, not sunset, Gita. Sunset sounds better, Gita muttered. Got to get the words right, Gita! Got to get the words right! Angus sensed another conversation going on here between these two. Mark picked up two silver coffee spoons then and light as kisses drummed a fancy rhythm on the rim of a fine bone china cup. He's good, Angus thought, he's bloody good. Pity we don't have a good guitarist for the gig next week, Jules commented. Or singer, Mark threw in over the dancing coffee spoons. I'm goin' to Grace Broz, Grace Broz, Gita sang, high above Mark's hypnotic fingers. Has the band really broken up? she asked wistfully. And then: Come on, Angus, it's your turn now.

I'm pretty rusty, he'd apologised, but all the same he'd managed to get out "Mr Bojangles" for her, and a couple of Beatles tunes, "Eleanor Rigby" and "When I'm Sixty-Four". She'd looked pleased, singing along with him once he'd got going.

It had been his father's harmonica; he'd taken it to the second world war, and when Angus went to Vietnam he'd given it to him. For good luck, son, his old man had said, tears in his eyes. Good luck! This memory always made Angus mad. One of life's minor tragedies, he muttered, measuring the depth of whisky in the bottle by the fire's glow. He'd have a humdinger of a headache in the morning: he'd put away far more than he'd realised. It must have been while the others were smoking grass. Hey, I haven't had any of that for I don't know how long, Gita had sighed, when at the end of the evening Mark had produced it. Okay by you, Angus? Sure, go ahead. Gita had offered him the thin, wet cigarette. No thanks, I've got my poison here. That set me apart from them right away, he thought. Generation gap. Them passing that cigarette from one mouth to another, and me drinking Scotch. Wasted, he muttered, savouring the bitter thought as he poured another nip. Wasted. Blown away like my mate Metcalf. I shouldn't have had those people here. Old, they made me feel old. All those wasted years. Stolen youth. Bloody government.

Bloody harmonica. She got me going on it again. And for the time they were here I actually thought . . . I actually felt life was possible. What a laugh. Away they go, and here am I, round and round in a bloody wasteland. I shouldn't have had them here. If her friends come to stay with her — fuck with her — what the hell business is it of mine?

He'd managed to say to her out of their hearing — he'd followed her out to the kitchen when she'd gone there with something — that the two blokes could camp at Springfield if she'd prefer that, room to spare here, Gita, if you'd rather they didn't stay at Marycote, you seemed a bit concerned this afternoon. And she'd leaned her head against his chest, her breath sweet with dope, her closeness this time nothing but the dope, and she'd said thanks Angus, thanks, but don't worry, it's okay, we'll maybe smoke another joint before we turn in. She'd begun to giggle. I want to tell you something, Angus — her giggles like chords of her dulcimer vibrating against his chest. No, I want to tell *you* something, he'd insisted. This afternoon . . . you . . . lamb . . . thrashing about, you know what I mean? At Marycote. And now . . . my glasshouse girl again. Gita? You know what I mean? She'd giggled some more. Yeah. Well. My turn now. Hey, maybe you ought to go easy on this stuff, huh? And she'd stood back and lifted up the empty whisky bottle. That was what she'd taken out to the kitchen, was it? You sound like Mary, he'd muttered, you sound like a wife. No, he hadn't said that at all, he'd said listen, Mary keeps it topped up with water, that's why. And then he'd laughed. One of life's minor tragedies, Gita. Jesus, Angus! You sure are pissed.

63   King Hit

He was surprised the next day when, mid-morning, Gita and Jules and Mark turned up at the glasshouse. "Can we come in?" Gita asked. So that's how the pieces fall today, he thought as she and the younger bloke came lightly into the glasshouse. "Look Mark, this is what I was telling you –" She stopped in mid-sentence. "Sure we're not in the way, Angus?" She frowned, looking at him.

"Go ahead."

She shrugged, turned away, began to explain her work in the glasshouse.

So you've missed out, mate, Angus thought, as the other bloke followed Gita and Mark. You and me both. He was arrested by the expression on Jules's face. What was it Gita had said about someone she knew? He scares the shit out of me. What else had she said? It's a power thing. A game. Gita, he won't let that silly kid have you without a fight.

"Are you plucking your eyebrows now, Gita?" Mark was saying, waving the tweezers.

"No, they're for a really smart idea Gita came up with for pricking out seedlings," Angus said proudly. "Stroke of genius there."

Gita looked pleased.

"Well of course it was, Angus," Jules said, smiling at Gita. "She had all that practice at the drug rehab centre. Didn't you, my dear? Months of practice in their native plants nursery."

Gita stared at him. Jules went on smiling.

You bastard, Angus thought. Look at her face. You bloody knew she wanted to keep that to herself.

He turned away and picked up the watering can. D'you think what you've just said is going to make any difference, you smart bastard? I ought to clock you one. I carry around enough baggage from my own past without worrying about hers.

That rabbit Mark dragged him into some silly argument then. It began with the word plantation. Was the idea to harvest the plantation for *profit*, Mark wanted to know, an edge to his question.

"No, what I'm doing right now is more of a permanent windbreak," Angus began, sensing he was being led into an ambush.

"I want to plant trees on the bare hill behind my place," Gita said suddenly. "Groups of yellow box and blackwood. Seven trees to a group."

"Ah! The magic number," said Jules.

"No, seven of the same species looks natural," Angus put in, surprised, and pleased, at what Gita had just said. "More natural than straight lines which is what we're doing this year. Five-row windbreaks along the boundary. To get back to your question, Mark. What I plant –" glancing at Gita – "we plant could be harvested if I – if it's gone about carefully. Replanting what's used. Putting in enough trees each year to cut down later for firewood."

"Or coppice?" Jules suggested, enjoying Angus's sharp glance at this bit of knowledge.

"Sure, that's even better. Perpetual source, then. And leaving the old dead stuff standing for things to nest in, Mark. Oh, and *pine trees*." Counter-attack.

"Pine trees!" Mark was appalled.

"Yes. Pine trees." He was right, Mark was one of those greenies ideologically outraged by the very word. "You could grow a stand of pines on, oh, two or three hectares and in thirty years' time you'd have a crop of high quality saw logs for house timbers and furniture."

"Crop!"

"I suppose running fine wool merinos is a sort of crop, too," Angus continued, laughing, sensing victory. "Isn't that a wool jumper you're wearing, Mark? And yours, Gita. Isn't it?" He ignored Jules.

Mark fingered his jumper, Gita said sulkily "It's yours, you should know."

This reference to Belle snatched away the advantage he'd just won over silly Mark. He turned to Gita. "People like me have their uses. Keeping you people warm. Remember what you said about all this being nothing but slaughter? Slaughter and breeding was how you put it."

"Are you on about that again? I told you, it was Crystal who said that."

Angus laughed. "No, Gita. It was you. It was that day you came over about a ewe that couldn't lamb. We were walking across to the house, I remember quite well because we stopped to look at some lambs playing, and I said something, and you . . . well, turned on me is a bit strong."

He stopped, conscious of Jules's smile.

Gita was looking puzzled. "*I* said? Are you sure?"

"Quite sure. In fact I remember your exact words, for what it's worth. You said what I was doing was all slaughter and breeding, and I said no Gita, breeding and slaughter."

"How come you remember all that?"

"Caught me on a nerve, I guess."

"That's our girl," said Jules.

"Enjoy yourselves," Angus said curtly, concentrating on the watering, when Gita told him they were off for a drive around the district.

She hesitated in the doorway. "There isn't anything here particularly that needs —?"

He shook his head. "I've got to catch up with some work with the sheep over the next day or so. Marking the lambs.

Ear clipping, docking their tails so they don't get flystruck over spring and summer, castrating the ram lambs," he explained for Mark's benefit.

"How do you do that? Bite out the testicles?" Jules asked.

Surprising the things this bloke had picked up. Angus laughed. "Not these days. We use a rubber ring."

Mark, as was to be expected, shuddered. "It all sounds barbaric."

"Want some assistance while we're still here?" Jules asked.

Angus, surprised, was very pleased to accept the offer. The job involved catching each lamb in a small, temporary yard and holding it still on a board on the fence while a rubber ring was placed on its tail and another, if it was a ram lamb, on its scrotum. On your own it was a slow job, and this time would be harder than it should have been because he hadn't got around to it until some of the lambs were pretty big and strong.

"So when do you want a hand?" Jules asked.

"If it's okay by you, day after tomorrow, unless it's raining. Tomorrow I'll get the yards ready. See you over at the shed at, say, no later than eight? A bit before, if you could. That way we should be all through by two and the ewes and lambs'll mother up again before dark."

"The day after tomorrow, then, Angus. We'll be off now."

Mark slipped his arm around Gita's hip and smiled at her. "We've got a good guide here."

Angus nodded at Jules. "Unless it's wet. Thanks. That'll make all the difference, having some help."

Watching them push their way along the overhung path, he wondered if she would take them past the potato farm. Bandicootin'. He wouldn't put it past them. Something Lou Catchpole said months ago hatched in his mind like a wasp's egg. *The rest of them, are they planning on moving in, too? . . . I reckon you want to be careful . . .*

The back of his head thumped. She's never trusted me. Day after day we've worked side by side at these benches and she's never said a word. Let me think that first morning that she'd never handled a plant in her life. What did she say one day? My teaching. Very flattering. Thank you very much. He lifted the watering can. Water sprayed wildly. Or if she did say something, I didn't take it in. Christ, what *did* she tell me? Using a substance is just one person's business. Of course it is. I've spent years learning how to mind my own business.

Well, if she's had some trouble with drugs I can sympathise with that. I could've easily become a boozer there a few years back.

He recalled how at the time he and Belle would seize on the most wounding words to hurl at each other. Aiming for each other's weakest spots. Real search and destroy mission, that marriage. He'd prided himself up to now that all that was past, that circumstances at the time had driven him to it, that never again, safe in his glasshouse at Springfield, would he need to be so brutal in his own defence. And this girl comes along and I'm too wrapped up in my own concerns to see beyond using a tenant to get back at Catchpole. Or using her to catch up with my work in here. What was it she said? There's using, and there's using, Angus. He clutched at the bench. He knew the picture. She uses some drug, and men use her for sex, and she tries to get away from it all at Marycote. So what happens? So yesterday he's angered by something she's come out with for reasons he doesn't take time out to discover and, having screwed her himself, goes and belts her with what anyone in their right mind would take as a sexual taunt.

The boy. Creeping up on him in the kitchen at Marycote. Is she very mad at me this time, Angus? She hadn't a clue where the boy was and she was worried silly.

Caring and nurturing. He's given the opportunity, and he king-hits her.

And you know why, don't you, you fool? Be honest, he told himself. You did it because when it's down to taws you're no better than that creeping jesus Jules. He thought of the three of them, gathered around her at Marycote. If she wants any of us, she'd better go for that wimp Mark. At least he's harmless.

64   Like One Who on a Lonesome Road

When, two days later, Jules and Mark had not turned up at the shed by a quarter to nine, nearly an hour later than arranged, Angus set out for Marycote in the utility. If they were on their way in Jules's van, he'd guide them to the spot in the paddock where yesterday he'd set up the yards.

Driving along the quiet road, where light pulsed transparently through each new leaf, he suddenly saw Gita's red gumboots, and behind Gita, the boy. She was carrying an armful of wattle bloom. Sunlight flickered across her face and across the full skirt of her dress — one he hadn't seen before, a bit flimsy for this cool morning, he thought, wondering as he drew up leaving the engine running whether it was a gift from Jules — or would it be Mark?

"Hi, Angus!" the boy shouted, running up.

Angus wound down the window and looked at the woman. She broke off a sprig of wattle and passed it to him. Smiled at him dreamily. Murmured " . . . miss all this, going back for the gigs. I haven't —"

Going back for the gigs. He cut her short. "Where are the others?"

"Jules and Mark? Asleep, I guess."

"They were supposed to be meeting me over at the shed to help with the marking. Are they coming or aren't they?"

Gita shrugged. "Maybe. Later, when they wake up."

"Later! Maybe! Good Christ, I've had the sheep yarded since seven. I've waited nearly an hour already. What is this, April Fool's Day?" Gita and the boy stared at him with alien eyes. "I should have guessed." *going back for the gigs* He began to reverse the utility.

Gita pushed Jarrah aside. "We could help you. Couldn't we? There's two of us." She had to walk along beside the moving vehicle. "Angus? We'll come."

"We'll come, Angus!" the boy shouted, trying to push under Gita's arm.

He jammed on the brakes. "You're hardly dressed for the part."

"Give me ten minutes and I'll get my scruffiest jeans."

He got out and stood beside her in the flickering sunshine. "You wouldn't be strong enough. Some of the older lambs are pretty big." He sighed. "Something else I should have done weeks ago."

"What exactly do we have to do? Catch them and hold them for you?"

"What are we going to do, Angus? Angus?" Jarrah ran around them, barking and springing.

"We'll be moving quietly, that's for sure. We'll be marking the lambs."

"What's that? Can I mark one? Can I put a mark on one?"

Angus laughed. Jarrah stopped jumping and scowled.

"Well, tell him," Gita said irritably.

Angus himself had grown up taking this sort of work in the yards more or less for granted. He wondered how much of what his parents had called the facts of life he was now being called on to explain. Not much, it seemed. It was the term marking the boy was unclear about.

"It's all the things I have to do today," Angus explained, reaching into the cabin for what looked like a pair of strong pliers. "See this? This stretches a rubber ring on to their tails. No knives, no blood. I'll be desexing the ram lambs with this too because I only need a few males for joining — mating — and as well I'll clip their ears with ear-clippers so I can put coloured tags in later. So I can tell at a glance what age they are, and what sex. This is called an Elastrator," he added, flexing the pliers. The kid loved words; took Angus back to when he was a boy, and then a youth, learning strange useless poetry for the sake of its music.

"I don't see how the rubber ring works," Jarrah was saying.

Angus smiled to himself. He's as interested in things as his mother, he thought, recalling Gita's eager questions in the glasshouse. Then winced *going back for the gigs* what else could I expect? Might as well use one of these things on myself. "It stops circulation," he said curtly. "The tails drop off." He reached into the cabin again. "These are the rings.

Here, don't try pushing it on to your finger, Jarrah!" He looked at Gita. "You won't go fainting or anything, will you?"

"Let's get going," Jarrah said. "Me and Gita'll take it in turns."

"Put your wattle on the back here with the dogs, they'll look after it for you," Angus said, lifting old Shep out of the cabin on to the tray with Bess. "You could grab some old clothes at the house," he went on. An old shirt and a sweater of his, and a pair of jeans from that room. "Save you going back to the cottage. If you're sure you really want to, that is . . . Well thanks, Gita, thanks."

"Me too, Angus, me too!" the boy shouted.

"You too, mate. Got the rings, Gita?"

As he turned back to the utility, he thought he saw Gita slip one of the small thick rings into her pocket.

He had set up the yards in a clean part of the paddock, a large yard to hold all the ewes and lambs, and a catching pen that had to be refilled frequently. He gave Jarrah that job. They worked in silence, Gita and Jarrah turn by turn catching the lambs, and Gita hoisting them on to the board where Angus, on the other side of the fence, waited with the Elastrator, rubber rings and ear-clippers. Lambs on his side of the fence sat down, or walked around calling for their mothers. He could hear Gita and Jarrah panting as the number of lambs in the catching pen grew smaller and cunning ones dodged behind the ewes. Gita's hair was falling loose; each time she pushed it back she left streaks of dirt across her face. He said he'd show her how to use the rings so as to give her a break from the heavy lifting, but she said she'd leave that part to him, she might make a mess of it.

"Sure all the lifting's not too much for you?"

"I'm fine."

It was round about mid-morning, just after he'd said "We're going well, team, we just might get them all done at this rate," when the ear-clippers hit a small vein in a lamb's ear and a thin stream of blood arched against Gita's temple and poured down her face on to her shirt.

"Oh God!" he breathed, snatching a handkerchief from his pocket and wiping her face. "Oh God!" He scrubbed at her blood-spattered collar.

"Hey! It's okay," she said, dropping the lamb on to the clean grass outside the yard. "It's only one of your old shirts, isn't it? I'll soak it in cold water, it'll wash out."

But he gripped her shoulder and went on scrubbing.

"What's up?" she said sharply. "Angus! What's up?"

"Sorry," he said at length. "Sorry — let's get this job finished."

"Pass that lamb, Jarrah."

She heaved it on to the board. It was a ewe lamb; he slipped the ring over its tail, reached for its ear.

"I don't know whether I can go on."

"Hey! Is it that blood on my face? Give me your hanky again, I never have one." She tightened her grip on the lamb and scrubbed at her face. "What is it, Angus? What's the matter?"

"The blood — all the blood —" To his horror he gave a choking sob. He grinned stupidly. "Sorry, Gita, Jarrah. Let's finish this job."

"Hey," she said. "You're all shaky. Have a break for a bit. Sit down on that bag, why don't you?"

She and Jarrah, holding their lambs, stood on the other side of the fence and watched him.

He sat looking at his trembling hands, then burst out "I didn't think — none of us thought —" Then, when she said nothing, he looked up. "The war. Didn't Mary tell you? She must have, she's always gasbagging. How do you think my hearing got buggered up? And my knee, it wasn't a tractor, it was a piece of shrapnel. Vietnam. I was in Vietnam for two years."

Gita nodded, about to say it wasn't Mary, I heard it in the pub, then shut her mouth.

It was Jarrah who exclaimed "You were in a war? What did you do, kill people?"

Gita turned on him. "Oh piss off, Jarrah! That's a dumb thing to say!" She stamped her foot. "Piss off!"

"What will I do with this lamb, then?"

"Hold it — put it down — I don't know."

Letting her own lamb go, she climbed over the fence and fell on her knees beside Angus.

"Hey mate . . . it's okay . . . okay."

"I didn't want you to know — women like you —"

She said gently "Heyyy! I'm not women like me. I am me. Trust me."

After a while, staring at his hands, he went on so low that she had to strain to hear. "What would you think of a bloke who lets his best mate get blown away in front of him? Blown up! Blown to little bits!" When she said nothing he looked up. "My best mate, Gita! And if I'd been a bit quicker I could have saved him. Metcalf would be alive today instead of a thousand little bits of bone and brain and blood that'll haunt me till the day I die."

She frowned, searching for a clue from all those sessions at that place. She said at last "But maybe you couldn't . . . I guess I'd need to know how it happened. If you want to tell me."

He looked up then and saw the child, and it was a lamb the child was grasping . . . fear on the child's face, panic — how could he ever tell Gita he'd been too slow at shooting a child? With a shuddering breath he turned his head into her shoulder.

"Oh Christ! Isn't it enough that I saw what was going to happen and I did nothing? I did nothing, Gita. I just stood by and let Metcalf get blown away." He began to cry again: choking, heaving sobs that shook his whole body and frightened Gita with their power. She flung her arms around him, holding him until he had cried himself out.

"It's okay . . . it's okay now."

"Thanks, thanks," he mumbled. "Sorry . . . sorry to . . . I've never told anyone else . . . not . . . not . . ." He stood up, steadying himself against the fence. "Better finish this job, I guess, now we've got so far."

"We could do it tomorrow, couldn't we?"

"Let's get it done. Gita — both of you — I'm sorry . . .

going on like this. What will you think – " He looked at Jarrah, rooted to the spot with his lamb. "Sorry, mate. Ready?"

"Don't keep saying sorry. It's good to talk." Gita grasped his arm. "It's good to cry. And I'm glad it was me that was here with you. Truly, Angus. And if you want to talk about it again . . ."

He put his arms around her then and hugged her with an immense feeling of relief, as though he had woken to find not a fiend but a loving friend on that lonesome road.

"Thanks," he said again, blowing his nose on the blood-stained handkerchief.

She touched a teardrop on his lashes and licked her fingertip.

65 My Bleeding Heart

When she and Jarrah returned to Marycote, Jules and Mark were in the kitchen cutting wedges of a huge chocolate sponge. Mark waved the bread knife. "Look what your old friend up the road just dropped in. Okay, Jarrah, wait your turn. Where've you been, Gita? You've nearly missed out." He stared. "That's – *blood* –"

"Doing what you two said you'd do. Giving Angus a hand with his lambs."

"So we did." Mark widened his mouth for a bite of cake. "He wanted us to cut off their little happy bits." Cream oozed over his chin. "Dear me, I am making a mess here."

"Poor little Bo Peep," said Jules, looking at her closely. "She went into the woods and met something nasty."

"Don't be a fool, Jules."

"You must admit, you do have funny friends."

"That's true. He's twice the guy you two are."

Mark sniggered. "That surly prick?"

"He's okay. He's got something to feel surly about. He was a conscript in Vietnam. And what happened there was so horrible it's still with him. Killing people, seeing people blown to bits. There's messy for you, Mark."

"My bleeding heart," said Jules, cutting a thick slice of chocolate cake.

"Hey Jules! She reckons she's staying on here!"

Even Jules was startled. "You're not coming back with us? For the gigs, Gita? What's made you change your mind?" Gita shrugged. "Aha! It's Bluebeard in the glass castle. You're starting to feel sorry for him and a woman who feels sorry for a man is a dangerous animal." He shook his head in mock dismay. "Gita! My dear!"

"Feeling sorry? I just like being here. I like my job in the glasshouse."

"Of course. Your job in the glasshouse. And after a while, when you've worn down your poor crazy vet with all that sweet pity, you'll screw the balls off him and then you'll move on because, Gita my dear, that's how you get your power kicks, isn't it?"

"Hey, go easy on her, mate!"

The bitterness in Jules's voice astonished her. She laughed. "Oh Jules! That's really got to you, hasn't it? That I had the willpower to walk out on you. That's it, isn't it?" She turned to Mark. "He's always on about being truthful and honest. Well let him try that for size! Oh, and something else, Jules." She reached into her pocket. "Try that for size, too. A consolation prize."

She flung the rubber ring at him.

As it bounced to a stop on the table he stared at it, then at her.

"You bitch!" He reached for the bread knife.

She drew back, and Jules laughed. The knife hovered over Mary's sponge. "Truth, my dear, isn't a cake you cut up and take a slice of." He spoke calmly but his pale face had grown paler. Gita shuddered. He's like a white worm you find under a stone.

"A cake? More like a cake of soap left in the bath, Jules." She paused. "And you're the bath. Yes, you're the bath,

Jules." She heard Mark's whinnying laugh. "And in the end truth just dissolves away until there's nothing left but a bathtub of scummy water."

"Dear me," said Jules. "We are in full flight today." He smiled at Mark. "All packed, mate? Let's go. I'll get your bike on the way."

"You really aren't coming with us?" Mark asked wistfully, lingering as Jules went out to the garage.

Gita shook her head, then threw her arms around him. "Take care."

"You too. You shouldn't have said that to Jules, Gita."

"He'll get over it."

"I wish we were closer."

"Me too." She brushed her lips against his. "But I'm staying here. At my place. 'I'm goin' to my place, my place.' "

"I guess you like him better than me."

She didn't answer.

"Do you? You do, don't you?"

"What of it? Why do you keep on about it, Mark?"

"You've spent a lot of the time we've been here talking to him, for all the things you say about him."

She shrugged. "I can talk to my friends."

"Yeah. All you want to do is talk."

"You seemed to spend a fair bit of time talking to him yourself."

"Well of course I did. It was pretty clear why, wasn't it?"

"No."

"Gita. I told you why. Don't keep on moving your face away from me. You don't really like Jules better than me, do you?"

"Jules? . . . Jules? Jules scares me dead. Listen mate, Jules ought to scare you, too."

"Is that why you ran away?"

"Maybe."

"Will I stay with you? The last few days have been good, haven't they?"

"Sure." She smiled. "But it wouldn't work. Not yet.

You've got a way to go yet, mate. We talked that out again last night, remember?"

"Fucking's better than talking. Isn't it?"

"Sometimes."

"Kiss me properly."

When they broke apart, they saw Jules standing in the doorway.

"Ready, Mark? Oh, Gita . . ." He turned back as Mark went out. "Gita. You might need this, my dear, one of these days."

He gave her a small brown envelope. She opened it. Inside were several foil packets, and inside each packet, she knew without needing to look, was a street gram of white powder.

"My dear Jules," she drawled, "I threw my syringe away."

"Come now, even our bucolic friend has noticed how resourceful you are."

"You fucking bastard. Fuck off, just fuck off!"

"Goodness, such paucity of expression! Whatever's happened to all that imagination?" He kissed her lightly, then, taking the envelope from her, he reached up on tip-toe and flicked it on to the top of the kitchen dresser. "My lovely Gita. As always, the choice is yours."

His parting shot.

66 Try That for Size

On the verandah they're discussing some sort of deal. Get your act together, we're relying on you, Jules says softly. You know a dulcimer's no good, Mark shouts at her, and Jules says I'll make sure she's there. She watches the bright blood rise. She opens her mouth, struggles to tell them I want out! I want out! but the words won't come. Crystal has to say it for her. Where am I? Gita manages to say. *Where am I?* she screams. I'll come with you, Jarrah says. Footsteps ring on the hollow earth. We'll all go, somebody says. As Gita moves away — floats — Jules's arm snakes out. He pulls her back. She disappears into his skin. *Try that for size, my dear*

67 Mulberry Cycle: Spring

Girls As Green Leaves
As green as love
    as leaves
        as glass
the girls appear
they laugh
    whisper
flirt with the wind
lift glass-green, grass-green skirts
    eye off the sun
        the breeze
        a passing shower
the girls don't care
    they ache with love
are quick with love
    with lust
        they crawl with bees
their secret places swell

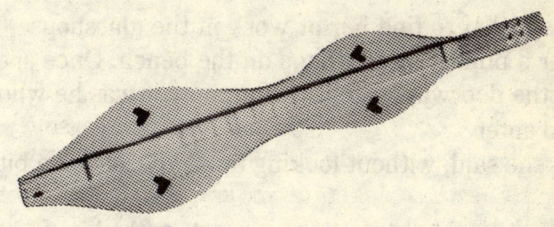

Aeolian Mode

As green as love, as leaves, as glass, the girls appear. They laugh, whisper, flirt with the wind; lift glass-green, grass-green skirts; eye off the sun, the breeze, a passing show'r. The girls don't care. They ache with love, Are quick with love, with lust. They crawl with bees. Their secret places swell.

68   He Was Startled

He was startled to find her at work in the glasshouse, head bent over a punnet of seedlings on the bench. Once she had stood in the doorway watching him, now it was he who was unable to enter.

"Hi," she said, without looking up. "These look a bit dry, Angus."

He went inside, tested a punnet with his fingertip. "Sorry." Adding casually "What are they up to today?"

"Right now..." – she concentrated on watering the punnets – "nodding off. Maybe. Who cares?" She shrugged. "They're not here, Angus. They've gone."

"Gone? For good? And you didn't go with them? But I thought . . . " *going back for the gigs*

Gita put down the watering can. From the chilly depths of her childhood, too deep to be penetrated by any rays from the present, there ventured to the surface a rare memory, a strange thing someone used to say to tease the small girl. She turned slowly.

"You know what Thought thought, Angus? Thought thought his toes were cold so he jumped out of bed to tuck them in."

Part Three

Fragments Dim of Lovely Forms

> . . . Then all the charm
> Is broken — all that phantom-world so
>   fair
> Vanishes, and a thousand circlets
>   spread,
> And each mis-shape the other. Stay
>   awhile,
> Poor youth!
>
> > – Coleridge, fragment of dream
> >   for "Kubla Khan"

69   Your Lips Your Breasts Your Lips

She opened her eyes. Where am I? she said aloud, or maybe she dreamed that she spoke. *Where am I?*

She turned her head, struggling against the old tide of panic. A chair, her clothes — folded: who did that? — a dressing table piled with papers.

"Gita?"

She raised her eyes and saw, standing in the doorway, Angus with a cup and saucer in one hand and a plate in the other.

"I looked in a couple of times, but you were dead to the world. I've brought you a bit of breakfast."

The night came back then. She looked at this man with pleasure, and laughed.

"What?" he asked, coming to the bed and looking down at her.

She laughed again, sliding up against the pillow and holding out her hands for breakfast.

"The contrast, the way you said that . . . here's a bit of breakfast . . . and last night."

He laughed himself then, putting the things down on a chair and bending to kiss her breasts lolling in the folds of the sheet.

"Take off your clothes," she murmured, rubbing her cheek against his head. She wanted to see him again properly, she said, last night it was too dark, all she could do then was stroke him, lick him — and he tasted what he smelt like, she'd recognise him anywhere — feel him moving inside her and that was good, good, hurry up Angus.

"The boy . . ." He nodded towards the door. "I told him as soon as I'd given you this I'd show him how I skin a dead lamb for a coat for that twin."

"Is he awake?"

"Been up for hours. Right now he's hoeing into a big plate of cornflakes."

"Shut the door, then." As he hesitated she said "He won't come in if the door's shut. He won't, Angus. He'll find something to amuse himself. Truly."

Well, I guess she knows, he's her boy . . . The thought

jabbed him: I guess he's used to it. All the same he went across the passage to speak to the child. At his step Jarrah looked up eagerly.

"I'll be with you shortly, I'm just talking to your mother."

Angus spoke brusquely. If the poor kid was disappointed, Angus refused to see it. He placed a chair against the door of the maid's room.

"This bed's a bit small for two people. Don't you have overnight guests too often?"

"I didn't notice it was too small last night."

"It's too small if you want to, what do they say, *sleep* together."

"Come off it, you slept last night." He heaved a sigh. "If I was twenty again you wouldn't have got much sleep."

"Hey! You aren't feeling sorry for yourself, are you?" She laughed. "Guess what, if *I* was twenty again, you wouldn't even like me."

"No?"

"No. I didn't like myself much."

Each time she breathed, she brushed against him. He moved his hand tenderly down her breasts and belly, drew his fingers through the crisp hair.

"But these days you do?"

She rubbed her heel indolently over the back of his calf. "I'm working at it."

"I like you."

"Yeah. I noticed."

He pulled her to him. "God, Gita, I love you."

"Don't! Don't say it, Angus."

She tensed, and so did he.

"Why? Don't you believe me?"

"Just don't say it, that's all."

"This isn't another one of your *signs*, is it?"

"Maybe I just think it's unlucky."

"I think I'm very lucky."

"Do you? If you knew the sort of person I am, have been I mean, you mightn't think so."

"Try me . . . Tell me what sort of person."

She moved her head back to look at him, asking some unspoken question.

"Trust me, Gita, don't you trust me? I need that more than anything. Your trust."

You don't open up much, do you? Oh come on, Crystal, what have I just been doing? *Sometimes it helps to talk* . . . Yeah? At that place, Crystal, we did nothing but talk. Yak yak yak. She sighed. "I guess we both do, Angus . . . Trust's easier to come to grips with than love, anyway. Love. What does that mean? . . . 'I hate you' — that's easy. But 'falling in hate' — no one says that, do they? And yet they're doing it all the time. But love . . . Falling in love, falling in lust, what the fuck's the difference?"

He laughed. "Here and now? Not much. Under the circumstances." He brushed her nipples, feeling them harden to his touch.

She twisted away. "Oh Angus, you always joke."

"Do I? I'm sorry. I thought touching each other was part of a conversation . . . I *am* listening, Gita."

She put her mouth to his ear as though to whisper. And ran her tongue inside the rim until he shuddered and pulled her close again.

"Angus . . . let's stop talking. Let's stop asking a whole heap of questions and then asking what the answers mean. One day at a time, remember?" She rolled over on top of him, reaching under the pillow, then rolled away again. "Hey! Do you wear pyjamas? I don't know *anyone* who wears pyjamas."

He sighed. "Generation gap."

"Oh come on, Methuselah, I'm not exactly one of the babes in the woods."

"Maybe I am. When it comes to living."

"Yeah. Maybe I am too." She scrabbled under the pillow again. "Here. What is it they say nowadays? Get your gear on, mate."

As she settled herself around him she watched him, watched with delight desire make his blue eyes darker.

"You look pleased," he murmured, holding her hips.

Maybe Jules was right: she was on a power-kick. She pressed against him. "So do you."

He grasped her buttocks. "I will say it. I love you, Gita. I love you!"

"If I'm going to stay over here," she said, " – and I'm not staying every night, you understand, Marycote's my place and I miss it – but if I'm going to be here sometimes, then we'd better use a proper bed where I can stretch out. I like space, Angus. What's wrong with that front room? There's a perfectly good bed in there. And a fireplace. I told you I love going to sleep beside a fire. Hey, and you like honey, don't you? Before we go to sleep, you know what I'm going to do to you this time?" She put her mouth to his ear and told him, then laughed as he reddened.

"My puritanical streak," he mumbled. "My calvinist forebears . . . Why not right now?"

"So . . . the front room. Okay?"

"The front room . . . okay. Let's get the fire going," he said, hoping she'd think his disquiet was just his puritanism. Or instant lust.

Each time they made love he felt renewed, like the swing of the seasons in their proper course.

One morning when he brought her breakfast to the bed and she gave her lazy laugh that shivered up and down his spine and he shut the door and pulled back the bed clothes so that he could gaze again at the slender generous body and she drew his head down into her thighs . . . that particular morning he murmured "Wait, I want to get you something" – and was astonished as he raised his head to see fear flicker across her eyes, the fear he'd observed when she caught sight of those two fellows at the cottage.

"What is it?" he asked. "What's the matter, darling?"

"Nothing. Nothing's the matter."

"When I said wait. You looked, I don't know, upset."

"Did I?" She smiled up at him. "Don't worry about it, Angus."

"Don't say that. Tell me what it was."

"Okay then. I'll try." She sighed. "I guess . . . saying wait, like that."

Puzzled, he sat on the edge of the double bed and himself waited. She reached for a piece of toast and chewed, her eyes on his face.

"Some guys — Angus, you wouldn't, would you? — some guys get you all stirred up and then they say wait, wait." Jules. *Jules, mocking gloating watching her body's despair until he chose to continue* "It's a game, it's like dangling you out over a cliff, hanging in space and you can't get back . . . You wouldn't ever, would you?"

If for a moment he recalled his own frustration that evening of the possum, the memory was gone before it surfaced. "Darling girl, I'm not a sadist."

"No. No. Hey and guess what? You're the only guy that's ever said things like that to me. Darling." As though he meant them.

"I just want to get you something. From the garden. Drink your tea while it's hot, I'll be back in a minute."

He went out to a sheltered spot on the south side of the house where winter roses were still blooming, their cool beauty surprising him with a stab of joy whenever he walked past. He picked a spray of each colour, delicate pink *pink for your lips, Gita,* green-veined white *white for your breasts*, and a deep plum *plum for those secret moist lips that hold me every time we make love.*

"Helleborus," he told Gita, giving her the flowers. "They made me think of you."

70 To Augment

Now that Jarrah's world had expanded, unless she'd been concentrating on every word Gita was often vague about just who was the subject of his long stories. Sometimes — usually — it was Angus; or one of the Catchpole boys; or even the dog over at Valley View Park, Mary's rock-chomping bull terrier that Jarrah had taken a liking to, or was it the other way round? Sometimes he meant one of the teachers (there weren't many men, Gita gathered, mainly old ladies), it might be the headmaster (who had a strap, the big kids reckoned, for the *reely* bad kids) or it might be Mr Gilford. Mr Gilford Gita heard more than once. He taught recorder and he could play a water pipe with holes drilled in it and the tap still attached to it and the big kids laughed at him because out on yard duty he'd be in the middle of telling them something, put your orange peels in the bin, and he'd pull a tiny recorder or a tin whistle out of his pocket and twiddle a tune — to *augment* what he was saying, Jarrah said he said.

Jarrah liked that word. Augment. He'd asked his teacher what it meant, and she'd sent him to the library where the librarian helped him look it up in the first volume of the big dictionary. "To increase." There was an awful lot of other stuff as well, but increase would do Jarrah. It also meant something musical, he noticed; that was its meaning for Mr Gilford, he supposed. One meaning for Mr Gilford and another meaning for him.

"Can I have a pet?" he said suddenly. "Gita? Can we have a pet?"

Gita, her feet hanging like two fish over the end of the sofa, looked at him in that way she had.

"Oh Jarrah, who d'you think'd end up looking after it?"

71 Still Doing His Own Washing

Since Gita was occupied helping Angus in the paddock, Mary fell back into the habit of dropping in at Springfield to whip around the house. A woman's touch, she thought, smiling with satisfaction as she dusted the rooms that Angus had opened up after all those sad years. It's what he needed. A woman's touch.

The boy had strewn some of his things around the room Angus slept in. She tidied them up and made the bed. Mopping the hall, she noticed that the door of the big bedroom,

George and Kate's room and then Angus and Belle's, was open, the bed in there slept in and unmade. Half way across the room she stopped abruptly. In each pillow was a dent where two heads had lain. Without touching anything, without breathing, she crept out and shut the door.

But he's still doing his own washing, she thought, putting a load into the machine. I will try to love her. I will, I will try.

72   You Had To Be Careful

Gita showered over at Springfield now, standing under the hot water till Angus hauled her out. I *think* under the shower, Angus, she said. Yes and after all that thinking *I* freeze. She also did her laundry at Springfield. Angus had a reliable old washing machine he said she was welcome to use. She carried the dry things across in her rucksack and he drove her and the wet washing home again. If it was late in the day he might stay on to have something to eat. And then he would linger, hoping their companionableness by the fire afterwards would take them to her bed when the boy had finally gone to his. But it never did. One time he asked her outright why not, said the kid was out of the way at last, he knew it wasn't her period, she enjoyed sex together as much as he did . . . at least he thought she did. Didn't she? She shrugged. Said don't worry about it, Angus. Said the bed's too narrow. I won't stay all night if you don't want me to, darling. No — look, just don't worry about it, I'll be over at Springfield again tomorrow, or the next night — soon. Don't *worry* about it. He looked around at Marycote's old firm walls, within whose confines once, in another lifetime, beautiful adolescent Belle to his terror and joy had let him go all the way. He hadn't told Gita about that, he hadn't thought about it for years. These were female walls, he told himself, reaching for his scarf and coat. Maybe there were mysteries he would never penetrate.

Gita still hadn't bought herself a bike to replace Mark's Peugeot so to do her shopping she waited until Angus was going into Currawong and got a lift in with him. Angus couldn't work out why she didn't want to take the Suzuki herself. She'd told him she'd been driving for years, just never got around to getting her licence. But when he let her try out the ute in the paddock and then offered to coach her for the driving test, she said "But it's *your* ute." "So what?" he said. She just looked at him oddly and said she'd walk.

He thought of buying her a bike himself, giving it to her as a surprise, but hesitated. Funny girl. He could never tell when she'd turn stroppy.

Like that time in the double bedroom: he was lying on his back, staring at the ceiling where there were faint stains he remembered from childhood when it was his parents' room, and he'd remarked "I was conceived in this bed. And my father, too, I suppose" and she'd jumped at him.

"Hey, you're not getting ideas?"

"No, Gita." He'd laughed. "No way. I've got my work cut out coping with myself, let alone trying kids with someone." He'd raised his head and glanced at her.

"That's okay, then." Her voice was cool, not at all jokey. "Just don't get ideas, okay?"

He had to mind what he said. You had to be careful with Gita.

73   Wonderful What You Get To Hear

The morning was a sliver of blue glass. There was a frost; grass crackled underfoot. Gita looked across the distance to hard-edged hills.

"Near the entrance to that new arcade might be a good spot to start busking, what d'you reckon?"

If he was surprised at this new idea, he didn't show it.

"Well, it's sale day. Plenty of people about. Want a lift in? While you're making your fortune I might drop in to the hospital for a few minutes to see my mother. Take her a few flowers from the garden."

"Your mother? Is she still alive? You never mention her."

He could have pointed out that she never mentioned her

mother, either, but said instead "She's in the geriatric section, been there for years. She hardly knows anyone. Not even me. Though she was having one of her lucid spells when Mary saw her the other day." He changed the subject. "How about a counter lunch when you're through singing?"

"Good idea. Will I meet you at the Horse and Harrows?" She laughed. "I've been in there. They didn't go off their brain."

She set herself up in the recessed entrance to the arcade, seated on a low wooden stool that she'd found at Springfield, with his battered Akubra at her feet for donations. Angus reached into his pocket and dropped a handful of change and a couple of five dollar notes into the hat, to encourage everyone else, he said.

She sang "Go Tell Aunt Rhodie" and "Dabbling in the Dew", and then a couple of her own pieces. People stopped to stare, or listen, then hurried past pretending they hadn't noticed the hat; a few dropped in coins; two girls nearly tripped over her, engrossed in some long story about Rodney; one or two people asked what the instrument was, or commented on the quality of her voice.

One woman stopped another one right on top of her but that wasn't for her music. "How's Rodney?" the first woman smirked. "Rodney? At the butcher's?" "That's the one." The second woman tossed her head and walked away. "I earn my own money!" *Well!* thought Gita. The old Currawong's coming to life.

A woman about her own age with a couple of little kids in tow looked promising. She smiled at Gita as the younger kid — just walking by the look of him — made a dive at the hat and spilt the coins. That's worth a donation, Gita thought, as the woman encouraged the kids to pick them up. The older kid refused, then started to howl, saying he's nothing but a pest, a pest. The mother squatted so that she was at the kid's level and said solemnly "Let's talk about this, Francesca." Gita stopped singing, just plucked a few chords so she could hear. "Perhaps you can think of something positive we could do about it, Francesca." Francesca stopped bawling. Wiping her teary face with the back of her hand, she hissed "Let's give him away!" The mother gave this serious thought. "Yes. That's one way. Now let's consider some other possibility, shall we?"

Gita laughed. She sang:

> Doggerel howls for the moon
> always beyond its reach
> shine on me, light my way soon
> I would take the brute to its kennel

One guy in a black coat stood leaning against the opposite wall for ages. Didn't bother with a donation, just stood there listening. At last he went away. Good. When she finished her song and looked up, he was back again. Just listening. Well screw you, mate! She gave him the old slow motion.

He lifted himself off the wall and came across. "I saw you in the Iron Bar."

She looked at him more carefully. Soft black coat around his ears. Soft yellow hair. "Yeah. I remember now. None too chatty, I recall."

"Ah . . . I had things on my mind that day. Nothing personal."

He was certainly more sociable today. Maybe this was Rodney.

"I play recorder," he told her. "A few other things, too, but I have to play the recorder."

"Yeah?" She plucked a couple of chords, running over the next song in her head.

"Yes. My job. Well, if I get a break. The way things are shaping, maybe not after this year. Maybe I'll end up busking like you. Make enough to get by, do you?"

She laughed, glancing down at the hat. "This is my first go in Currawong." She looked at the hat again, then back at him. He pulled some coins out of his pocket, selected one and dropped it.

"I might need the rest." He sighed. "After this year. I've been here so long now I thought I could end up being permanent. I mean, Mrs Bright's been away so long I good as am.

Permanent. Maybe something'll turn up. Maybe Mrs Bright'll drop dead."

"There's always the dole," Gita said, starting to sing again. She was losing customers listening to him.

As soon as she had finished her song, he continued "I like this place. There are some good people round here."

"Are there?"

He grinned. "Yes. Haven't you met any?" His face was okay when he wasn't grizzling.

"Not in the town. No, that's not true. There's the woman in the health food shop. She's good value. Actually I live quite a way out of Currawong. I'm working on a farm. And I busk because I like it."

She played a few bars of "Twinkle, Twinkle", pondering over wording because two women dressed up like Christmas trees in pearls and suits and two-storey heels were staring at her nose. She was startled to hear another instrument: the guy had whipped out a tin whistle and was joining in.

Good, he's good, she thought. Looking the two Christmas trees dead in the eye, she sang:

> Glitter, glitter, little stone,
> Through the gristle, not the bone –

"That's not true, of course," she tossed in, her aside making an accomplice out of the guy. "It's through the flesh part, but gristle scans" –

> How I wonder how it goes
> When you want to pick your nose!

He laughed. As he played something else at the women's retreating backsides she joined in with her own words: " 'Oh hark the cats are bolting, mate, we've scared them right away' " – wondering as she sang if someone made a donation now, would he want his coin back.

"You should hear me on the pipe and tap," he said, when they'd finished.

"Hey! I know who you are! You're Mr Gilford."

"Simon. Got someone at the school, have you?"

"Yes. Jarrah."

"Ah! You must be Gita."

"What's that little devil been saying now?"

Simon Gilford laughed. "Nothing incriminating. Though it's wonderful what you do get to hear." Please Mr Gilford — big grade three eyes wide with gravity — that new boy Jarrah said Eff. Did he, Tracey Ann? Just Eff, or the whole word? The whole *word*, Mr Gilford. But you didn't listen, did you, Tracey Ann? *No-o-o*, Mr Gilford. "Listen, maybe we could get together sometime, run through a few folksongs after school. What do you think? Do you come in to Currawong to pick Jarrah up?"

"I could. Sometime. Hey, that could be fun. A tin whistle sounds good with the dulcimer."

She gave him Angus's phone number.

He looked at his watch. "Shit, I'd better make tracks!" He strode off, then reappeared, hardly waiting for her next song to finish before saying "Maybe you'd like to drop in to a couple of my classes, be something different for them . . . What's so funny?"

"Nothing. Well, just that I seem destined to end up in front of the kids at that school, that's all."

"Might be a change from chasing sheep," he said sulkily.

"You reckon? Sounds like the same thing to me."

She grinned at his pained expression. She was sure, if she patted them, the soft yellow hair and the black coat would feel the same.

"I'll see what happens, okay?" she said.

Simon Gilford looked at his watch again, swore, and plunged off.

Gita played on. Several people dropped coins. There were a couple more notes. The woman who ran the health food shop stopped for a chat. "We're having a meeting soon?" she said, every statement a question. "Diane's going to speak on women's health issues? Diane? The new woman doctor? I can give you a ring as soon as we've fixed on the date?"

"That could be interesting." How in hell would she get in to a meeting? Well . . . something might turn up. Mary, maybe? She gave the woman Angus's number.

Just as the lunchtime crowds were thinning and she thought she might as well head off for the Horse and Harrows, Angus appeared.

"How'd it go?" he asked.

"Fine. I made a bit. If I'd hung around any longer I'd have been signed up for half a dozen committees, I reckon." She smiled. Simon Gilford . . . what a nut. They walked off in the direction of the pub. "How was your mother?"

"My mother?"

"You were going to the hospital."

"I haven't been there yet, Gita." He spoke so irritably her eyes widened. He began to walk faster.

Hey, she thought, hurrying to keep up. What did I do?

That guy Simon . . . irritable as hell in the pub: nothing to do with you, he'd told her this morning. Nothing to do with *you.* The women's guilt thing. *You should know better by now, Gita* and Gita leaning over the verandah rail at Marycote feeling ill because Jules – because she –

It's him Crystal he won't leave me alone it's all a power thing a game you don't have to play

When he stopped, so did she.

"It won't be much fun," he said.

She looked up. They were outside a group of new low white buildings set in lawns and bright flowerbeds.

"It won't be much fun." It was Angus talking to her, Angus's hand on hers, Angus, reaching in to the parked Suzuki for the bunch of sweet-smelling spring flowers he had picked at Springfield. "Gita . . . you don't have to . . . you can wait for me here in the garden."

His hand on hers was trembling. She squeezed it. "I don't mind."

At the reception desk they were asked to wait a moment, Doctor was doing his rounds. Gita could just make out the conversation in the ward. The names the male speaker was using caught her attention. "And how's Mrs Bear today, Sister? . . . Feeling better are we, Mrs Bear? Tell me, Maggie . . . March? . . . June?" And a female speaker: "Come on Maggie, be a good girl, you can do that for Doctor." The man again: "Good girl! She almost got it, Sister. Now listen carefully, Maggie . . ."

Jesus, thought Gita. I saw Maggie Bear the other night on TV at Springfield, she's that poor old duck everyone laughs at in *Mother and Son*! She glanced at Angus. He hasn't noticed, she thought. His hearing's not as sharp as mine.

The doctor came out, a very busy, very young man with a stethoscope bouncing against his white coat. Angus introduced himself, adding "This is my friend Gita."

The doctor shook hands with Angus, nodded at Gita, ignored her outstretched hand. "Kate's having one of her good periods this week, Mr Springfield," he said. "At this rate she'll soon know what day it is."

Shit, Gita thought, some old woman staring at the same four walls year in year out and she's supposed to know what fucking day it is! She glanced at Angus. His face was expressionless. Gita gave a mental shrug. It's his affair. It's his mother. It's none of my business.

They went into the ward. It was a bright, airy room, smelling like the arcade around the florist's shop. There were four high metal beds in here, all with their sides drawn up so that their occupants couldn't fall out − or run away, Gita thought, dull anger beginning to ache low in her belly as the slow eyes of the women turned towards the visitors. Anger at what? At heartless boys in white coats? At Angus for saying nothing? At life for playing games with you, turning a glowing face a man ached to kiss into a wrinkled seed potato?

Kate Springfield was in the bed furthest from the door. As soon as she heard steps she became restless, twisting her head, trying to sit up, giving inarticulate little cries.

"She thinks she should be rushing about putting on the kettle," Angus said bleakly. "Hello Mum," he said, bending to kiss the woman whose face had fallen slack again. "It's Angus, Mum. I've dropped by to say hello . . . I've brought you a few things from the garden. A few daffs and johnnies, look, and snowflakes still going strong near the old well. Remember them?" He glanced around the ward. It was full of flowers, Singapore orchids, carnations, proteas, roses heavy with fragrance. He tried again. "Mum, I've brought someone to see you. This is my friend Gita."

Gita walked around the bed and leaned across, level with Kate Springfield's empty gaze.

"Hello, Mrs Springfield."

Slow as snails Kate Springfield's eyes moved until they fixed on Gita's face. "Arabella!"

Gita heard Angus sigh. "Arabella was her sister."

His mother was muttering urgently. Gita leaned closer. "I never . . . Arabella, I never told."

Gita glanced at Angus, then smiled at the loyal sister. "Good on you, Kate. I've always appreciated that. Thanks."

The snail eyes sucked at hers. "And *I* got the whipping, Arabella!"

"Back again, Angus!" the barmaid in the Horse and Harrows said cheerfully. "What's it to be this time?"

So that's what he was doing while I was busking, Gita thought. She recalled his shaking hand at the utility.

"Orange juice for me, Jill, thanks."

"You might be wise at that. They reckon the new copper's dynamite."

"So I've heard." He gave a little laugh. "What'll you have, Gita?"

She was about to order a stout, then changed her mind and asked for red wine.

"I'm thinking of putting in grapes next year," Angus told her, sipping his orange juice. "On that northern slope near the house. Diversification. Something else besides wool and fat cattle."

"You told me."

"Did I?"

"Have you ever thought of goats? I've met people who breed goats." One of the people at that place bred Angoras.

He sighed. "One goat on the place is enough, Gita, I reckon."

She smiled, though he spoke with more than a tinge of self-pity. That guy Simon's another one, she thought. How come

I collect them? Simon Gilford . . . She lifted her glass and against the window stared at her wine's ruby clarity, then took a long sip, feeling its warmth spread down her arms, down breasts and belly, down to the tendons behind each heel.

"Penny for them," Angus said.

She smiled at him, studying the familiar lines that ran like eroding gullies down his cheeks.

"Can I get a job treading the grapes?"

The cook called their order number. There were only two other people eating a meal, a man and a woman whose eyes were fixed on the television set where horses were sweeping around a country racecourse.

Angus squeezed lemon on to his fish, took a forkful of salad, then put it down again. "Gita, thanks. Thanks for coming into the hospital. I'm sorry —"

"Don't worry about it."

They went on eating.

"Sometimes you find them again," she said suddenly, talking past his shoulder so that he looked around to see if someone was coming towards them. "Seed potatoes you've planted."

"What? What are you talking about?"

"Grown all shrivelled and mushy. Under the new plant. Part of it." She smiled, and took up her fork again.

"I can't follow you sometimes, Gita."

"Don't worry about it." She rubbed her leg against his. "It's okay, Angus. I've visited lots of people in hospitals. Friends who've OD'd. One poor guy on the way out with AIDS."

He thought God how little I know about her.

He leaned towards her. "You remember you told me I ought to ease up on the grog?"

"Did I? I must have been stoned."

"Maybe. And I was rotten drunk. But not too rotten to take in what you were saying. Go easy, you said."

"And you haven't touched a drop since, is that what you're going to tell me?"

"Fair go. I mean I woke up to myself."

"That's great. That's half the battle."

"Battle? There's no battle. Because there's no problem. Not really. Only when I start brooding."

"About the war?"

He shrugged, then laughed. "Well, I'm lucky, I guess. At least my drug's licit. And I can handle it." He laughed again. "Even if Mary thinks she has to keep topping up the bottle from the tap. It's a matter of willpower."

"Sure."

"And I've got plenty of that. It's up to me. I don't need to go on the wagon. I can monitor myself. Though there was a time there when things were getting out of hand."

Gita looked around. She lowered her voice. "Did you . . . did you really take a swipe at someone with a bottle?"

He stared at her, then laughed. "Who told you that? With a bottle? Hell, no! Maybe I wanted to. But I was too plastered to hit anyone with anything, and so was he. You don't want to hear that old story, do you?"

She shrugged. But she looked so relieved that he told her anyway.

"It's not very clear now, Gita. I remember we took a couple of swipes at each other, I gave the bastard more than he gave me, actually, and then he came back at me and by all accounts he slipped but what he fell against I don't know because I don't remember too much after that, only the publican telling me to bugger off, sort myself out. And when my head cleared the next day and I found myself lying under a pine tree in the park, I thought maybe he was right. There was nothing left for me in Currawong, anyway." He sighed. "I was in pretty poor shape. I mean I was drinking to sort out my head."

"I know what you mean. Drinking. Using. There was this guy, he used to talk to me all the time — in my head, I mean. That's crazy, isn't it?"

"I know the feeling. When I was angry all the time — before I came back to the farm — I used to argue with all those smart-arses every waking minute. In my head. All they did at the hospital was give me a handful of pills and say come back when they're finished. Useless bastards. I took a few of their pills and then flushed the rest down the dunny."

"Good for you. Pity Mary doesn't do the same with all that valium her doctor's pouring into her."

"Valium? Mary? Who told you that?"

"She did. In town one day. She was all tensed up about seeing the doctor, so I went into the surgery with her."

"Did you? That was nice of you, Gita." He sounded so surprised that she looked up, half smiling. "Poor old Mary. She'd really appreciate that."

He watched her crumbling the crust of her bread on to the tablecloth. She said after a while "You're lucky. If you really can control it. I couldn't."

He glanced at her keenly.

"I thought I could," she went on, making a ball out of bread particles then crumbling it again. She looked at him but she was looking through him. "I was kidding myself. Some users really can handle it, though. Straight people, the ones who don't use, I mean — oh, they might be drunk every second night or smoke like chimneys till their lungs fall in on them, but that's okay, isn't it, that's legal — they go off their brain if they hear someone's using. That's because they only hear about the worst cases, see some poor kid on TV that's OD'd at Kings Cross or something. They don't know about the ones who really can handle it, well of course they don't, obviously. Jules, for instance. He uses, but you'd never think so just to look at him, or talk to him, would you? You remember Jules?"

Of course he remembered Jules. "Junkie, eh?"

"No, Angus, he's *not* a junkie. That's just the point. Anyway, junkie's a term that people don't use any more."

"What do I say, then? Victim of society?"

"Jules? You're joking. He's no victim. I used to be dead scared of Jules."

"Not any more, though?"

She shook her head. "And I never will be again. You know how

I know? When he was here he left some stuff with me. Heroin."

"Did he really?"

"Yeah. So I'd start using again. But he's wrong, isn't he? I won't."

"Where is it now?"

"Over at Marycote."

"You mean you've still got it?"

"Sure. Don't look so shocked, Angus."

"What are you hanging on to it for? Why don't you just chuck the stuff out?"

"It's a test." As she said it, the idea became fact. "If I have it but I don't take it, then I'll know I'm free." She shivered. Of him.

"So . . . how long do you have to keep it? Forever? I mean, how will you know when the test's finished?"

"I'll know."

74   Trash and Treasure

"This Saturday," Jarrah told Gita, "there's going to be a Trash and Treasure by the old rotunda. Heaps of comics and white mice and fairy floss. Let's go."

"This Saturday," Gita told Angus, "there's going to be a Trash and Treasure. Coming? Give yourself another holiday." She smiled at the memory of that last one.

Angus laughed. "What, to buy a heap of boiled-up fruit labelled as sugarless jam that goes mouldy next day? Been there." He saw her expression change so added hastily "I'll take you in. What time?"

"Thanks. I'll walk."

"Please yourself."

Jarrah said eagerly "I'll come with you, Angus."

"Will you, mate? We'll give Gita a wave, will we?"

Saturday found Angus carrying bunches of locally grown broccoli and spinach, jars of rhubarb jam, pickled cabbage, home-made yoghurt, and the hand-knitted jumper she'd wanted but said was too dear and he'd nipped back and bought while she was talking to that bloke in the black coat. He felt a surge of contentment: the woman beside him, or lingering to turn over a heap of hand-crafted rings and bracelets, the boy somewhere about, chasing after his schoolmates, begging Gita for one more fairy floss then dashing off when Angus slipped him the coins.

"You're wearing what you had on the first time I saw you," he told her: the olive-green dress, black stockings, worn leather jacket with half the studs missing, little black leather cap perched on the back of her head.

She brushed against him. Her hair, caught back loosely with a velvet ribbon, glinted in the sharp sunlight as though she had rinsed it in tea. "Observant, weren't you?"

He returned her arm's pressure. "Farmers have to be."

He was surprised at the number of people she knew. "Hi," she kept murmuring, or would greet them with her enigmatic smile.

"I do come into town now and then," she said, when he commented. "You must know a few people yourself, don't you?"

"I suppose I do, really. Yes, I do."

It struck him then, he had come home.

They stopped at a stall that was selling garden seedlings. Gita wanted a pot of lemon balm.

"How's your tree-planting going, Angus?" the stallholder asked him. "I hear you've got great plans for windbreaks out there at Springfield. I've got a few trees here myself, local ones, I mean. Quite a bit of interest in them, actually, but I'm too busy with summer veggies and flowers to do much in that line."

"There you go," Gita said as they walked on with punnets of bergamot and salad burnet as well as the lemon balm. "Next Trash and Treasure, you set up your own stall. You're not the only greenie round here."

He laughed. "I've got enough on my plate as it is right now. There's that fencing we talked about."

"You mean so we could put that extra bit of plantation in this year? Good."

"I reckon we just about could, this spring. What d'you think, eh? But listen, even if we got extra help with it, there are still far too many seedlings. I don't know what I was doing, sowing so much." He shook his head. What a performance! Sheer willpower forcing him into the bush to collect the seed, and then all the frantic sowing earlier this year. Too busy even to wash down the glasshouse! "They're not even pricked out yet," he went on. "They'll just have to be chucked out, half those dillwynias and correas... unless you'd like to? And then sell them at the market here? Make a bit extra for yourself, I mean. Because you'd have to be the one to do it, I really am too busy for more than the occasional hand." He laughed. "Woodheap's getting low, have you noticed? Maybe we should think about putting in a couple of slow-burning stoves instead of lighting up all those open fires, eh?" He thought about the first time they had made love in front of an open fire, her skin as golden as the sweet potatoes from Mareeba. He went on "And I want to get the veggie garden going again, too, did I tell you? Springfield doesn't seem right without one."

"That pricking out," she said slowly. "In between my work at Springfield, you mean?"

"It seems a pity just to chuck them out, doesn't it?" he said cunningly, picturing her at the next Trash and Treasure, and the next, and the next. "Especially now, when people are wanting them. Because you're right, I'm not the only greenie. Give you a bit of extra independence, too," he repeated.

"It's an idea." She said she'd think about it.

75 The Hard Word

... But Angus, I mightn't be here, I don't know how long I'm staying here, do I? I might go tomorrow, I might go next week —

Don't say that, Gita!

But it's true. I might. Hey come on! I'm not planning on it, Angus, I'm not planning to leave, but how do I know? Anything might happen. You might get sick of me.

Never!

Never's a long time . . . There isn't any escape, is there, no plateau you reach and you can say *you're there*.

I don't understand.

I don't have a real home, I mean Marycote's my home but it's really your place, isn't it?

Listen darling, Marycote is your home for as long as you want . . . or if you want to move over here, this is your home too.

Don't hassle me, Angus. Don't put the hard word on me.

Gita! When have I ever done that?

All the time, Angus. Every time you look at me. Every time you smile.

76   Love Thy Neighbour

The afternoon drew on. Mary wiped down the sink again; straightened the teatowels. She should be back at Valley View Park, she should be making a start on that new recipe Belle had looked out for her. Mary sighed: a new recipe. But it was kind of Belle; she was trying to make up for the incident at breakfast time. Mary leaned against Angus's sink and stared out the window at the moving leaves of the saplings on the little rise. She shouldn't have said that to Lou . . .

"The runaround's still playing up, Lou," she'd begun hesitantly.

"That old rustbucket? No wonder."

"Rust now, Lou?"

"Haven't you noticed? All round the boot."

"The boot? That's all right then, I only use the front."

Lou had looked at her sharply. "So what's the latest worry?"

"That business starting it. It's no better. Rrrr-rrr, I don't like the sound of it." Angus was always so busy, she never had got round to reminding him.

"I told you what I thought that was. The points."

"Again!"

"What do you mean, again? I haven't had a go at it at all

yet, have I? Haven't had time." And he'd blown a puff of smoke across the table, whether deliberately or not Mary couldn't tell but it brought on her cough.

"Lou!" cried Belle.

"I think I know when I'm a nuisance..." – resolutely folding her serviette – "which is more than could be said of some people some years ago in some other men's houses."

"Mary!" cried Belle.

At last Angus came in from the paddock. Angus and the girl. Jarrah was with them, gazing up at Angus, telling him something about school. Angus was preoccupied, he wasn't taking any notice of the boy, so Mary said "That Mr Gilford sounds very nice, dear, a very nice teacher to have."

"And Gita's going to come to school and play the dulcimer. Mr Gilford said," Jarrah added quickly, as Gita turned on him.

"He what?"

"He only said might," the boy wailed.

"What about taking the wax off this pot of jam, Jarrah," said Mary the peacemaker. "I've made the tea, everything's ready."

"In the sitting room?" Gita asked. "I like the chairs in there. Light the fire, Angus."

Bossyboots! observed Mary. "Perhaps Jarrah could light it for you, I'm sure he's very sensible," she suggested, taking care as always to speak to Angus's good ear, but even so he didn't seem to hear. Is it something I just said, she asked herself, taking the tea tray through to the sitting room. After a second or two's hesitation she perched on the edge of Kate Springfield's armchair. Well, she always sat in this chair... and nothing official had been said... and anyway Gita without even a by-your-leave glance was already curled up in Angus's chair. Angus had to sit on the floor, leaning against his chair and staring into the fire with his feet in his holey socks stretched towards the flames.

"Where are you going to sit, Jarrah?" Mary asked, passing him a hot buttered scone on a plate, fussing a bit to make up for not lighting the fire. "Over here by me?"

The boy took the plate, smiling at her though he didn't answer. Pulling off his shoes so that he, too, was in socks, he sat down, legs outstretched, beside Angus. No one was very talkative, not even Jarrah. It's not like the old days, thought Mary, when it was just Angus and me. Unbidden there came to mind the image of the two dented pillows, side by side dumbly. She said "I must tell you about the sermon the new minister preached on Sunday. He's very nice, he's a bit modern, that's to be expected these days, isn't it — but he's very nice."

"What was the sermon about, Mary?" Gita interrupted.

"Love thy neighbour," said Mary, startled by the girl's abruptness. "Yes. That was it. Love thy neighbour. Your neighbour, is how he put it. Your, not thy. He is very modern. The rest of it goes on, as thyself. Love thy neighbour as thyself. And that was the important part." When the minister told the congregation what he thought Jesus had meant, Mary had actually started in her pew as though he'd just announced the Day of Judgment, or a safety pin had jabbed her. I know that! she had wanted to shout. I have always known that! But I didn't know I knew till now!

Of course that was much too boastful to tell anyone, that Jesus had said something she'd always known, unless you were telling someone really close, like a husband. Did Angus and Gita tell each other things in George and Kate's big bed? And so Mary had done the next best thing: called in the very next opportunity she had to tell Angus about the sermon, but not her revelation, and she'd had to wait till he came home and the girl was with him and he was in one of his moods — should she sneak a quick look at the level in the bottle?

"The important part?" Angus repeated, only half listening she could tell.

"Because you can't really care about other people, not really, he said, until you care deep-down about yourself — love yourself — he said. The new minister said."

Angus laughed. "Sounds a bit egotistical to me, Mary. Loving yourself."

While they were talking, Mary had noticed Jarrah's leg

gradually moving until it was touching Angus's leg. Angus shifted his leg away. Mary felt a stab of anger — against Angus? Surely not. "I wonder what it is that keeps us going?" she asked herself.

"Willpower," Angus said immediately.

Gita said nothing; her hand, reaching out, travelled slowly down the back of his neck, up again, and down.

Mary, eyes on the girl's spread fingers, had to look away. "What do you think, Jarrah?" She smiled at him. But the boy just shrugged.

"What do *you* think, Mary?" Angus asked, dragging himself back from wherever he was in the fire flames.

Pleased, Mary moved her shoulders in a deprecating shrug. "I suppose . . . self-esteem?" she offered.

Again she saw the child's leg move to touch the man's. Again Angus shifted. Oh Angus! The child wants a hug! He loves you. Give him a hug, Angus! Mary caught Gita's eye. Gita had noticed, too, Mary was certain. She looked hurt.

77 Gita Takes the Cake

An opportunity for Mary to say something nice to Gita, something to make up for Angus's unwitting hurt, came shortly afterwards in the kitchen while Mary was washing up.

"I'm glad there are things in Currawong for you to join in, Gita," she said as the girl put another dirty cup on the sink. "Otherwise it might be just too quiet for you." You know where the teatowels are, surely, Gita? "Your music will be a real asset at Jarrah's school."

"Jarrah's school!" The girl laughed, ignoring the substance of Mary's comment. "Jarrah's school has sent me a letter asking me — telling me — to make an appointment to discuss my son's playground language."

Angus, sitting on a kitchen chair and running one thumbnail under the other, looked up at that. He caught Gita's eye. "I wonder where he learns it," he murmured. Why was she so sharp with Mary? Got out of bed on the wrong side this morning all right: now she turned on him.

"I don't pretty up words for the body, if that's what you mean. 'Little boys' room'. God!"

"You're pretty free with a lot of words." Annoyed with himself for persisting: don't hassle me, Angus.

"You're pretty free yourself — bugger this, bugger that," she retorted.

"That's still more acceptable to a lot of people than some of the things you say."

That set her going. "Oh sure! It's all right to say bugger someone but not fuck someone, and you know why, don't you?" She ignored his frantic glance in Mary's direction. "Because buggery's men's business, it's something men can do with other men, but fucking involves a woman and men are so scared of women and anything sexual to do with women that fuck has to be banned and if you could you'd ban . . . you'd ban . . ."

While she was speaking Mary had walked out of the room. "How's the fire, Jarrah?" the old woman said automatically, giving the back log a bash with the poker. Men's words. Bar room words. She couldn't think what she had said to bring on such an outburst.

"He's going to let me light up a big heap of cypresses one day," the boy said.

She put her arm around the thin shoulders and gave him a hug.

"Ban what?" Angus asked.

He couldn't catch what she muttered.

He breathed tuh! like Crystal. "There wasn't any need for that performance in front of Mary, was there?"

"*Mary's* upset, is she?"

He laughed. "Don't kid yourself I am. I've met plenty of women with mouths like you."

"Have you, *my dear*? So much for what you told me last night."

"God, Gita! Women take the cake when it comes to using

what other people say to suit the moment! You know what I meant last night."

He limped out of the room — his knee was always worse when he was upset, she'd noticed. She could hear his voice: they were coming back to the kitchen. She ducked over to the doorway in time to hear Mary saying "There's no need for you to apologise for your friend, Angus. I'm sure if she wants to say something herself, she will."

"*Je*-sus!" She clenched her hands together and rolled her eyes.

Just then the phone rang. As Angus and Mary entered the kitchen Gita was saying "Hey, that sounds great, that sounds fun, it's what I really miss up here . . . Oh — walk, my bike's broken down . . . *Will* you? That's good of you, Simon, thanks. One way's not too bad, but back again . . . Sure, I'll have time for a bite to eat first."

"I couldn't help overhearing, Gita," Mary said diffidently, when Gita showed no sign of telling Angus about the phonecall. "If it's something in Currawong you're going to, I can keep an eye on Jarrah over at Valley View Park. He gets on well with the boys, and I'm there . . . Belle doesn't have to —"

"Would you, Mary? Okay, thanks. Some people I know are playing music after school tomorrow and then eating Chinese afterwards. Thanks, Mary. Thanks."

Angus shook his head: Mary apologetic, Gita nonchalant. You take the cake, Gita, he thought. You really take the cake.

She hadn't asked *him* to mind the kid. He didn't particularly want to — but she could have asked, couldn't she? Who the hell was Simon? He doubted that she would tell him.

78   He Said — He Said

He said "It's been a long day — too long. I'm turning in."
He said "You're looking done in yourself."
He said "You've sung those words dozens of times. 'He-e-ey funny money!' What's the problem all of a sudden?"

"*This* is a *new* tune." Jesus, Angus — you've played the old tune yourself on the harmonica!

And still he hung about — placed the guard in front of the fire — asked her again what the problem was, she didn't usually worry herself silly like this, was that what set her going this afternoon with Mary.

Cramped over the dulcimer as though she was haemorrhaging, in a too-cool voice she said: "I can't get the tuning right. These new melodies just . . . happened — and I can't get the bloody tuning right!"

"Give it a rest," he said.

"Find a bit of inspiration in bed," he said.

She stood up then. Took the fire-guard away. Said when she'd fixed the tuning maybe she'd walk back to Marycote. "I'll see what happens," she said. Whereupon *he* said "And the boy? You're going to wake him up and make him walk too?" and she said "He's okay here," upon which he said "I see!" and she said "What does that mean, Angus: I see?"

He turned away then. "I can't take this bickering."

"Who's bickering? . . . Okay, you want to know what the problem is. If I tune it to the key I want, I can't get D flat. And if I change the key then I can't get something else. It's the dulcimer, it's limited —"

"It's a lovely instrument —"

" — useless! — " *she knows a dulcimer's useless*

" — like running water. Makes me think of that first afternoon down by the creek, did I ever tell you? You had mist in your hair —"

"Oh shit! Oh shit! Why did they just come like that?" *Grace Broz Grace Broz Grace Broz* "They need a guitar."

"Then we'll get a guitar," he was saying. "No obligation to stick to the one instrument, is there?"

"I won't have a fucking guitar!"

If he said "Don't cry-y-y, baby," if he said anything at all . . .

He said nothing. Just went out of the room. Later, when the sitting room fire had burned itself out and she'd got no further with the tuning, she went to bed herself. The room was freezing. He never lit the fire if she was going to sleep over at Marycote. She put her cold feet against his leg. He didn't stir.

79 Trust

Gita hammered two stakes into the ground, then slipped a plastic sleeve over them and with the third stake stretched it neatly around the seedling.

"Each one's got its own little greenhouse," she commented.

Angus was ahead of her, digging half a dozen holes with the tree spade, then coming back to pour in a splash of water and slip a seedling into each hole. They weren't talking much; up in the plantation they often worked together for long stretches in companionable silence.

"That must give it a good start," she went on, unaware of his rigid back. "All that extra warmth. As well as protecting it. Doesn't it?"

"Start? Sure –" He swung around. "How was your music?"

"What? Oh – great. There's quite a group in there. Folk, mostly. It was fun."

Hey, that song of yours is great, they'd said. But you'd have to tune the dulcimer to a different key half way through it, wouldn't you? Your melody's much more complex than the folk songs.

"What do they play?" Simon, what does Simon play?

"Banjo. Flute. Guitar." Here, try it on the guitar, they'd said. It's more versatile. For that melody. Sure, she'd said, no obligation to stick to the one instrument, is there. "Tin whistle. Vocal. Hey, I'm getting ahead here. Get a move on there, Angus. Yeah, it was fun," she repeated. "You should come sometime. Bring the harmonica."

So she was going again. He muttered something about being too busy. I'm losing her, he thought, she's drifting away, her too, what else could I expect?

* *

Their love-making that night pushed back the limits of pleasure (like two travellers through space, she thought), the responses of their bodies unrelated to the desperation he felt as he held her, saying over and over I love you, I love you. The beginning of the end, he told himself, the beginning of the end. As they drew apart she began to cry, breathless sobs that alarmed him. Leave me, leave me, she wept when he tried to comfort her. What is it, he begged her, Gita, what is it, but she only moved further away until she was on the very edge of the bed, it's all right, Angus, it's all right — laughing a little — just leave me. Frightened, he moved to his side of the bed, staring at the stains on the invisible ceiling.

I came back. You can go there with someone you trust and still come back

He had drifted into a tormented half-sleep in which Metcalf kept trying to tell him something, when she nuzzled her head into his neck.

"I want to tell you something . . . Angus? Are you awake?"

I don't want to hear this, Gita.

"Angus?"

"I'm listening."

"Remember one time we were talking about screwing — and you said, I guess you wanted me to say I love you."

"I remember."

"And I couldn't. Angus?"

"You don't have to tell me."

"I want to tell you why. You."

Like one who on a lonesome road — he scrabbled in his mind for the rest of the stanza to block out the pain. I've been down this road, Gita.

"Remember I told you my cop-out, that day up by the rocks? Disappearing? Going right away outside myself till there's nothing there? And that's scary. What if I went so far I couldn't get back?" *But I can. I can come back. You can go there with someone you trust and still come back* "So you know how I made sure I was still there? You really want to know?

Do you?" She moved closer. "Are you asleep? Put your arm round me, Angus . . . Well, by using things. Substances, I mean. Speed, smack. Sex. Yeah, sex. I mean I needed the sex for the smack."

When he realised what she was *not* telling him, he said, glad with surprise, "But I guessed that a long time ago."

"Did you? You couldn't guess the half of it."

"Tell me, darling. I'm listening."

"Yeah, well . . . It wasn't just sex for smack thanks goodbye. That would have been okay. That would have been easy. But I'd end up getting into a relationship with some guy and often he was my supplier and I'd despise him because usually he was a shit too, or even if he wasn't, if he was just someone like Mark for instance, Mark's okay, he's an okay sort of guy when he's not mooning round after Jules . . . But I don't want to talk about them. What I'm trying to say is, after a while, whoever the guy was, if I started to feel something for him and he was a shit then I'd despise myself too, I'd end up hating myself, you know what I mean? Falling in love with a shit? And if he *wasn't* a shit I'd still end up despising myself."

"Gita!"

"I've never told anyone this before — anyone, not even at that place in the special sessions where everyone was shouting and raving and it was supposed to be good for you." She shuddered. "I hated those sessions. So I cleared out. Packed up Jarrah's and my things and hitched back to Melbourne."

He saw a road stretching from horizon to horizon and two tiny figures on it, her thumb stuck out and the anonymous cars flashing past.

He hugged her. "I'm glad you wanted to tell me . . . trusted me."

She lay still and tense for a long time. "So . . . where was I?" she said at last.

"Feeling something for someone."

"And I'd end up despising him. Whoever I was sleeping with. 'Falling in love' with. But at the same time because I could still feel something — hate, contempt, whatever — I'd know I was still alive. You know what I mean? That I hadn't . . . disappeared.

And that was good. I needed those relationships, I was hooked on them too. Because I'd know I was still alive. And then I'd get out of it. Out of the relationship. Always on the move." She sighed. "Yeah, always on the move. And I ended up being scared of loving anyone, caring I mean. Does that make sense?"

"Yes. That makes sense." He felt immensely tender towards her, traveller on the loneliest of roads.

And at the same time was suddenly chilled. Was that how she felt about him? Just . . . proving she was there?

80 Stone Axehead

Conscripted then dumped. How many times had he been over this patch? He glanced at her. She was picking at her bowl of porridge, ignoring him, ignoring the kid who kept on whining at her to sign something till Angus could have cuffed him.

"It's for the excursion, Gita. If you don't sign the form today I'll miss out."

Gita looked up vaguely. "What form? You haven't given me any form."

"I forgot."

Angus rarely interfered with the kid, he was Gita's business not his, but when Angus had opened the kitchen window earlier because he'd burned the porridge, the papers from the bench flew all over the floor and he felt fed up.

"Have you seen the axehead that used to be here, Jarrah?"

"No. You have to sign it today, Gita."

Angus spoke so sharply that both Gita and Jarrah stared. "So where is it, Jarrah?"

"*I* haven't got it!"

"He said no, didn't he, Angus?"

"I meant what he wants signed."

"At home. She has to —"

Home. Marycote. "In your bag, is it? And how long has it been sitting there? Not the first time, is it? Maybe if you miss out, you'll remember next time." Wasn't that what his parents used to say? How the hell did anyone know how to bring up kids? Gita's method was hit and miss.

The kid gave him a sulky look, and started nagging his mother again. "Gita, you'll have to come home with me. If I have to get it and bring it all the way back here, I'll miss the bus. *Please,* Gita."

And if he misses the bus he'll be back here grizzling all day, Angus thought sourly. "Want me to run you over to Marycote in the ute, Gita?"

Gita smiled at him from some distant landscape. "Come on, Jarrah, I'll race you."

Angus got up from the table and seized his hat. Work! Work till he dropped!

"What's he in a shit for?" Jarrah grumbled as Gita signed the grubby form.

Gita shrugged. "Who knows? . . . Listen, have you got that stone axehead of his? Because maybe you could —"

"I told you, no." When she looked at him doubtfully he added "But I know who does."

She looked even more doubtful then. "Well then," she said, smiling like a teacher, "wouldn't it be nice if it just turned up again in the kitchen . . . or somewhere where he'll see it . . ."

"You don't believe me, do you? That's 'cause you —"

"Here's your bus," she said, giving him a shove. "You better get going, Jarrah, or you'll miss it this time for sure."

81 Joy

The cottage grew calm. Its stillness was something she could put out her hand and touch like a fabric in a shop. No nagging boy to rip it, no guy swearing about a burnt saucepan. Marycote creaked faintly, shifting its old limbs as the day warmed them. Gita closed the back door behind her, then stood in a patch of sunlight, watching nothing, thinking nothing. A fly drifted past, its slow drone becoming part of her senses so that even after the noise had ceased, she could still hear it, follow it. She grew further away.

She started to walk back to Springfield the long way, down the road and along the winding drive under the pinoaks. At the bridge she stopped and stared at the rushing creek. The noise of water and the light wind in the treetops roared over her softly. Leaves turned and glittered. The sun flew across the sky. In the distance one of Angus's cattle bellowed twice, then fell silent. Nearby a magpie was stepping, its bright eyes intent on the grass. Every now and then it paused, head cocked to one side, then jabbed its bill into the soil and pulled out a worm. Its bill was full of worms. Gita looked down at her feet. Several curious ants were running over her boots. Ants stopping to touch feelers then running on ceaselessly had made a distinct track through the grass. There's a whole world underfoot, she mused, just like the world up here that we see every day. Worms, grubs, ants, roots of growing things, all busy in their invisible underground world, and up here, walking across it, I am part of that world, I am alive, I am I. She grew even stiller. She felt herself flow out to this world and the morning stopped and the shadows at her feet stood still.

82 Manipulator

She became conscious of an intrusive noise. Looking up, she saw an old blue car coming down the hill. Mary Springfield. She'd given her a hard time the other day. When the car came level, she waved. Mary drew up.

"Are you walking into town, Gita? Can I give you a lift? . . . doctor again . . . X-rays he insisted I have . . . must remember what he tells me . . . another little pain I get, too. In my side. Actually that was what I went to see him about last time, but somehow the other things came up . . . all those X-rays."

Oh dear now I'm talking too much again, thought Mary Springfield, as the old pain in her side nipped her like a watchdog. She makes me so nervous I chatter on like a magpie because I never know what she'll come out with next.

Gita saw that chill surgery with the elderly people patiently waiting on the hard grey chairs. She heard Mary's warm voice: This is my friend Gita . . . my friend Gita . . .

"Would you like me to come in to see the doctor with you, Mary? To help you remember?" she offered on the spur of the moment.

Mary said again "This is my friend Gita," and explained that she was there to assist Mary's silly old head. The doctor, spinning his chair slowly behind his big desk, indicated irritably that she sit next to Mary. I suppose it's the way I'm dressed, Gita thought. Well, at least my ears are clean: I won't miss what he tells her.

"Well Mary." The doctor shot Gita a cunning look as he put the X-rays in front of Mary and broke into a spiel of jargon. Mary looked blank. Gita, putting on what she hoped was an informed expression, nodded occasionally.

"I've always lived such a healthy life," Mary said sadly when he had finished. "Years on farms."

"Farms!" He laughed. "It's a wonder you haven't picked up brucellosis and hydatids along with the rest. Now . . . is there anything else bothering you? . . . Farms!"

Gita saw Mary bridle. "No," she said. "I don't think so, Doctor, thank you." She glanced at Gita.

"What about that little pain . . .?" Gita murmured.

"There is something they told me at home I should mention. In my chest." Gita frowned: I thought you said your side, Mary. "Sometimes. If I'm hurrying uphill. It's nothing really, but since I'm here —"

The doctor's chair spun to face her. "*Now* you tell me! You come in here and in passing you tell me you're walking round with heart disease!" Gita saw Mary's chin begin to tremble. "You watch TV, don't you, Mary?" He sounded kind now. "You've seen all the publicity?" Mary nodded. He gave a nod, too, and continued gently "I bet you and Miss — Miss — here were heading off for a nice cholesterol-making cream cake after this? Eh?" Mary nodded again, too distressed to speak. The doctor shook his head. "I've just shown you the X-rays and — if they aren't enough — now there's your heart." He sighed, still shaking his head. "In other words, Mary, you're a mess."

Gita caught her breath sharply. The doctor raised his eyebrows.

Keep your cool, Gita. You're here for Mary, remember? "That's a bit . . . strong, isn't it? Telling someone they're a mess?"

"You think so, do you?" Staring at her. I'm not going to drop my eyes, Gita thought. You shit.

Smiling, he turned back to his patient. "I have to rouse on you, Mary, you know that, don't you?" Smiled. Waited. Gita saw Mary try to smile back, try to nod, or perhaps it was her head trembling. "All my old ladies need a bit of a rouse now and then." Next, that smile at Gita. "Mary understands me, she knows when I'm joking. Don't you, Mary?"

"Are you laughing, Mary?"

But Mary just pleated her fingers and wouldn't look at either of them.

That was when he told Gita to get out of the room.

Startled, Gita looked at Mary questioningly. If you want me to go, Mary, just say the word. And you probably will. This prick's a snake. He's got you hypnotised.

Mary's eyes jumped from the doctor to Gita and back to the doctor. She said, faintly but firmly, "No Doctor. I want her to stay."

Well three cheers for you, Mary!

The doctor seemed to be as surprised as Gita. After a moment he said "All right. As long as she says nothing." The chair spun to face Gita. "Understand?"

Gita nodded. Listening was what Mary had asked her to do, anyway. She concentrated on what he was telling Mary. What on earth was PAT?

She realised with a start that he was talking to her again.

"Why are you staring at me? I don't like the way you sit there staring at me."

This guy was surreal. She could hardly keep the laugh out of her voice. "Mary wants me to listen. You've asked me not to speak." He gazed at her . . . trying to stare her out again. She gave him the old slow-motion.

He turned to Mary and continued his talk, larding it as before with technical terms. In the library at Springfield there was one of those old medical books that convinced you you had everything when you dipped into it. She'd look it up for Mary.

"Faulty evacuation," he was saying. That was okay. Suddenly he turned on Gita. "Do you understand?"

Gita nodded. "Sure." Now he seemed to be waiting for some comment, so she added, extra polite, "Perhaps some change in Mary's diet . . . ?"

This was the cue for a rave against diets, fads, dietitians raking in fortunes.

Mary looked so upset that again Gita came to her defence. "Mary eats sensibly."

"Does she? How do you know? Do you live with her?"

"She was telling me." She, she.

"My dear *Miss*, people *tell* you things every day."

My dear Miss . . . My dear she. Gita couldn't hide her anger. "Tell him, Mary. Tell him what you eat. Your muesli, for instance. You were telling me one day. Tell him."

Mary's voice was a faint simper. "Breakfast . . . muesli . . . a good helping of muesli."

He said "And why do you eat muesli, Mary?" Cold as a snake.

Glancing at Mary, Gita saw that the poor old thing was beaten. She watched her putting on a bright brave smile, dropping her eyes deferentially: after all he's a man, they know.

"Well, because . . . " She gave a false little laugh. "Because it's muesli!"

The doctor looked triumphantly from one woman to the other. "There you are! You people — you see something on TV, you rush out and buy the latest fad. Muesli!"

* *

"These are Mary's, I think," Gita said, holding out her hand for the X-rays as they rose to leave.

"Of course." He smiled as one does at a passing stranger, sighed, said "I've had a heavy week . . . problems . . ."

Gita gave him her best Jules-smile.

As they left the surgery Gita took Mary's arm. The old woman was shaking. "A good ginseng is what you need, Mary." She felt pretty stirred up herself. Mary said nothing, just let herself be guided into Gita's favourite shop in the arcade.

"He was very rude to you. I am sorry, Gita."

"He's a monster, Mary! A monster!"

"He's not usually like that. I do apologise for dragging you in with me." Mary glanced around to see who might be listening, then leaned forward. "I think he has problems, Gita."

"Does he ever! Is he on drugs or something? He's a manipulator, Mary."

Mary picked up her teaspoon and stirred her ginseng. "How do you mean, dear?"

"For starters, the way he gets people to give back the answers he wants. Like the muesli, for instance."

Mary's face crumbled. "Did I say the wrong thing again? I'm so glad you were with me. Such a support. What are all those things I've got wrong with me?"

"Mary, you've got to change your doctor . . . At least get a second opinion." She had an inspiration. "I'm sure that's what Angus would tell you."

How smart of you to think of that, my dear. You learned a lot from me

"Would he?" Mary smiled at her wanly. "You're fond of Angus, aren't you?"

Gita smiled back. Angus would do the trick.

"Angus has had his share of problems," Mary was saying as she stirred and stirred. "In the past, I mean. A slight problem. But I haven't seen so many –" again she glanced around, lowered her voice – "*empty bottles* on the hearth lately. You must be a good influence, dear."

Gita felt a weight fall on her. A good influence. A good woman. The womanly touch.

"Angus is okay," she said abruptly. "But let's talk about you. You don't have to change doctors. If you don't want to. Just show the X-rays to someone else — here they are — and see what they say. There really is a good doctor just five steps from here, why not give her a go? Right now? I'll come with you . . . It's okay. Truly. I've got all day." Angus can wait.

"What a nice young person!" Mary exclaimed as she drove Gita back to Marycote. "And very reassuring. She said the shadow on the X-ray was nothing. And the other things — perfectly normal for my age. I'm a very healthy woman, she said. Next time, Gita, I will tell her about that pain in my side. And those chest pains, which I hardly ever get anyway, what did she say about them? Just use my common sense, don't hurry up hills, put my feet up when I feel like it."

"She said a woman who's worked as hard as you have all your life deserves a bit of fun, Mary."

She had another inspiration then: she would make a ballad about someone like Mary, about all those old people she'd seen waiting in that power-mad guy's surgery, terrified into their graves by some crazy they worshipped. *Using:* she'd call it "Using" and sing it at her first gig with Simon Gilford's Grace Notes.

She came back to hear Mary saying "I do feel sorry for him, Gita. Especially if he's . . . taking things."

"Don't quote me, Mary."

As they drove along the leafy road Mary kept pointing out interesting things: there in the middle of a paddock a clump of hawthorn or an old nectarine where a house had once stood; here a chimney, all that remained of the cottage where poor old Syd Jones had died a bachelor. Mary knew who'd lived in all of them. She's like a dog let off the chain, Gita thought, as Mary talked on, the runaround weaving across the road so that Gita kept her hand ready to grab the wheel.

"See that bluestone cottage?" Gita saw four stone walls and a chimney amongst grazing sheep. "Old Billy Smith lived there. He played the fiddle at all the weddings. Those weddings! Nothing but wine trifles and cream puffs and fruit salads and sponges nine inches high, and then dancing till dawn to Billy's fiddle." Mary laughed. "When Agnes White married that nice Reverend Godwin, all the boys kept disappearing out the back for nips of Ma White's dandelion wine, Billy Smith too, and the tunes got wilder and wilder, and the Reverend never stopped dancing till Agnes told us she'd have to drag him away."

"Nothing wrong with your memory, Mary."

"But that's just it. You remember the old things."

Mary thought for a moment about how people her age went over and over the past, which was all you could do at her age with any reliability, take hold of the past, and even that was pretty risky: holding it up to the light like a well-worn garment, pulling threads together, making a patchwork out of it all — to wear as your winding-sheet?

"You love this old place, don't you?" Gita was saying as they turned into the drive at Marycote. "It suits you, Mary. You should be living here."

Mary looked surprised. "You're surely not leaving us, Gita?"

Gita laughed. "I'll see what happens."

Mary thought about the big house across the hill, its rooms gradually coming back to life. She felt more cheerful than she had for a long time.

83 The Smell of Hate

By the time Gita went over to Springfield it was well into the afternoon. After Mary had left she had spent some time preparing a block of tofu which she was planning to roast that evening. It was her own recipe, one that had occurred to her when she'd ducked into the supermarket after the ginseng with Mary. I bet he's never had anything like this, she thought, squeezing lemons to add to the tamari and white wine that the tofu was soaking in. Next she chopped herbs, tomato, onion, capsicum and celery and added them to a bowl of home-made breadcrumbs. The tofu she cut in half, proceeding to remove the inside so that she was left with a hollow box. This was a slow business as the tofu was rubbery and resistant. What she removed she chopped to marinade further until she was ready to add it to the stuffing. Should be good, she thought. He'd better like it.

She found Angus by the shed, in front of the garage. He was cutting ribs for the dogs off the sheep's carcass hanging from the old lucerne tree. He looked up in surprise.

"Thought I wasn't going to see you again today." Thought I'd never see you again.

She told him about going into town with Mary. "The man's evil, Angus."

"You might be right at that. Good God! She should complain to the AMA."

"Mary?" Gita laughed. "She feels *sorry* for him. If I hadn't been there, I think she'd be going to him for the rest of her life."

He put down the butcher's knife and came over to her, wiping his hands on his trousers. "Gita . . . but you *were* there." He put his arms around her and felt her relax against him, her arms go around him. "I thought you weren't coming back," he muttered against her hair.

Jarrah, back from school, ravenous because he'd gone without his lunch, came around the corner of the shed and saw those two chewing each other's faces again. He dumped his bag on the ground. They took no notice. And he had something important to tell them: Jane Catchpole had Angus's axehead in her rock project, the one she'd taken home from school this very afternoon, she'd been boasting about her A plus all the way home in the bus and she'd let some of her friends see the project and he'd poked his head through a heap of arms and he'd seen it for himself: bits of yellow and brown and green rocks and in the middle of them, Angus's axehead that she'd snitched from his kitchen.

Blow trying to tell those two now. He left his bag where it was and went into the garage, pulling the double doors shut behind him. Now that both sets of doors were shut, it took his eyes a moment to adjust to the dimness. The Ferguson was parked in the bay beside the Suzuki. It was a big tractor, with a rollbar and safety hood. It looked like something Dr Who might ride round in. He climbed up on to the bony, ridged seat and pretended he was driving, he was Angus, he was Dr Who racing across the paddocks brmmm brmm. He forgot he was starving, he forgot about those two mushing each other outside. Leaning forward, he saw that Dr Who had left the key in the ignition. "Brmmm brmm," he said, hand on the key.

She drew her head back to look at him. "My place or your place?"

"Your place." Hardly believing. "Now?"

She laughed. "Tonight. I'll turn on something special, will I?" Laughing again, rubbing herself against him. "To eat, I mean. I bought some tofu in town this morning. How does stuffed tofu grab you? My own special recipe. I'll —"

The tractor burst through the garage doors with such an explosion it flung Angus twenty years back to Vietnam. He and the woman fell apart. He swung around, and in slow motion watched the splintering wood, the tank edging forward to crush something fallen in its way and tear from a hook a naked corpse, coming to rest at last as the old lucerne tree slowly toppled.

Beside him the woman was screaming.

A kid leapt off the tank, white-faced and shuddering.

"You bloody little fool!" Angus yelled. "You could have been killed! Don't you ever — ever —" He turned back to Gita and shouted at her. "Look at my tractor! Look at what he's done to that tree! Kid needs a stick around his tail a bit more often!"

Gita shouted back. "If you ever lay a finger on him — ! If you ever touch him — !"

As she flew at him *he could smell the village women's hate* he grabbed her arms.

"Stop it! Stop it, Gita!"

Hearing these two whom he loved best in the world shouting at each other, seeing them going to hit each other, Jarrah turned and fled.

His hands were like a vice. "Let me go, Angus!"

He watched as she rubbed her arms.

"You shouldn't have done that, Angus."

"Okay, okay, keep your feathers on."

He lurched away, feeling sick.

84 Silver-spangled Sebright

"Hello, Jarrah," Mary said, surprised to see the boy still at Valley View Park. "Getting a bit late, isn't it? You'd better be off home soon or your mum will be worried."

She gave him another rock cake. Poor little fellow, he tucked into it as though he'd had nothing all day.

"Off you go," she said, letting him out the kitchen door. She smiled at the upturned face. "Quick sticks, now. See you tomorrow."

"We're going to have our baths now, Jarrah," Elton said, coming in to the bathroom ten minutes later and finding Jarrah floating leaves in the handbasin. "You better go home."

"Aren't you going to ask Jane if I can have a bantam? You said, Elton. Didn't Elton say, Keiran?"

"Yes, you did say, Elton."

"Yeah, I'll ask her. After our baths maybe."

"Couldn't I wait till then?"

"Nah . . . Mum'll get mad. Better go."

"Yeah, you go," Keiran echoed, giving Jarrah a push.

Jarrah wandered along the passage. Funny how Elton's face didn't jump when he was home at his own place. He gave his own mouth a couple of twists. When he came to Jane's room he paused. Looked up and down the passage. Listened. Stepped into Jane's room. It was there. Standing up on her desk. Her project on rocks. The one she couldn't stop boasting about. The one with the axehead. Jarrah listened again, then darted across and began to unpick the thin wire attaching the rocks to the particle board base. She'd tied them on very carefully, but eventually he had the axehead free before anyone caught him.

He could show Mary — the axehead and the space in the project. He bet old Jane had never shown the project to Mary.

He had another idea. Maybe, if Angus had his axehead back, maybe they could all be friendly together and it would be like that first afternoon with the skateboard when Angus had called him son.

He had an even better idea. Jane would be at the chook house feeding the Sebrights. He'd heard Mary reminding her, and Jane making the mistake of swearing at Mary in her father's hearing. Mr Catchpole got mad then, said if Jane wanted to go to Sue-Ellen's sleepover tonight she'd better do what she was told and wash her mouth out with soap while she was about it.

He slipped the axehead into his coat pocket. He could run faster than Jane. What he was going to do was pretty cool, pretty risky, but if he succeeded he'd have both his Sebright and the axehead to return to Angus.

Jane was still at the chook house, chucking grain around in the big wire-netted yard. Jeez, she looked mad!

"Stay out of the yard, Chomp," he said to his shadow, Mary's grinning bull terrier. No need to stir Jane-oh up too soon. "Can I hold this chook?" he asked, scooping up the prettiest Sebright hen as she pecked grain near his feet. Jane shrugged. She hardly ever talked to Jarrah. He was just one of the little kids. Jarrah stroked the bantam's head and white wings diamond-edged with black feathers, then walked outside the yard.

"Hey!" he said through the netting fence, careful in spite of the wire between them to keep on his toes in case old Jane made a sudden dash. "See this axehead?"

She spoke then all right. "Give that back, you little toad. You pinched that from my rock project."

"Yeah 'cause it isn't yours. It was somebody else's till you got hold of it."

"Well it's mine now. I found it."

"Yeah, on Angus's kitchen bench."

"Liar!"

"You're the liar, Jane-oh. And a thief." He took a step backwards as he saw her measuring the distance to the gate. "Your teacher'll give you Z minus I reckon when I go up to the high school and tell her you stole it."

"You? Go up to the high school? You wouldn't dare." But old Jane-oh sounded a bit doubtful. Didn't everyone know how he'd got himself to Currawong and then enrolled himself at the primary? She tried another tack. "You're the one who's got it now. I'll tell everyone *you* stole it."

"I've got *witnesses,* Jane-oh." He moved a few steps: Jane was edging towards the gate.

"Stop calling me Jane-oh!" she shrieked, and made a rush after him.

He was ready but old Jane, plump as she was, could really go. Downhill towards the gate he raced, Chomper at his heels, but Jane cut him off screeching "Thief! Thief!" and he had to veer along the fence and he'd never get over that holding the poor scared Sebright, she was gaining on him so reaching into his coat pocket he stood facing her, ready to fling the axehead into the thick bush growing along the roadside. Jane, red-faced, stopped a few yards off to catch her second wind.

"Listen," he heaved. "You reckon this axehead should go back to the —" his trick had come to this, too bad! — "to the real owner, okay?"

"Yes, you nerd." Puff, puff.

"If I give it back can I keep the Sebright?" Puff, pant from Jane. That was as good as yes. "Promise? Cross your heart?"

"Jeez you're a kid!" She spat on her hand and rubbed it over her heart. "Satisfied? Now just give me the rock, will you?"

"To its real owner – yes!" And he flung it over the fence.

Away bounded Chomper, back towards the gate.

If he thought Jane would give him a breather by hunting around for the axehead in the roadside scrub, he was wrong. She gave another roar and flew at him, shouting "You bloody little cheat!" No good continuing along the fence. Mr Catchpole's fences were much too tight to scramble through. He turned and ran uphill, back to the house, back to Mary. To his relief she suddenly appeared, walking towards the fowlhouse.

"Mary! Mary!" he wheezed. "Look what Jane give me! A Sebright all for me!" He nearly knocked her over, shoving the bantam at her.

Jane came up, savage as a hopper ant.

"That was nice of you, Janie," Mary said. "That's really generous of you, dear. Mum and Dad will be pleased, won't they?" Really laying it on, Jarrah thought. Old Jane must be a real old minge. Jane stretched a smile tight as an elastic band across her red face. "I came to see what was keeping you, Jane," Mary went on. "The Browns'll be here to pick you up very soon. Better hurry along to the house and get ready. Have you finished here, dear?"

Jane didn't say a word to Mary about the axehead. She just turned and sulked back to the house.

85 A Thousand Circlets

Angus was in the kitchen when the phone rang. He was planning to go across to Marycote shortly. He was sorry he had shouted at Gita and the boy: sorry, and shocked at himself. Lord, how she'd sprung at him! He laughed to himself at the memory. He'd go across and apologise to both of them, explain to the boy. He was a good kid. He recalled how just a few days ago by the fire the boy had stretched out his leg beside his, touching him, needing contact. The boy hadn't had enough of that in his life, that was obvious. And Angus too had failed him — moved his leg away irritably, too wrapped in his own griefs to feel the boy's touch for what it was: a gesture of love. Well, his mother was fond enough of him, that was clear, even if she didn't show it when things were going well. Only when something threatened him. Funny sort of life she must have had. He wondered if she'd open up about it sometime, the way she had about the heroin . . . He smiled. Just thinking about her brought her alive along all his senses.

The phone rang. It was the boy. "Mary told me —" he began. Angus heard a murmur in the background. "I mean, I'm sorry I did that today with the tractor, I won't do it again, I really am sorry, I mean, it isn't just Mary —"

"That's all right, mate," Angus said. "I'm sorry, too. I'm sorry I did my block, it's just sudden noises sometimes, you know? I don't mean to jump at people, the words just come out and afterwards I wish like hell I'd held my tongue — you know what I mean?"

"That's okay," the boy said after a moment. There was a short silence as each tried to think of something further to say.

"You're over with Mary, are you?" Angus said eventually.

"Yes, I'm going to stay the night here. Mary's invited me. What, Mary? . . . I mean, if Gita says I can. And Angus —" the boy's voice grew excited, ran on so fast Angus could hardly understand him — "guess what? Jane give me a bantam, she's a beauty, she's called a silver-spangled Sebright. She's white with black edging on her feathers and they look all silvery, do you want to see her? Jane give her to me."

"Sure, I'd like to see that bantam, Jarrah. First thing tomorrow, eh? Where's she going to live, by the way? Might be a bit lonely for her all by herself at the cottage. Want to keep her over here with my chooks?"

"Okay. If she'll be safe there."

"We'll take a look together in the morning, will we?"

He's a good kid, Angus thought. And then: she's by herself tonight. We'll be together, just the two of us again. My place or your place? I must have passed some sort of test. He hardly heard the boy say "Mary wants to talk to you now." He couldn't remember, when he put the phone down, what it was Mary had said, except to confirm that the boy was staying the night at Valley View Park.

Before he went across to Marycote he salvaged what he could of the crushed dogs' meat for Bess and Shep, then hurried inside for a shower and a shave. From the saplings on the rise behind the kitchen he picked some gumtips, pinching a couple of the glossy leaves between his fingers to breathe in their fragrance. She liked something fresh in a jar. He decided to walk: he needed a walk. He went the long way, his feet springy, along the Springfield drive and up the moonlit road to the Marycote entrance.

As he opened the gate he saw the vehicle.

Lou's Range Rover.

His head suddenly tight, he walked like a shadow up the drive and around the side of the cottage. Glancing in the sitting room window, he caught sight of her. She hadn't even bothered to shut Mary's curtains. She was laughing, picking up some piece of clothing then dropping it and throwing her arms about to emphasise what she was saying. He couldn't see Lou, just Gita. He walked closer. He still couldn't hear her actual voice but he could imagine it, its rise and fall, happy, eager. *Voices. Women's voices* Catchpole was keeping out of sight. Then, dropping whatever it was she was holding, Gita held out her hands and moved towards him. Angus, sickened, turned away – turned away before the flame-thrower spat, the women screamed, the children wailed. He ran stumbling around the back of the cottage, across the creek, uphill and down into the Springfield valley, keeping to the edge of the jungle until he'd reached the safety of the house.

Spy. Betrayer Back in his own kitchen he felt so chilled with the shock of finding himself still alive that he took several gulps of whisky to warm himself through. He banged the bottle down on the sink. He should have burst into the cottage and beaten Lou dead – her too – no publican present this time to ring the police. *If you didn't blow the bastard's brains out in a frenzy of rage or grief within the first few minutes then he was safe, he would live, you couldn't shoot him at all* Coughing, choking, he took another swig of whisky. He couldn't stop shivering. He took down his rifle from behind the kitchen door and automatically began cleaning it.

86   The Age-old Dance

"There was no need to shout at her, Lou."
"She gets up my nostril."
"Maybe, but she's a great help to me."
"Is she?"
"You'll end up driving her away."
"Things might fall into place a bit better round here if I did."
"I should stay in the kitchen, is that what you mean? Hands in the sink, dish up your dinner, give up —"
"I didn't say that. Look Belle, just don't put words in my mouth, will you! No wonder . . ." He snorted with disgust and turned away. Belle came after him. He slammed out of the kitchen and of course the old woman was listening, cleaning the kids' shoes on the verandah but listening all right.
"No wonder what, Lou? Lou? I know exactly what you were going to say."
"Oh you do, do you! Then why bother asking?"
Belle didn't reply, just stormed after him along the path so that he nearly went arse over tit over that useless bull terrier. He shouted over his shoulder "All right! What was I going to say?"
"No wonder Angus," she muttered.
He turned furiously. "There you go! Putting words in a man's mouth . . . No *wonder* Angus!" he smirked at her, triumphant.
And so they waltzed on.

87 Runaround

The boy didn't want to go home.

Wouldn't go home.

Burst into tears and said he was sick of all the *screamin'* he was going to run away nobody loved him.

So Mary, excited by anxiety and responsibility and the feeling that only she could do something, put down the shoebrush and went inside to ask Belle to let him stay the night on a fold-up bed in the sunroom. Belle agreed readily enough. She and Lou looked like a pair of ruffled roosters.

"But first we must ask your mother," Mary told Jarrah, once the difficult apology call had been made to Angus. She took the runaround's keys from their hook. "Yes, we must, Jarrah. All right, you stay here, I'll go by myself."

In a few minutes she was back in the house.

"I can't get anything out of the engine except rrrr-rrr-rrr — not a thing! My poor little runaround's dead."

Belle shot an accusing look at Lou. "I'll run you across to the cottage, Mary," she said magnanimously. And have a look at the woman while I'm about it. "I'm taking the Range Rover, Lou. I don't trust the Fairmont up that awful drive."

The woman was chopping a heap of weeds on the kitchen table. Just as the children had said, she had a great stone in her nostril. And, dangling from each ear, a crystal that swung and caught the light each time she moved her head. She smiled at Mary from under a mass of loose dark hair (Belle unconsciously put her hand to her own manicured golden crown), and gave Belle what Belle could only describe as an ill-bred stare.

She said "I guessed he was with you, Mary." She didn't say thanks for letting me know. She didn't say thanks for having him and thanks too for all the afternoons he's been stuffing himself with cake and biscuits over at Valley View Park. When Mary said the boy seemed a bit upset over a spot of bother with something of Angus's, she just laughed, sliding the chopped greens into a saucepan.

"Spot of bother? Yeah. He took a joy ride on the tractor without opening the shed doors."

Belle wandered into the sitting room and looked around. When Mary and the woman came in she said "Did you know Angus used to try to entice me out here on Saturday afternoons when we were kids, Mary?"

"Did he?" the woman said softly. "That must have been a long time ago."

You bitch. Angus is welcome to you! Belle turned away with her bright smile.

"Sure, Jarrah can stay," Gita said absently, thinking Angus will be here any minute; thinking I'll have to open all the windows, that perfume she's wearing's making me choke; thinking that was a very ageist thing you said to her just now, Gita. Sorry, Crystal!

"So I thought I'd come and get his toothbrush," Mary was saying since Gita wasn't making much effort to look for it herself. "What about a change of clothes?"

Gita began to collect things of Jarrah's which were draped over chairs to air, picking them up and putting them down again. We'll have the evening to ourselves. "Don't know if he's even got a toothbrush."

"I'll look for it," Mary said. Belle walked out with her, saying "I wonder if that old copper . . ." From the bathroom Mary called "Actually, Gita, Jarrah rang Angus to apologise. Wasn't that nice of him? Angus told him not to give it another thought. He was in a bit of a hurry, on his way out, I think."

Gita laughed. Seizing an armful of Jarrah's clothes, she went to meet Mary. "He sounded very happy," Mary added, meeting her in the sitting room doorway. Gita didn't answer, just laughed again and, dropping the clothes, put her arms around Mary and hugged her.

88 Voices

As the evening wore on she thought something's held him up − a sick animal. He's forgotten − but he couldn't forget! He's changed his mind. He's still in a rage, he doesn't want to come. She moved the soup to one side of the stove, glanced in the oven and basted the tofu. He's had an accident!

Pulling on her tracksuit, she set out towards Springfield. Hurrying over the frost-glinting paddocks, she was part of some huge breathing moon-drenched creature.

As she approached the house Bess and Shep began to bark. The house was in darkness. He's not there, she thought. Perhaps he's on his way in the ute. Or lying ill. The dogs continued their clamouring. She heard the kitchen window fly open, Springfield's shrill sharp whistle, the rattle of chains as the two dogs, subdued into silence, crept back into their kennels. The window slammed shut.

Well, screw him! she thought, back again in the warmth of Marycote. Taking down the dulcimer, she sang the "Spider Song", then tried her new version again on the guitar she'd borrowed.

Sure, she thought, use whichever instrument the song demands. She threw another log on the fire and, stretching out on the sofa, fell asleep.

Voices. Women's voices And then a man's voice calling "Gita! Gita!" and a pounding on the front door. She woke, thinking he's here, he came! She slid off the sofa, stumbled half-asleep along the passage and threw the door open.

"Hi, Gita," said Mark. He kissed her in greeting, then kissed her again. "Look who's come to see you."

There were two women with him, Sylvie who lived around the corner from the squat, and a girl called Heath who knew Jules.

"Long time no see!" said Sylvie. "So this is where you've been, huh? Marcus said you were hibernating amongst the lambkins."

Marcus: Gita glanced at him. Then she kissed each woman. "Come on in."

Sylvie looked around the sitting room and then at Gita again. "Hey! I like the jumper. Taken to knitting, too, have you?"

Gita flung a log on the fire. "Something like that."

"Something smells good," Mark said, following her out to the kitchen. "Look what I've brought." He held out two bottles of red wine. "Grange Hermitage 1982."

"Huh?"

"From Jules's cellar. But don't let on." He grinned at her, a kid who's scored. He went on eagerly "Hey! That's a guitar you've got in the sitting room."

She smiled, the old slow-motion, shaking her head at the unstated question. "Diversification, Mark, it's called diversification. I borrowed it from a friend. For a new song."

"Where's the loo, Gita?" Sylvie interrupted. "Is it one of those wonderful old pits where redbacks bite your bum and you're shit-scared of falling through the hole? . . . Hell, a flush toilet! Where's the alternative life?"

While the two women were out of the kitchen Mark said "I didn't even know if you'd still be here. Why didn't you write?"

"Why didn't *you* write?"

"I wasn't sure of your address. But you knew mine."

"You mean Jules's address, don't you?"

"I'm not there now. But he would have sent it on."

"Would he? Oh Mark . . . ever trusting."

"Don't be like that, Gita." He dipped a spoon into the saucepan. "Hey, this is good soup."

"Dandelion. Stirs up the blood. And stuffed tofu to follow."

"And I've got some really good weed. Oh Gita, it's terrific to see you again!"

"We've brought sleeping bags," Sylvie said, hours later – or was it minutes? Gita couldn't tell any more, time was the tofu, collapsed on to itself on the plate.

"It'll have to be the floor," she said, and giggled.

"Fine. Here by the fire? Come and give me a hand, Heath."

Mark followed Gita into her bedroom and watched while she tried giggling to light the fire. Succeeding at last, she sank cross-legged on to the bed while he leaned against the mantelpiece saying "Want to hear about Jules?"

"Not much. But you want to tell me."

"He chucked me out."

Gita shrugged.

He went on plaintively "Said I was a risk. Put him at risk. And I couldn't go back to your place because three lesbians had moved in and they wouldn't have me."

Gita laughed.

"Don't laugh. You've no idea what it's been like." He rubbed his nose, the old familiar motion, open hand up over his nostrils. Him and Heath both.

"Poor Mark." He was staring at her, that pitiful look. She giggled. "Want to sleep soft, Mark?" She patted her bed. "In a proper bed? You're too sensitive to sleep on the floor. You'd feel every knot-hole, like the princess in that . . . in that . . ." She couldn't stop laughing.

"You've no idea," he began again, falling beside her on to her pillow. She pushed him against the wall and curled up beside him. She began to laugh at what he was saying, bits and pieces that seemed terribly funny, bits about Jules, bits about Sylvie, bits about Heath who was dressed entirely in black and said nothing. The words floated in front of her, huge, hilarious; if she put out her hand she could eat them. Her mouth was crammed with laughter.

When she woke later there was a harsh taste in her throat. She felt chilled. Someone had thrown her sleeping bag over her, but she was still on top of the blankets. She felt about for Mark. He was not with her. And then she heard him in the sitting room – heard someone – Mark, or was it a woman, women's voices? Whispers, a gasp, little laughs. Mark with Sylvie? Mark with the silent Heath? Or was it Sylvie and Heath? She turned her head, watching the dying fire. They hadn't bothered about shutting doors. Here she was planning on the big night of passion with Angus, and Mark turns up. That's fate for you. She pictured Angus arriving as planned, then, finding the others there, too inhibited to press on regardless, unlike whoever was hard at it across the passage. She had another thought about fate: if Angus had turned up, maybe Mark — Marcus, she corrected herself, recalling the look on Sylvie's face — maybe fate wouldn't have sent *Marcus* and Co at all. Maybe. As someone groaned she pictured Angus's hands, those broad farmer's hands, searching out the secret places of her body as surely as he knew every inch of his land, every log he threw on the fire. She touched herself, growing moist as her thighs clamped around her wrist. Angry tears ran into her mouth. Her teeth grasped the pillow, her head rocked from side to side.

Afterwards, breathless, the irony of it struck her: here she'd been thinking she was landed for the night with second best, poor old Mark, always somebody's second best, and all the time the joke was on her.

89 Buttercups and Orange Peels

When Gita woke, grey light was seeping through the window. She heard a scraping noise, and her heart skipped: something had got into the room. She lifted her head. Someone was going through her rucksack.

"Hey! What's going on? Who's that?"

Mark said "Have you got anything? Any stuff?" And when she didn't reply: "Come on, I know it's here somewhere, Jules left some, didn't he?" He stood up and came across to the bed. "Jesus, I'm hanging out for it. And I'm skinned. Jules won't help me any more." She stared up at him. "I owe him, Gita. Jesus, do I owe him! And he's putting the hard word on me." He looked around desperately. "I'm going to take the mantelpieces."

"Oh no you're not! I *live* here, Mark."

But he began to tug at the mantelpiece in her bedroom, knocking a jar of wattle bloom into the fireplace. As the glass shattered Gita jumped out of bed. "Stop it! Stop it, will you!" She grabbed the nearest thing to hand — the dulcimer — and took a swipe at him.

"Don't, don't," he whimpered, dodging. "Have a bit of

pity, Gita. You never used to be so hard. What's got into you?"

Gita caught sight of the two women watching from the passage. She turned frantically, clutching the dulcimer against her belly like a child.

"Is he always like this, Sylvie?"

"If he doesn't get a hit first thing, yes. He's okay then for the rest of the day." Sylvie shrugged. "You know how it is. He just needs a hit like some people need their cup of coffee."

"Jesus," muttered Gita, watching Mark chucking her clothes about. "Okay," she said. "Just hold on, Mark, will you? Just relax, okay? Sure I've got what you want. Sure, Jules left some with me. You're welcome to it." *You poor sod.* In the kitchen she climbed on to a chair and from the top of the dresser took down Jules's dust-covered gift. "Jules said I might need it one day," she told him, giving him one of the foils. *Jules, Jules.* She watched as he unwrapped it greedily.

They went back into the sitting room. Sylvie had restoked the fire and was sitting on the sofa with Heath. Mark nodded; they moved apart so he could sit between them. Heath handed him the belt and the fit.

Came all prepared, did they? They didn't come to see me at all.

Heath looked up. "Sure you don't want to?"

It was about the only thing Gita had heard her say apart from yes and no.

She shook her head, but all the same she felt the old lust stir: just watching the blood rise in the syringe was enough to get it going.

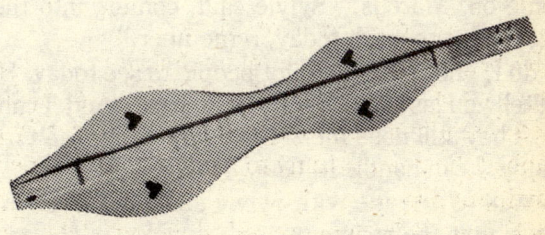

Rhumba

"Listen Mark," she said later as they were leaving. "Take the rest of this stuff since you're so desperate, take it and leave my bloody mantelpieces alone, leave me alone, okay? I mean it, Mark. I don't want it. But if anything happens to these mantelpieces the cops'll track you down, don't think they won't. I'll make sure of that. You haven't got it in you to be a crook, Mark. You're not like Jules. You're too bloody nice to be a crook." She hugged him. Shit, I needed a screw last night! She hugged him again. "This shit's for old times' sake. And if you try dealing it, for Christ's sake don't get busted. And listen, there's no point in coming back for more. This is it, this is all that shithead gave me apart from some story about buttercups and orange peels. Okay?"

"Come on, Marcus," Sylvie said, coming into the room. "I've got to get to work today, remember."

"So do I," he said. "I've got people to see today. Hey Gita — did I tell you last night? — I'm still in the band. I can handle it, Gita. They still need me. That's something, isn't it? That's something. I can handle it, Gita."

Gita walked outside with Sylvie and Mark. Heath was already sitting in the hearse.

"That's something, Mark," Gita agreed. "You stick to it, mate."

90 Mulberry Cycle: Completed

She found the bloody syringe by the sofa. She wrapped it carefully in the last of the newspaper from the pile by the stove and threw it into the old pit toilet. Then she dug up a bucket of soil from the recently turned herb bed and threw it into the pit to cover the parcel. Bury your own shit. Bury what's passed out of you.

She built up the fire in the sitting room and began to pick out a melody on the guitar, and then on the dulcimer. Thank God she hadn't hit Mark, she might have damaged it. She stared into the leaping flames. If he'd asked me last night, she said to herself. If he'd asked me last night, if they'd got out the shit instead of the grass, would I have joined in? It was fun last night, all of us sitting round together, it was like old times, no Jules there, just Mark and me and a couple of friends, a group of us together. It was because it was this morning − it wasn't the right time . . . if he'd said last night . . . I don't know. Maybe. I don't think so. For old times' sake. Oh shit. Oh shit. And then I nearly busted the dulcimer except that he ducked. If I'd hit him . . . That's twice in two days I've done my block with someone . . . Anger feeding on anger like maggots in meat.

Well, she could make a start on those spare seedlings this morning. She wanted to do that job. Get them into pots in good time for the next Trash and Treasure. She'd go over to Springfield in a minute. It wouldn't matter whether or not he was there. She knew which punnets. And if he'd changed his mind, said she couldn't have them after all, she'd put a rock through his glasshouse for him. She wasn't really a violent person, though. The crossest she'd got for a long time was yesterday when she'd yelled at Angus, and then swinging the dulcimer this morning when Mark tried to rip out the mantelpiece. She began to laugh. My property. Protecting my property.

She'd go over to Springfield soon. "The Sun Grows Warm", that was her new song. She began to sing:

> Rosy-wrinkled
> nipple-sweet
> the mulberries ripen
> to his heat

Ionian Mode

[Musical notation: Ro-sy wrink-led, Nip-ple-sweet, The mul-ber-ries ri-pen To his heat.]

She'd go very soon. And maybe, when the seedlings were finished, put in the ground, her share sold, maybe then she'd take a trip back to Melbourne. She'd like to see a few old friends again. Some of them. Not Jules. Not Mark. She was through with them. Jesus, all those head fights she'd had with them! With Crystal too. Was that all they were – head fights? And that argument with Angus – twice, or was it three times now? – about who'd actually said "slaughter and breeding", herself or Crystal. Angus was convinced he was right. If she thought about it, she could see those lambs in the house paddock, one after the other bounding stiff-legged off that black stump and then herself trailing after his retreating back wondering what the fuck she'd done wrong – but had Angus fed that picture into her memory? *It wasn't Crystal who said it, Gita* Maybe it wasn't Crystal who'd said a whole lot of things. Or Mark. Or Jules. Do we just invent what people say, invent our friends? Was Angus her invention? She recalled something he'd said one time after they'd fucked: "You've given me back to myself." Had she created him for himself? Done a bit of manipulating there? Power, did she really have a lust for power?

91 Angus Brooded

Angus brooded and dozed by turns all night. He didn't bother going to bed, just sat on a kitchen chair by the stove. He held his rifle across his knees and cleaned it, and then cleaned it again. He didn't need a light. His fingers knew exactly what they were doing. Sometimes, more and more frequently as the night grew colder, he took a swig of whisky. And then he would fall asleep, twitching and dreaming. *You want womans?* When he woke, his thoughts were little different.

Towards morning he got up stiffly from the chair, leaned the rifle against the sink, and pulled the kettle into the middle of the stove. Harlots, all. Come and take, come and go. He stared out the window. That TV documentary: thousands of lush acres sprayed out of existence — what grew there now? Useless coarse stuff: American grass, they called it. And this land too? On the windy rise behind the house the saplings' leaves glittered. *Eyes, eyes everywhere* Ghosts of the former occupants of plundered land, hundreds of ghosts, shadows you hardly saw passing in front of your eyes. What a joke, replanting a few acres. Go — they would all go. She'd pack her rucksack and her dulcimer and she'd go, back to wherever she'd come from, or to a new place with new faces. He wouldn't be able to go near that cottage. He'd shut up Springfield again. It was too full of memories, moments of joyous surprise, false hopes all of them. Lies, lies, night after night of disinformation. The kettle was boiling but he pushed it off the stove: he didn't want tea. He glanced at the clock. Catchpole ought to be up by now. He went to the phone. "Marycote," he said. But when it came to the point he couldn't bring himself to say outright "You can have it, Lou, just as soon as we agree on a price." He mumbled through a mouth fugged with whisky "That step in the fence, Lou — that dog-leg. I've been thinking."

"What? What? Who is this? Have you got half an idea what the bloody time is, mate? Jesus!"

Angus was overcome with revulsion against that thief, that despoiler of dreams. "What's wrong with you? I've just told you, she's yours. That's what she wanted, isn't it? The sooner the better." He fumbled the phone back into its cradle. It was done. The cottage would be bulldozed, the fence straightened, the big trees axed and the sprouting seedlings on his side of the fence ploughed in as surely as his dreams. Lou never did things by halves. He opened another bottle of whisky.

92 Bush Lawyer

Lou sat down heavily at the breakfast table. Mary, busy at the stove, glanced at him. He was never the best first thing. Whoever could have annoyed him so early in the day? If she'd been quicker she could have got to the kitchen phone before Lou picked up the one at his bedside. And now she couldn't remember how he'd had his eggs yesterday. Poached, was it, or fried? Was it fried today, or . . .

She said automatically "Have you got everything you want, Lou? Milk? Stewed fruit?"

"That bloke's off his chump."

"What bloke?" Belle yawned, pulling her dressing gown around her as she came into the kitchen. "Who was that ringing before, Lou?"

"Springfield. Off his chump."

"So what's new? . . . Thanks, Mary." Belle yawned again as Mary put a steaming cup in front of her.

"I mean, he's been bloody-minded for years about that bit of dog-leg fence round the cottage, that step, and now he wakes me up at sparrow's fart to tell me he's changed his mind, I can have it — at least I think that's what he meant. Is he on the booze again, Mary? You should know, you seem to keep in touch with him."

"Of course he isn't drinking," Mary said sharply. "What do you mean, Angus said you can have the step?"

"Seems he's come to his senses at last . . . Thanks, Mary. Nice if we could have poached for a change."

"The step, Lou? But that would mean . . . Lou, that would mean pulling down the cottage to straighten the boundary."

"Correct. Put a 'dozer through the old place."

"But you wouldn't!"

"Too much trouble any other way, Mary."

"It's a perfectly habitable cottage, Lou. Someone's living there right now." Mary's voice quivered as she thought about those daydreams of living there herself.

"Well she'll just have to get out, won't she?" And Lou snickered, picturing himself going over and telling that sulky slut to move on. This time she'd see who was boss! "I reckon we've had about enough of this conversation," he said abruptly, shutting up all argumentative women. "Any more toast going over there?"

"Wouldn't you want the timber out of the cottage, Lou?" Belle asked. "I noticed some nice pine lining when I drove Mary over yesterday."

"Too much trouble."

At the thought of Marycote pushed into a heap like kindling, Mary said "There must be some mistake."

"No mistake, Mary. That was Angus on the phone. She's all yours, he said. Those were his very words: she's all yours, mate." Weren't they? The bastard sounded so plastered Lou could hardly make out what he was saying.

"People change their minds," Mary said.

"You're dead right they do. Angus for instance. Dragged me out of bed to tell me, didn't he?"

"People can change their minds," Mary repeated.

"Look, get this straight, Mary. I'm not changing my mind."

"Angus. Angus will change his mind." He's had a row with her. Something went wrong last night. It's a lover's tiff.

Lou laughed.

"Don't be too eager with the bulldozer, Lou," Mary said stubbornly. "People's promises are not worth the air they're . . . they're . . . " She couldn't think.

"I'll get it in writing. Think I'm a fool?"

"And then by law he'll have three days to change his mind." Wouldn't he? Mary began to shake.

Lou raised his eyebrows. "Since when did you become a bush lawyer?"

I'm going across to ask him myself, Mary thought. He *can't* let the cottage be broken up like an armful of sticks! It's my home! He as good as said . . . Tears came to her eyes. She had to turn away to the sink and wipe them on the corner of the dishcloth. "Get your bantam out of its box," she said to Jarrah who was enjoying a late breakfast. "We'll go over to Angus's right now and show him, will we?"

"We'll have to walk," she said. "But it's not far if we go across the paddocks. Here, borrow Elton's gumboots."

"But she said — Mrs Catchpole said —"

"Never mind that now, just put them on."

What was she in such a grump about? "This is a lovely chook," Jarrah said, stroking the silver feathers as they tramped through the early slanting light. "Angus will like it. There's lots of chook houses at Springfield. He said I can keep it there with his chooks. D'you think he will *reely*?"

"If he said so, Jarrah, of course he will."

Jarrah looked at her reproachfully; her lips were moving silently, as though she was talking to herself. No one tells *her* not to drone, he thought. "Come on," he urged. "Angus wants to see my silver-spangled — what's it called?"

"Sebright."

"Is that s-e-e or s-e-a?"

"I really have no idea. Why don't you run on?" she suggested, as he danced about her impatiently. "Take Chomper with you," she said. "The silly thing's got another stone ready for you to throw."

That pain was back in Mary's side. If she walked slowly, she would have the strength to get to Springfield and talk to Angus.

93 Child with Gift

Calling the dog, Jarrah dashed away, holding the bantam carefully close to his chest. He could feel her heart beating rapidly under his fingers. Tick tick tick. "It's all right," he said, stopping to stroke her. "You live with me now. You're my pet. I've never had a real pet to look after. You'll like that, won't you? And maybe one day I'll get you a friend so you won't be lonely. You'd like that, wouldn't you?"

He grinned, wondering how he could trick another Sebright out of old Jane.

He ran on, following sheep tracks across the hill and between the trees. He enjoyed going through the bush, but he had to be careful of his step. One time when he stumbled he dropped the bantam and had to chase her through the undergrowth until she gave up and let him catch her. He decided to carry her inside his coat.

Chomper came up and sat at his feet, chawing on his rock, licking it, pushing it with his nose. "Hey, you've got that stone axe!" Jarrah exclaimed. "I'll have to throw it away again. You can carry it till we get a bit closer."

At last he came within sight of Springfield. He could see smoke coming out of the kitchen chimney. "I hope Angus's got some breakfast going," he told Chomper. "You might like rocks but Mary didn't give me time to finish my toast. Hey! You better let me have that axehead now before you get sick of it. Good Chomp."

Angus, supporting himself against the sink, saw a child dodging amongst the saplings on the rise. He was carrying something. Bringing a gift and it was lethal. Angus opened the window. *This time, Metcalf.* He reached for his rifle. Reached for the ammo. Loaded and sighted along the barrel. Bloody trees — he kept losing him. And then he was in the open again, he was standing still. This time, Metcalf, this time, my best mate . . . Just as he had him the bloody kid moved. Stand still! That's a good kid, in front of that sapling, that's it . . . his head right in the cross-hairs —

94 Range Rover

Lou Catchpole, snickering to himself, backed the Range Rover out of the garage for its second trip to Marycote in less than twenty-four hours. His fingertips tapped the steering wheel. His lips grinned in anticipation.

95 Two Little Half-chicks

Two little half-chicks. You could make a song out of that.

> Two little half-chicks
> hopping through the dew
> each said to the other
> let's dig plant and screw

Well, she'd just have to see. She'd go and prick out those seedlings and see what happened. Nice of Jarrah to ring up and say he was sorry. Must be about the first time ever! Good kid, Jarrah. Wonder if Angus appreciated it. I guess not, or he'd have come across and told me. What a nerd. Sulking there in the dark and whistling at his dogs.

I'll go over to the glasshouse very soon but first I'm going to write a letter. I'm going to write to Crystal. And she sat dreaming into the fire, her fingers plucking idle notes from the strings, the words of her letter forming themselves in her head. Dear Crystal . . . This is a surprise, huh? I guess you didn't expect to hear from me. I haven't disappeared, Crys – quite the contrary. Didn't we have good talks? Gee, I miss them! Any chance of getting away from things for a while and coming up here for a weekend? The country's good, Crys. I haven't found too many . . . She paused, leaning into the fire, a faint smile like shadows of flames dancing across her mouth.

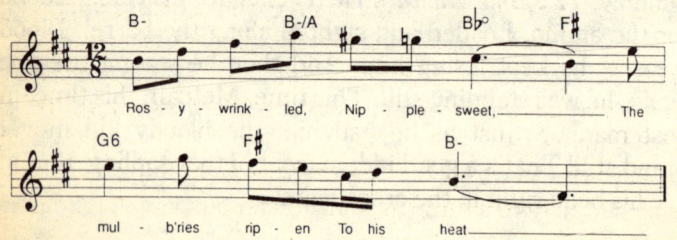

96 Child With Gift

The kid comes towards them, face lifted in welcome, one hand behind his back, the other outstretched. "Hi, kid!" Metcalf calls, holding out a bar of chocolate. "Want this, do you?" and the child nods, the child runs forward, his hand flicks out and Metcalf is screaming, squirming, his body disintegrates and Springfield from the safety of a wheel rut is forever punished knowing that if he'd believed what his eyes were telling him, Metcalf would be alive, it would be the kid not his mate who was wasted.

At this point Angus always wakes up. He lies there shaking, sobbing, he might get up and heat some milk, make a mug of cocoa, resist the temptation to get stuck into the grog again. Because if he drinks, he always falls back into the same dream – wakes up, dreams again. This time he knows what is coming, *watch it Metcalf* he screams, and he lifts his rifle to blow the kid into a thousand bits before he can offer his treacherous gift to Metcalf but it is too late, it is always too late, the child runs forward, stops, one hand holding on to something inside his coat while the other flicks out –

97 The Forests Protect

– one hand flicked out and a dog ran, a white dog went bounding into the bush and leaves blew across the child's face. Eucalypt leaves. Through the sights of the 222 Angus saw clear as daylight they were eucalypt leaves and if they hadn't moved . . . *He had almost wasted a child.* This was no nightmare. Here at Springfield he'd come one hell of a lot closer than ever he had in Vietnam to murdering a child.

I've been trying to tell you, Springers you obstinate bastard: is that what we thought we were fighting for — to waste kids? I've been tellin' and tellin' you but you wouldn't listen, groggin' on there by yourself —

Oh Christ he was right, Metcalf was right, Mary was right – he had to take a jump at himself and quick. Gita had done it, she'd got on top of a habit but first of all (and she'd done her level best to make him see) you had to admit to it — grog, anger, despair —

Hey Springers, cop this, will you: you've got to let go, my best mate. You have — got — to let me — go!

Metcalf's voice. Women's voices.

He had to let go.

He unloaded the rifle, thrust the round in his pocket, ran to the boy.

"Angus! Angus!" Jarrah was shouting. "Here she is! My silver-spangled Sebright. Hey, don't squash her."

For Angus had seized him, was hugging him. "You dear kid!" he was saying, sobbing. "You dear, dear kid! Oh God I love you!"

"You should hear her heart," Jarrah said.

98   Why Shouldn't Our Dreams

Mary, coming over the rise as Angus reached the boy, saw him hug him, saw the boy show him the bantam, saw Angus seize him and hug him again. She watched as the two walked towards the kitchen, Angus's arm around the boy's shoulder. She smiled. Lou had it all wrong. There was no other explanation. Angus wouldn't dump Marycote like an armful of kindling. She walked on slowly. If Gita was already at Springfield, Mary would refuse to speculate; if she wasn't there, Mary would whisper to Jarrah to run over the hill and fetch her. And while she and Angus were waiting she would slip a batch of scones in the oven and make sure the kettle was boiling.

The pain in her side was really biting now but if she took her time she would beat it.